FINDING RAVEN

BIRDS OF BOSTON: BOOK TWO

S. E. EMORY

Published in the United States by S. E. Emory Books in 2025

Finding Raven
–Birds of Boston Series–
www.seemorybooks.com

ISBN: 979-8-9910768-2-1 (Paperback)
ISBN: 979-8-9910768-3-8 (Hardcover)
This is a work of fiction. Unless otherwise indicated, all the names,
characters, businesses, places, events and incidents in this book are
either the product of the author's imagination or used in a fictitious
manner. Any resemblance to actual persons, living or dead, or actual
events is purely coincidental.

Requests to publish work for this book should be made to
s.e.emorybooks@gmail.com

Cover Design: Disturbed Valkyrie Designs
Editor: Jenny Sims www.editing4indies.com

—BIRDS OF BOSTON SERIES—

Before you go on this journey with Gage and Colette, please be aware there are some themes that may be triggering to some readers. These themes include explicit sexual scenes with choking and light bondage, explicit language, memories of sexual abuse by a parent, scenes of self-harm, scenes of sexual assault, and loss of a parent. If you or someone you love struggles with these issues, just know that you are not alone.

-S

For all the men in this world who hold back tears,

who wear a mask,

who are silently screaming for help—

I hope you find healing in your Chaos.

"Brother" | Kodaline

"Train Wreck" | James Arthur

"Little Bit Better" | Caleb Hearn, ROSIE

"It's You" | Ali Gatie

"Half a Man" | Dean Lewis

"What's Left of You" | Chord Overstreet

"Give You Love" | Alex Warren

"Ghost Town" | Benson Boone

"Monsters" | Timeflies, Katie Sky

"Already Gone" | Dermot Kennedy

"I Don't Want to Lose You" | Luca Fogale

"i'm yours" | Isabel LaRosa

"Work of Art" | Benson Boone

"Storms draw something out of us that calm seas don't."

-Bill Hybels

gage

Four years ago

L eora Laney, or should I say Leo Phoenix.

I've found her. She ran from my brother and I four years ago, and I have been searching for her since. This task has proved incredibly irritating since I'm one of the best hackers the FBI has.

And for *four fucking years*, she has evaded me. Until now.

I could cope with the fact that a young eighteen-year-old girl who didn't even own a cell phone could slip past my system. She could have and probably did use cash for everything, worked under the table, and never opened up a bank account—it's possible. But the one question that only she can answer, the one I could never find a reason behind...Why did she run?

She and my best friend Everett were head over heels for each other, and then she disappeared seemingly out of nowhere with no explanation. Taking my best friend's heart and my fucking sanity with her.

Finally, now I know. My knuckles turn white as I grasp the ceramic coffee mug that holds my bold Americano—made perfectly by the only barista who could make such a smooth, sweet espresso. Extra hot, just how I like it. The barista who now clings onto a little wild-haired, scrawny boy.

They embrace each other how a mother should embrace their child. Lovingly, with their entire body and soul. A comfort I can only imagine. The quiet, shy, shell of a girl I once knew now beams as radiant as she was when she was with my best friend, but now it's directed at this little boy.

My hands shake with the anger coursing through my body, and I force myself to release the mug before it splashes over and burns my hand. The breathing ritual I use to calm my mind fails me as I think about Leo and how happy she is with her new family. Even when she was with Everett and me, there was always a glimmer of sadness in her eyes. But now, looking at her as she gazes down at this boy? She is shining. And thank fuck for that, but jealousy eats at my heart because I miss the fuck out of her, and I wish she could have found that happiness with my brother.

But she didn't. She found it with someone else. And now they have a child, a family. Fuck.

We were her family. Why did she think that she couldn't have had that with Everett? I—he needed her.

Her laughter fills the room as she throws her head back at something the boy said, and at that moment, I know I can't tell Everett. This will ruin him. But on the other hand, how am I supposed to keep this from him? He'll continue to ask me about her, ask me if I have any leads, and I'm going to have to tell him I don't.

Breathe in one, two, three. Out one, two, three. Shit. I still feel the urge to launch my coffee mug across the room. Plan B is digging my nails into my fists. I feel the bite of pain, and my body calms. Pain releases pain.

Bringing the warm mug to my lips, the hot, bold liquid coats my mouth, and I feel it travel down my throat, allowing it to heat my chest as I take in the little shop she has created for herself. The coffee shop Leo now owns, Henry Leo's, a combination of her and Ski's name, is everything I knew one day she would create. A tranquil environment filled with love and laughter. I knew she would do something simple but overwhelmingly wholesome with her gifts. This place has a nostalgia to it, with its recycled tables and mismatched chairs, the uniquely horrific coffee mugs, the warm lighting, and large pane-glass windows revealing a busy Boston street. It combines the soothing hum of the city with the peaceful calm that is Leo.

I wish Everett could see it.

Maybe he'll find her on his own. This little shop is only a few blocks from his apartment, and the man has a coffee addiction. Although, he doesn't need the caffeine. Everett has more energy than a hopped-up golden retriever on cocaine, but the coffee brings her back to him—at least that's what he tells me when I ask him about his late-night coffee habits.

Maybe he'll stumble upon this little shop, and I'll be saved from having to lie, but the man would also have to go more places than just work and his apartment for that. And let's say he does come across it, finding her on his own. That doesn't change the fact that she still moved on. Tore his heart from his chest and fucking trampled all over it. Ever since she ran from us right before graduation, he has been a fucking ghost. From the outside, he seems like the normal Everett, but I know him better. He hasn't played ball in years, not since he graduated undergrad. He doesn't crack jokes or drag me out to social events anymore. Honestly, he has become like me—a fucking nightmare who prefers the company of darkness over anything else.

But the Leo-sized hole in his chest threatens to keep him from who he truly is, a fucking light in this dark, dark world.

A shriek pulls me from my trance, and my eyes fly to a beauty behind the counter. Her hands are entwined into her long, dark, twisted hair with small gold rings threaded throughout. Her golden, chestnut skin glows under the warm lights of the shop. I wonder if her skin tastes as rich as it looks.

Shit.

"Oh, fuck me sideways, LJ! I can't get this stupid thing to stop pouring the espresso!" She takes her fist and begins banging on it, making a loud metallic sound ring through the shop. Her wildness and unashamed abrasiveness cause my lips to pull up to the side, but I catch myself and quickly get rid of that pesky expression.

I'm intrigued by her—her foul mouth, her chocolate skin, her raven hair. God, she is stunning. Like an exotic fucking creature, dark and wild. There is also a softness to her eyes, but I don't have to speak to her to know she would immediately give me a headache. Maintaining my sanity solely relies on avoiding loud, wild things like her. My routines and life are orderly and refined. There is no room for such a chaotic little thing. At least…not for more than a single night.

Leo runs behind the counter, laughing as she presses a few buttons and then looks at the chaotic beauty. "Cole, you forgot to press the stop button."

Cole.

Say her last name, Leo. Come on, make it easy on me.

But she doesn't. Why would she? No matter, I can find out anything I want about her with just a first name. But maybe I shouldn't. Maybe I need to leave all things Leo and her life alone. Better not torture myself.

The tantalizing creature lets out a huff of air. "Well, it's not my fault this ten-thousand-dollar machine doesn't label its buttons properly. Seriously, they couldn't have labeled the Stop button with the word stop. No, instead, they had to use that foreign hieroglyphic symbol only the ancient Egyptians could fucking read." She talks a mile a minute, and I find myself being challenged to keep up with her ramblings.

Throwing her hands up, she walks to the back but slips as she rounds the corner. Another shriek leaves her lungs, and she quickly catches herself on the doorframe. "Seriously, this is why you do the coffee shit, and I handle everything else, LJ. Don't make me fill in again."

She continues to say something, but now she's too far for me to hear as she retreats into a back room, huffing and puffing. Leo is just giggling as she cleans up the mess left behind in that tornado of a woman's wake.

As I watch Leo, she looks directly at me, and I quickly turn to look out the window, concealing my face behind my black baseball cap. Full-on Joe Goldberg style. What a brilliant man...

When I sneak a glance back from under the bill of my cap, Leo is busy behind the counter again. The shop is packed, and a spark of pride fills my chest at her success. Am I livid with her and how she left us? Yes. But I can't deny that seeing her happy and successful makes me proud. I know where she came from because I came from the same life. We didn't let our past define us, and that is something I will always root for, no matter who you are or what you have done.

When I finish my Americano, I return the mug to the dirty bin on the counter and attempt to leave Henry Leo's, but a letter posted to the bulletin board next to the main door catches my eye. It's a delicate soft white paper folded in thirds. A deep green wax seal with a raven imprinted in the wax conceals the contents. Something about it piques my interest, so I unpin it from the board.

I recognize the bold, ink letters as ones stamped on it from a typewriter. Running my fingers over the letter, I can feel the slight indent. Whoever wrote this didn't print it from a computer but spent their time delicately and patiently typing this out on an old-school typewriter. A human after my own lost, dark heart.

Standing in the busy coffee shop, the snap of the wax seal narrows my attention on the letter before me.

October 29th, 2020

My dearest stranger,

Do you believe in fate?

Well, I do. I believe that this letter found you for a reason.

Five years ago, my dad went missing, and I have been lost ever since. No one knows what happened to him. No one has any answers for us. No one can help me. But I'm hoping you can. I know this will seem crazy, but since you picked up this random, unlabeled letter, I think you must have a little crazy in you. I am asking you to write back to me but as my father. Maybe I can feel like I got to say goodbye. Like I got to hear from him one last time. I'm drowning. And I pray that through you, I can find myself again.

Please, if you choose to help me, post your letter in the same place you found mine, and I'll know it was you.

Shuffling the top page to the back, I continue to read.

Daddy,

I miss you. I long to hear your laughter again. To feel your arms wrap me in your hugs. I'm so lost without you. You grounded me. You were my home, my peace, my person, and without you, I don't know who I am. What happened to you? They call you missing in action. In two years, you will be re-classified as killed in action. Stupid titles and timelines that don't give us anything. You are gone, they are sorry, and we are left with more questions than answers. But I feel you. I know deep in my heart that you are somewhere out there. If this is goodbye, then at least I will get to tell you one more time…I love you. Always, your little raven.

Under the signature, a stamp of a raven inks the page. A smile tugs at the corner of my mouth as I take in that unique signature. My own typewriter has a custom arrow key. A strange quirk to it that I assumed was a custom modification.

Maybe fate is real as it brought me to a letter signed by a custom key, not much different from my own. But alas, I don't believe in fate. It's a fuck ton of bullshit people use to justify things they can't explain with rational and logical findings. It gives them hope that everything will work out as it should. Here's a fucking tip: don't leave your life up to fate. The only way to get shit done is to do it yourself. Nobody is going to help you. No one is going to save you.

I pin the letter back onto the board and head outside. At the crosswalk, the light turns from green to red, halting my feet at the intersection. A car horn blares, and the shuffling of feet and whisper of wind through the skyscrapers are a murmur in my mind. Whispering to me. That letter. Her desperation, her fear, her loneliness and loss. It's like a reflection of my own soul.

Who is she?

"Fuck," I mutter and turn, then catch the scolding eyes of a mother clutching the hand of a small child. I pull at the hair on the back of my neck, already mad at myself for my poor decisions. A compulsory need to reply but also a fear that my reply will be inadequate plagues me, and I don't like the feeling of my impending failure.

The little bell rings above the door to Henry Leo's, but I snatch the letter quickly before Leo can welcome me. Tucking the letter inside my coat pocket, I make my way out onto the chilly, spring Boston street once again. There is no doubt in my mind that I want to reply, but what do I say? I had a fucking shit father, so how would I know how a good father would respond?

***

"Good afternoon, Mr. Eros. Nice night for a walk?" The old man greets me as I walk through the lobby of my apartment complex. Herold has been the front desk attendant since 1803. The old bastard needs to retire, but he is kind enough and doesn't pester me about shit, so I tolerate him.

"Not really. Any mail?"

"Not today, sir." He nods his head, and since I'm feeling nice-ish, I nod back.

During the entire ride up in the elevator, the letter is like a weight in my coat pocket, and although I want to write back, I'm exhausted and need sleep.

Walking through the front door of my dark apartment, the cold air and the soft whirl of the fan immediately comfort me. It's been a long, shit day but nothing like my routines to ground me. I place my keys in the bowl on my entryway table, hang my black wool coat and scarf on its hook, and slip my black boots off just under my coat.

One deep breath in, and then I'm off to shower. The outside world is fucking filthy, so the first thing I do is shower off the day. The heat singes my skin, and I relish the burn as it turns my pale skin red. Although, you really wouldn't be able to tell anymore with the amount of ink I have decorating my skin. As I take my phone out to plug it in, a notification pops up on my phone, and I fight the urge to launch it across the room. Deep breath in one, two, three. Out one, two, three.

Hale: Get your ass to headquarters.

There's been a breach.

Me: I'm off tonight.

Hale: Gage, get your ass in.

We need you on this one.

Fuck. Who knew the FBI would be so fucking needy? Fuckers can't do anything without me.

Chapter Two

colette

Present Day

*D*on't come to my door. Don't come to my door. Please don't be coming to my door.

But I know they're coming to my door.

The two Marines walking up my front porch steps have their heads held high, but their eyes are dull. My nightmare has become a reality as their white hats and blue pants make their way to deliver the news that is only communicated in person. Any military family's worst nightmare is playing out before my very eyes. The bright sunny June day, and the profoundly recognizable Marine uniform. The birds outside chirping happily while unknowingly providing what will become a triggering sound.

Dad has been deployed for nine months of his twelve-month tour. But I know, when they ring my doorbell, he won't be coming home.

As I wait at the front door, my hand is glued to the doorknob, refusing to turn it, shielding me momentarily from heartbreak. I watch them through the window. Their eyes meet my own, and my world stops.

"Who is it, honey? Why haven't you opened the door?" Mom gently nudges me to the side.

Don't open it, I want to scream, but nothing comes out.

The door creaks as it swings open, and I watch her break before any words are spoken. I watch her break. Everyone knows what two Marines in their Dress Blues at a front door means.

My thunderous heart almost drowns out my mother's cries. Almost.

"Mrs. Corvina. I am deeply sorry to notify you that Captain Michael J. Corvina has been classified as Missing in Action as of June 4th, 2015."

My mother's scream almost drowns out their words. Almost.

My daddy almost came home. Almost.

My eyes fly open, and a sharp inhale burns my lungs as if I were drowning and I just resurfaced. Tears track down my face, and my throat burns with what I know are the echoes of my screams. My sheets stick to my body from my sweat. The cool air hits my legs as I fling them off and stumble to my closet. Grabbing the wooden hat box, I hurriedly rifle through it till I find his letter. And when I do, I clutch it to my chest as if it were my father, my life raft in the storm I drown in almost every night.

My shaking hands open it, and I wipe my tears before they fall and stain the delicate paper.

November 24th, 2020

My little Raven,

I wish I could come home to you. I long for nothing more than to hold you in my arms, smell your sweet hair, and kiss your perfect cheeks. I miss you more than the stars miss the shine of the moon on a new moon night, more than the ocean misses the beach during low tide, more than a plucked flower misses their roots.

But my little Raven, you are not lost. For how could someone be lost who is found? You know who you are. You do not need me for that. You are my daughter, and I am with you always. I'm with you in the wind that brushes your cheek, I'm with you in the smell of the dahlias that flower in summer, I'm with you in the sunset and the sunrise, I'm with you always in your heart.

If one day, I never hold you again, do not fear, for I never left you. I'm with you always.

-Your Father

My father's words, even though I know they weren't written by him, silence my storming heart. I re-read those stamped words as I have done countless times before, running my fingers along their indented edges. Anytime I need my father, I have him here in these words. All thanks to the stranger who gave me this four years ago.

I tuck that letter away and continue to Arrow's letter.

Dearest Raven,

I don't know who you are, how old you are, or where you are in life. In fact, I know nothing about you except that you are hurting. But I hope that you found your father's letter to be everything you needed. I hope in a small way, it gives you peace. Maybe some closure as well.

I did not have a good relationship with my own father, and although I felt I was not the right person to respond to your letter, something about it drew me in, and I couldn't leave it alone. You don't know me, not in the slightest. I could be an eighty-year-old man or a thir-ty-two-year-old single mother. I could be anyone. But I guess one thing you should know about me is that when I feel a pull in my mind toward something, I cannot nor will not let it go. I could not let you go. I tried walking away, and I couldn't. I don't understand the compulsion to write to you beyond your father's letter. I don't believe

I have written or even spoken this much to anyone in a long time, if ever. Maybe it's the anonymity of it all…

I guess all I'm trying to say is that I know what it's like to be lost. If you need someone to anchor you, ground you, and listen to you, just write to me, and I'll be there. You can confide in me, and I promise when you're lost, I will find you.

Arrow is the one I turn to when I'm lost, and he always finds me among the storm that is my mind, leading me back to the surface.

My dad used to be that person for me, but with his absence, Arrow has stepped in. We have never met in person. For me, and I assume for him as well, the anonymity of our relationship is what makes it so special. There is no pressure to hide our truths or be dishonest for the sake of saving face. We can be ourselves.

In many ways, I have fallen in love with Arrow without even seeing him. I feel as though I know him on a soul level, and if I were to meet him by chance, I believe I would know it was him. At least I hope I would. He feels too ingrained into me to pass on the street and not feel him.

Sometimes I watch the people who linger at the bulletin board, my curiosity getting the best of me, but then I remind myself that

I love our relationship as it is and want to keep it this way. I don't want to know him face-to-face. I think that's mostly my fear talking, though. She can be an insecure little bitch sometimes.

The doubts she whispers into my head creep in whenever I get the courage to ask Arrow to meet. What would happen if he knew who I was to the outside world? Would he like me? Would he hate me? Would our letters end? Would I fall even more in love with him?

"Cole, sweetie?" My mom's wobbly voice filters in along with a soft knock on my closet door. Her citrus scent grows stronger with each step she takes toward me. Strange woman loves the smell of artificial fruits, and I hate it. Another thing we contradict on. She's summer, warmth, and vibrance. I'm cold, soft, and dull inside.

"Another nightmare?" she asks as she enters my closet, wrapping her arms tighter around her waist. I used to correct her—not a nightmare but a memory—but I've stopped. They come too often, and each time I remind her that this is our reality, I watch her eyes die a little more.

"Yeah. About Daddy." I look up at her, wrapped in her fluffy plum robe, her hair bonnet crooked from her own restless sleep. She kneels next to me and places her cold hand against my cheek.

"Me too, baby. Me too. Are you sure you're ready to leave?"

"It's time I fly the nest, Mama. I'm ready. I can't stay with you forever, trapped in this house with him surrounding me. It's not what he would have wanted for either of us." I've wanted to move out a few times and even tried to convince my mom to do the same. But we're stuck in this house, waiting for a man who is never coming home. Every time I look at apartments, my heart begins to race, and

I feel sick to my stomach. Nothing has ever felt as right and as wrong as home.

But it's time. I need to learn to fly on my own. It's been nine years. If he was out there, they would have found him by now. Two years ago, they changed his classification from MIA to KIA, and that's when we buried an empty casket.

"Come now, let's get some coffee in us. We are looking forward to exciting things today. We will speak good things into existence. You're going to find the perfect place." Mama pulls me into a hopeful hug, and I breathe in her optimism, only choking slightly on the watermelon lotion she put on last night. Fuck positive affirmations, they never work, but I hope she's right about finding the perfect place.

Fingers crossed.

gage

"EEEEKKKK!"

A shrill squeal wakes me from my sleep. My deep green velvet curtains block the light, but nothing can block the god-awful screech of the fucking banshee next door.

"For fuck's sake." I fling the covers off my body and step into the gray sweats folded at the foot of my bed. I didn't get home until almost three o'clock this morning. There was an unexpected break in the case we've been working on for months. Apparently, I'm the only one competent enough to hack into the servers they needed information from. Fucking idiots, the whole lot of 'em.

The clock above the oven tells me it's eight in the morning. I hadn't planned to go into headquarters till noon, and we have a debrief at two that I have to be at, but thanks to the fucking banshee, it looks like an earlier start to my day than I had planned. Ritual is vital in keeping my sanity, and there will be hell to pay to whatever creature just woke me.

And speaking of the vile creature, another squeal penetrates my apartment walls, and I groan. "Yes! It's perfect! Can I move in this weekend?"

Fuck. No.

Not. Happening.

The vacant apartment across from me has been a blessing, something I absolutely had a hand in. And will continue to have a hand in until I vacate this complex myself. I don't do well with kind and curious neighbors, loud noises, or people in general. And I will not, under any circumstances, have a fucking banshee that sounds like a dying cat living next to me.

Running my hand down my face, I swing my front door open with a determination to demolish any happy dreams of this being Little Miss Noisy's new home before she can sign the damn lease. But I stop in my tracks when I happen upon someone I was not expecting in my hallway.

"Leo? What the fuck are you doing here?"

"Gage! Hey!" She tries to peer around my body that fills the doorway, and I subconsciously move to block her view. I like my privacy, even from my best friend's girlfriend, who is also my best friend. Ex-new best friend...it's complicated.

"Do you...live here? Oh no..." The excitement that was written on her face is quickly replaced by horror, and now she won't make eye contact with me.

I narrow my eyes, and she shrinks away. "Leo," I warn.

Suddenly, the chaotic beauty known as Colette Corvina, or as I like to call her, utter fucking chaos on tall, perfect legs, runs out of the vacant apartment door directly across from me. "LJ! It's perfect, and he said I can move in this weeken—"

She finally notices my looming 6'4" frame in the doorway, but she doesn't miss a beat. Crossing her arms over her chest and cocking her hip, she sneers at me. "Why the fuck are you here? And where is your shirt?" Despite her malicious tone, I see the way her deep brown catlike eyes trace over my tattoos while my own trace over her tongue as it darts out to lick her lips.

Fuck. Stop. Not that creature. Anyone but her.

I snap out of it quickly. "Fuck. No. You are not moving into *that* apartment." Pointing my finger toward the open door, I step into her space.

And to my surprise, instead of stepping back, she steps up toe-to-toe with me, her head craning back to look me directly in the eyes, a challenge and spark in them that almost makes me smile. "The fuck I'm not. You're not the boss of me. I'll live wherever I want."

I bite down on my back teeth to keep my anger under control. Breathe. In one...two...three. Out one...two...three. I'd love to just wrap my hands around that pretty little throat and make her writhe beneath me till she's begging to do anything I please.

Fuck, breathing isn't working.

I keep my eyes locked on hers but speak to Leo. "Control your friend, Leo, before I do it myself."

My nails bite into my fists as I back away, taking the high road, but Colette Corvina is like an annoying little chihuahua that doesn't know when to shut the fuck up and back off. "What, Gage? You going to spank me? Bring it on, buddy. I'm not afraid of you!" She steps toward me, almost across my threshold when Leo places a hand to her shoulder and pulls her back.

"Be careful what you wish for, Chaos." And I slam the door in her face as her jaw drops with what I'm sure was going to be a smart-ass comment. If she wants to open her smart-ass mouth, I'll give her something to fill it with.

I cannot have her living next to me. I can barely stand her in the same fucking city. Not only is she loud and obnoxious but she's also dangerous. Ever since I saw her four years ago, I've been obsessed. Despite her being everything I detest, I feel a tug in my mind toward her. A curiosity. She is a plague that has stained my brain, and I can't scrub her clean. And then she mouthed off three months ago at Henry Leo's, and I've dreamed of no other mouth but hers. The image of her on her knees, those pretty, pretty lips wrapped around me. Fuck. She really is a nuisance.

No matter what I do, she pops into my head with her loud, uncontrolled laughter and challenging amber eyes. She makes me want to simultaneously run as far from her as I can and be close to her. And I have never wanted to be close to someone like I do her. I just haven't decided whether it's because I want to fuck her or get fucking rid of her.

Trying to sort the clusterfuck that are currently my thoughts, I start my espresso machine to make my Americano. A knock sounds at my door, and I resist the urge to throw my cup at the damn wall. Can't people just leave me the fuck alone? One day, that's all I want.

I swing it open with a huff, not trying in the slightest to conceal my irritation. "What the fuck do you want?"

"Oh wait, let me just put these on." Hale pats his jacket pockets, then pulls out and slides his sunglasses onto his face. "The sunshine coming out of your ass this morning is truly blinding." He stands with a drink holder in one hand, two cups of coffee keeping it balanced. His loose tie and rumpled suit tell me that he slept at his desk last night...again.

He doesn't wait for an invitation before he moves past me and takes his glasses back off, tucking them into his pocket.

I follow him, slamming my door shut and snatching the coffee he's now holding out to me. "I'm always a ball of sunshine. You didn't answer my question. What do you want?" I make my way back into the kitchen, tossing his crap coffee in the trash and finishing up my drink. Fuck his bribe. Bringing my Americano to my lips, I inhale the rich scent of espresso and turn to face this demanding ball of stress I call my boss.

"I need you at HQ with me. Now." He leans against my kitchen island and sips from his own cup. My taste buds literally revolt at the thought of what cheap gas station, piss-poor coffee he's sipping. I'd offer to make him something, but I just don't want to.

"No."

"It wasn't a request, Eros."

"I was there until three in the fucking morning, *Knight.* Get someone else. Jones, Marcus, Jesus, even sweet old Mary. I don't give a fuck. Just not me." I stare him down, using his last name since he used mine. Apparently, he's all business right now. But the special agent doesn't scare easily. I've also been working with him for years, and although he knows I'm just as much bite as bark, I hardly ever mean it with him.

"You know that you're the only one with the skill set we need for this case. The other hackers aren't as good."

"Then you shouldn't have hired them. Not. My. Problem." I take another sip and so does he, silence filling the space as we both challenge the other.

"What's crawled up your ass and made camp? Normally, you don't give me this much shit." He digs his thumb and forefinger into his eyes, clearly under an immeasurable amount of stress, but also not my problem.

However, he's right. I am giving him more shit than usual. What can I say? Colette has inspired me this morning. Usually, I do what he wants because I can do it faster than it would take me to argue the matter, but I'm in a bad mood this morning. My routine has been thrown off, and he and the rest of the world can fuck right off.

I don't answer him as I stare out my large, floor-to-ceiling window overlooking the Boston skyline.

"Is it that smoking hot little firecracker I just saw down the hall? She seems loud and just your cup of tea," he mocks with a smirk.

"I fucking hate tea." My jaw clenches, and I narrow my eyes at him. One thing about Hale; he reads body language like it's his first language, so it didn't take him long to pick up on which of my asshole glares were serious and which he could poke at.

This one is serious. I do not, under any circumstances, want him looking at Colette, nor do I want to talk about why the thought of him checking her out makes me see red.

He raises his hands in a placating gesture. "Alright, alright. No more about her. Off-limits. Message received loud and clear. I'm not interested anyway. You know I'm more into blondes." He makes his way to my door. "Be at the car in ten, or I'm having Mason assist you on this."

Oh, fuck that shit. That little weasel isn't getting anywhere near my setup. Whiny little cunt. I do not have the patience for him today, okay . . . any day. I run my hand down the nape of my neck and pull at my hair there. The pain releases some of my tension, then I get my ass moving.

Hale: 1 Gage: 0.

Bitch.

December 24th, 2020

Arrow,

Merry Christmas Eve.

I don't know your story, what you believe, or where you are, but everyone deserves to have a Merry Christmas.

Christmas is my favorite holiday. It has always felt special. My mom lights a million candles in our home. She decorates with fake snow and ugly thrifted Christmas decorations, but she always makes them look cute and cozy. We have a huge mantel over our fireplace that she sets a little village across.

But my favorite Christmas tradition? My dad and I used to go to our local coffee shops and order the sweetest Christmas drinks we could find. We'd drink them all in one night as we walked the city and looked at the lights.

I haven't done that since he's been gone. I miss him so much. Especially today.

But your letter helps. I've read it countless times and even more today. I wanted to say thank you, but those two simple words don't seem to hold enough impact for what you did for me.

Whenever I am lost in my grief, I read your letter, and you find me.

But it's not just my father's letter that you wrote.

It's yours.

Your honesty, your vulnerability. I get the sense that you aren't vulnerable in real life. You wear a mask.

Like me.

In my life, to the outside world, I'm joyful and full of life, but on the inside, I feel like I'm drowning. Lost in my mind. My grief and sorrow are incredibly heavy, and I'm weighed down. The mask I wear with those I love is always in place, only coming off when alone. So I do my best to never be alone. But your letter lifted a piece of my grief off my shoulders, and for the first time since my dad went missing, I felt like I could take a deep breath. See, how can two little words express that?

I would like to know more about you, my stranger.

Who are you?

Chapter Four

colette

My. Own. Apartment.

Holy shit on a stick.

I'm doing it.

I'm moving out, and I'm healing. Well, I wouldn't say healing, but I have definitely put enough Band-Aids on my wounds to try this whole being-on-my-own thing.

Plus, this apartment is stunning. The floor-to-ceiling windows overlook a charming little park. It's not so high that I feel the Boston wind sway the building, but it's not low enough I have to worry about people breaking my windows. It has old exposed brick walls combined with new appliances and modern fixtures. The ceilings are exposed pipe and beams that have all been painted a sleek black.

A typical twenty-five-year-old who co-owns a coffee shop probably wouldn't be able to afford this place. But I'm anything but typical. I took the money I earned and invested. I have the brains for finances. Money just clicks in my head; it always has. It's why I do so well with LJ and the shop. She handles the hospitality, and I handle the numbers. A perfect machine. I didn't go to college, and my car is paid off. I don't really have any major expenses, and I'm frugal. I don't spend outside my needs, and I thrift a lot.

This apartment is probably the first thing in my life I've splurged on. Could I have gone with something less expensive? Yes. But I felt I deserved it, and maybe something I truly love will keep me here. The only downside would be my grumpy, butt-nugget neighbor. I can't believe he lives right across the hall. He's going to be a royal pain in my ass. But that's okay. I can handle him. I really don't see what LJ sees in him. She says he's sweet once you get to know him, but I highly doubt that.

As I push thoughts of Gage to the side, I roll up to my new parking spot in the apartment parking garage. The spaces are a little tight, but my little VW Bug has no issue squeezing in. Grabbing the seat belted hat box in my passenger seat, I make my way to the lobby to let LJ and Everett in.

Before grabbing them, I ask the front desk attendant, Herold, to open the service elevator door. The old man grabs a key and makes for the back, leaving me with a genuine smile and nod of his head. I think Herold might be my favorite part about this place. That or the beautiful fireplace in the lobby. I can definitely see myself snuggling up in front of that thing with a good movie. I wonder if they would let me decorate it for Christmas?

"Miss, uh. I'm afraid I'm not able to get the service elevator working. I checked this morning, and it was fine, but . . ." He fumbles with the keys in his hand and looks at his feet. "Well, I'm not sure. I'm sorry."

Fuck.

"Well, I guess we'll just use the regular elevator. It will just take a few more trips." Resting my hands on my hips, I decide that this little hiccup won't rain on my parade. But speaking of raining on parades . . .

Gage walks through the lobby doors with LJ and Everett in tow. The happy couple is smiling, and hell must have frozen over because the devil himself actually has a smirk on his face that instantly drops when his hazel eyes meet mine.

"Thank you, guys, for coming to help." I give LJ a small hug, but she's unable to wrap both arms around me because her fiancé still clings to one of her hands.

"Of course," her sweet voice replies.

"Unfortunately, the service elevator is down, so we will have to make more trips using the regular one." I motion over my shoulder to the much smaller elevator.

"What a bummer. That's going to really suck." Gage's impassive expression makes me see red. What an ass! LJ intervenes before I can fire back with something cheeky as she places her hands on my shoulders and directs me away from Gage. "Let Ev handle him. Come on, let's go grab the first boxes."

As we walk out front, LJ slows, running her fingers over one of my braids. "I'm so proud of you. This is a big step, girl." She fingers a particularly special gem in my hair, a small gold phoenix she got me as a birthday present a couple of years ago. It's my second most prized charm. The first being the little gold raven my dad got me.

On the verge of tears, she sniffles and takes a deep breath. She knows how difficult my journey has been with moving out and processing the loss of my father. She doesn't know the true extent, but she knows enough. I could never let her see how dark my storm truly is.

"Please don't start crying. If you cry, then I cry. That's the deal, and I can't show weakness in front of my new neighbor." I let out a small laugh through my tears.

"I can't help it. Are you really going to be okay?" She opens the passenger door and hands me the bag of snacks and drinks she brought over.

"Yeah. I have a good feeling about this place." And strangely, it's not a lie. It's everything I have always seen for myself. It seems to fit my personality like a glove, and it's in the perfect location.

"Maybe this will be the place where you find your one true love. I've seen a few hotties in the lobby."

"Oh god." I let out a fake moan, and it makes LJ slap my shoulder as she shushes me. "What? I would sell my soul to find a man who knows how to please me in bed."

I've made a million and one questionable choices in men. I can't help it. I'm human, I'm lonely, and I'm fucking horny. A bad combination that will inevitably lead to a bad decision that usually leads to a faked orgasm and me kicking Mr. Can't-find-a-clit-to-save-his-life out the door.

"You're going to find your man. Just give it time." I roll my eyes at her response as we ride the elevator up to my new apartment, thinking to myself I already have. Arrow is everything I want . . . except I've never met him. Semantics.

"I don't need anyone serious right now."

The elevator dings, the doors open, and when we get to my door, I notice it's open. Everett and Gage are already lingering inside, talking about some dumb man shit, I'm sure.

"How did you get in here?"

"The lock on this apartment can be troublesome. The last tenant made multiple complaints, but it just seems to be problematic," Gage says as he walks by me, and my lungs fill with his clean scent. God, he smells good.

No, Colette. The most dangerous flowers smell the prettiest.

He stops next to me. His gaze slowly travels down my body, and I swear I feel it everywhere. I want to punch him in his pretty face . . . but also want to ride that same face. It's conflicting. I'm confused. Sue me.

Even though I know exactly what he's trying to do, I don't back away but challenge him with my eyes. He leans in slightly, and his grin could melt my panties right off. "Would be a shame if someone just walked in here in the middle of the night . . ." His thumb tugs down his bottom lip just before he shoulder-checks me and walks away. "Might want to consider a new apartment."

When I turn my body to watch him retreat, my braids fly around me, and I flip him off even though his back is to me. "Fuck you. You can't scare me off. But nice try."

"You two are going to be trouble . . ." Everett snorts, and I flip him off too.

After unloading half my belongings, I call for a break. I leave the front door open because I'm nosy and want to see who else lives on this floor. All three of us plop down on the floor and have a little

McDonald's picnic. Everett is shoving his face with multiple chicken nuggets at a time. And LJ dips her fries in honey mustard as I sip on my extra crispy Sprite.

We joke and laugh, and I feel that this is a small blessing in this apartment. Starting off with strong, happy, silly memories is exactly what I need in my new place. That is until Gage emerges from his own apartment.

"Hey man, come here!" Everett calls out, and I resist the urge to punch him in the face. Why did they have to be best friends? LJ too. *Traitor.*

Gage saunters in like he owns the place, his stride more confident than I like. What an arrogant butt face. He doesn't say anything. He just glances over each of us and then looks at our McDonald's wrappers splayed out over the dark wood floors. The raise of his eyebrow tells me he doesn't approve.

"Where are you headed?" Everett asks.

"Work." His answer is clipped, clearly wanting to evacuate this conversation before it's even had a chance to start.

"You have to work on a Saturday night? Didn't you just get off this morning?" LJ chimes in.

"You work on Saturdays. And Sundays."

"True. But not every weekend. Leo has others to help out. Who do they have besides you? You need a break, man."

Gage scoffs at Everett's response. "You know what they say: if you want something done right, do it yourself."

Everett just shakes his head, and Leo smiles sadly at Gage. The arrogance of this man is outstanding. Really. His head could fill the entirety of Texas . . . no, the United States.

"Well, we're having an unpacking party tomorrow if you want to join?" Everett mentions, and I throw a fry at his face. Stupid quarterback reflexes allow him to bat it away, and I snarl at him like an annoying little sister.

"No," Gage and I say at the same time, then he turns on his heel, hands tucked into the front pockets of his black dress slacks.

"Gage, you live right across the hall. Come over," LJ adds on now, throwing a crumpled-up wrapper in his direction.

He looks over his broad shoulder at her and grins. "That's disrespectful, Leo. I have shit to do." Then he walks out my front door and slams it closed.

LJ looks at me and shrugs. "I tried."

"Don't worry about it. I don't want his help unpacking. He would probably fuck with something of mine just to drive me crazy. He seems like the type."

"Hey now, that's my brother you're talking about. Be nice," Everett chastises jokingly as he throws the same fry back at me. My reflexes fail me, and it hits me directly in the forehead. Fucking awesome.

"Yeah, the brother who kept LJ and Rune from you for four years? That's who you want me to be nice to? No. Not happening," I not so subtly remind him as I get up and retrieve the wrapper LJ threw, tossing it into the trash.

Everett's green eyes narrow, and his brows pull in. When he responds, his voice has dropped an octave, and I get the rare but serious side of Everett Rowan. "We have settled that. And I would appreciate it if you didn't hold that over him. Gage had his reasons, and he has suffered enough. Leo and I have forgiven and moved on. Frankly, what happened between the three of us is none of your business."

Truth be told, I've already moved on from that. I don't really hold grudges well. Life is too short, and you never know who and when you'll lose someone. But still, I won't let him see that, so I roll my eyes instead. "Fine. But he's still an ass."

"True. But he's ours." LJ smiles and reaches up on her tiptoes to kiss Everett's cheek.

"Barf. You guys are too cute. Go away," I mock with a smile as I head out the front door to finish the rest of this torture people call moving.

By the time we're done, it's four in the afternoon, and I'm exhausted. We were able to get my bed up, and I found the box with the sheets, so after LJ and Everett leave, I take a quick shower and collapse onto the bed.

I can't believe it. I'm on my own.

Now for the hard part. Sleeping.

February 18, 2021

Raven,

  I apologize for the delayed response. I wanted to write to you sooner, but life seems to be getting in the way. Funny how that happens. Life keeps you from truly living. All the mundane tasks we are required to do to "live" are really the things that keep us from actually living.

  I'm glad to hear that my letter helped, and strangely, I'm happy you wrote back. I keep to myself mostly, but I would be lying if I said I wasn't hoping you would respond. I don't believe in fate, but I can't shake the feeling that you and I were meant to connect.

  As far as holidays go, I don't celebrate them. What's the point? People decorate their lives with frilly things, put on themed songs, and pretend that just for a short time, their lives aren't completely fucking dull. It's just another lie we live. So no, I don't celebrate Christmas.

  But if it brings you joy, who am I to say that just for a moment, the facade isn't beneficial? I guess we all need something that makes us forget.

I don't know if I can answer your question. Who am I? I'm many things on the surface, even fewer to my core. I'm a man; I can confidently tell you that. I'm twenty-three years old. I have a demanding job. I enjoy the city and hate the country. Don't take me camping or anywhere near nature in its rawest form. I enjoy coffee and computers. Specifically hacking into them. I don't own any pets, significant others, or children. That's my surface.

Deep down . . . I'm a simple man. But that's all I'll give you because for some reason I want you to keep writing to me.

But I will turn your inquisition back to you. Who are you?

gage

S hould I have been the friendly neighbor and helped Colette move in? Yes, probably. Definitely. Should I have, at the very least, not hacked into the service elevator and caused a temporary malfunction? Also, yes.

Am I or will I ever be a friendly neighbor? Abso-fucking-lutely not. In fact, I'm not kind or friendly to anyone. Except Everett, Leo, and occasionally their son, Rune. He's a little too touchy-feely for my liking. But he's a child, so he has an imperceptible amount of forgiveness from me for his ridiculous invasion of personal space.

The cool air of my apartment hits me as I step through the doorway. Going through my usual ritual, I put everything away, but even following my routine, the day still nags at me. We're working on a case currently; a few girls have gone missing in a six-block radius, and the same vehicle has been spotted around the time of their disappearance. Normally, when we have such a common denominator, it's a pretty cut-and-dried case, but this one is giving us difficulty. Or rather, it's giving me difficulty since I'm the one working on tracing the vehicle. You would think a task as simple as that would be easy, but it's proving aggravating. I can't find that fucking car anywhere. Of course it has unmarked plates, and to top it off, it's one of the most common vehicles in the city, a white Honda Civic.

I have a love-hate relationship with my work. On one hand, I went into this field not only because I was recruited due to my god-like hacking skills, but I went specifically into the human trafficking division because of my own past. The men—yes, men get trafficked too—women and children that we find have gone through indescribable trauma, and I can relate. I want to save them before it's too late. Sometimes we do. Sometimes we don't.

Plus, working in this field gives me a unique opportunity to find the sick fucks who traffic and rape these innocent humans, and if the justice system fails...well, I may or may not get their information into a less than legal justice system. Either way, they get what's coming to them.

Running a hand down the back of my neck, I head to the shower to rinse off the day. I can't believe that the dying cat—oops sorry, I mean chaotic banshee—moved in. I tried talking to Leo, seeing if she could convince Colette to steer clear of my space, but Leo explained that this is the first time she has seen Cole so excited about a place.

Leo gave me those blue puppy dog eyes, and then Everett gave them to me as well. Let's just say I couldn't deny them. I relented and told them I wouldn't sabotage her lease agreement, but I made no promises when it came to fucking with her after she signed the lease.

Before hopping in the shower, a text catches my eye. And because of my perfectly normal OCD tendencies, I can't have a little red dot above any of my apps, or I will literally lose my ever-loving mind. I open it just to clear it but find Hale in desperate need of a reality check.

Bitchass Knight

> Come get drinks with us tomorrow night. O'Riley's 9 p.m.

> You don't drink.

> I drink water. I'll buy.

> Do we need a refresher about workplace harassment? Leave me alone.

> Jesus, stop being a whiny bitch and come out with us.

> I don't associate with that name, and I have better things to do. And for the record, you're the bitch in this relationship.

After I wash this day away, I finally lay in bed. I'm set on trying to get some sleep, but as soon as I feel myself drifting, a ping on my phone makes me want to throw it across the room. Thank fuck I have better self-control, or I would have gone through at least ninety-nine phones by now.

"For fuck's sake," I mumble as I roll over.

Co-Daddy

> Hey. Leo, Rune, and I are headed out of town today. Can I bring Muffin over . . . say 8 a.m.?

> It's 3 in the fucking morning. Why are you awake?

> Just got off.

> I will only wake at 8 a.m. for an Americano from HL.

HL is what we shorten Henry Leo's to. And Co-Daddy is what he put himself under in my phone when we both decided to co-parent an annoyingly messy but irresistible dog, Muffin. I'm not an animal person; however, Muffin is the laziest dog I have ever met. He sleeps, eats, and shits. And that's it. On a rare occasion, he will get the zoomies around the apartment, but that lasts for all of two minutes.

> Yeah, but my face first thing in the morning should be more than enough. Right?

> You're sounding needy. Go snuggle your girlfriend.

> Fiancée.

Technicality. And yes, that is fine. I have to go to work for a meeting at 10 anyway.

Seriously? Haven't you been to work every day this week? They work you like a dog, man. Hey, great idea incoming…

You could come on this little trip with us!

That sounds like an awful idea. I'm fine. I'll see you in the morning.

Love you, Gagey-Wagey.

Fuck off.

Co-Daddy added Leo to the chat

Babe, Gage is being a dick. Put him in his place.

Leo

Ev. Stop adding me to your guys chats. Leave Gage alone. Let me go back to sleep.

Co-Daddy

You're taking his side? Do you see how he treats me? He told me to fuck off. Rude. By the way, I'm making sure Brooke makes you a normal temp Americano in the morning.

Leo

> If you force my employee to serve sub-par coffee, I'll withhold sex for an entire month. Don't test me.

Co-Daddy

> Yes, ma'am. Gage. See you in the morning. I have a pretty bird to beg forgiveness from. She really isn't a morning person... even worse when I wake her in the middle of the night. Unless it's with my mouth on her pussy.

> I'm utterly disgusted right now. I did not need to know that.

Leo left the group chat.

Despite the annoying fuck of a best friend I have, I can't help but smile at his ridiculous antics. He has always been the opposite of me in every way. Outgoing, obnoxious, kind, welcoming. And Leo, well, she and I are cut from the same cloth. We both suffer a pretty fucked-up past, and although she's a bit more caring than I am, she's still pretty closed off. That's why we get along so well.

"No. Please! Don't leave me!"

What the fuck? I jump out of bed at the sound of . . . is that Colette?

February 28th, 2021

Arrow,

It's funny how that happens. Tell me, Arrow, what would be your truest and happiest form? Who would you be if life didn't get in the way?

I cannot and will not accept that you have never celebrated Christmas! Didn't you ever celebrate it with your mom and dad?

I will not be friends with someone who has never sat by a fire in Christmas pj's, drank hot chocolate, and watched Elf. So you have a task to complete. In your next letter, include a picture of you doing this. It doesn't have to have your face in it if that makes you uncomfortable, but I need hard proof you have done as I have asked. Pinky promise?

I love surface-level facts, but I also want to know you. Give me the gory details, Arrow. You won't scare me away. I promise. Give me your greatest fears and your greatest insecurity. Give me your true goals and dreams. Tell me about your family and friends. I want to know it all. I'm nosy like that. Sorry. I mean, what do you have to lose?

As for who I am? Well, you already know I lost my dad. And isn't that the most accurate word? Lost. Because it's true, he's lost. He was never found. How does someone just become lost?

I just turned 22. I have a job I enjoy, but it's not my passion by any means. I graduated from high school, barely. I was a bit of a reckless teen after losing my dad. I never attended college. I grew up in Boston so I can agree on the nature thing. I don't do well with animals and bugs. I don't have a significant other either, or children, or pets. I guess it's just my mom and I, and my best friend. That's my surface.

Here are my deepest waters. I'm terrified of being alone. I surround myself with people and noise because if I don't, I feel I'll be just as lost as my father. And despite how I act outwardly to the world, I have many insecurities and flaws. I put on a front of confidence, but inside, my mind battles me. I second-guess myself constantly. I fill my head with doubts and fears, most probably irrational to everyone else, but to me, they are very real. And they are terrifying.

For my goals and dreams, the sad thing is I don't have any. When my dad went missing, all that I had to give I needed to survive. And when I finally felt a micro-ounce of normalcy in my life again, the world and life had moved on without me. I never thought about more because I never wanted more. Not until now. Not until your letter. Before my dad's disappearance, I wanted to go to beauty school, like my mom, but now that I think about it, I really only wanted that to feel closer to her. My true passion lies in art. I used to love painting, but I haven't picked up a brush in years. I don't know that I ever will again.

I'm looking forward to your next letter, Arrow. These small moments of you make me feel a little less lost.

colette

"*No! Please don't leave me!*"

The sound of my own scream pulls me out of my nightmare. My heart is racing, the tightness in my chest not allowing me to take in a full breath. I feel like I'm drowning. I can't breathe. Oh god.

I need my letters.

When I fling the covers off me, the sting of the cold air intensified by my damp skin makes shivers break out across my body. I race to the living room in search of him. My letters. But all the boxes. Where did I put them?

My chest tightens even more.

No. No. No.

The room begins to close around me. My chest hurts. God, everything hurts.

I can't breathe. I can't—

I need to feel. Something. Anything.

I need to feel. I need to feel more and less all at the same time. In the absence of my letters, my panicked mind reaches out to my old habits. My letters always calm me in times like this, but without them . . . I need to find a release elsewhere. Where I used to before Arrow.

Stumbling into the kitchen, I find the box cutter I left on the counter. Then I climb onto my kitchen counter and rest my legs over the sink. Always over a sink or in a tub, so it's easier to clean up the blood. I run my fingers over the raised scars on my thighs. Remembering the panic I was in when I made each one, remembering the release I felt as I scarred my own skin. Sliding the blade up, I press it to the soft flesh, already feeling the bite of the blade pull me from my mind.

But before I can draw blood, a banging on my door startles me, and I drop the cutter into the sink. "Fuck!"

Practically falling off the counter, I snatch up the blade. Who the fuck is here at this time of night? The door flies open before I can catch my breath.

"Gage." My chest deflates, my shoulders drop, and with it, my arms drop to my sides. Strangely, at the sight of him, I don't feel so panicked anymore.

His eyes run from my pink tie-dye satin scarf, to my old stretched out T shirt to my boy shorts and I feel the caress of his eyes all over me as they inspect me.

"What the fuck is wrong with you?" He steps toward me, and I take a small step back.

"Nothing. I'm fine." I pull my T-shirt down to cover my scars. I don't know if he saw them or not already, but either way, I need more coverage around this man. He's shirtless, in a pair of black joggers, and his hair is a mess. He looks drool-worthy, and I'm well . . . I could be compared to a homeless person.

"You typically scream at the top of your lungs at three in the fucking morning?" He takes another step closer, his eyes searching for something or someone.

"It's really none of your business," I remind him. "How did you even unlock my door?" I cross my arms over my chest to put on a brave front, but the box cutter remains open, and I stab my bicep.

"FUCK! That hurt like a son of a cock-sucking bitch!" Dropping the blade and grabbing my arm, I try to stop the bleeding, but it seeps through my fingers.

"For fuck's sake, Chaos." He runs his hand down his face and turns back to his apartment.

"What help you are . . ." I mumble as I make my way to the sink. Fuck, I don't have any towels unpacked. But I'll bleed out before I ask Gage for one. Asshole—

"Sit," he commands, and I look over my shoulder. He stands like a pissed-off bull just inside my kitchen, fisting a first-aid box and a bottle of whiskey. He nods to the counter next to the sink, and I follow his command. I do my best to scooch up onto the counter while holding pressure on my arm.

He comes up to me, his body hovering next to my cold legs, his heat radiating off him and warming me without even touching. His warm presence is a complete contradiction to his cold attitude.

Holding up the bottle of whiskey, he nods at it, and my eyes follow. "Drink."

"I don't—"

"Trust me, it helps," he reassures as I grab the bottle with my bloody hand and bring it to my lips. I watch his gaze fall from my eyes to my lips, then my throat as I swallow the burning liquid.

I wince a little at the taste, then he takes the bottle and brings it to his own. I watch him as he did me.

Jesus. That was hot.

No. Stop, Colette.

Setting the bottle on the counter, he pulls out gauze, a needle and thread, and some other items, then begins cleaning my wound. "Ouch!" I hiss. "I thought the whiskey was supposed to help?"

"Keep still. And not for this part." He tightens his grip just below my arm, and I wince, but he doesn't seem to care all that much. Snatching the bottle from next to me, I take another drink.

"You're a fucking idiot, you know that? Why would you cut yourself with a box cutter?"

I roll my eyes as he inspects my wound now that it's clean. "I didn't do it on purpose, Einstein. It was an accident. I forgot it was in my hands. I was a little . . . never mind."

"My point still stands. What kind of idiot forgets they are holding a fucking box cutter."

I take him in while he's concentrating on threading the needle. He really is beautiful. Now that I'm closer, I can see his eyes are a hazel that almost reflects some green. His skin is smooth, almost translucent with how pale it is. But only on his face since he's covered in tattoos from his neck down. His cheekbones and eyes are feminine, while his straight nose and sharp jaw look like they were copy and pasted out of a *GQ* magazine. And his smell? God, he smells good. It's a clean smell with a hint of some kind of spice. It's intoxicating.

"Stop staring at me." His voice is taut and irritated.

"Sorry," I mumble but continue to stare. The whiskey begins to warm my stomach, and I feel myself loosen slightly.

"No, you're not," he grits out as he inspects my arm.

Despite his abrasiveness, he leans in closer to me slightly. My arm is burning, my heart roaring inside my ears, and I have to clench my legs together to keep myself from squirming at the sensations now pulsating in my horny vagina. Great, add masochist to the things wrong with me.

"You're not about to—" He stabs the needle into my skin without warning. "Fucking shit on a stick. That hurt!"

"You have quite the creative mouth on you," he says, not even trying to hide his annoyance at my colorful vocabulary. His eyes remain on my wound, focusing on his work.

"You know you don't have to be so mean. My mind was a little lost when you showed up. It was an accident." *This one at least.*

His amber eyes briefly meet my own, understanding flashing in them. "Either way, remind me never to be near you while you have a sharp object nearby."

Wait. Was that an attempt at humor?

I watch him as he expertly stitches the deep cut on my arm. I didn't realize how badly I got myself. Oops. Well, at least the pain replaced the current storm overtaking my mind. Goal achieved. What can I say, I'm an overachiever.

"How did you get so good at this?" I ask him gently. My voice is quiet so as not to disturb him.

"I've done this a few times." His voice is numb, and I should leave it alone. But I don't.

"On you or other people?"

He ignores me.

"What do you do for a living? Are you in the medical field? You seem to know what you're doing. You do know what you're doing, right?" At this point, I'm only speaking to distract myself, and not from the pain but from his closeness and my urging desire to reach out and touch him.

"Why are you so nosy?" he responds without looking at me. He continues to pull the thread through my skin, the sensation almost a tickle now that the whiskey is coursing through me.

"Just trying to get to know my neighbor who apparently knows advanced first aid. You could be a murderer for all I know. So how did you learn to do stitches? Come on, tell me, or I'll just keep asking."

"My father was a doctor. And would a murderer fix the wounds he inflicts?" He uses his teeth to tear off the thread. Well, that doesn't seem sanitary. It jostles the wound, and I hiss in response. He ignores that and doesn't even apologize.

"Could be your kink, I guess. Fix them after you torture them. Then kill them once you're, uh . . . satisfied."

His gaze meets mine, and I swear he leans into me more, or am I leaning into him? "I have many kinks, Chaos. Killing isn't one of them, and neither is fixing people. But the torture . . ." He trails off suggestively.

Wait, what? I'm 90 percent sure my jaw just dropped, and my panties are now wet—more wet. With that, he steps away, and I almost fall off the counter, and yup, it was me leaning into him. *Shit.* I find myself opening and then closing my mouth like a fish out of water. I don't think I've ever met a man who's left me speechless.

He packs his kit back up and grabs his bottle of whiskey, then makes for the door. "Wait! Why do you keep calling me Chaos? And what do you mean you like to torture people! Should I be worried! You can't leave after dropping a weird fucking kink bomb on me like that! We should talk about this! I have questions!"

He continues to walk, not even looking over his shoulder. "Go to bed."

He slams his door, leaving me utterly confused. And horny. And my vibrators are packed up.

Fuck that bastard. I hate him.

May 5th, 2021

My Raven,

Your clever way to commit murder by Christmas festivities failed. Although as I sat there drinking the nauseatingly sweet hot cocoa, I was near death. Also, did you know they don't stock Christmas-themed pajamas if it's not around Christmas? I had to order them online. Guess what? They were delayed. Fucking postal service. Then I had to buy the movie Elf and hot chocolate. And then, to top it off, I had to start a fire. My apartment doesn't have a fireplace, so I had to use the one in the lobby. Did you know that required me to go down stairs, in front of people, in Christmas pajamas, with a mug of hot cocoa and my laptop open to Elf. If that wasn't embarrassing enough, I had to ask the front desk attendant to help me start a fire.

But here is your damn photo. Savor it because you're not getting any more, Raven.

I hope you're happy with my suffering.

On the surface, it seems we have many things in common; however, our cores are vastly different. I thrive in solidarity.

I don't like people or loud things. And yes, I'm aware I live in a city. But the city's noise is soothing. Loud, obnoxious people get on my nerves. I don't have many insecurities; I'm not afraid to admit I'm a confident person. I'm not cocky, but I know what I want and when I want it.

As far as family and friends, I don't have the former, and only one of the latter. My mom died when I was five. My dad was in my life until I turned eighteen, but I haven't talked to or seen him since, and I never want to. I have a single friend who has been by my side since we were kids. He's like a brother to me. I had one other friend, but she's gone.

Fears? Don't have them. Well now, Christmas pajamas and Elf.

Goals? Singular. Save as many people as I can.

I'm a simple man, and I like it that way.

I'm sorry to hear that you struggle with your mind, Raven. I won't tell you it will be okay because I don't make empty promises. I would hold you, though. I would help you battle the storm that plagues your mind. I know what it's like to fight your own mind.

I can tell you that it can get better. Not that it will. And being alone isn't so bad. Conquer your storm, then you will find peace in your isolation.

I will help you however I can. I'll find you in the deep recess of your mind, and I'll drag you back to the surface. Kicking and screaming if I have to.

You gave me a task, so here is yours. Paint me something. Don't tell me who you are, show me.

Words mean nothing.

gage

"The Alessi twins are in town." Hale is rocked back in his cheap government-issued chair, his hands loosely interlocked behind his head. His tired eyes are wracked with concern. I can practically see the wheels turning in that head of his. Anything to do with the Alessi family is trouble, so that means I'll be working even more overtime.

I guess the bright side is that I won't be stuck in my apartment, tempted by the chaotic little creature across from me. What the fuck was she doing with a razor blade? At three in the fucking morning.

Being so close to her this morning, her blood dripping down her arm, the smell of vanilla mixed with her sweaty skin, the small noises she made as I pierced her skin with the needle was intoxicating. Like watching a fucking storm on the horizon. You know you should run and take cover, but you can't help but watch it build. A storm I'd love to take control of . . .

Fuck me, I have to stop my train of thought before I pop a fucking boner right here in Hale's office.

The Alessi family.

Yeah, that will do it. Boner gone.

The Alessis run one of, if not the largest, sex trafficking rings on the West Coast. Their father has run the business for years, and his father before him and so on. The twins, his maniacal little hit men, do all his dirty work. Rumors have been running that Papa Dearest is getting a bit paranoid. He won't leave his mansion in Seattle, so the twins have been doing more and more. I'm sure they're preparing for when they take over. But if I know anything about Dante Alessi, he won't be giving up his throne easily.

"Why are they in Boston?" I ask as I sip my Americano. The view from Hale's office window calms me. When I see the bustling city below, all the people and noise focus my mind.

"Fuck if I know. But they are, and we have our eye on them. We need you to dig around and see what you can find. We need to know why they're in our city."

"Do you know where they're staying?" Turning from the window and finding a seat across from Hale, I fall into it and cross my ankles atop his desk. He smacks them off, and I chuckle.

Touchy touchy.

"Yeah, the Copley." He opens the file resting on his desk and slides it toward me. I flip through the photos they have captured so far. Nothing seems obviously suspect, except the fact that it's the fucking Alessi twins. The dark-haired Italian twins dress to the nines. Always in their sleek suits, high-end watches, and foreign sports cars. Fucking douchebags, living in extravagance off the lives of innocent men, women, and children.

But when I flip to the next photo, my brow raises, the only indication I'm surprised. What. The. Fuck.

"What? Why do you have that look on your face?" Hale immediately recognizes my change in demeanor.

"This girl in the photo, the blonde. What do you know about her?"

"What do you know about her?" He fires the question back at me with narrowed eyes. Suddenly defensive. *Strange.*

"I asked first."

"I'm the boss."

My only response is the glare I fire at him and my silence.

"Dick," he says as he gets up, coming around to look at the photo I'm staring holes into. His presence looms over my shoulder, and if I was a different man, it would be intimidating to have Hale Knight at my back. The former Navy SEAL is intimidating as fuck to everyone except me. I know he's a little fucking softy at heart.

"Natasha Baldwin. Heiress of the Baldwin empire on the West Coast. Good ole Daddy Baldwin owns a series of hotels down the coast. And if she's involved with the Alessis, we can only assume her father is too. We honestly don't know much more about her. No record. Currently works at a dance studio as a ballet instructor. Grew up in a small town on the outskirts of Portland but recently moved to Boston. As far as we can tell, she's clean. Which begs the question, why are the twins interested in her."

"I'll figure it out." I stand and make my way toward the door.

He nods. "Let me know what you find out about her."

One thing between Hale and me is that we completely trust each other to do our jobs. There is no second-guessing if it was done or how it was done; it gets done. I have his back, and he has mine.

Leaving his bright, bland office, I head into my own. My fortress of solitude and the highest caliber tech. No windows and sound-proof walls leave it a dark haven for my mind. I can control the fucking world from here.

Booting up my monitors and security cams, I begin digging. I could just ask Everett for Natasha's contact but what fun is that. Plus, I need to keep him out of this world as much as possible, especially if the Alessi twins are involved. He just got his happily ever after. I can't ruin that.

After minimal effort, I have Natasha's whole fucking life in my hands. All the way from birth to the present, I know everything about her. Seems like Daddy Dearest didn't invest in protecting his little princess. Nothing was securing her most private information. And to my surprise, Natasha's bank accounts are relatively empty. A whopping $246.89 to her name. Strange with her being an heiress to the Baldwin empire.

The twins are a little more difficult to pull information on. They have security measures on all their accounts, which is no shocker. It's the same as it has been each time we've looked into them. They are good. But I'm better.

They arrived in Boston two days ago and checked into their high-rise with only two guards in tow. No out-of-the-ordinary transfers or withdrawals coming in or out of their accounts. Whatever they're here to do, it seems like it will be a quick trip. Either way, I don't like it.

We don't dig too much into them; the Seattle office mostly handles them, but on the rare occasions they cross those state lines and travel to our city, we keep tabs. But now they are somehow connected to Natasha, and that hits a little too close to home for me. My fists ache to hit something as I think about her being in their crosshairs. Not for me, I couldn't give two fucks what happens to her, but if she gets hurt, Everett will be hurt, and that I can't fucking have.

Time to pay my high school nemesis a little visit. According to her Google calendar, her first class of the day ends in twenty minutes, and I'll be there to greet her.

I head down to the studio and park my ass in the coffee shop right across, giving me a good view of the entrance of the little brick studio. I can see her teaching tiny spawns through the large glass windows. She looks happy, and it sickens me. This vile ex of Everett's was a nasty little thing in high school. If anyone tried to come between her and Everett, it was hell to pay, which is what I experienced when I became his best friend. It only got slightly better, and by better, I mean her completely ignoring me, when Everett got tired of her bullshit and put his foot down. At the threat of losing him, she eased up on me. Not that I cared, but I think it bothered him. Always the protector.

As the little children in their pink leotards and tutus filter out with their parents, I slip in.

"Nice little gig you got here," I say as I step into her studio, hands tucked into my pocket, fidgeting with my coin.

"Well, look who the cat dragged in. I haven't seen you in a while. What brings you to my studio, and how do I get you to leave?" She places her hand on her hip and flips her long blonde braid over her shoulder. The fully mirrored wall behind her showcases her entire tight body. If I didn't know how much of a bitch she was on the inside, I might actually find her attractive.

Beating around the bush isn't my style, so I get right to the point. "What are you doing with the Alessi twins, Natasha?" But her reaction tells me that it's not my bluntness that has her spooked.

She goes pale, and her eyes shoot to the front door. My guard is immediately up. Why is she spooked? If she's working with them, it's not by choice. She clearly knows they're dangerous, so who's forcing her?

"How do you ev—never mind, it doesn't matter. You need to leave. And don't bring them up again." She comes toward me and reaches out to grab my arm, I'm sure to lead me out, but I step back.

I raise my chin in defiance and look down at her. "Why are you scared of them?"

"Gage, please." Her tone is hushed, her eyes darting around. I've never heard her beg before. Oh, how quickly the queen falls when in the real world. She's desperate, and as much as I despise her, Everett cares for her so that means I will protect her.

"I'm not leaving this be. Give me something if you want me to go."

She finally relents letting out a breath, her sweaty chest sinking in. "Fine. I'm . . . with them." She doesn't make eye contact. Her hands are fidgeting with her tights.

"Lie. Give me the truth."

"Ugh, you're such an ass! I'm not lying, and you need to leave." Turning from me, she goes and grabs her bag, then shuts the lights off. I follow her out the front door, unwilling to let this all go.

But I pull up short when a tall, dark figure steps out of a blacked-out SUV. It's one of the twins although I can't tell which yet. Flicking away the cigarette he was smoking and buttoning up his suit jacket, he steps up to Natasha.

"Can I help you, Agent Eros?"

Ah. Too formal to be Enzo.

I hold this asshole's gaze. "Just visiting a friend, Rafael."

Nat's eyes dart to mine. "Agent?"

Rafael wraps his arm around Natasha's slim waist, pulling her in tight. "Ah yes, your friend here works for the FBI, specifically the human trafficking division. He's quite efficient in what he does. And quite a nuisance to my entire existence."

I don't miss Natasha's trembling hands as they clutch to her duffel bag or the way her eyes won't connect with mine. "I didn't know he was in the FBI. I didn't—"

"Hush now." He silences her with a tightening grip to her waist, and my fists clench. My nails dig into my palms, and I release a deep breath, trying to remain cool. "I'll see you tonight, like we talked about."

Confusion flashes across her face, but she doesn't say anything. I'll text her later and have her meet me at the gym. Enzo and his brother, Rafael, aren't stupid. They know we're watching them, and now they know I'm watching Nat. They won't do anything to endanger her, not while she's in Boston at least. So now, I just need to keep her here and figure out what the fuck they want with her.

November 13th, 2021

My Arrow,

  Thank you for the photo. The Henry Leo's mug was a nice touch. It's my favorite place to get coffee. In my opinion, it's the best coffee in Boston. But I'm biased. I hate to hear that you didn't like the movie! Or the experience. Maybe you just need someone to experience it with.

  I'm sorry it has taken me so long to write you back. Your task was more challenging than I ever expected. Every time I lifted the brush, I felt as though I couldn't breathe. It took me six months to complete your task. But I did it.

  See, when I told you I loved to paint, I didn't tell you that it was my father who taught me. It's what he and I bonded over. Anytime I was lost in my mind, he would bring me to his art room, throw a canvas in front of me, and tell me to let it all out on the canvas. And then we would talk, my mind and words flowing out of me like the art I was making. But I haven't, not since he left.

I didn't realize how much I needed it until you reminded me. Until you reached into my mind and pulled me from the deep, suffocating waves that told me I could never feel connected to him again because he wasn't here to paint with me.

Thank you, Arrow. Thank you, thank you, thank you.

I have to say, I'm rusty, so please don't judge too harshly. I could pick out a million flaws in this painting, but I felt like you would have wanted it real and raw without alterations. I had to paint on paper since I didn't know how to fit a canvas into a letter, so I hope you like it. But typically, I paint on canvas with acrylic paint.

Here I have for you a watercolor. I hope you like it.

I'm sorry to hear about your mom. I can't imagine losing someone so important at such a young age. And your dad, why would you not want to see him? He raised you, no? I can't imagine knowing my dad was out there and never speaking to him. I need to know, as someone who didn't have a choice in losing her father, why would you willingly give up yours? He can't be that bad. After all, he's your father. I'm sure he loves you in his own way. I've learned that forgiveness is vital for survival. We have to let it go and move forward. We have to forgive. It's not worth it not to. You never know when you won't have the chance again.

I admire your goal. Are you a first responder? How do you save as many people as you can? And how do you find peace in the chaos of your mind? Let me be one of the ones you save.

colette

"**F**uck, shit, damn, ball-sucking cunt!" I could scream right now! Oh wait, I fucking did. Where the fuck is my box of letters?

I have unpacked this entire apartment, and they are nowhere. I brought them with me, safely belted them into my passenger seat, and carried them up myself to avoid this exact situation. I can't lose those letters. They are my lifeline, my connection to Arrow. I read them anytime I'm feeling lost, and he saves me. Without them, I'll lose my mind.

"What a foul mouth on such a pretty thing." Gage stands in my doorway, looking as sexy as sin with his arms crossed over his chest. His black shirt stretched over his muscles and now I want to punch him or fuck him. Maybe both, in that order.

"Don't call me pretty." I huff at him as I collapse onto my new-to-me couch. Thank you, Goodwill, for the ratty, floral-print grandma couch.

"What's wrong, Chaos?" He comes and looms his tall frame above me, hands tucked into his pockets as usual.

"Why do you care? And stop calling me Chaos. It's creepy, and I'm not chaotic." I pout as I fiddle with the hem of my tank top.

He pulls his hand from his pocket, and I get a good look at the backs of his hands. Are those coins tattooed into his veiny hand? Silver rings adorn his fingers. I never in my life thought I would find jewelry sexy on a man but consider me corrected. His fingers grip my chin as he lifts my face so I'm looking up at him.

His hair falls back into his eyes as he looks down at me. "I don't care. But I need sleep, and you're loud. If I can fix your problem, I get to sleep. And you're chaotic. Probably the most chaotic person I have ever met. Now answer my question. What's wrong?"

If he wasn't so damn hot, and if I wasn't secretly hoping to put his dick to good use, I'd punch it right now. Yet I can't help but want his help. Something in me needs to give in to him. Letting out a breath, I decide to let him help.

"I lost an important box. I've looked everywhere, torn apart every larger box, looked in cabinets, under my bed, fuck, I even looked in the shower. Nothing. I need that box."

He drops my chin and peers around, taking in the chao—nope . . . not going to prove him right. The . . . messy living room and kitchen. I really did make a mess trying to find those damn letters.

"What does the box look like?"

"It's an old hat box. It's, uh . . . wooden and has the letters MJC carved into the top."

"Alright, come on. I'll help you look." Gage begins circling my apartment, lifting clothing and blankets, opening boxes and moving stuff around. After only a few minutes of watching him, I notice he's organizing items as he looks.

"Are you . . . categorizing my things?" I mock him.

"You're a messy creature. I can't help myself," he replies without even looking at me. I just smile to myself. And then it hits what he actually said.

"In my defense, I'm in a crisis right now. I'm not usually this bad."

"Doubtful." That's his only response as we continue to look through items. He has sorted out a few piles, one for the kitchen, bedroom, bathroom, and living room, and one with random things that don't seem to belong anywhere.

After what feels like hours but has really only been half an hour, Gage breaks the silence. "Colette."

I turn to find him standing with an old shoebox, and my eyes bug out of my head with embarrassment. "Don't look in there!" I lunge forward, hurtling boxes as I try to reach him.

"Too late. You have quite the collection of toys. The white sparkly one is my favorite." If I wasn't so mortified, I would melt at the smirk he's giving me. I reach him as he holds the box high above his head, and despite my average height, I still can't reach it, even when I jump.

Fucking tall people.

"You're such an ass-wipe! Give me that back!"

He doesn't. He just continues to chuckle. "Nah, I like watching you work for it." His gaze heats as I realize my boobs are about to fall out of my tank top.

"I'm going to shove EC so far up your ass, you'll feel him in your ears! Give me—"

"You named your dildo EC?" He finally drops the box and hands it to me. I take it with a huff. "I went through a *Twilight* phase. Sue me."

Confusion crosses his face, and then it hits him as he doubles over laughing. Holy shit, I thought he was sexy as sin with a scowl on his face, but when he laughs, that bright smile, that deep, raspy tone . . . fuck me sideways and take me to church . . . he's stunning.

"You named your sparkly white dildo Edward fucking Cullen." He continues to mock me despite my absolute fuck ton of humiliation right now.

"Shut up! Shut up! Shut. Up! Don't hate on EC. He's way bigger and better than you!" I smack him on the shoulder and cover the bottom half of my face with the shoebox, trying to hide the blush creeping up my neck as I can't help but imagine him using EC on me.

He rights himself now, a smirk still on his face as he tries to catch his breath. "He's comparable, without the sparkles of course."

I fumble my box of toys, almost dropping it, at the image I just got of Gage with an eight-inch girthy penis. "There is no way. You—no." My eyes travel down, and I'm caught red-handed checking him out.

The cocky ass just smirks at me as he continues going through boxes. "You'll never know."

"Well, you don't vibrate. EC does." Take that, Mr. Eros. I proudly walk back toward the area I was clearing, an extra sway in my hips.

"But EC isn't pierced."

"Wha—Fuck!" Gage's comment has me tripping over myself, literally. My feet get caught up in a blanket on the floor, and I find myself falling face-first into a large box. The cardboard edges scrape along my arms.

"Ugh! I hate you, Gage Eros!" I cry as he comes and looks down on me, not even offering me his hand to help me up.

I want to shove EC straight into the stupid, smug, perfect smile he's giving me right now. I crawl out of the box and sit on the floor, pouting, feeling completely hopeless, and now embarrassed.

As he sits in front of me, knees up, resting his tattooed forearms on them, all I can think about is his pierced, comparable-in-size-to-EC cock, and I just want to see it.

Just a peek.

For research purposes.

The tips of his slip-on Vans meet my bare shins, and shivers run up my legs. I drag my eyes along his ink, taking note of all kinds of images. God, this is really unfair. He's so pretty.

"Hey, you will find your silly little box." He nudges my leg with the tip of his shoes.

"It's not silly. It has letters in it. Really important ones. Ones that can never be replaced."

He looks to the side, and I notice his eyes narrow, focusing on something that has caught his eye. When I follow his gaze, I find him staring intently at my dad's old typewriter perched on my bookshelf.

"Do you use that?" He gets up, going to it before I can even answer. I follow and see him tracing his fingers over the keys, then landing on my dad's custom raven key.

"Sometimes," I say as I press my body into his, but he moves slightly to the side, creating space between us. He runs his fingers over all the keys, then settles on the raven key and presses down over and over again, imprinting the ink into the paper. He studies it like a secret code, and I'm drawn in by the small crease between his dark brows.

"Why a raven?" His voice is a whisper. The first time I have ever heard Gage's voice vulnerable.

"My last name, Corvina, it means raven. This was my dad's. He was . . . killed in action when I was sixteen. He used to write all his letters on this, signing it with the raven key instead of his name. He was a pilot. His callsign was Raven."

Gage's eyes meet mine finally, and for the first time, I see his mask drop. The fear in his eyes is palpable, like he's seeing a ghost. He shakes his head as if to clear it of a fog and makes for the front door. "I need to go."

"Are you ok—" I don't even finish my sentence when my front door slams closed. What the hell?

April 18th, 2022

Raven,

Your painting is exquisite. As beautiful
as I imagine you to be. It's dark and soft,
alluring and comforting. It's simple but
incredibly profound. The strokes of your
brush seem so soft, yet the image is bold.

I'm glad to hear that you were able
to paint again. I hope you felt closer
to your father as you did so. Whenever
you struggle to find a connection to him,
paint me something. I can imagine you,
set up in a dark room, maybe in front of
the window, sitting atop a wooden stool,
in messy paint-ridden overalls. I see the
image, but I can't see your face.

And stop with the flaws. There are no flaws
in your art, just as there are no flaws in
who you are. Just because we have struggles,
scars, and monsters does not mean we are
flawed. Everything we are is made up from
all we have been through. Could you imagine
how boring life would be without a little
darkness? I, for one, love your "flaws" as
you call them.

And yes, the coffee at Henry Leo's was delicious. Reminded me of a little place I used to go to back home. The burning homesickness I felt in my chest as I sat there was almost too much to bear. I'm afraid I'm weak in that sense. I cannot stand to be in there, but I will go for your letters. Briefly, I will endure that pain for you.

The topic of my father is a sensitive one, I'm afraid. In fact, after your choice words, I was not sure if I could write you back. That's why it has taken me a while to respond. But I could not let him take another beautiful thing from me.

You have no idea what you speak of, though. Not everyone had a good father growing up, dear Raven. I understand you did not have a choice in losing yours, and I'm sorry for that. However, I would have given anything to lose mine. I would have rejoiced and danced upon his grave. I don't speak to him; I don't ever want to. He does not deserve my words, my voice, my attention, nothing. So please, if you want to continue with our relationship, you will not bring him up again.

As far as my job, it's not something I really discuss with people. But I can tell you that I'm not a first responder. I don't work in the medical field. But I do use my specific skill set to help innocents who need saving.

Finding peace in the chaos of your mind is simple, sweet Raven. Make friends with your monsters. Don't hide them, unleash them. They are a part of who you are. When you're able to do this, you will see that peace comes easily.

And when you need me, I will always find you. But I have a feeling that you will be able to save yourself one day.

←———◁

gage

R aven.

My Raven.

No. That loud, obnoxious, foul-mouthed, chaotic beauty cannot be my Raven. But like fitting the last piece of a puzzle in place, the picture is suddenly so clear. Her dad. Her last name. Leaving our letters at Henry Leo's.

But my Raven is broken, fragile, sweet. Colette is . . . well, she's her. She doesn't have a fragile bone in her body. Her mouth is quick and smart. She's challenging and temperamental. Or just mental.

I try to wrap my head around the fact that the girl I have been anonymously writing letters to for the past four years not only lives across from me but is Leo's best friend. Flashes of Raven's letters come to mind, and Colette begins to blur into Raven seamlessly.

In my life, to the outside world I'm joyful and full of life, but on the inside, I feel like I'm drowning in my demons. Lost in my mind. My grief and sorrow are incredibly heavy, and I'm weighed down. The mask I wear with those I love is always in place, only coming off when I'm alone. So I do my best to never be alone.

I put on a front of confidence, but inside, my mind is battling me. I second-guess myself constantly, I fill my head with doubts and fears, most probably irrational to everyone else, but to me, they are very real.

Could Colette really be my Raven? They are two completely different people. Raven is special to me. She's mine. Completely and utterly mine in every way except physically. I can barely tolerate Colette. But that's not true, is it? There is a pull in my mind toward her. Ever since I saw her in Henry Leo's, something about her stayed with me. Like a fucking itch I couldn't scratch, she was there. The more we were near each other, the more she continued to infect me. Grow on me. She always pulled me in, just like my Raven did.

Holy. Fucking. Shit. As if fate is fucking me in the ass with its middle finger, it all falls into place. Who the fuck threw me into the script of a fucking rom-com, and how the fuck do I get out of it . . . yet it doesn't change the fact that Colette Corvina is my Raven.

Thoughts of how Raven always made me feel as I read her letters circles through my mind like sharks circling prey. I was safe with her, seen and heard. She was my outlet to express all the feelings that I typically repress.

And despite me not wanting it, Colette feels the same way. I'm so fucking confused.

Before I can even stop myself, I'm at her door. Knocking. Shit. I can't do this. What am I going to say? Take a breath, take control. This isn't you. You're in control. But now it's too late because when she opens the door, I see her in a completely different way. I think, for the first time, I'm truly looking at her. I know her soul, and now I'm matching her stunning features to it.

Her smooth skin is warm and flawless. The slight upturn of her eyes, which I once found fierce, are now so fucking vulnerable. The fire I once thought was in her eyes, I see now is sorrow and grief. Colette is a mask, and now, I see behind the facade. My Raven has been here all along. The foul mouth, the loud, obnoxious attitude, it's a shield.

Fuck. It really is her.

"Raven." It slips between my lips unwillingly. I don't even realize what I just blurted until Colette looks at me with her head tilted and a small lift to her brow.

"Are you okay? Did you hit your giant-ass head and not tell me? Do I need to call Everett?" She steps to me and lays the back of her hand against my forehead. Like being abruptly pulled from a dream, I snap back into reality. Stepping away from her touch is like closing the door to a warm, sunny day. "No. I'm fine. Did you find your box?"

She's looking at me like I have two heads, and maybe I do. I don't know what the fuck is going on in this reality right now. "Uh, no. Are you offering more help or . . ."

Fuck. Am I? No. I can't.

"I actually need to go."

"You're being creepy." She steps back and crosses her arms in front of her chest, pushing her breasts up. Don't look. Don't look. Don't look. Fuck.

"I need to go," I say more to myself than her. I walk away faster than I have ever moved before making a beeline to the elevator.

Jesus, get a hold of yourself, Eros. She's still Colette, the chaotic little banshee who drives you mad. Mad with annoyance and aggravation.

I need a distraction. And I know the perfect one.

I dial her number, and she picks up on the first ring. "You need a hit, baby?" She already knows. I never call her for anything else.

"Meet me in ten."

"You got it, sugar. I'll be ready."

Hopping into my Audi, I make my way to Joe's. The boxing gym that has saved my life on more than one occasion. Laying into the bags or other people—willing people—allows my monsters to come out and play so they leave me the fuck alone momentarily.

Any reprieve I can get from the monsters that haunt me is a blessing. I told Raven once to make friends with her monsters, and this is how I befriend mine. So as I let my fist fly and feel the pain in my knuckles, ribs, and face, I'm reminded that I'm alive and no longer at his mercy.

Pain is the only touch I can handle. Soft caresses across my skin remind me of the way he touched me. The way he used my body to please the darkest parts of himself and then the way he beat me because of how much he hated himself for his desires.

I can't do soft touches. But I can do pain. I need the pain.

The old gym with graffiti brick and old slide-up garage-style doors is empty. Closed for all but Sabrina and me at this time of night. B lives at this gym, literally. Allowing me to come at any hour. To fight or fuck. She's one of the best fighters I know and the only one who can come close to challenging me in the ring. She doesn't go easy on me, and I can give her what I can of myself at that moment.

And usually after, we end up fucking the adrenaline out of our bodies. She doesn't do soft touches or sweet words. She needs it quick and dirty, and that's all I can give. All I can give anyone.

My mind is in disarray. For years, Raven has haunted me. If I could see myself with anyone, it would be her, but I can't give her intimacy. It's not that I can't be gentle. It's that I cannot allow others to be gentle with me. And I've always known Raven to be someone who needs to give her love to someone. That couldn't be me. It never will be.

How could you form a genuine, intimate, loving relationship with someone who can't stand to be touched? You can't. Despite how much I was always drawn to Raven, she deserved a man who could give her those things. So I kept my distance. But now she lives right across from me, and I'm losing my ever-loving mind.

Pulling up to Joe's, B is already sitting with her hip cocked, leaning against the rusted doorframe of the fire station turned boxing gym.

"What's got ya in a tizzy, stud?" Her silky voice lures me in. Ready to fight. Ready to fuck.

"Nothing." She never deserves my attitude, but I can't help it as it leaks from every pore of my body.

"Fine. Whatever. Let's fight, big guy." She walks away, letting her confident stride lead me to the ring. Her short frame is thick in the hips and thighs from dancing across the canvas. Her waist is trim and tight. Her red hair is always in two braids running down her stubborn head to her tight ass. The silvery scar running down her back between her shoulder blades shimmers. I always mean to ask about it, but then again, it's not my business. She's a fiery little thing, but don't mistake her beauty for weakness. I have seen her take down men even larger than I am, and not just with her fists but with her attitude as well.

Besides Everett, Leo, and Hale, she's the only one I spend any amount of time with, but unlike them, we don't confide in each other with our words but with our bodies.

Stripping my shirt and wrapping my hands, I climb into the ring with her. Bouncing on the balls of my feet to warm up, I throw a few jabs, and she watches me, leaning against the ropes. Based on the sweat shimmering on her chest, she's already warmed up.

And then we begin our dance. She's fast, going for my ribs first, always the fucking ribs with her. She uses her small stature to her advantage, forcing me to crouch inward to guard my most sensitive area, then she comes for the face when I'm closer to her height. I've been fighting with her long enough that I know her tricks, but I still fall for them.

"You're slow today, baby. Fucking hit me!"

I growl at her taunt, then unleash myself.

As much as she tells me to never pull my hits, I always do with her. I could never lay my full power into a woman, even one who begs for it. She usually calls me out on it, but I don't give a fuck.

We continue our dance, exchanging blows till we are both collapsed onto the canvas, heaving for breath. Little bits of blood leak from my brow, and my ribs are bruised from her strong legs. A small trail of blood drips from her nose and from her brow since I opened an already healing cut there.

"Good fight." She extends her sweaty fist to me, and I tap it.

"You too, B."

She hums in response, both of us too out of breath to form any lengthy sentences. That's not really our style anyway.

"Want to hit the showers? That fight made me horny as fuck."

I scoff at her. Normally, I wouldn't hesitate to get a little wet with her, but now that I have Raven—Colette, fuck, whoever, in my life, the thought of rolling around with B makes me feel like I'm being unfaithful. I know that Colette and I have no relationship like that, but something just doesn't sit right in my gut at the thought of fucking someone else now.

"Not tonight, B." I lean up, resting my elbows on my knees to catch my breath.

"You're not pussying out on me, are you? Catching feelings and shit?"

Chuckling at her, I reassure her, "No. Not at all."

"Thank fuck. Did you finally find yourself a girl to call home?"

A person to call home. She and I have talked about what we would do if we found someone who felt like home. But both of us know we have too much fucked-up shit in our heads to feel that with someone.

But . . .

Raven always felt like home.

For the first time in my life, I'm unsure of my feelings. I have always been a man who knew what he wanted. I didn't second-guess or question my desires. I just went after them. But with Raven, I have no fucking idea what to do. I can't be who she wants, who she deserves. I'm too fucked in the head to give her a man who is worthy of her.

Colette, on the other hand, is a stunning little creature, and I'm highly attracted to her. It's her attitude that has always thrown me through a loop. Loud and eccentric, unashamedly foul-mouthed and brazen. She's nothing like my Raven, but she's my Raven. How fucked up is that?

"I don't fucking know."

B gets up and strips her clothing right in front of me, revealing her naked pale skin glistening with the sweat we worked up. A painting of bruises mars her skin, but I know without a doubt each bruise was earned. No one touches her without her permission. And she doesn't need anyone to protect her.

"Don't overthink it, Gage. If you want her, go get her. If you don't, leave her the fuck alone and move on. Don't drag her along, big guy."

I leave the ring following B's little pep talk, feeling physically exhausted but even more mentally exhausted. That fight gave me absolutely no relief, and her words left me desperate for answers. I hate feeling this way.

Fuck me.

May 2nd, 2022

My Arrow,

  Since I know you're dying to gaze upon my stunning face, I have included a self-portrait. Let your eyes feast on what I see in the mirror.

  But in all seriousness, I wish I was as beautiful as you make me sound. But I'm not. I do paint in front of a window, but I'm usually in ratty old pajamas, my hair thrown up in a nest atop my head. I can promise you it is not a pretty sight. But then again, I think that's what helps my creative hand flow.

  You say such pretty words, but if you really knew who I was, met me on the outside world, would you love me? I wonder. Because who I'm with you here, in these pages, is vastly different from the mask I wear to the world. I don't even know who the real me is anymore. This girl I'm here with you is my true self, but the girl I am to everyone else is who I want to be. Bold and confident. It's exhausting really, acting in a way that is not true to your nature. But they say the more you tell a lie, the more truth it holds. Maybe I can lie long enough that she will become my truth. And this scared little girl from the pages will disappear forever.

Have you ever thought of disappearing?

I'm sorry to bring up your father, but you can give me your story. I will keep it safe. I do want our relationship to continue, but I want it to be honest. I want it to be real. Don't hide from me, please. You need someone to listen to you. To love you and to truly love someone, you have to give them every part of you. The good and the bad.

I hope that you will write back to me, but I understand if you cannot. I'll still look for your letters. Every day, I will look. If it takes you a day or five years, I'll still look for you.

Chapter Ten

colette

"You're a goddess." LJ's spaghetti strap white silk gown falls to just below her knee and hugs her curves beautifully. The swooping effect of the neckline showcases just enough cleavage, but she still looks like a classy lady.

"Thank you. Are you sure it's not too . . ." She bites at her lip, and her cheeks blush. "Sexy?"

I come up behind her and fluff her curls as we both let our eyes travel the length of her body, assessing the simple yet sexy dress.

"LJ, it's perfect. It's completely you. It's sexy in the simplest way, and Everett will be drooling all over you all night."

I pin her headpiece behind her right ear, pulling back some of the curls from her stunning face.

"I can't believe I'm about to marry Everett," she says behind tear-filled eyes.

"Leo Jean Phoenix, if you cry right now and ruin the perfect makeup I applied to your face, you will be limping down that aisle. Shut it down!"

Matching her elegant dress, I did a light makeup look with a small wing on each eyelid and a red lip. I did mine to match, but she outshines me by a million stars on this day and any other. If I didn't love dick so much, I would totally be a lesbian for her.

"I'm sorry. It's just so surreal. After everything we went through . . . I never thought we would be here."

"Well, you are and stop second-guessing if you deserve it because I know that's what you're doing."

"But—" I round her so that I'm facing her now and squish her cheeks in my hands, silencing her.

"You deserve the world, and Everett will give it to you. Stop looking for the other foot to drop. Nothing is going to take this from you."

"Shoe," she says through squished lips.

"Yeah, I got your shoes." I let her cheeks go and bend down to help her into her silver pointed-toe stilettos.

She laughs as she grabs my shoulder for balance. "No, the phrase is for the other shoe to drop. Not foot."

I right myself and wave her away. "Whatever, losing a foot would be way worse."

A knock sounds on the door, and we both turn to look as it slowly opens. "May I come in?"

"Yes," LJ says as she steps down off the little pedestal. Ski walks in and wraps her in a bear hug. He's a tall man, and despite his age, he still seems to be pretty fit. If LJ hadn't told me he was a big softy, I would have been terrified of him. He just gives off that don't-fuck-with-me attitude.

"Leo." His eyes also fill with tears, and if either of them let those tears fall, I'm going to lose it. But then he takes in a big breath, collecting himself, and pulls out a black box from his suit pocket. "This belonged to my Millie, and . . . I know she would have wanted you to have it. She always wanted to give it to our daughter, and I never got the chance to with . . ." He uses a handkerchief to wipe the tears from his eyes. "Well, I'd like you to have it."

LJ opens the box to find a stunning silver necklace with an emerald-cut sapphire. The blue shines as bright as her eyes, and dammit . . . there go the tears.

"Ski, this is—I can't—" He takes it from her hands and moves behind her as he wraps it around her neck.

"Millie needed something blue on our wedding day, but I couldn't afford anything like this, so I found a little rock, painted it blue, and hung it from a chain. She wore it for our wedding then hid it away, rightfully so. The thing was hideous . . ." He chuckles as he continues to fumble with the clasp, so I quietly step in and finish for him, and he nods his head in thanks. "A few years later, I bought her this to replace the rock necklace."

I hand LJ a tissue so she can clean up the small tears running down her face. Thank Jesus for waterproof mascara.

"And this must be Colette?" Ski looks at me finally, and I don't wait. I walk right to him, and he envelops me in a hug just as he did my best friend.

"It's nice to finally meet you, Ski."

"Likewise. I'm glad she had someone like you, Colette. Thank you for taking care of my girl."

I'm not going to cry. I'm not going to cry. Dammit. I can't even respond with words because if I do, I'll just cry harder.

"Well, we shouldn't leave the groom waiting. He's already been waiting long enough for this day."

LJ loops her arm through Ski's, and they lead the way out of the room as I follow. They stop just outside the courthouse's double doors that lead into the small little chapel, and I go to excuse myself, but LJ catches my arm. "Cole. Thank you. For helping me with the dress, the flowers, the makeup . . ." She looks down at her feet. "For everything." Her tone and the love in her eyes tell me she means more than just today.

"Of course." I place a soft kiss on her cheek.

"One day, it will be reversed, and you will be the bride." A pang hits my chest at the thought of me walking down an aisle. Without my dad, who would even walk with me?

I've always wanted a big wedding—the dress, the flowers, the music, the family and friends—but then one day all that changed. My dad was gone, and I isolated myself. I withdrew into a cave of my own grief, and it left me with no one but myself. "Maybe one day," I lie.

In my mind, I know I'll never be a bride. Who would want to marry a fraud, a ghost living in an animated body? Whoever falls in love with me falls for the outgoing, vibrant persona I wear. No one loves my true self, my broken, shadowed soul. Even Arrow, the one who truly knows me, doesn't love me that way.

I walk into the little courthouse room first and see Gage standing next to Everett. His all-black attire is just about panty melting. I swear the man could give the devil himself a run for his money. We haven't talked since that weird incident at my apartment, but the way he's undressing me with his eyes currently has me blushing, and I'm not exactly sure what to do with these feelings.

"Are you nervous?" I whisper to Everett as I watch his hands move together.

"Fuck no," he says with confidence, and it brings a smile to my face.

The double doors open, and Ski walks Leo down the short little aisle. Before he delivers her to Everett, he places a kiss on her cheek and envelops the groom in a giant hug. I tune out the officiant as he says his rehearsed little speech but focus on Leo as she begins her vows.

"Ev, there is no way I could say all the things I'm feeling at this moment. So . . ." She reaches into the pocket of her little dress and pulls out an origami note. "I wrote it."

He takes the note and pulls his own from his pocket. Leo's little gasp tells me she wasn't expecting him to have the same idea. "Did you think there would be any other way I would say my vows to you, pretty bird? In reality, I've been writing my vows to you since that first day in chemistry. This is just a continuation of them."

She takes his note and they both put them back in their pocket without reading them. "Would you like to read them aloud?" the officiant asks, and Everett looks at LJ, silently asking if that's what she wants to do.

"Phoenix," she whispers.

"We will read them privately," Everett tells the officiant as he brings LJ's hand up and kisses her knuckles.

"Very well. I guess all that's left are the rings."

They exchange rings and do the fun little kiss-the-bride thing, and it's official. My best friend is married. I'm not going to cry. I'm not going to cry.

"You gonna cry, Chaos?" Gage smirks at me from behind Everett.

"Shut up," I quip, and Gage chuckles as he follows the bride and groom out of the courthouse.

November 22nd, 2022

My Arrow,

I told you that I would understand if you didn't want to reply, but I'm not okay with it. At all.

I miss you. You're all I have right now that is keeping me sane.

I'm drowning, and I need you back.

But I'm also so furious with you. How could you allow me to open up to you? How could you stand there and let me confide in you, take shelter in your words, and then leave me with nothing but these pieces of paper?

I see that you don't want to open up to me. I can understand that, but don't leave me. Stay with me.

Maybe I don't want you back. Perhaps it would be better to stop this little game we've started. Maybe it's better this way before I fall in love with you. But the thought of that makes my chest hurt. Makes me sick to my stomach. I still need you. And perhaps that makes me weak, but I never claimed to be strong.

Please, just come find me again.

gage

I fucking hate weddings.

If I had to root for any couple in the world, it would be these two, and still, I can't find any fucks to give about their wedding. Even when it's in a simple fucking courthouse. It's sickening. What the fuck is the point? Why does a piece of paper make people believe you're somehow more in love than you were the day before you said "I do."

Thank fuck Leo and Everett did a little last-minute courthouse wedding because if I had to plan any best man waste-of-money shit, I would have killed myself. Lie. I would have done it all begrudgingly because I love the shit out of both of them, but I would have complained the whole time.

Everett was fucking beaming like a kid on Christmas as Leo came down the aisle in a simple white dress. Her wild curls were down, and a little origami folded note was pinned behind one ear. She was stunning. As radiant as she has always been. If anyone ever says I shed a tear at seeing those two finally happy, I'll deny it until my last breath.

And to top it off, the assholes dragged me to a fucking club. With people. Drunk people. Do they know me at all? They'll be lucky if I make it out of here without breaking someone's fucking nose. If anyone fucking touches me . . .

Silver lining? I get to sit at this bar, whiskey in hand, as I watch my chaotic beauty swirl her hips and throw her head back in sweet serenity. She's utterly oblivious to how fucking crazy she's making me. Her tight deep-purple dress hugs her hips, and the ruffled sleeves fall off her shoulders. The tight neckline of the dress suffocates her breasts. I don't know what kind of fabric it's made from, but whatever it is, it clings to her curves. The only thing it would look better on would be my floor.

"Fuck," I mutter. The images running through my mind are ungodly.

"She's hot, huh?"

"Jesus fucking Christ." I jump in my seat. No one sneaks up on me. Ever. But Colette had me so utterly distracted I didn't even see my best friend sneak up on me.

"Leo. I see the roles have been reversed. Sneaking up on me now?"

"Not my fault you're eye-fucking my best friend, and you didn't notice me." She jumps onto the stool next to me. And yes, she actually has to give a little hop since she's so short.

"I wasn't eye-fucking her," I lie through my teeth, but Leo could always sense my lies.

She simply tilts her head and raises her brow at me. "You can admit it, Gage. You like her." Leaning into me, she bumps my arm with her shoulder. Her eyes are glassy from clearly drinking a little too much. But I don't judge because she deserves to let loose.

"Why aren't you out there dancing?" I inquire as I try to change the subject.

"Don't change the subject."

Shit.

"I needed a break. I'm not as free-spirited as Cole. Plus, she doesn't need me. She dances to the drum of her beat. Own beat. Dances to the beat of her drums," she slurs, and I don't bother correcting her while I continue to watch Colette.

"You should go dance with her." She nudges me with her shoulder.

"Do you even know me?" Her eyes drop, sorrowful for a split moment as she remembers the past eight years we've been apart. Right. She might not know me. But this has not changed. I don't dance. Or do social events. Or speak to people outside of my little family.

"I do know you, Gage. I know you're attracted to her, and she's exactly what you need."

"Oh, please do explain how I need a chaotic, loud, stubborn, infuriating creature in my life. I already have you and Rune to fill those roles."

"Oh, silly boy, don't you see? There is no one quite like Colette Corvina." With that, she gets up and makes her way over to where Everett is ordering another drink from the bar. She jumps into his arms as he turns to her, his eyes completely lighting up at the sight of his girl. He's a lovesick puppy dog and putty in her hands. What a pussy. I'm so fucking happy for them.

"Ohh, are we getting shots!" The music vibrates in my chest, but upon her coming into my space, the noises blur and quiet. When she stumbles into me slightly, I reach out, catching her by the waist and righting her. My heart now pounds with the music at the feel of her skin on mine.

"Oopsies, sorry," she mumbles close to my ear. Her breath tickles my ear, making my fists clench. Memories of my father flood my mind.

"I'm sorry, Son. I wish I could stop," he whispers in my ear.

My reflexes push her away, and the hurt in her eyes pierces my chest. Fuck. Take a breath. Take control.

Everett's hand clamps down onto my shoulder, his eyes looking for me. Finding me like they do when I fade away into my memories. The four of us stand in a circle as Leo passes around shots. Colette raises her glass, and I see the shine of her eyes; she's about to fucking cry. Then I look at Leo. Fuck, so is she. I finally look at my best friend, searching for even an ounce of testosterone, but he stares down at his wife, also about to cry.

What a bunch of fucking pussies. I'm surrounded by hopeless romantics. Great.

"To this day. July seventh, 2024. The day my best friend and the love of her life finally tied the knot! You guys have been through more than any humans should have had to in order to be together. But you made it!" she shrieks, and I wince as my eardrums about burst. "You're beautiful, and you made a beautiful little human, and I'm so happy to be part of your love story."

And the tears fall. All three of them wipe tears from their cheeks as I knock my shot back before any of them can guilt me into making a toast. I need more of these if I'm to survive this night.

The night continues. I remain in my seat as I sip my whiskey and watch Colette move effortlessly. My eyes are eating her up. Devouring her deep honey-colored skin, practically fucking glowing in the lights of the club. The slit in her dress rides higher and higher the more she moves. I beg it with my eyes, just a little higher. A little more. What can I say? I'm a greedy bastard.

Leo and Ev are off at a corner table, kissing and enjoying their night without Rune. And I've had just enough alcohol to think my next move is a good idea.

My eyes aren't enough. My hands need to be on her. In her. Fuck, they would settle for near her at this point. I stand, and Colette's eyes immediately meet mine. She's eating me up, just as I am her. She continues to sway her hips, dragging her hands up her thighs, raising her tight dress even more. Fuck me, she's doing this on purpose. What a little tease.

I move toward her, my pace steady and my eyes locked with hers. When I finally meet her, only a breath away from her, she raises her hands to wrap them around my neck.

When I catch her wrist in my hands, her warm skin lights me on fire. Her pulse hammers under her skin, and I wonder if it's out of fear or something else swimming through her veins. "I don't think so, Chaos. Hands to yourself." She lets out an adorable pout, and I resist catching that sweet lip between my teeth.

Circling her, I keep her hands in mine. With my palms laying against the soft, delicate skin on the back of her hands, I bring them back to her thighs and run both our hands up her inner thighs, trailing along her center, then up her flat stomach, to her full breasts, then finally that perfect, silky neck. I want her to feel how alluring her body is, how perfect.

She tries again to wrap her hands around the back of my neck, but I just can't have that. Intertwining our fingers, I bring them back down to her waist. Our arms are crossed around her waist, her ass pressed against me.

"You're so stiff."

Tell me about it.

"Move your hips like this." She begins to sway her hips back and forth. I resist at first, causing her to rub her ass against me. Nope. That's not a good idea. I begin to sway my hips with hers, wrapping my body even more around her warmth. The smell of sweat and her sweet vanilla scent makes my eyes roll into the back of my head.

Fuck, she's an intoxicating little thing. Keyword being toxic . . .

"There you go. Move with me," she says as she tries to turn in my arms and remove her hands from mine, but I hold her hostage.

"Let me touch you," she whispers into my ear as her head lays back on my shoulder, and my own lips graze her neck.

"In your dreams, Chaos."

"Gage, please." Her plea almost makes me relent. Almost.

"I can't, baby girl," I beg her. Hoping with everything that she understands without me having to say anymore. If she knew who I was, she would know why I can't let her gentle hands caress my skin. She would know. She should know.

"Colette, I . . ."

My body is forced away from her as a large form stumbles into us, spilling their drink all over Colette. I immediately push him off her as he catches himself on her fragile frame, and she stumbles, trying to hold his weight and hers.

"Don't fucking touch her." I inhale through clenched teeth, my chest expanding, the confines of my button-up pulling tight against my skin. I step between them. He can't touch her, not without her permission. I feel my monsters claw at my mind, rippling under my skin, begging to be released.

Her hand on my chest pulls me from my nightmares. "Hey, it's okay. He just tripped."

He's tall but shorter than me. Average build. Blond surfer boy hair and douchy fucking polo. Clearly more intoxicated than he should be. "Yo man, chill. It was an accident." He looks at her now, and I have to dig my nails into my palms to keep from breaking his fucking jaw. "Sorry, I didn't mean to."

She keeps her hand on my chest and steps between the drunk asshole and me. "It's okay. Really. I'm fine. You should go."

He glances once at me, gives her a smile, and walks away. He fucking touched her. His hands wrapped around her small arms. My breathing is heavy, filling my muscles with the oxygen I need to defend her. I will protect her.

"Gage, look at me."

I watch him retreat into the dark crowd. His tall frame, black suit, dark hair. It's him. He hurt her. I won't let him touch her like he touched me.

His touch. My cheek. My skin breaks out in goose bumps.

"Gage, look. At. Me."

My eyes meet hers as she steps in front of me fully, pulling my face to meet hers. But she's blurry. It's all so clouded. Like I'm underwater.

"Gage." Everett's stern voice and firm hand on my shoulder pull me from the waters. I look to my side; he's standing as steady as he has always been. His eyes search mine, and then he nods when he sees I'm with him.

"What the fuck was that? Where did you just go?" Colette's voice is sweet. The poor thing has no idea about the fucking storm brewing in my mind.

"You ready to head out?" Everett asks, ignoring Colette.

"Yeah, but you stay. Enjoy your night with your new wife. I'll talk to you tomorrow."

Everett pulls me into a quick hug. A hug that to most would be the bro equivalent to I love you but to us is so much more. He's grounding me. Telling me, as he has done since we were six years old, that he's got my back. That he's my brother, and he will always save me.

June 22nd, 2023

My Raven,

  I could not respond to you earlier. I
wanted to, but I couldn't. You confessed
in your letter that loving someone means
giving them every part of you. Giving you
the truth about my past wasn't what kept me
from responding. That wasn't the terrifying
part.

  The terrifying part, the part that paralyzed me for a year, was that I realized you
were right. I wanted to give you every part
of myself. Without question or hesitation,
I was ready to give you the deepest parts
of my soul. I've never felt that compulsion
before.

  I'm terrified. You terrify me.

  And that's crazy, right? But you do.
You terrify me because you made me wear
Christmas pajamas and watch Elf while I
sat in the lobby of my apartment complex
drinking hot cocoa. You terrify me because
you fill me with joy and laughter and
happiness. Fill me with feelings I never
want to feel. Because when you feel those

things, you can lose those things. I don't want to lose that.

I'm terrified to find out what would happen if I lost you.

I'm terrified because I have never wanted to make someone as happy as I want to make you.

I was set on never writing you back. I had made my peace with it. I was going to let you go before I could lose you. But I couldn't. I'm a selfish bastard, Raven.

But I'm going to give you my truth, and I'm going to make you promise you will not ask me to do this again.

My truth is that my father was my abuser. And it took me a long time to be able to say that. A really long time. I lost count of how many bones I have broken and how many times I have stitched myself up. My dad was a doctor, so I was never taken to the emergency room. There was no one I could turn to in my life until my best friend came along. He saved me, and he doesn't even know the full extent of the abuse. No one does or will. By the time I was sixteen, I was finally strong enough to fight back.

I haven't spoken to him since. I left at eighteen and never looked back.

So you see, sweet Raven, he haunts my mind. All I know is the pain he has left me with. The same pain I now need to survive. It's all I can take. All I can give.

I cannot and will not allow you to live with my monsters. They are mine and mine alone, and although I have accepted and made friends with them, I will not share them, baby girl.

I will find you in your darkness, but let me remain lost.

Chapter Twelve

colette

"**W**ork fucking sucked dirty balls today, LJ. If I didn't love you so fucking much, I would quit." I'm slumped in front of our complex's grand white brick fireplace in the lobby. My phone is squished between my shoulder and ear, drawing pad in hand as I furiously scribble lines to release my frustrations.

"You can't quit, Cole. You're a co-owner." LJ's stupid voice of reason reminds me of the terrible mistake I made going into business with her. And by terrible, I mean amazing. It's just terrible today.

"Yeah, well, I can't handle people who don't know how to send out shipments on time. We aren't going to get the fall blend in time. It won't arrive until late August now, and I know you like to start the fall menu in late July. By the way, that's fucking stupid. Don't take my summer drinks away when it's still summer."

"Who handles the coffee?" she quips.

"You," I retort, unpleased with the reminder.

"Exactly. I know what I'm doing. I've been in the business since I was a teen, and I was taught by the best. Leave the coffee to me. And I know you will figure out the shipment thing. You'll whip our distributor into shape, and I bet the shipment will end up being early."

She's damn right I will—after I pout and whine about it. "Whatever."

"How is living across from Gage going? It's been a month, and he's still alive, so I assume well?"

"Well, considering I haven't seen him since your wedding, great! He completely avoids me. First, the EC incident, then the weird freak-out, then he was all sexy and all over me. Now he's a ghost. If I do see him again, I'm going to kill him for leaving me all hot and bothered that night."

"Is he a good dancer?" Her suggestive tone makes me regret opening my mouth about him at all. I should have brushed her mentions of he-who-shall-not-be-named aside.

"He's—god. He's . . . you know what? He's an asshole, and it was nothing." *Liar.* It was the hottest thing I have ever experienced. I was tingling all over, like a fucking sparkler. The hottest guy I'd ever laid eyes on was running his hands all over me. His lips brushed against the skin of my neck, and holy mother of Jesus, it was like nothing I had ever felt.

I find myself digging my pencil harder into the paper, imagining it's his face.

"It doesn't surprise me he danced with you and is now ghosting you. He was eye-fucking you all night, but he has . . . well, let's just say he's always had a hard time with people. It's not my story to tell, but just give him some patience."

"I'm not a patient person. I'm more of a poke them in the fore-head annoyingly until they do what I want kind of gal. And speaking of getting people to do what I want, I better go before my hot date shows up."

"Ugh, please tell me it's not Jeremy. That guy is a dick."

"Yeah, I don't care. He has a nice one, and he doesn't bother me with emotions and shit. Sometimes EC just doesn't cut it. I need to be tied up and span—"

A throat clears behind me, and I turn to find the Grinch of Christmas himself looking as cool as a fucking cucumber, a cucum-ber I could go for a ride on . . .

Nope. No, Colette, you have Jeremy for that. No hot then cold, Gage.

"Hey, your dickhead best bud just interrupted. I'm going to re-arrange his pretty face. I gotta go."

"Tell him I said hi and to be nice!" LJ shouts before hanging up.

I watch as Gage comes around and sits next to me on the extrava-gant white velvet couch. His thigh almost brushes up against mine. His black jeans, slip-on Vans, and hoodie completely contradict my neon pink crew neck sweater that says "Absolute Delight" across the front.

"LJ says hi and to be nice," I say as I look at his profile, his head resting on the back of the couch, hands tucked behind his head. His irresistible features make me jealous. Jealous they aren't mine. Jealous I'm not kissing them. Then my eyes travel down to his neck and Adam's apple. Jesus, why does he have to be so pretty? Add on all the tattoos and his bad boy attitude and he's a walking orgasm on a stick, make your pussy pulse sex god.

"She doesn't know me at all, does she? I'm never nice." His gravelly voice pulls at me, and I instinctively lean a touch closer to him. Wait, what were we talking about? Oh yeah, him being nice.

"I think you have the potential to be nice." I look down at my leggings and begin fiddling with the cuffs of my sweater. For some reason, mentioning what happened recently makes me nervous. "You helped me look for my letters . . . you danced with me."

"That was purely for my benefit. I needed sleep, and you were being loud and annoying."

"I was not!" I slap at his shoulder, and he lets out a chuckle.

"I specifically remember the words fuck, shit, damn, and ball-sucking cunt being screamed at the top of your lungs." His reminder is met with me crossing my arms in defiance.

"I wasn't even that loud. I can be way louder than that."

He lazily rolls his head to the side to look at me now. "Oh, I bet you can." I don't miss the sex dripping from his voice. Okay, he needs to go away before I drag him upstairs and do naughty, naughty things to him.

"Creep."

He lifts his head, a small chuckle leaving his lip. I notice him staring at the fireplace now and follow his gaze. I take in the details of the wood mantel. The brick pattern is horizontal on the top, but it changes to a herringbone pattern under the mantel. The mantel itself is a beautiful, rich brown with small flaws in the wood that only add to its beauty. Arrow once told me how our flaws make us who we are. I see it in the wood and in my friends but not myself. As

I stare at the fireplace, something about it is incredibly familiar, like I've seen it before, but I can't place it.

"Do you come down here a lot?" I ask as I glance at Gage but notice that he's already looking at me as if he is studying me.

"Once."

"I like it down here. My mom's house had a fireplace like this. Brick with a beautiful mantel. She decorates it around Christmas to look like a little village." I smile at the memory; he just hums in response. The vibration in that one note makes my heart race.

"What are you drawing?" Both of us glance down at the scratchy lines that mar the page.

"A self-portrait," I reply, only half joking. Sometimes, this is exactly how I feel on the inside. A dark raven with a scratched out face. I know who I should be, who I once was but the reflection in the mirror is a mess of harsh lines these day, blurring and distorting the image. It's similar to the portrait I sent Arrow so long ago. Funny how years have passed, yet nothing has changed.

"I like it." The sincerity in his voice takes me by surprise. I meet his burning amber eyes and see understanding in them. Does he know what it feels like to battle the monsters in your head? Does he see how lost I feel? Does he understand looking in the mirror and not recognizing the person looking back?

We are stuck at this moment, just looking into each other's eyes, and I feel something shift in my chest. Almost as if I know this dark, mysterious, cluster fuck of a man. His presence and his aura feel so familiar. Like coming home to a dark house with a single light on, he feels safe.

His eyes dart to my lips and stay there, and I wonder if he's thought about kissing me like I have him. "Do you think we've ever met before? I mean, before LJ and Everett?"

His eyes widen, letting his mask fall for a split moment, but just as quickly, it's replaced with his usual cold stare. He looks back at the fireplace. "No, I don't think I have met a creature quite like Colette Corvina."

I go to ask more, but Jeremy steps up and places his hands over my eyes. "Guess who," he whispers in my ear. Removing his hands before I can even guess, he grins down at me, then looks at Gage with an innocent smile.

"Hey, Jer, I'll, um. This is Gage. My . . . neighbor." I stand, introducing the two. Why do I feel so awkward? Why do I feel a sense of guilt meeting up with Jeremy now that I have had this conversation with Gage?

But my not-so-friendly neighbor doesn't say anything. He just stands and narrows his eyes on Jer, then looks at me. "Planning on getting tied up and spanked tonight, are we, Colette?"

I practically choke on my own spit. What the fuck did he just say?

"What the hell, man?" Jer tries to sound tough, but there just seems to be an edge that is lacking. He isn't quite psychotic enough to really match Gage's level of crazy. I can see it, and so can Gage based on the way his eyes light up with mischief, and he begins running his thumb along his bottom lip, teasing Jer and me at the same time but in completely different ways.

"Does he like to use your toys on you too, Chaos?" Gage continues to taunt.

"I don't need to use toys, pretty boy. I can make her—"

I watch as Gage's body tense, going from playful to downright intimidating. I step between them, needing their alpha male competition to end. "Okaaayy, that's enough. No need to whip out your dicks and start measuring."

Gage ignores me, pressing closer to me. "Hmm. Poor JerBear, you don't know yet? Toys are an asset, buddy. Just a tip for your next girl." He looks at me now. "Haven't you shown him EC, Colette? I'm surprised you haven't. EC is fun."

"What is he talking about EC? Who the fuck is EC?" Jer is frantically looking at me, like Gage has gotten to experience something he hasn't. I turn to give him a piece of my mind, but he's already walking away. That fucking asshole.

I hate him.

October 4th, 2023

My Arrow,

How do I respond to a letter like this?
How do I put into words how I wish I could
hold you and show you that everything that
happened to you was not your fault? I'm so
fucking sorry. Thank you for sharing that
with me. I can't imagine it was easy.

I don't know how I terrify you. I'm no
one to be terrified of. In fact, I'm no one
special at all. You don't terrify me at all.
I think you're used to pushing people away,
but you can't do that with me.

I'm not scared of your monsters, Arrow. I
think you're going through something. Let
me go through it with you, and maybe we can
heal together.

How could I let go of the man who got
me to paint again? The man who writes me
the sweetest letters, who finds me in my
darkness without even seeing me.

Share your monsters with me. Let me find
you.

gage

Jeremy Carter Reynolds. What a boring fucking name for a boring fucking guy. Born June 18th, 1997. Works as an EMT for Boston Fire, been there two years. Big dummy was wearing his cute little name tag on his cute little uniform. I have access to his entire existence from a name tag.

You know, he should really be careful where he wears his uniform. Someone could use that information against him.

Leaning back in my chair while gazing at the multi-monitor setup, I could ruin this man's life with a touch of a key. The man has a clean record, graduated with good grades, and volunteers at the local elementary school doing first aid and fire education. Seems like a pretty stand-up guy. Seems like a good match for Colette.

I should leave it alone. I should let them have their fun. I should move on and accept that she's better off being with a man like good ole JerBear the EMT. I should be the good guy who lets her go.

But I'm not a good guy.

I pull up the security cameras in the lobby as well as the ones in the main elevator and our hallway. The complex has no idea I have hacked into and have access to all their cameras and security measures. Weak-ass systems are just begging to be broken into.

I spot them in the hallway, just stepping off the elevator. Looks like my little chaotic beauty is sucking up to JerBear. I'm sure she's reassuring him that he can please her in bed without the need for toys. Pussy can't take a little criticism, it seems. What fuckhead doesn't use toys on their woman? What an insecure little bitch.

When they make it outside her door, I see him pull her in by the back of the neck for a kiss.

Let her go, Gage.

I watch as she fumbles to unlock her door as his lips move to her neck.

Let her fucking go.

Just as she's opening her door, I see him lift her shirt and his palm grasp her breast.

Nope. That's it. Fuck what I should do.

If Colette wants to get loud, I can help with that. With a few clicks of my mouse, the fire alarm blares throughout the entire building. What a bummer, JerBear. Guess she won't have to fake an orgasm to placate your large ego. Shucks.

I close out my systems, then head out my front door to evacuate. Stepping into the hall, I wait patiently for Colette and her fuck boy to exit. But as people pass me by in their own evacuation, the two I'm looking for stay inside. Do they think this is a false alarm? I mean, it is, but that's not the point. Are they that desperate that they are going to ignore the fire alarm? You'd think EMT JerBear would take a fire alarm seriously.

This just won't do.

Pulling out my phone, I work a little more magic. Then I hear a familiar, high-pitched shriek, and out comes my chaotic little creature, covering herself with JerBear's white uniform shirt.

"What the fuck! Why are the fucking sprinklers going off! There isn't even any smoke!"

"Well, they actually respond to heat, not smoke. Maybe we were just too hot." He winks and smirks like he just came up with the best pickup line. What a fucking nerd. Seriously, dude? Fucking kill me now.

A soaking, fuming Colette looks me up and down as I lean up against my doorframe. "Why are you not wet?" she snaps.

"Strange. I have no clue." I begin making my way to the stairs as Colette stops at the elevator.

"No can do, babe. The elevators won't work when the alarms are going off. You'll have to take the stairs." Jer smiles like he's delivering some monumental knowledge that will impress Colette. Is this guy for real?

"Fuck that shit. I'm going back to my apartment. I bet you there isn't even a fire. Probably just some prank. I'm not walking down all those stairs."

She walks back, and EMT Jer just shrugs his shoulders, making his way through the stairwell door.

"Where the fuck are you going? Not going to make sure your girl is alright, EMT Jeremy?" I snide and he gives a soft laugh like I'm kidding.

"She's scary when she's mad. And she's probably right. But if you want to go after her, you got it, bro." He lays a hand on my shoulder like we're friends, and I somehow resist the urge to punch him in his damn throat.

"Don't fucking touch me." I fire back at him and shrug him off. What a hero. Remind me to max out some credit cards in his name. Pussy.

I chase Colette and stop her with my hand around her bicep. "No can do, Chaos. Fire alarm says to evacuate."

She spins on me, and I stand corrected. It looks like there is a fire, but it's all in her golden eyes. Fuck, she's sexy when she's wet and pissed. I need to do this more often . . . "I'm not walking down eleven flights of stairs! This apartment complex can suck my nonexistent dick! Plus, since I seem to be the only one soaking wet, they can also reimburse me for the damage their defective sprinklers caused! And I want the fucking penthouse while they fix the water damage!" She actually stomps her foot and crosses her arms over her chest like a petulant child.

I step into her but avoid getting close enough to touch. "You have three seconds to get your stubborn ass down those stairs," I whisper so she has to listen carefully to hear me.

"First of all, dick bag, I can't make it down in three seconds, and second of all, I. Don't. Want. To." She pokes me in the chest with each word.

She doesn't even need to evacuate. There is no fire. I know that. But now she has challenged me, and my control is already hanging by a thread.

"Colette, get your ass moving. Now."

She steps into me, our chests brushing. "Make me."

God, she's magnificent. But that small thread of control I had? Well, she just fucking snapped it.

I lean down, wrapping my arms around her thighs, and throw her over my shoulder. She yells and kicks, but I don't give a fuck. "Gage! Put me down, you asshole! I'm going to beat the ever-loving shit out of you!"

Jesus, that mouth just loves to do dirty things. Her small fists pound against my back if only she knew I fucking love it. I lay a sharp smack to her round ass, and she screams out again, "Gage! I'm going to fucking kill you!"

"What's wrong, Chaos? I thought you liked to be spanked?"

Her punches have lightened, and her kicks have stopped. "As soon as you get me to the bottom of those stairs, I'm going to slap you into next week!"

"Hmm, how did you know I like it rough?" I chuckle under her, making her thighs and ass jiggle. The urge to turn my head and bite that perfect ass is almost too irresistible. Almost.

Eh. Fuck it.

I bite into her thigh that's right next to my mouth. My teeth sink into her flesh, and I have to strangle the growl that almost leaves my throat. "Oh my god! Did you just bite me! You're fucking crazy!"

Accurate.

I hurry down the stairs, needing to be rid of her body against mine before I turn right the fuck around and tie her to my fucking bed. Finally, we make it downstairs, acquiring many strange looks from others, and I set her down on the street. She wraps the large white shirt around her body, trying but failing to hide that black lacy number pushing up her perfect breasts.

Fuck. Now I have to try to hide my raging fucking boner. First carrying her down the stairs, her ass right in my face, and now getting a delicious view of her tits—I didn't think this all the way through.

"You're an awful human. I hate you." By the way she won't make eye contact with me and the flush of her pretty chestnut skin, I know that's not true.

"Where is Jeremy?" she asks as she looks around the crowd gathered outside the complex. The firemen are already going in and out, searching for the reason for the alarm, but they will never find it.

She continues to search, but I'd bet my next month's paycheck that bitch dipped out as soon as he got down the stairs. After a few minutes, when she can't find him, she narrows her eyes on me.

"This is your fault."

"What is?" I innocently smirk at her.

"All of this! I know you did something to fuck with the system. And my apartment was the only one where the sprinklers went off. Everyone else is dry!"

I shrug, looking down at her. "You wanted to get wet tonight. I don't see the issue here, Colette."

She steps into me, eyes narrowed, pouty lips turned up in a smirk. "Are you admitting you set off the alarm and the sprinklers in my apartment?"

Leaning in, I let my lips hover just slightly over hers. "I admit to nothing, Chaos. But the way I see it, I have made all your fantasies come true. Well, almost all of them."

"How so?" Her voice is a whisper, luring me in like a fucking siren song. Are there still people around us? Who the fuck knows, who the fuck cares. I'm two seconds from ripping those clothes off her and seeing how wet she really is.

"You're wet. You've been spanked. Now all you need is to be tied up. Would you like that, Chaos? Would you like me to tie you to my bed and see how truly wet you are? But it wasn't from sweet JerBear, was it? No, it was from my hands on your ass and my words in your head. You hate it, don't you? You hate how much you want me, how much I drive you crazy. Admit it, baby girl. You're desperate for me."

She shoves at my chest and slaps me across the face. I hum in response as I turn to look back at her. Now she has me all riled up. She thinks slapping me is a punishment? Baby girl, I'm harder than I have ever been. "Do it again."

"You're fucking crazy." Her words don't match the desire in her eyes. But before I can pull her into me, an announcement rings out from some fuckface with a radio.

"All clear. You can all return to your apartments. We will put out a statement in the morning. For now, Boston Fire has determined the alarm to be false."

She turns from me, getting lost in the crowd. No worries, I'll always find you, my Raven.

December 24th, 2023

My Raven,

I should terrify you. You should let me go. You should find someone to give your heart to. Just not me.

But I'm a selfish man, like I said, so as long as you're writing to me, I will not be able to resist you.

Also, Merry Christmas Eve. Are you going to ask me to do something ridiculous again? If so, I will begrudgingly do it, but I will complain the entire time. Just so you know.

I know holidays must be hard for you without your dad. So here is a task for you. I want you to do something you have always wanted to do but have never done before. Go out and live in this crazy world. Embrace the chaos of it. Tell me about it in your next letter.

In fact, I did something new today inspired by you. I went into a coffee shop and watched all the people wearing Christmas clothes, and all I could think about was you. Are you in your own ugly Christmas pajamas, watching horrible Christmas movies? Are you drinking hot chocolate like it's water? I found myself smiling, thinking of you. I hope that you smile today, baby girl.

Anyway, I'm getting off topic. What I did that was new, was order the sweetest Christmas drink I could find.

And it was awful. Repulsive. Entirely too sweet. But I saw it on the menu, and I thought about you and your dad, and I ordered it. Before I had time to back out, she charged my card, and I was locked in. I absolutely regret it. And I blame you.

I'll be sticking to my Americanos from now on.

Merry Christmas Eve.

Chapter Fourteen

colette

"He did what?!" LJ's voice carries over the entire coffee shop as she whips her head around to look at me from the bar.

I'm sitting in my favorite spot, the table by the large window next to the street with my laptop. Catching up on budget reports has my mind wandering, and I might have let it slip to my best friend that Gage threw me over his shoulder, smacked *and* bit my ass, and whispered filthy things into my ear while I was soaking wet—in more than one way—and in another man's T-shirt.

"My Gage? Tall, dark, and handsome with a good helping of broody asshole? That Gage?" She continues to dry the coffee mugs. The shop is slow right now. Our morning rush is over and now the midday lull will allow us to get other things done before our after-work rush.

"Yup," I say, popping the P. "That's the one."

She giggles and shakes her head, her curls swaying with the movement. "I'm not surprised. Not with how he was undressing you on the dance floor at my wedding."

I slam my laptop closed. "Actually, can we have a real honest conversation about him because I'm really confused."

She looks at me now. I know she can see the sincerity in my face. And despite my silliness, I'm actually freaking out. I know I put on a happy face like nothing really bothers me, but I'm tired of that shit. I want some answers about this man, and I'm going to get them. But instead of being the brave, strong, independent woman I aspire to be, I'm going behind his back and ask his best friend.

Solid plan, Cole.

LJ comes and sits in front of me. "Okay, honest conversation. Let's go."

I sigh, gathering my courage. Where do I even start? "Is he a good guy? Truly?"

Her shoulders drop, and she tilts her head at me. "Would I be friends with him if he wasn't? Come on, Cole, if you don't trust him, trust me. Gage is an incredible person; he just has a really tough exterior. It was the same when I first met him."

I bite my lower lip, thinking about what she's saying. "I don't know, babe. He has me all confused. One minute, he's so vulnerable and flirty, and the next, he's . . . cold and detached."

"Yeah, that sounds like Gage—oh, hold on." LJ goes to take the order of the customer that just walked in, and I'm left thinking about him. LJ would not keep him around if he was as bad as he makes himself out to be. I know she wouldn't.

One thing I'm not letting her in on, though, is that not only am I confused because Gage is more confusing than fucking rocket science, but I'm also confused because I have feelings for another man—Arrow.

I haven't been in a committed relationship since Arrow because a part of me only feels safe with him. We haven't spoken about meeting, but I want to. I didn't before, but now? Now I see what LJ and Everett have, and I want that. I want that kind of connection with someone, and he's the only one I can imagine having it with. But I know him, and he won't want to meet.

At the same time, I feel like I'm wasting my time. I could be missing out on some incredible people because I'm waiting for a man who doesn't want to be with me. How fucking pathetic am I?

"Okay, where were we?" she says with a huff as she plops back down in the chair across from me.

"You were telling me what I should do about Gage," I remind her.

"Umm. No, I wasn't because I can't tell you what to do, but nice try."

She reaches over, placing her hand over mine. "Gage is an amazing person. I have never seen him look at a girl like he does you. Granted, I have a few years missing from his life, but when we were in high school, he never dated anyone. Never even flirted. Honestly, the thought crossed my mind that maybe he was gay . . . And since he has been back in my life, well, he's a private person. Shit, I don't even know if he's even had sex before—"

"By the way he talked to me, he's 100 percent not a virgin . . . or gay." I interrupt her.

"Okay. Ew. I don't want to know." She waves her hand at me. "But with all of that being said, I know Gage has some deeply rooted issues. He has been through a lot in his life, and if you choose to go after him, just know that you two will have some stuff to deal with. Being with Gage will not be easy. He's defensive because he has always had to guard himself. But once you break through those walls, man, will he take care of you."

"Should I? Go after him, I mean? He's hot as hell, but I don't know that I'm really . . . emotionally available to be in a committed relationship."

"I think you need to just talk to him and maybe spend more time with him. If there is one thing I've learned, it's that communication truly is key. If you don't talk to him, you may miss out on something amazing."

I laugh at her idea. "Talk to him? I feel like I can barely breathe around him!"

Now she laughs. "Seriously? Where did my feisty best friend go?"

"That's what I mean! It's like he has infected me. I'm all shy, heart-pounding, and thigh-clenching around him now. Even though I still want to punch him in his stupid pretty face."

"Ah, there she's—" The doorbell ringing overhead pulls her attention. "Sorry." She stands and leaves me.

"No, it's okay. I'll just die in my utter humiliation and confusion over here! Don't worry about me, bestie!" I shout to her as she walks away, giggling to herself.

Stupid boys. I hate them. I should become a lesbian. Girls can't be this confusing, can they? Who am I kidding, I love dick too much. But there are such things as strap-on's . . . No. No. I couldn't. Men may be infuriating as fuck, but I'm straighter than a gator. Is that even a saying, or does it just rhyme? Whatever.

I open my laptop to work on my reports again when an email comes through. If I have to answer another stupid question from our distributor, I'm going to scream. The company seriously needs to hire some new personnel. The ones they have now don't know how to do shit. But that's a rant for another time.

Opening it up, I see it's not from a distributor but my apartment complex. Finally.

Miss Corvina,

My name is Benjamin Knolls, the manager of Park View Estates. I cannot express my apologies enough for the malfunction with our sprinkler systems. Unfortunately, we were not able to detect why, in only your apartment, the sprinklers were activated.

We will of course reimburse you for any damaged personal items. Please send us a list of items so we can work on this as soon as possible.

Regarding your request for the penthouse, we do not have a penthouse here at Park View, and unfortunately, it seems all our apartments are listed as occupied. I'm doing further research into this as I had assumed we had a few vacant apartments to offer you while the damages were being repaired, but as of this morning, all are listed as occupied.

Until then, below are some nearby hotels. We would be happy to reimburse you for the cost of lodging from one of the places below.

When you have decided, please let me know, and I will do whatever I can to make this as easy and pain-free as possible for you.

Again, I'm terribly sorry for this situation.

The email goes on to list multiple hotels, and I begin googling the locations and pictures. God. I can't believe this is happening. No unoccupied apartments in the entire building? I have a hard time believing that. Well, I guess I'm going to pick the most expensive hotel from this list and treat it like a little vacation.

Unknown

> Don't even bother looking into any of those cheap-ass hotels.

> You're staying with me.

> > Who is this?

> Come on, Chaos. You're smarter than that.

Gage. He's right. I should have known. Now my phone is ringing Unknown across the screen.

"Hello," I say with a little apprehension.

"You're not staying in any of those hotels. Tell Manager Ben to fuck off. You're staying with me." His rough voice sounds through my speakers, and even without seeing him, my pussy throbs. Jesus, calm down, ya hussy.

"I'm not staying with you. And how do you—" It hits me then. Gage the tech wiz.

"Oh my god. Gage!! Get out of my computer, you fucking creep!" I shriek, and LJ turns with wide eyes to look at me. I try to tell her with my eyes that her best friend is dead meat, but then she just laughs. Actually laughs. What a traitor!

"Say you'll stay with me." There is a vulnerability in the way he begs. It makes my heart clench in my chest and I know I won't be able to deny him. But his invasion of my privacy is a major red flag.

"No! You used your big, egotistical brain to hack into my computer. There is no way I'm moving in with you! You, sir, are a stalker." It's a lie. I'm definitely staying with im but I wouldn't be me if I didn't give a little push back.

"Labels mean shit. Are you staying with me, or am I emailing Benny Boy back myself?"

"Don't you fucking dare!" I press the phone to my shoulder and try to reply to Ben, but my keys aren't working. My mouse is no longer coordinating with my strokes. But it is moving.

He has control of my fucking laptop!

"Gage Eros! I'm going to string you up by your toes and leave you there to starve! Give me back my laptop!"

My voice is louder than I mean it to be, and now I'm getting strange looks. Clearly because I'm yelling threats at a man to give me my laptop when it is actually sitting right in front of me. His little warfare is invisible to all but me. He's making me look crazy!

Then I see him begin his reply to Benjamin.

Mr. Knolls,

I will not be needing a hotel to stay in. My lovely neighbor has offered his apartment to me while repairs are being made. He's just the kindest person. Gage Eros. In fact, I think I would like to terminate my lease. I understand that the sec—

"Oh my god! Fine! Fine! I'll stay with you! Just please do not fucking send that email!" I cry out to Gage and see the email slowly erase, one letter at time.

"Send the email, Chaos, or I will." Then he hangs up the phone, and my laptop comes back to me. I quickly type out the reply to Benjamin telling him I will not be needing the hotels but leaving all the other pieces Gage wanted to add out.

What an asshole!

When I close my laptop, my screensaver has been changed to a picture of Gage and me. More specifically, a still shot from the hallway camera when Gage picked me up and threw me over his shoulder. It shows me, over his shoulder, his large hand on my ass.

I cannot believe him. I'm going to seriously hurt him the next time I see him. Who does this shit!

I slam my laptop closed and pout in my seat. Actually, hold the fuck up. Why am I letting him walk all over me? I'll stay with him, but I won't make this easy on him. Gage Eros will regret the day he invited Colette Corvina into his apartment. Time to take back the power.

I dial the unknown number back, right after I save it in my phone under the appropriate name of Stalker.

"Can I help you, Colette?" His deep timbre rolls through my body. I almost give in and lose my bravado. Almost.

"Yes. You can. Where are you? We need to discuss our new living arrangement."

"I'll text you."

With that, he hangs up. Does this man even know the word goodbye?

Not a second later, a text with an address pops up.

February 14th, 2024

My Arrow,

   Happy Valentine's Day. Will you be my valentine? Cheesy, I know, but I couldn't help it.

   If there is one thing you should know about me, it's that I rarely do as I'm told. In fact, telling me I shouldn't do something will surely make it all the more fun.

   Challenge accepted, dear Arrow. I will never let you go, and you will have my heart.

   And I do have a challenge for you. In honor of Valentine's Day, I want you to tell me about your first love. What girl or guy captured your heart first? Maybe I can get some tips . . .

   Regarding Christmas, you're right. It is an extremely difficult time without my dad. But we manage. We try to continue our holiday traditions, but it's hard. There is always a solemness to the traditions, a piece of our family missing. And you were right, I was in my pajamas which are not ugly but festive. Thank you very much.

I wish I could have seen your face when you tried that Christmas drink! So you're an Americano type of guy, huh? My best friend is a big coffee person. I'm not so much, but I'll usually have a cup in the morning. I don't have a fancy machine; I can never figure out how to get them to work. But my single-cup maker works just as well. I've never had an Americano; I'll have to try it sometime. I've seen them made, and they look awful. Water and espresso? But for you, I'm willing to try one.

Update.

I tried one. It's glorious. I had to add a little sweetener in there. My friend melted some brown sugar with the espresso before she added the water. It was delicious. Now I'm going to be addicted, and I'm going to blame you.

One day maybe we will wake together and sip our Americanos, snuggle up in a warm blanket and watch the Boston sun rise. One day, my Arrow. You told me what I shouldn't do. Now watch me as I do it.

We will find each other.

gage

I'm going to regret inviting Colette into my apartment. I just fucking know it. But the idea of her staying by herself in some shaggy-ass hotel has my skin crawling. There is no fucking way.

She's resourceful. I'm sure she could have found a safer place to stay, but I wasn't going to allow that to happen either. No, I need her close. And I need to teach her to defend herself. She's captivating and feisty, and that combination will only lead to her mouthing off to the wrong person and getting hurt. Plus, I've been watching her . . . not in a stalker way . . . okay, maybe in a stalker-type way, but fuck labels, I'm just looking out for her. The woman doesn't watch her surroundings. She's oblivious to not only me hiding in the shadows, but she puts herself in the most vulnerable positions.

Like when she was leaving the grocery store and stood right in front of an alley entrance, texting on her phone. Or when our doorman was on break, we typically use a key code to access our apartment, but she just held the door open for the man walking up behind her, letting him tailgate right in after her. My blood was boiling as I watched him smile at her.

When she asked to meet to discuss our living arrangement, I was already at the gym. Seemed like the perfect time to start her training. A notification pings on my phone that she has pulled up to the gym, so I roll up the garage door and lean against the rusty frame.

I don't have a shirt on, just some loose shorts, my hands wrapped and feet bare. I love the way she tries to hide the heat of her eyes when she spots me, and her cheeks flush. My Chaos. My Raven. My Colette. Fuck, she's beautiful.

Her black biker shorts hug her thighs, and the loose T-shirt she's wearing settles on her hips, only bringing to light her amazing curves. Her braids are spun up in a bun atop her head, making her high cheekbones stand out. But it's her eyes. Always her fucking eyes. They are what truly captivate me every time I see her. I'm obsessed with them. They are pissed right now, narrowed on me in a glare but behind that glare, the deep amber burns with something far more dangerous than anger.

"Is this where you lure me in to kill me?" She steps close to my body, gazing up into my assessing eyes. It takes everything I have not to wrap my hands around her and throw her over my shoulder again.

Eh. Who am I kidding? I've never been one to shy away from the things I want.

I chuckle at the thought, then give in. Bending down, I wrap my arms around her thighs, throwing her over my shoulder again. Her body is warm against mine; she's solid but melts into me as she should. She was made for me. I just wasn't made for her.

"Gage! I'm going to fucking kill you! You can't just manhandle people!"

"Save all that fire for the ring, Chaos."

She goes still in my grasp. "The what?" Lifting her head, she tries to peer behind her at where I'm walking but she just isn't quite that flexible.

Before she can protest more, I throw her down on some mats next to the ring, and she looks up at me from her back. Oh, I could get used to that view.

"Ouch. That fucking hurt, you ass."

"Toughen up." I kneel in front of her, and despite the hesitation in her eyes, her pretty thighs part for me as I move between them.

She leans back on her elbows, never letting her eyes leave mine. I can see the blush creeping up her neck and the slight increase in her breathing as her chest moves more rapidly up and down. Wrapping my hand around her ankle, I straighten her leg and push it toward her shoulder. I keep a close eye on her body language, making sure that this is okay. I don't want to make her feel uncomfortable, but by the way her chest stutters and her eyes heat, I don't think she minds. Plus, I know she would let me have it if she truly wanted me to stop.

"What—What are you doing?"

"Stretching you out." I let the innuendo drip from my lips.

"I—" She tries to stutter out a response, but for the first time in her life, I think she's speechless.

"You're going to learn to defend yourself. I'm going to teach you. But first, you need to stretch." I shift to do the same stretch on the other leg. But she kicks me away, her shock finally wearing off, and she's coming back to her senses.

"Get the fuck off me."

Ah, there she is . . .

"Oh, I like her. Can I tussle with her first?" B walks up, hand on hip, staring down at us. Dressed in her usual leggings and sports bra, scarlet hair braided back.

"Who the fuck are you? And no, I'm not fighting anyone! You all are batshit crazy, screws loose, cuckoo on the Cocoa Puffs."

Colette stands, but I grab her wrist and look up at her. A man on my knees and she's the only one I'd do it for.

"Please, Colette. You need to know how to defend yourself. B can teach you if you want." I nod to Sabrina, and Colette's eyes follow, shooting her a glare. "But I need you to be able to protect yourself. Just a few moves. For me?"

Something breaks in her eyes. And I can see the moment she relents. "Fine. But if I do this, you give me back my laptop. No more hacking into it." She points her finger in my face. Quickly, I grab her wrist and nip at the pad of her finger.

"Deal," I say as I look into her shocked eyes. Blown wide with surprise and a hint of heat from my teeth on her skin.

"I just want it known that I do not like this idea. I do not like violence," she says as she kneels to take her shoes off, matching the bare feet of B and I.

"I find that hard to believe." I watch her, bent over as she unties her sneakers. Imagining her bent over my . . .

An elbow to my gut ceases my train of thought. "Focus, G. No eye-fucking in my gym."

I give a grin to B. "But we can actually fuck?"

"Dirty bastard." B slaps the back of my head and pulls the ropes down to hop into the ring.

"Are you two. . ." Colette's eyes bounce between B and I.

"Not anymore, baby girl. Come on. Hop up." I pull the bottom rope down and reach my hand out to help her up into the ring. She not so gracefully stumbles over the ropes and lands on her hands and knees on the canvas.

"Alright, babe, to start, I just want you to bounce on the balls of your feet. Like this. This will help your blood get to pumping, and your muscles loosen up." B begins dancing around the ring.

"I'm not fighting your ex," Colette growls as she places her hands on her hips and glares at me.

"First of all, not his ex. And second, retract the claws. I don't want your man."

"He's not . . ." She lets out a huff, turning to me for help.

Giving her a grin, I remind her why we're here. "Bounce, baby girl." I begin to bounce as well, hoping she will follow. But she's stubborn, as usual. She crosses her arms, turning her head away from me. What a petulant child. Alright. Let's play.

I come in close to her body, bouncing on my feet. She continues to ignore me as I circle her and begin to nip at her skin with my fingers. Tickling her most sensitive areas. I get her in the ribs, the ass, her thighs, her neck.

"Stop that!" she says as she swats at me, but she's too slow. So I continue. It's time to entice my feisty Colette out.

"Make me." I stop bouncing, then come up to her so we are chest to chest. Reaching out, I tip her chin up to me. Our lips are mere breaths apart. I should be rewarded for the resistance I'm showing currently.

Fuck, if I just lean in slightly . . .

Her breath hitches. "I don't need you. I can protect myself." Her whisper grazes my lips, and I want so badly to descend upon her. But her safety is more important. She needs to learn.

As quickly and gently as I can, I grab her around the legs and slam her onto the canvas. I'm gentle enough so it doesn't hurt . . . too much. But forceful enough to give her the reminder. My hips press between her thighs, her knees spread wide to accommodate my body.

"Get off me!" Her words don't match her breathlessness at our proximity.

"Make me." Her little fists pound against my chest. Futile. It's laughable really how much she thinks she's doing but how little she's actually doing.

"See. This is why you need our help. You have no idea how to get out of this position, do you? What if I wasn't a nice man?"

"You aren't a nice man."

Her scent overtakes my senses as I lean in, and I feel like it's just us two. "I could be nice to you, Colette," I whisper in her ear, and her thighs tighten around my hips.

"Watch and learn." B comes up next to us, kneeing me in the ribs so I roll off Colette, clutching my side.

"Bitch," I groan.

"Get up, toots." B motions Colette into the corner. Despite the look of pure rage on her face, Colette complies and sits in the corner, her eyes never leaving B.

"Almost 100 percent of the time, your attacker will be larger than you. So you have to learn to use your smaller size to your advantage. Come here, big guy."

B lowers herself into the position Colette was just in, and I roll onto her, just like I was with Colette, but it feels entirely different. My hips pressed into B's body; my mind is in fight mode. When they were pressed into Colette's, my mind was ready to fuck.

I gently wrap my hand around B's throat to allow her to teach.

"Alright, love. First thing, you're going to take your hand opposite his that's holding your throat and wrap it around his wrist. Then take your other hand and bring it up, across his holding arm. Like this." She demonstrates and pauses. "See how I have him here and here." Wiggling her fingers, she shows Cole exactly where to hold.

"Then you want to take your foot, on the same side as his holding arm, press it into his hip and at the same time, bring your opposite leg up, as high as you can get it, up into his armpit. Your goal is to trap his holding arm and spin, so you're perpendicular to him."

She performs the move slowly so Cole can track her movements. "Then when you're in this position, bring that leg you used to push his hip away from you and wrap it around his head like this. You want to isolate this arm here."

She does it slowly again.

"Now, you've got him. All you do from here is lift those hips. He will roll and then pull with everything you have to break his fucking arm."

She flawlessly performs the move, rolling me onto my back, then bending my arm back till I feel it begin to bend in a way it shouldn't. I tap out, and she releases me.

"Easy peasy," she says as she gets up onto her knees. "It's your turn."

Colette's jaw is practically on the floor. "I can't do that. What the fuck did you even just do?"

"Sabrina?" A light voice filters through the gym.

"Hey, Nat! Meet me on the mats, baby! Be right there." B heads over to Natasha, who we have been training since I found out she was involved with the Alessis. Strangely, they have allowed her to do so. I'm not stupid enough to think she's giving them the slip. They know she's here. Question is, why don't they care? But that's a mystery for another time. Right now, my focus is on my girl. Not theirs.

"Come on, Chaos. Show me what you got." I wave her over, and I slowly walk her through the move again and again. She was hesitant at first like all the girls are. But as we practice, she becomes bolder and bolder. Before I know it, she's performing the move without me having to instruct her.

Once she's a sweaty mess, I call it, walking over to the corner and squirting water into my mouth. I watch her chest move up and down. The imagery of how else I could get her breathless and sweaty filters through my head. "You did good."

"That—was so—fucking—hard," she says between panting breaths.

I laugh and roll my bottle of water to her, which she happily takes and chugs.

"Come back tomorrow, and we can go again. I'll teach you how to get out of the most common positions men attack from."

Sitting up now, I see the drops of sweat trail down her chest. Fuck, I just want to run my tongue between her breasts and up her long neck. I pull my gaze away, checking on Nat and B, who are practicing combos on the bags.

"Why do you care so much if I can protect myself?" she asks with a timidness I know from Raven but never from Colette.

"Can I be honest with you?" I ask.

"No, please lie to me. I'd love nothing more." She rolls her eyes.

"Okay, brat. Never mind." I turn to walk away, but her sweet voice halts my retreat.

"I'm sorry. Sometimes I can't stop the brat from escaping . . . please, be honest with me." The look in her eyes tells me she means what she says and so, for reasons I don't even fucking know, I decide to trust that feeling.

"When that guy touched you at the club, I . . . lost it. I saw red when his hands were on you."

She tilts her head, and her brows dip in. "But that was an accident, Gage. Just a drunk guy who couldn't stay on his feet. It was harmless."

Taking a breath, I release it fully, letting my chest sink before I reply. "It was an accident . . . this time. If it hadn't been an accident would you have known what to do?"

She straightens her spine as her lips remain sealed, her silence the only answer I need.

"I don't ever want you to feel helpless. No one should feel that way. I want you to know that your size doesn't matter. You can always fight back."

"Well . . . thank you. For teaching me." She dips her head and begins twiddling one of her braids that had fallen out during our training. I love seeing both sides of her. The side she keeps hidden from the world but gives to Arrow. And the chaotic, fiery side that she loves to give me.

"Have you ever felt helpless before? Is that why you started fighting?" Her eyes meet mine again as I take another drink of my water and then come over to her. I hang my arms over the ropes and push between her knees that are dangling off the edge of the ring.

I lean in, and the ropes stretch with my weight, but she doesn't lean away from me. In fact, she leans closer as she reaches up and grabs the rope with her small hands. "I started fighting because if I didn't, I would have killed someone."

Her pretty eyes widen, and my lips lift at the corners. I love seeing her a little scared. I come up off the ropes quickly, and they snap, forcing her forward, but she catches herself before they hit her in the face.

"Asshole," she mutters as I walk away and to the locker rooms to freshen up.

colette

Rolling around with Gage in a boxing ring, him shirtless, muscles glistening with sweat, his dark wet hair hanging down into his eyes. Someone better take me to church and bathe me in holy water cause hot damn, that man just made me think of one thousand ways to sin with him.

It's odd. How unyielding Gage was about teaching me to defend myself. It's like what happened at the club spooked him. Like he's on a mission to make sure I can take care of myself. I'm not opposed to it. In fact, I kinda always wanted to learn some self-defense moves. But I don't know if I can do it with him. I'll jump his bones the second we are alone if he gets all hot and sweaty again.

"Hey, how was your session with G?" B who I have now learned is actually named Sabrina, walks up. Her perfect muscular body and cute, stupid face make my back teeth grind. I didn't miss the fact that Gage practically announced from the rooftops—okay, that might be an exaggeration—that they used to fuck. Even though he isn't my man, my jealousy still forces me to be a bitch. Truly, it's out of my control.

"Fine." My short response was meant to deter her, but I failed. Miserably. She plops her annoyingly perfect ass right next to my cellulite-covered one.

"Oh, I bet it was more than fine. G is sexy as fuck, and you got to roll around with him shirtless and sweaty."

Is this bitch for real? She can take her perfect petite body and stupid Boston accent and shove it up her ass.

Jesus, calm down, Colette.

"Excuse me?" I retort as I glare at her.

"Don't worry honey, I'm not after your man. G and I go way back. We used to fuck, but not since he met someone."

She has no filter. She doesn't see that any of this conversation is not appropriate. I look at Gage, who is speaking with Nat, the tall blonde who used to terrorize my best friend but now is somehow part of our little friend group.

"He met someone?" My heart sinks into my stomach, and I try to reel it back up. Maybe I've been completely reading all his signals wrong. It wouldn't be the first time. Cough, cough . . . Arrow. No, it's fine. He can meet someone. It's not like I wanted a relationship or anything. In fact, I hate him. This is fine. I'm fine. Really.

"Yup. He has been completely abstinent since he met her." She pauses. Looking at Gage and it's not longing I see in her eyes but respect. Then like a bolt of lightning strikes her, her spine straightens, and she turns her blue eyes on me. "Oh shit! You're his girl!"

I give her a look that says what the fuck are you talking about, and she easily reads it. "Yes! Fuck, I should have known! Of course! He never fights with the women he brings here."

"The women he brings here?" Great. Looks like I'm not as special as I thought I might have been. That really fucking hurts. Like an actual ache in my chest that brings down my entire mood. Why is he affecting me like this? Why am I letting him?

"Oh yeah. Every Friday nig—" She stops to look at me mid-sentence. "Oh no, sweetie! Not like that!" She lays a hand on my leg like we're best friends. I want to brush her off, but the act is actually conforming. "He teaches a women's and children's self-defense class on Friday nights. Usually brings in a new woman or kiddo each week. I don't know where he finds them, but they usually come from an abusive situation or have been attacked before."

My whole perception of Gage changes at that moment. He helps women and children learn to protect themselves? Looks like the tin man might have a heart after all. "How long has he been doing that?"

"Oh years. He showed up on our doorstep eight years ago, mad as hell at the world. My dad taught him to fight, and he hasn't left since. He started the classes about six years ago."

Something she said earlier comes to mind. "But he doesn't fight with the women?"

"Nope. He teaches and guides, but he lets them tussle with each other. I don't really know why, but he never rolls around with them. When it comes to the point in his program that they need to take on someone bigger and stronger, he pulls from my men's class. The only person he fights is me, well you too now."

I'm sitting in shocked silence at her words. Why doesn't he fight with the women? Why does he do this at all? I know there are many things I don't know about my dark, strange neighbor, but now I'm thinking that what I don't know isn't bad. And I'm going to find out. I'm too curious not to.

I had been fighting my feelings for Gage, scared of . . . I don't even know. Him? Commitment to someone who isn't Arrow? His secrets? But I think maybe, just maybe, Gage Eros isn't as scary as he wants people to think. Maybe under the mask he wears is just a man who wants someone to fight for him.

Gage looks at me, a small smile on his perfect face. God why does he have to be so pretty? And now he apparently helps innocent women and children learn how to defend themselves? Could he be more perfect?

"You ready to head home, Chaos?"

I get up from where I was sitting on the edge of the ring and walk up to him. "Could you stop calling me that? I'm not chaotic." Crossing my arms, I pop my hip out and put as much attitude into my body language to try to hide how turned on I am by him.

"Chaotic, psychotic, neurotic, exotic . . . ." His hand reaches up and snatches my throat, pulling me into him. "Erotic." He whispers the last one, and his hand tightens just a touch. My lips immediately curve into a small smile, and I watch as his eyes flash down.

"You're going to be trouble, aren't you?" he asks with a grin of his own.

"You're going to enjoy every second of it," I choke out.

He releases me just as quickly and pulls his black shirt over his head, then shakes his head to fluff out his wet hair. He unwraps his hands, slowly wrapping up the white cloth as he goes. My body hums as if his hands are still on me. But at the same time, a pang of guilt hits my chest because no one has ever made me feel this way.

What if I fall for Gage harder than I ever feel for Arrow?

How would I choose between the man who makes me feel safe and seen and the man who makes me come alive?

Chapter Seventeen

colette

Gage's apartment is exactly what I expected. Dark. Cold. Organized to perfection. Walking into the apartment, it's the same layout and has the same features as my own. Although his is currently a lot dryer than mine. Thank you, defective sprinklers.

Where mine is decorated in a hodgepodge of different textures and colors, his is black, black, oh and a little bit of black. Black couch, black accessories, black rug. But I will give him credit. There is a mix of dark brown leathers here and there. Like his expensive-looking leather recliner.

He walks in, placing his keys and wallet into a black bowl sitting atop a metal entryway table, then slips off his shoes. Then he turns on various lamps around the living space and kitchen. He doesn't turn the overhead lights on, giving the room a warm glow. It's peaceful despite the lack of decoration. I follow with my own shoes, trying to be respectful of his space and undefined rules.

"Question. Am I allowed to breathe in here because if I do, I might dirty it up a bit . . . "

He just shakes his head, ignoring my sarcasm.

"I'm pretty sure if I ran my finger along your ceiling fan, there wouldn't be a speck of dust," I say as I walk farther into the living area, looking around for anything that might be out of place.

"You wouldn't," he confirms as he goes to the hall closet and grabs a blanket and pillow, bringing it over and setting it on the couch.

"You aren't human. Who doesn't have dust on their ceiling fan? I'm concerned. You might actually be a serial killer. Should I call 911?"

He rolls his eyes, disregarding my theatrics, and fills my space with his tall, lean body. Looking down at me, he gently runs the back of his knuckles over my cheek. I think he might lean in and kiss me the way he's looking at my lips, then my eyes, then back to my lips. "Go take a shower. You smell."

"Rude! You don't smell like daisies either, ass!" I say as I push at his chest, but he doesn't budge.

"The towels are under the sink in the master bath. You can use anything you find in the shower. You can sleep in my bed." With that, he walks away from me, going to the fridge and pouring himself a glass of water. "Now, Chaos."

"But I-I don't have any clothes here," I protest. At this point, I want to argue with him just for the sake of it. I want to challenge him, to get him to touch me again. To get him to set his burning hazel eyes upon me and light my body on fire.

"I'll set some out for you. Go." He tilts his head, motioning to the master bedroom, and I heed his command. Who knew little old me would love to be bossed around so much?

After I shower, I go into his room, where he has laid out a pair of my pajamas on his bed. I'm not going to question why or how he got into my apartment to get them. I giggle a little at his choice. He could have easily grabbed a sexy, skimpy pair, and I would have no choice but to wear them, but no, he grabbed my red Christmas pajama pants with cows in Christmas hats all over them. I smile when I see he also remembered to grab my satin scarf.

Walking out of his bedroom, he's stretched out in his recliner, tapping away on his iPad, his long legs extended. He's shirtless, again, his black sweatpants sitting on his hips perfectly. But that's not what gets me. No, what has my pussy throbbing and my panties wet are his square-frame black glasses resting on his nose.

Great. Not only is he brilliant, sexy, and teaches innocent women and children how to fight, but now he wears glasses and is all nerdy.

"Fuck. So hot."

He looks up at me. "What was that?"

Shit. Did I say that out loud? "Nothing, I . . . it's . . . hot . . . in here. Not you. Well, you too but. Just." I pause, trying to collect myself. "You put me in my ugly Christmas pajamas. In the middle of July. It's hot in here, okay? Stop looking at me," I say as I try to hide my face, heading to the kitchen to get a drink of water.

He comes up behind me as I face the sink, chugging my water to attempt to cool myself off. I'm not physically hot. Gage's apartment could compete with fucking Antarctica. But the images rolling inside my mind, holy cow.

His hands wrap around the edge of the counter, trapping me between his muscular, tattooed arms and the counter. He presses his body into my back. "They aren't ugly. They're festive," he whispers into my ear, sending chills down my spine.

I spin in his arms, but he doesn't pull away. He stays close to me. His eyes are assessing. Taking in every inch of my face. But I don't shy away. No, I give it right back. Studying him. Memorizing him. His features are delicate and strong, masculine but pretty. I reach up to touch his face like he did my own not too long ago, but he catches my wrist in his hand, startling me.

"I don't like to be touched." He holds my gaze, the softness turning dark.

"Why not?" I whisper.

"Go to bed, Colette." He walks away from me, our moment now lost. Just as brief and fleeting as the other ones that have taken my breath away.

"Good night, Gage," I say as I head to his room.

He doesn't respond, but I feel his eyes on my back as I retreat.

I take a sip of my water, setting it on the bedside table. Then tuck into his silky sheets. I inhale the smell of him. The clean smell with hints of a spice I can't name but know somewhere in my memory.

As I search my brain for why Gage is so familiar, I drift off in sweet peace.

"It's empty."

"What?" the man, who I've never met but somehow knew my father, replies.

He's older, maybe in his early sixties. I've never seen him before, but here he stands, looking down at the black casket. Most people have left already. Nobody likes to see the casket lowered into the ground. I hug the American flag that was folded, then handed to my mom. She then handed it to me. I imagine she felt disgusted holding it. My father died for this flag. It's supposed to be a token of honor. My mother sees it as a reminder her husband is never coming home.

"The casket. It's empty," I tell the man again. He looks over at me, and I can see his confused gaze in my periphery.

"What?" he repeats again.

"They never found his body. We have nothing to bury. The casket. It's empty. I'll come to the grave and visit my father, but it's empty."

I'm empty. It's what I want to say, but I don't. Nobody really cares to know how you're really feeling. Then they would feel obligated to make you feel better and try to help you. I don't want their attempts; they would be useless. Only my dad could ever help me, and now he's gone. His casket is empty.

The man looks at me, shakes his head, then walks away. They begin to lower it, and Mom and I watch as it goes down, down, down. The empty casket. She's sobbing. I'm numb. I just stare at it. Down, down, down.

"I'm sorry for your loss," the preacher says.

"Loss," I repeat, not making eye contact with him. Then I laugh. "Loss. That's funny 'cause the casket is empty. Where is he?"

I wake in a startle. My body is sweaty. The sheets below me soaked. My chest feels heavy. Like something is crushing my lungs, I'm not able to inhale fully. My letters. I need my letters. His letters.

I throw the covers off me and begin to make my way to my closet but remember that I'm not at home. My letters.

Gage's apartment. My letters. Lost. I need . . . release.

Trying to calm myself, I open the bathroom door and find a razor in the drawer. The blade. My letters. My brain is only thinking in fragments. Moments.

I take my pants off and climb into the empty tub.

Easier to clean the blood.

Empty.

I press the blade to my inner thigh and gasp as I drag the blade across my skin, releasing my lungs. Releasing the emptiness and pain that was bursting at the seams. Like cutting open a festering abscess, the initial bite of the blade is harsh, but the relief is welcomed. It gives me breath.

I can breathe. I can feel. The pain. I feel it.

Closing my eyes, panting, living in the moment. I run my fingers along the open wound, then along my old scars. Before I had my letters, I needed this almost every night.

But my letters are gone. Lost. Just like my father.

I don't hear him. But my eyes snap open at the feel of his hand on my wrist. The strength in his grip forces me to drop the blade.

"Gage."

"Baby girl. Why would you do this?" His eyes are glassy. Tired. Did he even fall asleep? Or is his sleep also haunted by nightmares of the past?

I bow my head. I don't have an answer that would make any sense to him. It barely makes sense to me. Pain releases pain is what I want to say. The only way I know how to describe it.

He runs his fingers along my scars. "My Raven. So lost. So broken." It's a whisper. Probably not meant for me to hear, but I do. Am

I delusional? Has my exhaustion from restless nights of sleep and the adrenaline pumping through my system from the blade clouded my mind? Did he just call me his Raven?

"Gage." His hazel eyes meet mine, and I want to cry. I want him to hold me. He's the first person to see this side of me. Oh god. What will he think? Will he take me to the hospital? Tell them I tried to kill myself. It's not that. It's just a release.

"Come here," he says, and I lean up as he slides in behind me. His legs surround me as he stretches them out as much as he can in the tub. Wrapping his arms around my chest, he holds me tight. My head falls back against his shoulder, and his head leans into my own.

"You will not do this again. Do you understand me?"

"I have to, Gage. I need to feel. The pain, it . . . helps me. When my nightmares come, I feel so lost. The pain brings me back to reality."

"Is this what you were doing with the box cutter that night?"

"Yes." I turn my head into his neck, whispering against his skin. I feel him stiffen beneath me. All the muscles in his body go rigid, but he doesn't move away.

"No more, Colette." His voice is stern but comforting. It's not a demand to seek control of me but to protect me.

"But I—"

"I said no more. When you need pain, you come to me."

"My letters used to help me. I had someone helping me with all of this, but I lost his letters. I would read them instead of . . . well, this. But I can't find his letters, and he hasn't written me back since my last one. I need his letters, Gage."

He can't possibly know that I already have someone to find me. But my letters are lost. Can Gage fill that void in the meantime? Arrow hasn't written me back. It's been five months. The long gaps are not abnormal for us, but I don't have any of his other letters to get me through right now. I need another as much as I need oxygen. I'm drowning without them.

Gage stays silent at my back. He probably thinks I'm crazy. Cutting myself with his razor blade, talking about letters.

"I bet you regret making me stay here now, don't you?" I say with a chuckle, trying to lighten the mood.

"I'll never regret letting you into my life," he whispers.

gage

Fuck, I'm tired. I was up all night. After I heard Colette crying out, I knew she was having a nightmare, but from personal experience, I also know it's better to ride them out. To not wake someone in the middle of one. But then I heard her go silent. I felt an uneasiness crawl over me, and I needed to check on her.

Her bright red blood dripping down her perfectly scarred skin is imprinted into my mind. I never want to see her bleed.

I never knew how much our letters meant to her, but I knew I needed to find them, so I went into her apartment and looked and looked. And finally, after I tore the place apart, I found them. They were packed in a box, in a box, and that box was shoved into the back of her closet, then covered by mounds of clothes. How they got there, I have no idea, but knowing my chaotic little creature, she didn't remember putting them in that box in the first place.

By the time I got back to my apartment, I laid on the couch for two seconds before my alarm went off. I contemplated the entire time I was looking about telling her that I was Arrow. But nothing has changed. I still cannot give her the kind of relationship and love she deserves. I still can't stand the idea of someone touching me. Loving me. It makes my stomach turn.

"Gage?" Her raspy morning voice draws my eyes to hers. Her delicate hands rubbed the sleep from them, still in her ugly sweater but no pants, just her boy shorts. The white gauze still taped to her leg from when I cleaned her up and bandaged her wound is a stark contrast against her rich, dark skin.

"Hey. Did you sleep okay? After. I mean?" She stands in front of me as I make her coffee, still rubbing at her sleepy eyes, and I wrap her in my arms. *What the fuck?* I didn't mean to do that. It's as if my arms instinctively dragged her into me. Wanting to feel her body pressed against mine.

"Thank you for last night." She looks up at me. Her eyes are tired, but I see the spark in them that was gone last night. It's my Raven who's in my arms right now. My gentle, fragile Raven.

"I made you an Americano," I say, nodding toward my espresso machine and releasing her so she can pick up the mug.

She hums, and my dick immediately responds. *Shit, down boy.* She's not allowed to make those sounds unless I'm inside her in some way. My fingers, my tongue, my cock. If I'm not in her, she cannot sound like that. I'll lose the small amount of control I'm barely hanging onto.

Taking her first sip, her eyes close. "I love these. Did you put brown sugar in here?"

"I know, and I did." Her eyes open, and she tilts her head.

"How do you know that?"

Fuck.

Time to change the subject. I clear my throat and nod to the coffee table. Her eyes follow, and as soon as they land on the wooden hat box, they begin to water.

"Oh my god. Gage. You found them?" Setting her drink down, she runs over to the box and opens it. Quickly thumbing through them all as if she's making sure they are okay.

I remain silent, just taking in her reaction. The peace and happiness on her face brings a smile to my own. Then she's running up to me. I brace for impact as she leaps up and wraps her legs around my waist and her arms around my neck. I instinctively wrap my hands around her ass and hold her there.

"Thank you, thank you, thank you! You have no idea how lost I was without those letters."

She pulls her face from my neck and looks at me. I rest my forehead against hers, taking in her scent, her warmth, her. "I told you I would find you."

Before I can even open my eyes to gauge her reaction, her lips are on mine. Their softness soothes a broken piece of my heart. Before I can chase that feeling, she pulls back.

"Shit. I'm sorry. I didn't—"

I don't let her finish; I slam my lips back to hers, and my heart jumps as she opens up for me. Allowing my tongue to tangle with hers. The taste of espresso and brown sugar makes me moan. She feels effortlessly perfect in my arms. Her skin against mine; her weight settles into my body.

Her fingers run up the back of my neck and into my hair.

"Your hair is soft, boy. I love the way it feels in my hands. How you feel in my hands."

His touch. "Stop." I drop her, and she lands on her feet but stumbles slightly at the abrupt change in position.

"I'm sorry. Did I—" She looks at me, such vulnerability and hurt in her eyes. It tears at my heart. This is exactly why we can't be together. She wants to give her love to me, her soft touches, her gentle caress. Herself. But I can't handle it. I can't feel her without also feeling him.

"Stop, Colette. This was a mistake."

"Gage." She reaches out for me, and I take a step back. I don't want to live in my memories. She can't touch me. I won't let her.

"I'm late for work."

Grabbing my keys and walking out the door, I leave her behind. This is how it should be. I shouldn't have gotten close to her. I need to stay away. For her sake. And mine.

***

Slamming the door to Hale's office, he jumps slightly in his seat. "Fuck. You scared the shit out of me. You could knock first."

"Where are we with the Alessis?" I don't acknowledge his comment. It doesn't matter because I never knock anyway.

He runs his hand down his face, his stress pouring out of him in his tired eyes and wrinkled suit. "They are being . . . upstanding citizens. Nothing suspicious. They follow Natasha around, grab lunch with her, sometimes take her to dinner. It's like they are fucking courting her. According to their texts, they are set to fly back to Seattle soon."

Going over to his large windows, I look down at the busy Boston street. "That's on par with their usual routine when they come to Boston. Do we know if Nat is going with them when they leave?"

"You mean Natasha?" His narrowed eyes are inspecting me.

Oops. God, I'm a fucking mess right now.

"Yeah, Natasha."

Thankfully, he drops it.

"Not a clue. They don't seem to be hurting her or forcing her to do anything. I'm not sure what is going on. You said that she told you she was "with them"? He does little air quotes with his fingers.

"Who knows what the fuck that means. I've had B training her. Just in case. Not that she could ever be a match for the twins, but it's better than nothing. They haven't followed her or come to the gym like I had expected."

He comes over to me, and I turn to look at him. I see the wheels turning in his head. His hand is stroking his beard in deep thought. He hates a puzzle he can't finish. "What are you thinking?"

His brows furrow as if confused. "I'm just wondering how someone like her could get wrapped up in the twins. It has to be connected to her father."

"Maybe she was payment? Is there any evidence that Mr. Baldwin has been dabbling in the sex trade business? He had a debt he couldn't pay so he sold his daughter?"

"Well, I don't fucking like that at all." Hale stiffens. Rage like I've never seen crossing his face. Strange . . .

I turn on my heel, heading for the door. "Where are you going?"

"To get some answers."

On my way to Joe's, I call Everett and pick his brain about Natasha's past. I had to bring him in on a little bit of what was going on to get him to give me as much detail as I demanded. But eventually, the puzzle started to become clearer.

"Eros, what did you find?" Hale's deep, tired voice reminds me the man works entirely too hard and often, but now along with a heavy dose of drowsiness, there is also urgency.

"According to a close friend of Nat's—Natasha's, the Baldwins had an arrangement with another wealthy family in Oregon since Natasha was little, the Rowans. The Baldwins wanted an heir, not wanting Natasha to take over the business when Daddy Dearest retired, so in exchange for political support, Natasha and the Rowan son were to marry and have a son. All went to shit when the Rowan son backed out."

"So she isn't the prize pig, he's using her like a fucking breeder?" Hale's voice deepens. Fuck, he's pissed.

"If that's still his goal, it sounds like it. But I think Natasha might be able to fill in some gaps."

"Find out, Eros," he commands, and I know when and where not to mess with Hale, and for some reason, when it comes to Natasha, he's not to be messed with. Looks like another thing I'll need to look into when all this shit blows over.

"I always do," I say, just before I hang up. My foot drops, accelerating my Audi to reach the gym before B is done with Natasha.

Arriving at the gym, I find Natasha and B just finishing up, laughing and acting like best friends. I stalk up to her, tired of all the damn questions. Grabbing her by the elbow, I pull her away from B.

"What's the deal with you and the Alessis?"

She jerks her arm out of my grip. "Jesus, Gage, hi to you too."

"I'm tired and don't give a fuck about pleasantries. Give me something. Despite how much I despise you, Everett cares about you so that means I need to protect you. Help me, help you."

She stares at me, questioning if she can trust me, I'm sure. After what feels like forever, she gives an inch.

"Fine. I can't give you every detail, but I belong to the twins. For now. They made an arrangement with my father. They don't hurt me. I'm safe. Can you trust me?"

"No."

"Well, you're going to have to," she says as she flips her braid over her shoulder and looks quickly at Sabrina.

"We know a deal was made, Natasha. The question is, what kind of deal and were you a willing participant? Do you know what kind of business they are in, Nat? How can I trust that you will be okay?"

She lets out a sigh, like a teenager who was just told she couldn't go to prom. "I know their history, Gage. I'm not stupid. And I'm not one of their girls. Leave it before you get hurt."

"Your father wants an heir to his empire. A male heir. If that's what the twins are meant to provide him, you're one of their girls. It doesn't matter that they treat you to expensive dinners and nice clothes. You're still their whore."

She steps back, her eyes catching on a form behind me.

"Agent Eros. Pleasure to see you here." Rafael's voice rings out. Turning, I see both the twins looking at me with murderous eyes.

"The sentiment is not returned. What do you want with Natasha?"

"That's our business. Plus, why would you care so much about our *whore*? As you so eloquently put it."

"A bit harsh, don't you think, pretty boy?" Enzo chimes in, stepping toward Nat and I, but B steps between us.

"Okay, boys. No fighting in my gym, and Nat isn't going anywhere she doesn't want to go," B sings out in her sweet voice, but her eyes send daggers to both the twins.

Enzo looks down at the small hand she has placed on his expensive tie. Then raises a brow at her. "Cute. But I don't listen to little girls who think they are tough shit. Move." Enzo grabs B's wrist, attempting to remove her hand, but she reaches up, forcing the butt of her other hand into Enzo's nose, instantly breaking it. But he doesn't make a sound as his head snaps back. When he looks back at her, blood pouring from his nose, his eyes are hungry.

"Don't fucking touch what isn't yours." She sends an equally murderous look at Enzo as he steps into her, but Rafael grabs his shoulder.

"Control yourself, brother."

"Oh, but I like her. I want to see her cry. Come on, let me play." A sickening grin graces Enzo's face as he licks the blood off his upper lip. He's known to be a bit unhinged. Clearly, the rumors hold true.

"Jesus. Everyone, calm down. I'm fine. Trust me." Natasha looks at me, giving me a reassuring nod, and I don't know why, but something in her eyes makes me listen to her. For some odd reason, I do trust her. Something tells me that Natasha is tougher than she lets on.

Rafael turns with his arm slung over Natasha's shoulder, and Enzo backs out, keeping his eyes pinned to B, and I don't like the look he's giving her. As if she's his new toy that he can't wait to play with.

"Well, that was fun." B bounds away like she didn't just break Enzo Alessi's nose.

How many fucking women do I have to try to keep safe? Too fucking many.

colette

My letters.

Clutching them to my chest like they're my lifeline, I breathe in the scent of the worn paper and ink. When Gage found them, I couldn't keep from flinging myself into his arms. Like a desperate fucking teenager. Then I don't know what happened after that, looking into his eyes, his strong arms holding me, knowing in my heart he would always care for me, even if he's a grade A asshat.

I kissed him.

Then he rejected me.

God. How stupid could I be?

Gage is a good guy; I know that now, but he clearly doesn't want me in that way. I catapulted myself from the friend zone and was completely obliterated when I hit the ground. Literally, he dropped me so fast I thought I was going to fall on my ass.

How embarrassing.

It's been two weeks, and I haven't seen him. He's avoiding me. And I hate it. How I got into this position where his absence from my life feels like a knife to my chest is beyond me. I literally hated the guy not that long ago, but now, he's all I can think about.

Don't even get me started on the clusterfuck in my brain of what to do about Arrow. Having his letters back made it that much more real that I was falling for two different men. And hey, funny thing, neither of them wants me. So that's great . . .

The guilt I feel for loving Arrow but also having feelings for Gage is eating me alive. I had determined that Arrow would be the man I settled down with. Even though we hadn't met, I just couldn't see us dying and never meeting, and I was going to wait till we were both ready to meet in person. But then walks into my life Gage *fucking* Eros and I'm more confused than a chameleon in a bag of skittles.

After our one night, I didn't stay with Gage as he had demanded. I thought he would text me or call me and make me come back to his place, but he didn't. I definitely didn't wait next to my phone waiting for his call. That would be pathetic . . . So I stayed with my mom and watched re-runs of *Friends* until I was crying . . . laughing.

Last night was my first night alone again and I had another nightmare. For the first time in years, the first thing I wanted wasn't my letters.

It was Gage.

I wanted Gage over my Arrow. But Gage isn't an option now. I need to just let him go.

And that's how I find myself thumbing through my letters, sitting on my bedroom floor, crying . . . again. I don't even know what I'm crying about anymore. Gage, Arrow, my dad. I'm such a fucking mess, I can't even keep track of what is making me sad.

Arrow hasn't responded to my last letter. Ouch. Gage rejected me after I kissed him. Ouch. And my dad is gone, leaving a giant hole in my heart. Triple ouch.

As I'm packing away my letters, determined to paint my face with the happy, joyful Cole who everyone loves, a picture falls out of one of the letters. I smile at the memory. I remember asking Arrow to do this silly Christmas tradition when I found out he never celebrated Christmas. What a Grinch.

I stare at the picture, his Henry Leo mug in hand, his ugly Christmas pajama bottoms with elves chasing reindeer, the white brick fireplace—

The. White. Brick. Fireplace.

What. The. Fuck.

I shoot up from the ground, grab my keys and run down to the lobby. Picture in hand, slippers on my feet. Hair in my bonnet.

Standing in front of the fireplace, I hold up the picture. Fuckin' fried shit on a stick! It's the same one. Even the coffee table Arrow has his feet perched up on is the same. The brick pattern is the same. Arrow fucking lives in this apartment complex. Or at least he did. This picture was from years ago. Who knows if he's still here.

No wonder this place felt like home when I first walked in. God, how could I not recognize it?

Holy shit. What if I have seen Arrow and not even realized it? What if we rode in the same elevator? Passed each other in the hall?

A giddy sense of excitement fills my chest at the possibility. But it's quickly swept away when I realize that even if I want to meet him, he may not want to meet me. He may be content living without me.

You know what? Fuck him. I'm going to find out who he is, and I'm going to show him that I'm worth it. And when he meets me, then he can decide if he wants me or not. As friends or more. Then I will be able to make a decision about Gage.

Bottom line, I need to find Arrow.

I walk with determination up to the front desk. Herold is there, sipping his morning coffee. Dressed in his fancy tux, he has his gray hair slicked back.

"Good morning, Miss Corvina. How can I help you?"

"Good morning, Herold, do you know the person in this picture?" I show him the photo and he pulls his glasses down to the tip of his nose and squints his eyes a little then looks at me like he might be missing something.

"Uh . . . I don't believe so. Miss, all I see is a hand?"

"Yes. Yes, I know. Silly question. Umm—do you know who might have taken this picture? Do you recognize the pants or anything about his hands, the mug? Any detail could help."

"Well, I know that not many people use the fireplace, miss. The pants are Christmas-themed, so I assume it was taken around that time but so many people use the fireplace for photos around the holidays. And the hand, well, it appears to be a man's hand."

I sigh in frustration. Way to point out the obvious, Herold. "But you helped this man start this fire."

He pushes up his glasses onto his nose, and his shoulders drop with a sigh. "I'm really sorry, miss. My memory isn't what it used to be, and it wouldn't be the first time someone needed my help with the fireplace. I hope you do find him, though."

I let my hands fall with exasperation. Damn, I thought I had something. "Thanks. If you see anyone with that mug or in those pants, could you let me know? It's really important."

"Sure thing," he says, nodding.

I head back up to my apartment to get ready for work. My mind is racing with who he could be. After work, I will go through all the letters again, see if I can find anything that might sound familiar.

Entering Henry Leo's, the small bell announcing my arrival, I do my best to tuck away all thoughts of Arrow and Gage. Time to focus on work.

"Well, good morning, sunshine."

"Why are you so happy this morning?" I narrow my eyes suspiciously at LJ. She's not a morning person, and I usually am greeted with a groan and moan instead of a good morning.

"Nothing. Just happy, I guess."

I throw my bag down on my desk and take the coffee cup LJ extends toward me. "Well, good for you. I'm miserable. Just rub it in."

As I sip her perfectly made Americano with brown sugar, a small piece of my anger falls away. But then I'm reminded that me and a certain man on my shit list share the same favorite drink, and I want to launch my cup across the room.

But that would be a waste, and I have more self-control than that, so instead, I throw myself in my desk chair and pout like the grown-ass woman I am.

"Oh stop. Why are you miserable?" My best friend rolls her eyes as she perches her butt on the corner of my desk.

"Because of your stupid *best bud Gage*," I mock in a juvenile tone; I don't even care at this point. "And Arrow hasn't replied and—"

"Arrow?"

Shit.

"Uh, yeah." I try to move past the slip of my traitorous tongue and open my laptop to begin working, but I'm stopped by LJ's "mom voice."

"Colette Corvina." She slams my laptop closed. "Who the fuck is Arrow?"

Double shit.

"I'm going to need a muffin first. Blueberry, please?" I bat my eyelashes at her, and she sighs, getting off my desk and walking to the front of the store. When she comes back, I notice we have thirty minutes till Henry Leo's opens, and I finally word vomit to my best friend about the man I've loved for the past four years.

"Holy shit, girl. I can't believe you've hidden this from me all these years."

"I'm sorry. I'm an awful friend."

"Hey." She lays her hand on mine. "You don't need to apologize. You're under no obligation to tell me your whole life. You're human. You need things for yourself. I just wish you would have told me you needed help. I would have done anything to help with how you felt about losing your father. I had no idea you were struggling so much."

Biting at my lip provides me with enough pain to distract my mind from someone actually acknowledging the shit I've been dealing with. This is why I don't share. It makes me feel weird when someone sees your vulnerabilities and . . . accepts them. "I wear a good mask."

"But you don't need to. I love you no matter what state you're in. I'll always be there for you."

"I know. I guess I just didn't want people treating me like I was fragile. Like they couldn't have fun or be happy around me because I was so lost."

"It's okay to be fragile, Cole."

I give her a smile, a genuine one.

"And you said this Arrow guy, you think you love him?" She continues when I remain silent.

"I do. I just don't know if it's as a friend, or maybe it could be more. I know he's important to me. I want to meet him, but he has been through—well, something traumatic, and it has left him with some issues. But honestly, I want to help him through that. I want to be there for him."

LJ suddenly looks conflicted. "What about Gage?"

"What about Gage?" I counter with a bit more attitude than I meant.

"I don't know, I thought maybe you two were . . . getting along. Maybe moving toward something more?"

"Definitely not. He doesn't want me like that."

"I wouldn't be so sure. I've never seen Gage look at anyone the way he watches you. I think you have more of a hold on him than you think. The question is, do you want something with him?"

I have no words to express what I want, so I stare toward my bookshelf and try to really feel in my heart what I would want.

LJ's hand brushes my cheek as she turns my head to face her pretty blue eyes. "I know Gage has a past, one that is similar to my own and when you have the kind of monsters we have . . . " Her eyes glance down, and I watch as she swallows hard. I can tell by the scrunch of her brow and the break in her voice that what she's saying doesn't come easy. "Gage and I are hard to love. But I know he's worth it."

I stay in silence for a moment, thinking about her words. Sounds like Arrow. "You know, you're worth it too," I remind her in a whisper as I stare at this woman I have the honor of calling my best friend. She gives me a half smile and gets up to leave.

"You'll have to choose, babe. The only way past it is through it."

"Can't you just tell me which to choose? I don't like this game," I plead jokingly, and she laughs a little.

"I can't do that. Just don't be afraid. Okay? Don't run away like I did."

The bell ringing overhead signals our first customer. LJ and I make our way to the front, me to grab some napkins for my muffin and her to ring up our first coffee addict.

But a letter on the bulletin board catches my eye.

August 2nd, 2024

My Raven,

  You want to know about my first love? I'll
tell you.

  She's electric, transcendent, wild, loving, and kind. She challenges me, pushes me
to the brink of insanity, and then tackles
me over the edge, laughing as we fall
together. She irritates the fuck out of me,
drives me up a wall, makes me question all
my choices.

  She's everything I never wanted and everything I need. I'm addicted to her. Her
smile, her laugh, her eyes.

  I knew her before I fell for her, and I
think that's why I fell so hard. So fast. I
knew her before I knew myself.

  But she's also beautifully broken. She's
fragile, and she elicits a need in me to
protect her. But at the same time, I know
deep down, she doesn't need me at all. She's
fearless enough to do it on her own if I
only give her the way.

  That's the hardest part about loving her.
When I teach her how strong she is, will she
still need me? Will she still love me when

she realizes I'm even more broken and cannot be fixed? That I cannot give her what she truly desires. Someone she can fully love.

She reminds me very much of you, Colette.

colette

The first thing I notice as I read Arrow's letter is he's using present tense. His first love is his only love, and she's in his life. She's his. Not me.

He doesn't belong to me. Maybe he never did.

The next thing I notice is he knows who I am.

He knows, and he doesn't want to meet me.

In the end, it doesn't matter who he is or what he wants. It matters what I want, and the last thing I realized while reading his letter? Everything he confessed about his love is how I feel about Gage.

Arrow's letter solidified everything for me.

Arrow may hold a piece of me, something that will always belong to him, but Gage is who I want.

And I'm going to get him.

gage

"**A**lright, ladies. It's the final part of your program. You all have been practicing taking down women, people similar in strength and stature to yourselves. But as we all know, when the time comes to put your skills to use, it most likely will not be a fair fight. Now, it's time to take on the men. For many of you, this will be the hardest part of your program. This may elicit memories of your past, but to move forward, you must face your fears. If you don't feel ready, that's okay, you can pair up with a woman, but I highly encourage you to try."

I look out on my women's class. Many of these women are from domestic abuse or sexual assault backgrounds. I have been doing this class for years, and this is the hardest part. They are put into situations that bring back their trauma. The question is, can they push past their memories and think clearly to save themselves? Or will they be consumed by their monsters and falter? They don't graduate from their program until they can take down the men. It's a mental game more than it is a physical one.

The men line up, and some women look eager, ready to conquer their fears. Others are already retreating into their memories. But all of them step up and choose a male partner. Pride swells in my chest.

There are always a couple who need more time, but for the most part, by the time they are in this stage of their program, most are equipped with the physical and mental strategies to push through.

As I watch them on the mats, evaluating and assessing techniques, I see a dark beauty lingering in my peripheral vision.

Speaking of pushing through your trauma, I've been a bit of a hypocrite. Avoiding her has been the only way to keep my mind strong and my hands to myself. If I put them on her, she will return the sentiment, and I can't feel her touch. I can't be hers like she wants me to be.

I wrote her as Arrow, although I still haven't decided whether it was a mistake or not. Did she put the pieces together? Could she see me behind the pages? Now that she knows that Arrow knows who she is, will she give him up or demand more from him? From me.

"Gage. Can I join?"

"The men's and women's classes are combined tonight. I'm sure B is free to spar." I don't make eye contact with her. I know I'm being a dick, but I can't look at those fucking whiskey eyes of hers. I'll crumple under her gaze. The war in my head is raging. And if she captures me in her chaos, I won't make it out without hurting her.

"I don't want to spar with B. I want to spar with you."

"I can't. I'm bus—"

"Oh, I got this, big guy. Go tussle with your hottie with a body." I glare at B as she wiggles her fingers at me, waving me away.

"I hate you," I whisper to her.

"You love me," she says as she turns her back to me with a little too much sass.

Walking over to Colette, I feel nervous, which is just fucking bizarre. I've never felt nervous around a woman before. Is this how teenage boys feel when they talk to their crush for the first time? It's awful. I hate it.

"Hi." Her voice is timid. My Raven is here. Maybe she knows that I'm her Arrow.

"Hi," I return as I stand close to her, my head tilted to look down on her beauty. I didn't mean to get this close, but here we are.

"I'm sorry. About—" she starts, but I don't deserve an apology. She does.

"Don't." I see her back teeth grind. Her eyes light with fire. Shit. Now I have my Chaos.

"Don't interrupt. It's rude." She gauges if I'm going to let her continue, and for some odd reason, I'm going to. I want her fight and her fire. I have always wanted it.

"As I was saying. I'm sorry I kissed you. I shouldn't have. I just was . . . overwhelmed. I understand that I'm not your type, and you don't want me—"

"Stop."

"What did I say about interrupting?" Her arms cross over her chest, and I know she's angry, but I can't have her thinking I don't want her. I do. More than anything. But I can't have her, for her sake. There is a difference, but I will never let her feel like there's something wrong with her.

"I'm a rude person. You know that. But Colette, it's not that I don't want you or that you aren't my type. I just . . . It's something wrong with me. Not you. Never you."

The confusion crossing her face tells me that she fully believed it was her that I wasn't attracted to. "But you said it was a mistake."

"I know. It was. But not because of you, baby girl." I brush my wrapped knuckles along her flawless skin. "Because of me. There are so many things wrong with me, and I can't let them hurt you."

"That was a dick move."

A grin pulls at my lips. "I never claimed to be a nice guy."

She reaches up to grab my hand, but I pull away. "Come on, Chaos. You missed last week, so you have some making up to do."

She undresses down to her biker shorts and sports bra. And I wrap her hands. I help her warm up by practicing her combos, and I'm pleasantly surprised at the force she has behind her hits.

After, we move to the mats to practice defense maneuvers. Tonight is all about getting out of an attack from behind. I have my arms wrapped around her neck, her hands clawing at my forearm.

"The first reaction for most people in this position is to panic and pull away. What I'm going to train you to do is stay calm and get close," I whisper in her ear.

"Why would I want to get close?" she questions.

"Panicking gives him more power. They are after your fear. Your struggle. Don't give it to them."

She's breathing rapidly, her instincts telling her she's in a dangerous position, and she is . . . in more ways than one.

"First, tuck your chin into my arm and protect your throat as much as you can. Then, step to the side, into the arm they have around your throat." I loosen my grip enough to allow her to think clearly, and she does as I command. "Then, hit them in the groin, either with your elbow or fist. This will force them to bend forward, and as they bend forward, bring that elbow up and straight into the fucker's face."

We go through it slowly a few times. "Good. This is a dangerous hold, Colette, so you need to be fast. Let's go again."

With each run through, she gains confidence and speed. The last time, she's so sure of herself she actually gets a hit into my nose, making it bleed slightly. The pain shoots straight to my dick, and I feel it harden.

Fuck, that's my girl.

"Oh shit! Gage, I'm so sorry." She comes up to me, placing her hands on my cheeks and inspecting my face. Grabbing her wrists, I pull her off me and take a step back.

She looks hurt at my retreat. "I'm sorry," I say without even thinking.

"Why are you sorry? I just busted your nose." She keeps her distance, though, clearly reading my discomfort at her touch.

"Let's run it this time, but if they lift you up from behind. Many attackers will try to get you off balance by lifting upward, getting you off your feet."

"Okay." With awareness of the tension now between us from her touch, she comes back into my hold.

I show her how to swing her legs when I lift her from behind. With her momentum, she knocks me off balance and quickly gains her freedom. She's such a fast learner, and I'm so fucking proud of her, it's borderline unhealthy.

After getting some water, I check in on my women's class as they end their session. Only two were unable to complete the task and will come back next week to continue to try. I dismiss them and head back to B and Colette, who are laughing and giggling at something. Probably talking shit. Little fuckers.

"What are you two laughing at?"

"Nothinnnng," B says with a singsong attitude. I give her a look that says don't try me, but of course she does. "Just how you're actually a sweet little teddy bear under all those tattoos and DGAF attitude."

"I'm afraid you have been misled," I remind her with a ruffle of her fiery-red hair. She returns with a punch to my gut, and I double over since she never takes it easy on me.

"Bitch."

"Pussy," she replies as she walks away.

Groaning as I stand to my full height again, Colette has a grin on her face, clearly amused at my pain. "What are you smiling at, Chaos?" I groan out as I rub at my abs, which are now going to bruise.

"I love that she's not afraid of you."

"Never has been. One of the reasons I can stand to be around her." I begin to unravel the wrapping on my hands and watch as Colette traces my movements.

"I'm not afraid of you," she says with a tone that makes my dick pulse. She steps into me and takes the white wrapping from my hand, unraveling it herself. I watch her, stunned at her boldness. But I don't know why it shocks me because Colette Corvina is bold to her core when she wants to be. That's one of the things I lo—like most about her. She's a complete contradiction to what everyone wants her to be. She's daring and timid at times. A comfort but also makes you want to push yourself beyond your comfort zone. She loves deeply but isn't afraid to hurt your feelings.

"Can you stand to be around me?" She looks up at me with innocent eyes. Eyes I get lost in every time she challenges me with them.

"No."

"Why not?" She leans in, and her hands blindly continue unwrapping my own rough hands.

My body leans into hers like fucking gravity, and I can't resist her tempting mouth and fiery eyes.

"Because you make me want things I can't have, baby girl." I'm so close to her I can see the pulse of her heart fluttering beneath her neck. Right where I want to sink my teeth in.

"What are those things?"

"Your touch," I whisper without even thinking of lying to her.

She drops my hand and seals our lips together. The softest of kisses. Just a graze of her full lips against my own.

I'm paralyzed by her softness, her gentleness. Her.

The lights suddenly shut off. "Would you two just fuck already and get it over with?" B's voice rings out from the balcony overlooking the gym.

Colette smiles, her cheeks flushing with a deep red against her skin. She looks at her feet then back up at me, clearly waiting for my reaction.

I flip B off and slam my lips to Colette's, taking in every taste and sensation that makes her, her.

I pride myself on my patience, but this woman makes me lose it. Pulling away from our kiss, both of us panting, I scoop her up, her thighs wrapped around my waist, and I walk her to my car. My plan was to put her in the damn passenger seat and put some distance between us so we can have a conversation, but the breathy moan that escapes her as she bites down on my neck obliterates my plans.

Pinning her between the passenger door and my body, I look into those eyes and decide to give her what I can. Because let's be fucking honest, I can't stay away from her. She's too alluring, too captivating. She has drawn me in, infected me, and consumed all my thoughts, and I'm tired of fighting it.

"I want you, Colette. But I can't—" I stop, struggling with how to word what I want to say. I've never been the type to hesitate. I don't sugarcoat my words. But I've also never cared if I hurt someone's feelings. With her, I do.

"I don't like to be touched."

"But you fight. We touch when we spar, when B spars with you."

"That's different. It's rough. It has a bite of pain. I can't do . . . soft touches."

"I'll take whatever you can give, Gage. Just do something because you're driving me insane. If you want me, take me. If you don't, tell me so I can move the fuck on."

My knuckles graze her cheeks. "You need to know what you're signing up for. I'm not gentle. I'll bind your hands so you can't touch me. It won't be loving. It won't be tender. I'll take and take to fill my needs, and you will be left, begging and wanting. If you're a good girl, I'll make you come so hard you see heaven, but you will not touch me, kiss me, or love me. If you do, this ends. Do you understand?"

"Yes." She releases on a breath.

Wrapping my hand around her throat, I tilt her lips up to mine. I growl against them, unable to control the rumble that releases from my chest at her submission. "Good girl."

colette

Fuck. Fuck. Fuck.

I knew I wanted Gage. Knew I wanted him to want me, but what the hell did I just agree to? I can't touch him? Like at all? I can't kiss him? Can't cuddle him? I'm a stage-five clinger. What the hell am I going to do if I can't touch him?

Well, I'm shit out of luck 'cause I already feel myself breaking the rules. I already feel the desire to place my hand on his as he shifts his Audi, racing us home. I already feel my lips burning with wanting to lay them against his pale skin. I already feel my heart being ripped apart.

I'm in so much fucking trouble.

But the thought continues to pop into my head. He doesn't like to be touched. Why? Is it a dominance thing? Is it a trauma thing? Either way, I have agreed to his rules, and now I'm going to get a piece of Gage I'm not sure I'm ready for.

He all but drags me into his apartment, his grip tight on my hand. Once inside, he spins so fast, I run into his chest. He grabs me by my throat and pushes me against the door. His lips meet mine aggressively. Devouring all I have to give him. My mind is spinning with the hungry side of this man that I have never seen but am soaking my panties for. *Jesus.*

I feel as if I have released a part of Gage he was repressing. A monster within.

Make friends with your monsters. Don't hide them, unleash them.

Arrow's words float inside my head. Shit, I shouldn't be thinking about him while kissing Gage.

I reach up, going to wrap my arms around him and drag my fingers against the skin on his back, but he freezes. Every muscle in his body tenses.

"Don't," he growls against my lips.

"Sorry. I don't know how not to touch you. I don't know how to do this." The confession leaves my lips, and I'm terrified that he will change his mind. But I know any relationship that starts with lies is not one that can last.

"Then let me remove your opportunity." With that, he grabs my thighs and lifts me so my legs wrap around his back, then his fingers intertwine with mine but not gently. His grip is tight and rough, just like he promised. He pins my hands above my head and pushes his hips into mine. Pinning me against the door.

He continues to kiss me, his tongue demanding every breath I have. His lips move down my neck, biting and sucking, and I moan at his body against mine, the nips of pain mixed with pleasure. It's driving me wild. Not being able to touch him, to return his kisses, is a completely new form of torture.

His erection presses against my core, and I find my hips moving of their own accord. Dancing across his hips, seeking friction, seeking release. "Fuck. If you don't stop doing that, I'm going to come in my pants like a fucking virgin."

I chuckle at this description. "You poor baby." I pout my bottom lip out, and he catches it with his teeth.

"Watch it," he warns, then pulls me away from the door. Walking me to his bed, he throws me down on it. I bounce a little at the force and smile. He unbuckles his belt and pulls it from the loops in one swift motion.

Kneeling on the bed, he pulls me up by my throat and lays a quick kiss on my lips before collecting my wrists and securing them with his belt. He hovers in front of my face. I lean forward to wipe the distance between our lips away, but he pulls back, and I chase him slightly, leaning in.

"No kissing." He grins.

"But you kiss me," I plead as his hazel eyes challenge me.

"I'm allowed to. You aren't," he says as he lifts his shirt off his torso. My mouth drools at the sight of his toned body and black ink tattoos.

"Such a hypocrite," I say as he pushes me, and I fall, unable to catch myself. My braids spill out around my head as he grabs the waistband of my shorts and underwear and works them down my hips, then my legs. His eyes never leave mine. Watching me.

Is he looking for me to break his rules?

Then he unzips my bra, the zipper in the front making it easy for him, and my breasts spill out.

Once I'm laid out on his bed, hands bound and above my head, he steps back, assessing me with those dominating eyes. They run from my face to my chest, down my stomach, pausing on my pussy, and then running down my legs. I've never had a man look at me the way Gage does, with such intensity and focus. His possessive gaze makes me feel vulnerable and delicate but also on fire at his approval. I can see it in his eyes and the bulge of his jeans that he likes what he sees.

"Are you going to stare all night, or are you going to fuck me, Mr. Eros?"

His eyes fly to mine and turn dark. "Don't be a brat, Colette."

He circles the bed, a predator sizing up its prey, and I squirm under his gaze. I'm dying for his touch—for his body to cover mine and his lips to sear my flesh—but he continues to stare. Teasing me without a single finger touching me.

After what feels like hours, he unzips his pants and pulls himself out. I watch as he strokes himself, his hand running from base to tip, and my mouth waters at the sight. He's big but not overwhelmingly so, and I raise a brow at the fact that he wasn't wrong. He's comparable in size to EC. I let out a whine when I see the silver bar through the tip of his head. Fuck. He wasn't kidding. I wonder what that will feel like inside me. I clench my thighs together at the thought.

"Gage. Please," I whine, and I don't feel an ounce of shame at how weak this man has made me.

"Please what?"

"Touch me," I growl at him.

A devilish smirk graces his pretty face, and I want to smack it right off. "Apologize," he commands, and I about lose my shit.

"For what!" I shriek. "Let me out of these bindings. I'll give you something I should apologize for!"

Okay . . . maybe I did lose it a bit . . .

"Being a brat."

"Aw. Is Gage a sensitive man? Did I hurt your feelings?" I want to goad him, pull out the darkest parts of him. I want to see if the man who controls everything would lose it for me.

"You're asking for it. Are you sure you want to go there? Remember what I said about being a good girl?"

"You don't want me to be good. You love it when I challenge you."

He raises a brow, then comes closer. Yes. Finally. Wrapping his left hand around my throat, he pins me in place. His right hand goes to my pussy, teasing me with his long fingers as he circles my clit, slowly and gently. The sensation makes my hips lift, sending shivers over my entire body. Something about the way he touches me makes me feel electric.

I moan out, closing my eyes, chasing this high. Fuck. He's a musician, playing me like the god he is. My core begins to clench as my orgasm builds. I can feel myself on the brink of destruction when he pulls away.

My eyes fly open as my orgasm dissolves, and my heart thundering inside my chest begins to slow. No. No. No! "Gage, please." I'm almost crying at this point.

"Apologize," he says right before he sucks his fingers into his mouth, and his eyes roll back.

Be strong, Cole. Don't give in. It's just an orgasm. Nothing I can't give myself. "If you're not going to fuck me, give me EC, and I'll do it myself."

He laughs, actually laughs. "You want EC?"

He tucks himself back into his dark slacks and leaves the room, not even bothering to put a shirt on. I hear his front door shut and open again. Stepping back into the room, he smirks and holds EC up. "Is this what you want, baby girl? You want me to fuck you with your toy? Make you come so hard your body feels like it's betraying you since you and I both know it belongs to me now?"

He turns EC on, and the vibration makes me wetter. Like a fucking Pavlovian response. He places the tip of EC against my nipple, circling it, stimulating it until it's almost painful before moving on to the next. My hips are writhing, doing anything they can to chase some kind of friction. He drags EC down my stomach, the vibrations tickling my flesh, then finally he reaches my clit, and I let out a loud moan at the sensations flying through my body. I instinctively open my legs, asking, no . . . begging for him to slide EC inside me.

I think my wish has come true when he presses the tip of EC right at my entrance and pushes just the head in. But then he pulls him back and circles my clit again. He does this over and over and over. My core is tight, right on the edge of an orgasm, needing something to fill me up, to push me over the edge, but he denies me over and over again.

"Are you ready to apologize, baby girl?" His eyes heat and the urge to smack that smirk right off his face surfaces.

I stay silent, letting my whimpers fill the silence, but I can't hold on any longer. "Yes. Yes. Please, Gage. I'm sorry. Okay? I'm sorry I was a brat." I beg him with my eyes, and he rewards my submission.

As he pushes EC fully inside me, filling me, his warm tongue meets my clit, and I see stars. My orgasm crashes into me like nothing I have ever felt. I close my eyes as my body shakes and writhes beneath his tongue. He holds EC inside me, pressing on my lower belly with his arm, the vibrations hit that special spot inside as his mouth sucks and teases even more from me than I ever thought I could give.

When he promised he would make me see heaven, he wasn't kidding. I have never felt an orgasm so deeply, so fucking strong. As I come down from it, he withdraws EC and kisses my pussy. "Such a good girl. See, that wasn't so hard."

"Fuck. You," I say between heavy pants.

He just hums in response. I curse myself for my attitude. My eyes stay closed, feeling unable to even move those small muscles. But I drag them open when I feel his hands on mine. He pulls them to my stomach and releases the belt. Then he places gentle kisses on my wrists, the delicate skin stinging at the touch. I look at him, taking in his dark hair and pretty face. What a sight to fall asleep to.

My eyes begin to close, sleep pulling me under, but then I remember . . . "Wait, you didn't get to finish."

"Watching you reach the stars was all I needed. Go to sleep."

I try to argue with unintelligible words, but my eyes won't open, and my body is relaxing faster than I can protest.

In my half-sleep state, I feel his knuckles brush my cheek and lean into him. "Good night, my Raven."

colette

The dark room is silent. I don't sense Gage's presence next to me, which makes me wonder where he is and why he isn't with me. I have to admit that I'm a little disappointed that he isn't snuggled with me in bed. I crave his warmth, his scent, just him.

Rolling out of bed, I bring the sheet with me, wrapping it around my body. I want to find him and drag his grumpy ass back to bed with me. I'm needy like that, and if he wants me, he'll have to get used to it. I need snuggles.

When I enter his living room, I see it's six in the morning on the oven. The sunrise is coming, making the sky a light gray. I find Gage lying on his couch, one arm across his stomach, one above his head. He's shirtless and beautiful. His eyes are closed, his face peaceful. His hair is a little ruffled. He's so captivating it's annoying. Some men are handsome, some sexy, some hot. Gage is ethereal; he has a feminine masculinity that makes both men and women jealous of his features.

"Stop staring and go back to bed." His rough morning voice makes me jump.

"Come with me."

"I don't snuggle." He opens one eye and peers over at me.

I drop the sheet, revealing my naked body to him. His eyes open fully at the gentle sound of the sheet hitting the floor, and his head turns slowly. Hazel eyes run from my feet to my face and back down. I feel his eyes on every part of me, goose bumps erupting where his gaze lands. I remain silent, letting him take in his fill. Finally, I turn and head back to the bedroom.

"Come on, pretty boy." I fill my voice with seduction and sway my hips with confidence. My mind may be a weak little bitch, but I know my body is sexy. I *feel* sexy in it, and that is something I'm going to lure this man into bed with.

"You will be the death of me, woman," he says, and I hear the leather couch creak with his weight leaving it.

When he enters the room, I can see the uncertainty on his face. Actually, all over his body. He's tense, stiff as a board. Why?

I pat the bed next to me. "Come on, I won't bite."

He runs his hand down the back of his neck and pulls on the hair there. "I think I would prefer it if you did."

How can someone not want to be touched, to feel another loving them in that way? I don't understand it. Physical touch is one of the five love languages. We all need it in some form. What happened to this man to make him completely cut off something so vital to our existence?

"We don't have to touch. Just lie next to me."

He steps forward, trusting me with this, and it's at this moment I realize how truly special that is. To have Gage's trust.

He lies on his right side, facing me as I lie on my left.

"This technically isn't snuggling," he reminds me.

"I know. But just having you near is enough."

He closes his eyes, whether with the intention of going back to sleep or processing what is going on, I'm not sure. But I'm naked, he's half naked, and my mind is racing too much to sleep.

"You're getting too close."

"I haven't even moved." I giggle a little at his absurdity.

"Not your body. Your heart." His voice is cold, and I feel it like an icicle growing inside my chest.

"Would that be so awful for me to have feelings for you?"

"Yes."

I'm taken aback. I wasn't expecting such bluntness, but I'm not sure why. Gage doesn't filter his thoughts or words. He would have to care to do that. And clearly, he doesn't. Not about my feelings anyway.

"Wow. Okay."

"I told you I couldn't be with you. It's not you, Colette. It's me."

"Yeah, that's what they all say." I roll onto my back, not wanting to look at his stupid pretty face as he rejects me. I stare up at the ceiling and force the question out that's been on my mind. "So all you want is my body then? This is just sex."

"It can be a friendship too."

"I can't be your friend, Gage. I can't . . . just be your friend. I already feel too much toward you. Mostly anger. But also other things." I turn back to face him. I needed to see his reaction to my honesty.

He lets out a sigh. "I feel more too."

A spark of hope lights in my chest, hitting me like a lightning bolt. "But I can't allow myself to lead you on. I can't be with you in the way you deserve, Colette."

I've heard that before. What the hell is wrong with me? The two men I have ever had strong feelings for both claim they can't be with me.

The thought escapes my lips before I can push it back down my throat like I've done countless times before. "What's wrong with me, Gage?"

"Nothing." He grazes his knuckles along my cheekbone. "Nothing is wrong with you. It's me. I'm . . . defective," he says that last word with a furrow in his brow as if he isn't sure that's exactly the word to describe himself.

"Let me help you." I reach out to touch his high cheekbone, but he captures my wrist.

"You can't."

"Let me try." He doesn't release my wrist, but he allows me to push my hand forward. I lay the pads of my fingers on his temple and slowly drag my hand down. His eyes pinch as if in pain, and my heart breaks for him.

"That's enough." He pulls my hand away, and when his eyes open, they are unfocused. As if he isn't even looking at me but through me. His breathing is harsh, his nostrils flaring. The mask he's hiding behind at this moment is the same one I saw in the club on LJ's wedding night. Or maybe this isn't the mask at all? Maybe this is his true self.

"Gage, look at me." When his eyes focus on my own, I see his stone-cold affect slip back into place. But I don't want the cold-hearted man or the lost one. I want the flirtatious one who makes my heart race. But how do I get him back? "Let's try a different touch."

Pulling my wrist out of his grip, I move my hand to his cock and grip it over his sweats with a firm touch. This doesn't seem to bother him. In fact, I can feel him growing in my hand at the rough way I'm handling him.

A groan leaves his chest, and I smirk. I love seeing how much pleasure I can give him.

I lower myself on the bed, settling between his legs, and pull his pants down just enough to pull him out. I'm trying my best to keep my touches rough. The tip of his piercing hits his stomach, and the sight of it against his abs and the strong cut of his jaw from this angle makes me want to capture this image and paint it later. God, he truly is gorgeous, a masterpiece. My mouth salivates at the image of him on his back for me.

My eyes connect with his when I stroke him. A devilish smirk graces his face. "I've been dreaming about shutting you up with my cock down your throat for months, baby girl."

I narrow my eyes at him. "Asshole."

"We could do that too." He winks as he covers my hand with his and increases not only the pace but the pressure as well.

"Absolutely not."

He scoffs as if I'm joking. And just to be the brat that I am, I run my tongue up the underside of him, flicking his piercing with the tip when I get to the top.

"Fuck," he groans.

I do it again, continuing to stroke him but never putting him fully into my mouth. Watching him struggle as I tease him fills me with confidence. "How do you like being teased?" I mock him.

"I don't." The vibration in his voice is a warning, one that makes me clench my thighs together.

He gets up faster than I can process. "On your knees," he says as he points at the floor in front of him.

"Make me." I cross my arms in protest.

"You really want to go there?"

I shrug, but before I can fully complete the action, his hand wraps around my throat while his other cups my pussy. He presses his palm into my clit and slides two fingers inside me. The pressure he has on my throat and my pussy has me letting out a whine.

"If you're going to tease me with that mouth, I'm going to put it to use. You better understand one thing, Colette. You want to come all over my hand, my face, my cock, then you do as you're told."

Oh fuck. This is everything I've wanted and more. Gage is the first man to ever give me what I want. I want to be used. My reality is full of making decisions and carrying burdens yet in here, with him, I want him to take away my choices.

I know that's fucked up—a dark and twisted fantasy—but I can't help what I want. And I know Gage would never truly take away my choices. It's an illusion. The real power lies with me because I know when I say stop, he will.

The grip he has on my throat tightens, and he begins to pull his fingers out slowly, then pushes them back in just as slow. "Do you understand, baby girl?"

"Yes," I whisper, and he releases me completely.

I crawl down and kneel on my knees before him. Then he cradles my jaw in one hand, tilting my gaze to meet his own. "Good girl. You're learning."

I stare up at him, looking up at his sculpted abs and pecs, his body before me is terribly unfair. His black and gray tattoos heavily ink his skin. I barely see any blank canvas left, but if there was an open spot, I would love to put my mark on him. Paint his skin with my brush.

"Open up and stick that temptress of a tongue out."

I do as I'm told, and he runs the tip of his cock against it. Without warning, he plunges inside my mouth, straight to the back of my throat, and I moan around the intrusion, my eyes closing on instinct. Fuck, he's big. He stays there, completely still, and I'm forced to breathe through my nose.

As my eyes water, he pulls out, then pushes back in after I suck in a breath. He guides my hand up and down, my tongue circling him as best as it can.

"Touch yourself," he commands.

Again, I do as I'm told. I'm concentrating so much on not gagging that I don't have it in me to disobey.

The faster and deeper he goes, the more wet I become. The way he dominates me, takes control, but also reads my body and gives me my breath when I need it is incredibly hot, and I can't help the moans that escape my throat as I look up at him and see his pleasure written all over his body. His head is thrown back, his neck flexing as he tries to control his own body as well as mine.

Tears begin leaking down my cheeks from the depth he's hitting, the cold metal gliding along my tongue such a contrast to his warm skin.

Finally, he looks down at me, tracking the tears running along my cheeks. He rubs them away with his thumb, releasing his grip on my hair. "When This is the only time you will ever cry for me, baby girl."

With that, he pushes deeper, then I feel him swell inside my mouth and the taste of him explodes along my tongue and down the back of my throat. As he finishes, so do I. My body tenses, and it takes all I have not to bite down on his cock. But I do end up grazing my teeth a bit against his taut skin, and his eyes flare with heat at the small amount of pain I'm sure I'm causing him.

I swallow him down like the good fucking girl I am and lick my lips after he pulls out.

"I knew that mouth was good for something other than annoying the shit out of me."

I stand and give him a kiss on the nose before he can pull away, "You love when I annoy you."

"Whatever. Get dressed. I'll make us coffee." With that, he tucks himself back into his pants and turns around. As he walks away, for the first time, I notice two large wings cover his entire back. Black feathers like a dark angels . . . Or a raven.

gage

C olette and her mouth.

Colette and her mouth.

Fuck.

The espresso couldn't brew slower, could it? It's torturing me because all I can think about is getting back to Colette.

I'm a fucking pussy. Who the hell have I become? Wanting to spend my morning with a girl? Letting her touch me? Lying with her in bed and not fucking? Well. That one is a bit of stretch; we didn't lie long. But the point remains that no other woman could get me to do any of these things. But Colette fucking Corvina has bewitched me.

She makes me want things that I shouldn't, just like my Raven did. It makes sense they are one and the same.

A part of me knows I need to tell her—be honest with her—but I can't bring myself to. She'll want a relationship, a real one, now that she's getting involved with Gage and falling for Gage. If I tell her I'm also Arrow, she'll go over the edge. She'll want it all, and that isn't something Gage can give right now. It's not something he's capable of.

Fuck, now I'm thinking in third person.

The Americanos are just about to finish brewing, so I press the button on my machine to stop them. The symbol brings back the memory of when I first saw Colette, screaming and pounding on the machine at Henry Leo's because she couldn't figure out which button to press to stop the pull of espresso.

"What are you smiling at?" Her voice hits my ears, and I try and fail to mask the smile.

"I was just thinking I should teach you how to use one of these." I place my hand on my second most prized possession.

"Fuck those things. Plus, why would I need to know when you're right across the hall?"

I sit on the couch next to her, handing her a mug. We look out the floor-to-ceiling windows as the sun begins to come up. "Mmm, this is so good. And with the sunrise. All that's missing is some snuggles." She looks over at me suggestively, but as quick as it came, it's gone. Replaced by a furrow in her brow.

"What's wrong?"

She blows on her coffee, then takes a small sip, not looking at me anymore. Finally, she releases a small breath. "Nothing."

"Don't lie to me."

Keeping the mug in one hand, she begins fiddling with one of her long, dark braids with. "I made a promise to someone. That one day we would sip Americanos, cuddle, and watch the sunrise together."

I remember that in her last letter.

"I guess I just feel a little guilty."

"Why do you feel guilty?" I'm confused by her admission. She has nothing to feel bad about. She isn't in a relationship with Arrow. She may love him in a way but loving someone and being committed to them are not synonymous. Just because she loves Arrow doesn't mean she can't enjoy her time with me.

"I love him. But I also . . . well you. I want you." Silence fills the room. I'm not sure what she's trying to say exactly. I don't even know if she knows what she's trying to communicate.

"I'm not saying I would rather have him here than you. I just . . . I guess I've never had feelings for two people before. I don't know how to navigate it all."

"I see, and if this man wanted you the way you want me, and we were both standing in front of you, what would you want?" I recognize how unfair it is for me to ask her this, but there is a small insecurity within my fucked-up brain that worries she loves Arrow more. Even though we are the same, Arrow is not someone I'm readily able to give. He has been and only ever will be hers. He's not for anyone else, and I fear if she knows I'm him, she will want me to be more like him to everyone else, and that isn't me.

"I guess that's why I need to know what we are. If there is something here, something we can build, I want that. I want you. Arrow . . . he has another person he loves, and I'm good with that because it made me realize that I want you. But it's still difficult to think you'll have a life with someone only to find that it's not going to happen the way you envisioned."

I look down at my own coffee. This is exactly what I never wanted. Complicated feelings and shit. Why did Colette have to be my Raven? Why did I have to figure out it was her?

"I don't know what we are, Colette. I know that I can't give you the life you envision, but I can't give you up either."

"Why not?"

I can see a whole future with her. I just don't know how to get there. How do I make her understand?

I must have been quiet longer than I thought, lost in my own head.

"Answer me, Gage Eros, and don't you dare lie to me." Her body is fully facing me now, challenging me with her eyes. I couldn't lie if I tried.

"I do want you. More than I have ever wanted anyone, baby girl. But I don't know how to be with you the way you want me to be. Can you really be in a relationship with someone you can't touch? Who won't cuddle you? Sleep in the same bed as you because he's too afraid that your hand might brush his in the middle of the night? You don't deserve that, Colette. That's what I'm trying to protect you from. Can you just take what I can offer?"

"No."

There it is. She can't be in a relationship with someone like me. I knew it to be true, but it still kicks me in the fucking chest. Tightening and taking my breath away.

"I can't take what you offer. I want more. And now that I know you want me too, I'm going to take and take and take. I'm going to make you love me, Gage Eros." There is a teasing uptick to her tone.

"You terrify me," I say as I pull her in for a kiss by her throat. Not a gentle one, never a gentle one. She moans into my mouth, and it takes all I have to pull away.

"How do you plan on making me fall in love with you?" I whisper against her lips.

"By making friends with your monsters." She pulls back slightly, letting her eyes burn her truth into my soul.

"How do you plan on doing that?"

Shrugging like it's that easy, she replies, "By getting to know them, silly."

"Oh, look at the time. I need to go to work." I go to get up, but she drags me back down, and before I can protest, she's straddling my lap. But she isn't touching me with her hands.

"We're going to play a little game. I'm going to ask a question. You can answer or not. But if you choose not to answer, I get to touch you. Just a single time for a few seconds. I'll answer any question I ask you. And if I don't answer, you can touch me."

My body tenses, readying to fight. I clench my teeth, and I feel nauseated.

She notices because her eyes soften. Gone is the playful little siren. My Raven is sitting in my lap now. "I'll never force you to do anything that feels like too much at one time. But I won't give up on you. You're so lost in your head, Gage. Let me find you."

She's right. I have lived with my monsters for so long and made friends with them that I started to think I was fine. Everything I had done and gone through was fine because here I am, a functioning adult in society, but here is a woman sitting in my lap who wants to give me her heart, and I can't take it because her gentle heart will break me.

I give her a nod. The bravest act I have ever done so far in my life. Relenting to her questions, to her touch.

"Let's start easy. When is your birthday?"

"July 28th, 1998."

"Ah, a Leo. That explains your confidence." She smirks. "I'm an Aquarius. February 14th, 1999."

Pretending I didn't already know that, I plaster a look of confusion on my face. "You were born on Valentine's Day? That explains so much," I mock her.

"Shut up, you ass!" She gives me a playful smack on the shoulder but continues to keep her hands to herself outside of dishing out a little pain.

"Okay. Next question. A bit harder. What's your deepest fear?"

"Being forced to watch Christmas movies," I say before considering the consequences.

She throws her head back laughing, the column of her neck exposed, and it takes all my restraint not to lean forward and bite at her perfect sepia skin. Her laughter is like music to my ears, and I want nothing else than to hear it more. When she stops, I move my hands from her ass to her ribs and squeeze. She lets out a squeal and tries to slap me away. "Stop! This torture tactic—will not work!—You will—answer my questions," she says between laughter.

My cheeks hurt from the smile on my face. "Don't you remember, one of my kinks is torture?" But despite my words, I cease tickling her, resting my hands back on her thighs, running them up and down with firm pressure. Feeling her skin warm my hands.

After she catches her breath, her features fall. "Mine is losing people I love."

"That's understandable, given what you have gone through," I say as I move my hand up, tracing her collarbone with my fingers.

"Moving on," she sing-songs after a moment of silence between us, clearly not wanting to dive deeper into those feelings.

I run my eyes over her perfection. Her upturned brown eyes. Her full lips, the top just a little fuller than the bottom. A unique, odd little quality. Her high cheekbones, the dark brown, almost black braids that adorn her brilliant head and fall to her lower back. Braids I love to run my fingers through. I wonder what it would be like to run my hands through an exquisite mess of curls instead? She's a magnificent creature that I want to continue to explore and learn about.

"Earth to Gage." She snaps her fingers in front of my face.

"Hmm?" I sound out, but don't look her in the eyes as I continue to trace her features, too lost in her beauty.

"What are your parents like?" Now my eyes meet hers. Grinding my teeth, she reads me like a book, hyperfocusing on the hesitancy written on my face.

"My mom is dead. She died when I was young. I don't remember much about her. I only know she had dark hair like mine, and people tell me she was incredibly beautiful."

"And your father?"

I stay silent.

My silence is answer enough. She reaches her hand up, slowly, as if trying to tame a wild animal. My heart is racing inside my chest. My breathing picks up to match it. My chest heaves. Am I really about to let her do this again?

"This terrifies you." It's not a question so I don't answer her. "Who did this to you?"

The gentleness in her voice is resounding. It's a roar inside my head that echoes off my empty chest, bouncing off the hollows of my rib cage.

Her fingers trace just above my eyebrow, brushing the hair away. Revealing the small scar that runs through that eyebrow.

"It's not right for a boy to have such a pretty face. If you weren't so pretty, I wouldn't want you like I do. It's really your own fault."

"Dad, stop!" I whimper, but my small, high-pitched voice does nothing to deter him. It never does.

"That pretty face…" His hand brushes my jaw as his other clutches a glass beer bottle. "It makes me want you. But I don't want to want you! Let me fix it for you."

I watch as her eyes focus on it, furrowing slightly. Probably wondering how I got it.

"One."

"Two."

She whispers, then her fingers leave my skin, and my chest caves in as I release the breath I was holding.

When I can pull in air again, I answer her. "A broken beer bottle. When I was nine."

"Was it an accident?"

"No."

She looks down at her hands. She will never know the pain her hands cause and the memories they evoke. I want to rewire my brain so I don't think of him when I feel her, but I don't know how.

"Tell me about your parents." Everything of note about her parents I have already done my research on, but I want to hear about them from her lens. In fact, I think I'd like to see the entire world from her lens.

Her eyes light up thinking of them. "My mom is incredible. Even if I didn't always think so. She's sassy and kind. She will always put me first. She's fierce and loyal, generous and compassionate. She gives her best but isn't afraid to be vulnerable. She has taught me so much, and I don't think I've ever thanked her for it."

"She sounds like you," I remark, and she gives a small laugh, relaxing into my lap even more, her shoulders drooping slightly.

"Yeah. That's why we always butt heads."

"And your father?" I use my fingers to trace small circles on her outer thighs. Letting her know through my own touch that I'm here. I'm here for these difficult memories.

"If my mom is fire, he was her ice. He was calm, collected, and patient. I've never seen him mad. He was a pilot in the Marines, so he was tough. But only when and with who he needed to be. He listened to me. Inspired me. Challenged me in the best way. He always saw something in me that I could never see in myself. He kept me grounded. Kept me out of my head and in the present. Every time I fucked up as a teen, I always thought, *this will be the time he loses it with me*, but he never did. He always met me with love and understanding where *I was*, never where he thought *I should* be."

I watch as her face changes from joy to sorrow as she remembered him. "I miss him."

"I know. He's always with you," I say as I brush one of the braids that had fallen into her eyes behind her ear.

"One more question."

I nod, giving her permission.

"Why don't you like to be touched?"

I don't want to answer. But I don't want her to touch me. I don't want another memory to surface. I still feel on edge from the last one. I feel like I'm treading water, so I reach out to the hand she's offering, deciding to give her a piece of me.

"My father used to touch me. It brings back memories that I have fought hard to suppress."

I see her own breathing pick up, her chest moving up and down faster than it was a moment ago.

"What memory came back when I just touched you?"

My chest feels like it's about to implode as if the walls around me are slowly moving in, but I try to fight through it and stay in the present for her. "I thought you said just one more question."

"Please?"

She isn't going to take my deflection. I have fought with sweat, blood, and tears to push him to the back of my mind and lock it all in a box, and now this chaotic beauty is forcing me to open that box, and I hate it. But I don't hate her.

"I can only give you so much, baby girl. You're asking a lot of me right now."

"I can't imagine what you have been through. But I can see that your father still haunts you, Gage. Let me share your pain, your burdens. Let me take some of it away. What memory did you just see?"

My mind escapes back into the memory that I pushed away. I try to open my mouth to give it to her, but nothing comes out. The weight in my chest consumes me, and I feel like I'm suffocating. Like a fucking elephant is sitting on my chest. Fuck. I can't breathe. I can't—pull in enough—air.

"Gage." Her hands on my neck bring me back to her. Her grip is not gentle. It's firm and demanding. "Look at me. I'm right here. Breathe, baby. With me." She grabs my hand, laying it over her heart. I feel her chest move up and down below my palm, and I begin to match her. "You're with me."

"He came into my room after a shift. That's usually when he came. I woke to him touching my forehead, where you just touched. Brushing my hair back, then down my jaw . . . then—"

I feel her chest rise under my hand, and mine automatically does the same, synching with her.

"He told me that I was pretty. He always said I had such a pretty face. A face that didn't belong to a boy. That if I wasn't so pretty, none of this would be happening to me. He wouldn't have the urges he had. After he . . ."

I pause, wondering how much she can take of my past. But she asked for this, and I've never had the capability to refuse her. "He did what he needed to do to feel . . . satisfied. And like he always did, he punished me for his desires. He wanted to make my face a little less pretty. I remember wishing that he would disfigure me. Make me so incredibly ugly that he would never touch me again. But he didn't. He left a small scar but kept my face pretty enough."

I expect disgust at the knowledge that, as a man, I was raped. That's what the world would think, isn't it? Because men are too strong to be raped. We are too strong to be victims. We are too strong to seek help. That's not very manly. Am I less of a man because I've been forced to do things that made me gag till I threw up? Am I less of a man because my body has unwillingly pleasured another man?

Am I less of a man?

But she gives me none of that. She leans forward and places a soft kiss on my scar. Her vanilla scent invades my nose at her proximity. "Mine," she whispers. Then she places a gentle kiss on my lips, cradling my jaw in her warm hands.

"Mine, not his. Do you understand me?" I don't answer her. I can't. I'm on the verge of a breakdown. I want to escape. Hit something. Be hit. I want to feel anything but what I'm feeling right now. I'm drowning in panic. So many emotions filter through me. I'm feeling them all, their weight carrying me down. Fear. Hate. Love.

Being loved.

"And you have a terribly ugly face."

She smiles at me. And I resurface.

colette

"What is that?" Gage leans back on his couch, shirtless and oblivious to how sexy he looks in his glasses. He's fingering something, moving it back and forth across his knuckles.

"A coin."

I move toward him, his eyes tracing my legs as I walk. When I get to him, I straddle his waist and take the coin from his fingers.

"Excuse you," he protests but doesn't move to remove me or take his coin back.

His large hands fall to my thighs. I'm only in my underwear and a baggy T-shirt since we're about to go to bed. For the past two weeks, we have fallen into a rhythm all our own. He's already up with coffee made in my apartment by the time I wake up. We haven't had sex yet, but damn, he sure knows how to use his fingers and tongue to bring me to earth-shattering orgasms nearly every morning.

I go to work utterly and blissfully happy, and when I return home, he has dinner ordered and on the way for me. When he gets off in the evening, he meets me here, where we play our questions game or watch a movie or read together. After he tucks me into my bed, he heads to my couch, where he stays through the night.

His work schedule has been a tad bit difficult to navigate. I work normal daytime hours, but Gage doesn't have set hours. He works when he's needed and can really work whenever as long as he completes his tasks. I have discovered that he's a night owl, usually choosing to work in the evenings and sometimes into the following morning, but I've also noticed he has been home with me more at night.

I'd like to think that has everything to do with wanting to spend time with me instead of working, and if that's the case, then I'm happy to contribute to a healthier work-life balance for the once workaholic.

He still refuses to sleep with me, though. But I have convinced him to lie with me for a movie or to read, which is progress in my book. Baby steps. And as long as we are taking steps, I don't care how slow we go. As long as he continues to do this journey with me.

"Is this what you're always fiddling with in your pocket?"

"Hmm." He hums and nods his head.

"Why?" I try and fail to twirl it between my knuckles like he was just doing, and it lands on his chest, tails up.

He glances at it, then at me, expecting me to pick it up. "I'm not going to pick it up. It's tails. It's bad luck if you pick up a coin that's tails up."

He picks up the coin and begins flipping it again, staring at it as it travels across his tattooed knuckles.

"Someone once told me that they always take a chance on tails-up coins. She said she couldn't imagine all the worth lying about, never picked because of others' fear that one simple coin would bring them bad luck. So she picked up this coin and gave it to me."

He continues to watch the coin, lost in his memories, and I give him the silence he needs to continue. Because for once, I think that this memory is a good one. One he needs to be lost in.

"I keep the coin to remind me that every person has two sides. A side that everyone wants to see and a side that no one wants to take a chance on. But both sides hold the same value." He flips the coin again and leaves it on the tails-up side in his palm. "When I feel overwhelmed, like I want to give in to my monsters and let them have me, I flip the coin and think about how easy it is to turn it over. To see the other side, to see worth in both the heads and the tails of the same coin."

"Is it that easy? To see your worth on both sides?"

"Never. But that's why I keep the coin." He holds it out to me, tail side up, and I take it from his hand.

"Give me your worst, Gage Eros."

"Be careful what you wish for, Chaos." He smirks, and I instinctively grind down on him.

His eyes travel down to where I'm moving my hips against his hardening length. Fuck, he feels so good. He's pushing his hips up into me as he grips my own and takes control of them. Moving them back and forth in a rhythm he and I both appreciate.

"You like that? Hmm? You like rubbing yourself all over me, baby girl? Is it driving you absolutely feral that I'm not inside you right now? How fast do you think I can get you to come for me with our clothes still on?"

I whimper, not even able to put together words at his filthy mouth. I keep moving my hips, begging him to go faster and faster as he guides me. I feel the pressure building all over my body. It's practically vibrating. Just a little more . . .

He lifts my hips, pulling me away from the pressure. "No," I whine.

"What was that? Like five seconds? Come on, Colette, I thought you had more fight in you than that. You're going to let me destroy you that fast, huh?" He chuckles under me as I level him with my eyes.

"You. Are. Such a jerk!" I grip his throat in my hand, pinning him to the couch. I know he could take control at any moment, but he doesn't. He lets me grip him as I pull down his sweats and pull him out.

"Hmm, there she is." His throat vibrates under my hand.

I stroke him up and down as he keeps his eyes narrowed on me, but I see his jaw clench, trying to hold in his pleasure. His stubbornness collides with my own. Neither of us wants the other to win, but we both want to be destroyed.

I hover my hips over him and end up having to remove my hand from his throat so I can pull my panties to the side. I watch his eyes darken as I barely place his tip inside me, teasing him just as bad as he does me. I grin as I see the disappointment in his eyes when I keep my hips elevated.

"You don't like being teas—" He grips my hips and slams me down onto him. He enters me with such a delicious force that I gasp and then moan out long and loud.

"Fuck. No. I don't like being teased, Colette," he growls as he rolls my hips with his large hands. My eyes roll back in my head as his pelvis grinds into my clit. It only takes two strokes before I'm shaking with the strength of my orgasm. I'm out of breath as he continues his torture, rolling my hips and thrusting up into me. My hands fall to his chest, and he moves his hands from my hips to my wrists, trapping them behind my back. He holds them in one hand, then moves the other to my throat.

I feel like liquid as he moves brutally in and out of me. "Fuck. Fuck. Fuck," I whine with each thrust.

"Jesus, Colette," he whispers as he takes my lips in his, continuing to thrust, faster and harder.

Another orgasm hits me like a fucking train, and I can't help but collapse forward onto his chest.

One more thrust has him groaning out his own release. "You feel so fucking good, baby girl. Like you were made for me."

"Hmm." That's the only noise I can manage. I'm dead weight on him. I can't even think of any sassy or crude comments, which is how we both know I have been thoroughly fucked . . . literally.

He slaps his hand down onto my ass, the sting waking me slightly from my almost slumber that I nearly fell into on his chest—his heartbeat underneath me like a lullaby.

"Come on, let's get you cleaned up." He chuckles.

"No," I protest. "Let's stay here."

"Colette. I don't snuggle," he warns with a growl, my happy Gage now long gone, before sliding out from under me.

Asshole.

colette

I'm fucked.

Literally and figuratively. This man has a sexual appetite that would exhaust a whorehouse. But that's okay. One thing I have discovered is I love being his whore.

There, I said it. Judge away! I am who I am, and Gage makes me feel like that is the only person I need to be.

But I'm also fucked because I'm in love with him.

But, Colette, it's only been two weeks? Yeah well, I was born on Valentine's Day. Of course I fell for him in such a short time.

My mom used to tell me, when you know, you know. That's what Gage feels like. He feels like home. He feels right. I feel safe. He feels like forever. I have never laughed or smiled as much as I have with him. I'm tearing through his walls like a fucking wrecking ball, and I love to see him laugh and smile as I do. And let me tell you, when he smiles? Holy hell. That's probably why we fuck so much 'cause sweet baby Jesus that smile is a panty dropper, let me tell you.

He has opened up to me more and more, and I'm seeing the side of him LJ always ensured me was there. He's incredibly kind and sweet. He takes care of me. Physically, emotionally. My nightmares are less frequent, and when they do come, he's there—holding me. Whispering in my ear, telling me he's there. He doesn't sugarcoat things. He never tells me it will be okay. He just reassures me that I'm not alone because he knows my deepest fear.

But we are still working on some things. He still won't sleep in my bed with me. He still won't allow me to touch him. Although I have noticed he's less careful. Sometimes he brushes against me when we're cooking together. He doesn't tie my hands as often anymore, trusting that I will respect his boundaries. He allows me to give him small kisses, but just on his face.

We still play our talk or touch game, and I'm either asking harder questions, or he's getting more comfortable with my touch. But either way, I have now been able to touch him a little longer. Although that is still hard for him, and each time, I ask him to share with me his memories.

They break a part of my soul that I will never repair. But if they affect me that much, I can't even imagine what his soul looks like.

It's Saturday now, the last day of the month, and I'm having brunch with my mom. We decided to have brunch together on the last day of each month to keep us close.

I brought Arrow's and my first letters to each other. The one that was written as if it was my dad. I don't need it anymore. I have Gage. And I know in my bones he would never leave me. Call me crazy. Call me stupid. But he won't.

"Here, Mom. I wanted to give this to you." I hand her the letter and explain what it is. A tear falls from her delicately aged face.

"This is so special, honey. Are you sure you want me to have it?"

"It did its job for me, Mom. And now I have Gage. He fills that void. Now it's time it heals a part of you."

"Tell me about him?"

And I do. I tell her everything. Well, almost everything. She doesn't need to know how he uses EC on me, or how he ties me up and spanks me and bites me and makes me see heaven when he makes me come. How he edges me when I'm a brat, or how when he goes down on me, I see stars.

Yeah, we can leave that out.

But I do tell her about his trauma. How he won't let me touch him.

"That poor boy." She shakes her head as I tell her a little bit about his story.

"I love him, Mom. But I'm afraid he doesn't feel the same. I'm afraid he won't ever let himself feel that way toward anyone."

"I think he already loves you, honey. But he has never felt love. He probably doesn't even realize that is what he's feeling."

I never thought about it like that. In my naive mind, I thought everyone knew what love felt like. But what about when you've never experienced it from the people who are supposed to show you what love looks like? But I know Everett and LJ love him. Maybe he can feel and accept a platonic love, but what we have is more. Can he feel that?

"You're a wise woman." I grin and mock, and she just rolls her eyes at me.

"You're just figuring this out? That's what I've been trying to teach you since you were born."

By the time brunch is over, I'm practically vibrating at the thought of being with Gage again. God, he has me addicted to him. I'm literally having withdrawals. Bastard.

Before I make it home, a text comes through from Everett asking me to stop by and pick up Muffin, the dog that Gage and he share custody of. I'm not an animal person, but Everett knows I'm practically living with his best friend at this point, so I'm basically Muffin's bonus mom. LJ being his real mom.

Running up the steps to the Phoenix residence since Everett took LJ's last name, ditching the Rowan name and expectation, I knock on the door, and it opens to Everett's smiling face.

"Hey, come on in. I just have to grab his leash, and he'll be good to go." He excuses himself to go to the kitchen as I step in, noticing that Rune and LJ aren't home.

"Where are my favorite humans?" I ask as I bend down to scratch behind Muffin's ears.

"Well, I'm right here, and Gage is at work . . . "

Rolling my eyes, I snarl my lip up at him, mocking the comment he thinks is so funny. He just laughs and hands me the leash. "Leo and Rune went to get ice cream. They should be back in a few if you want to wait?"

"Nah, I'm good. I'll see her on Monday." I hook the leash to Muffin's collar and am about to head out when a thought pops into my brain. Because I'm a dummy and occasionally listen to my intrusive thoughts, I go ahead and turn back toward Everett.

"Can I ask you something?"

"Of course," he says with a sincerity that I find rare in men . . . okay, humans these days. That's one thing about Everett I have always liked. Even when Leo and he were trying to figure things out, I never felt like he was disingenuous. I know he made some mistakes, but so did LJ, and I have never ever questioned his love for my best friend.

But I also know LJ's past, and he loved her through it. How did he make her see her worth? How did he show her that she's worthy of love because that's the battle I have been fighting with Gage. Even though there has been progress, it seems impossible to have what LJ and Everett have. And that terrifies me.

"You and LJ . . . her past and her trauma, it's heavy . . . " Damn, what am I even asking? How do I ask it?

"LJ told me that loving someone with as much trauma as she and Gage have is hard . . . so how did you know that you could do it? How did you always have faith that you would find her?"

He looks down and shakes his head, his hands braced on his hip. "That woman."

After taking a deep breath, he looks up at me. "Loving her is the easiest thing I've ever done. It's easier than breathing. Love like that isn't something you have to work at. It's as much a part of you as the beating heart inside your body. I'm not saying our relationship doesn't require work because it does. But our love isn't a choice we made, just like your heart beating isn't a choice you can make."

He pauses a moment, but I can tell he has more to say, so I remain silent as Muffin collapses onto my feet, clearly tired of waiting for his humans to stop talking.

"That man is my brother, Cole. He's just as broken as Leo once was, even more so, I think. Before you decide you want to fix him, you better ask yourself if loving him is as easy as breathing."

"It is," I say without hesitation because despite everything, Everett is right. There was never a choice. I love him without thought or question, and that can be dangerous with someone like Gage.

He's a storm I love to watch, beauty and power, a love that is unpredictable and one you can easily drown in. But I'm used to drowning.

When I get home, I unleash Muffin and go to grab a snack, but there is a note on my counter. I pick it up, and my heart drops in my chest.

Last minute work trip came up. I'll be gone for two weeks. No phones where I'm going. See you soon, baby girl. Be good. -G

Two weeks? No phones? Jesus, is he going to the fucking moon? Where could he be going where he can't call me?

My insecurities and fears begin to crawl up my chest, infecting my brain. Is this him leaving me? Am I too much for him? Does he need space from me?

No. Gage wouldn't do that. He would tell me straight up. He wouldn't run.

Would he?

I dial LJ, and she rushes over with Rune as soon as I tell her I need her. As Rune plays with puzzles at my coffee table, I pace the kitchen. "Is he really on a work trip?"

"As far as I know. That's what he told Ev." She's running her fingers over the lip of her mug.

"What does he do for work? Is it dangerous? He's going to come home, right? Oh my god, LJ. He's going to come home, right? I can't lose him."

"Breathe, babe. He's going to come home. He works for the FBI as a computer person or something. Honestly, I don't even know what he really does, but he doesn't really do the dangerous stuff. He probably just can't call due to security reasons. He works on some top secret stuff."

"Okay. Yeah." I swallow, trying to push down my fears. I don't know why we've never discussed his job in depth. I knew he worked with computers and never talked much about his work, but honestly, it never mattered what he did for work. "Yeah. He'll be fine. But he couldn't have called? I need to hear his voice."

"Auntie Cole? Are you okay?" Rune's sweet voice breaks through my fog, his hand slipping into mine. I bend down and give Rune a big hug. "Yeah, buddy. I'll be fine. I'm just a little sad is all."

Rune escapes my arms and runs to his backpack. "Uncle Gage told me that when Auntie is sad, I should give this to her."

He hands me a letter, typed out on an old-school typewriter. God, he even found a typewriter 'cause he knows how much they mean to me. And like the big, emotional baby I am, I start crying. "I hate him, LJ. I fucking hate him."

"Yeah. Sure, you do." She gives me a hug and a kiss on the forehead, then leaves with Rune. She's letting me read my letter and be an emotional wreck by myself because she knows I hate being vulnerable in front of people.

Colette,

Didn't I tell you that the only time you're allowed to cry for me is when you're on your knees? Why are you crying, baby girl?

I'm not leaving you. I'll be back in two weeks. Do you understand me? I'm not leaving you. Drink your Americanos, annoy the shit out of Everette for me, use EC, and paint me something. I'll be home before you know it.

It's my weekend with Muffin. Ev should have dropped him off or had you pick him up. Let him give you all the snuggles you need.

I'll come home to you.

I promise.

-Yours, G.

Chapter Twenty-Seven

gage

I hate her.

She has fucking infected me. She's all I can think about. Now I'm on the mission I have been waiting for, for years, and all I can think about is how I need her near. Every second, I'm wondering what she's doing. Actually, I don't even need to wonder. I know her like the back of my hand. I know her schedule, her habits, when she wakes, and when she finally falls asleep after fighting it off.

I know that because I'm gone, her nightmares are going to return, and I'm praying to a God I don't even believe in that she doesn't hurt herself again. I'm a mess. And it's all because I'm worried sick about her and missing the fuck out of her.

It's been twelve fucking days, and I'm itching at my skin like a fucking druggie, needing a hit of her. Three more days. Three more days and I'll hear her laugh again, feel her body again, and see her eyes again. Three more days.

"Alright, Eros. You demanded to be here. You wanted in on this. Let's go." The man in command calls over to me as I sit, biting at my nails with the anticipation of getting this mission done.

I do my best to push her out of my head so I can work. This is too important to fuck up. I get my systems set up and begin my scans. Searching for that one open door I need to hijack their shitty security measures.

And there it is. Hidden in plain sight. Fucking amateurs.

"I'm in."

"Good." The man running this operation speaks into the radio, giving the go-ahead to send the men in to retrieve our package.

Moments of muffled sounds and distant voices fill the small tent we are in, just on the outskirts of where the operation is taking place. Shouts, then gunshots. Our voices stay silent. Waiting.

When I hear that the package has been secured, I let out a breath. I'm never this invested in these things, but this one hits close to home.

"Sir, we—" *Static.*

"Get comms back up," he shouts to me.

"I'm trying."

"Try harder!" he demands.

"I can't fucking connect to something that isn't there. His comms aren't down; they're gone."

"What the fuck do you mean they're gone? Get them back!" he demands, and I watch as my screens go black. The static in the room is the only sound among all the men ensuring this mission goes smoothly.

"They're gone," I confirm again as I try to find an alternate route, but there is nothing.

A loud explosion rings out in the distance, then another closer to our hideout.

"Get down!"

The ringing in my ears disorients me, and I reach out to find anything to focus on with my eyes, but I can't see or feel anything. All I see is black as it swallows me. And for the first time in my life, I fear the possibility of never coming home. I promised her. I can't leave her.

Chapter Twenty-Eight

colette

"LJ, it's been a week since he was supposed to be home. Have you heard from him? His phone is going straight to voicemail."

I'm pacing in my kitchen. He promised me that he would come home to me. He should be here. Something is wrong.

"Calm down, babe. We're doing everything we can to find him. His boss isn't saying anything. We can only do so much. Everette is raising hell. We—" I hear some whispered voices, but I can tell LJ has her hand over the speaker. "We're coming over."

"Did you find something?" My heart beats faster than it ever has. Why are they coming over? Did they hear from him? Did they hear from someone else? Is he okay? Why can't they tell me in person? A million and one things race through my head. None of them are good.

"We'll be there in a few minutes." Then she hangs up.

I'm bawling my eyes out, preparing myself to hear those words. I know they're coming. Just like I knew what was happening when those Marines walked up on my front porch. LJ found out he's dead; she's coming to tell me in person.

My mind is a blur as I pace my kitchen. I don't even realize the passage of time until I hear them knock.

That knock on my door transports me back to that day. If I don't answer, it won't be true. But then the door opens. I forgot I gave LJ the code, and I hear Everett and her walk through.

"Cole?" LJ calls, and I round the corner from my bedroom into the kitchen. "Hey. I heard from someone. Gage is alive."

My chest collapses as do my knees. I hit the floor hard. "Holy fuck. I was sure you were going to tell me he was dead."

Everett comes over to me and lays his hand on my shoulder, then helps me stand. "No. He put me down as an emergency contact, and they called me when you were on the phone with Leo. They just got Stateside and got him settled into his room."

"Stateside? Room? What the fuck happened?" My eyes bounce from LJ to Everett, begging for answers that I logically know neither of them has. But logic is out the window right now. I'm only thinking with my heart at this point, and it wants Gage.

"Come on. They gave me the address. We can go see him."

Luckily, they transferred to a hospital here in Boston so we don't have to travel far, but I fucking would have. I would have gone anywhere to see him.

When we get to the hospital, LJ and Everett hang back since only one person is allowed in at a time. When I walk in, the tears begin to fall again. Actually, I'm not sure they even stopped. Who fucking knows.

His eyes are closed, and scrapes and cuts mar his perfect face. His leg is in a cast that comes up to just above the knee. His arms are just as bruised. But despite it all, he's beautiful. Just seeing him, safe, breathing. Here.

"Stop staring, Chaos." His voice is hoarse and deep, as if he hasn't spoken in a while. Fuck. The sound of it makes my whole body thrum with relief.

"You fucking asshole! I hate you!" I cry at him as I throw my arms around his neck and bury my head in his shoulder.

"Ouch—Shit, baby girl."

"Fuck. I'm sorry!" I pull back, but he grabs my arms and pulls me back into him. Holding me there.

"I'm fine. Don't go."

I crawl in bed with him, on his good side, and curl up into him. "I was fucking terrified, Gage."

"I promised you I would come home," he reassures me as he trails the tip of his finger in a figure eight against my temple.

"If your leg wasn't already broken, I would break it so that you could never leave again. Where did you go? What happened?"

"I can't tell you that, baby girl. But it doesn't matter. I'm here now." His muscles tense under me, and I know he's hurting. My added weight is not helping.

"Don't do that again," I say as I lean off him slightly.

"I don't plan on it. This fucking hurts." We both laugh, then he winces. "Fuck me."

"Not in your condition. You need to rest up."

"Nah. You can ride me. I won't even tie your hands." He looks down at me, the smirk almost convincing me to do as he suggests.

"Dirty, dirty boy. Let's at least wait till you get home." I trace a small cut on his cheekbone with the tip of my finger. I see him begin to pull away, but then he stops himself. His hand reaches up and takes my wrist, placing a kiss to it, and my breath catches in my throat. He can be so tender sometimes.

"I missed you." His words hit me in the chest, and my heart practically explodes.

"You what?" I say in disbelief as I stare into those golden eyes of his.

"I missed you, Colette. So fucking much, it was fucking torture."

"You going soft on me, Eros?" I mock, but inside, I'm bursting with happiness. He missed me?

He chuckles, the movement of his chest rattling me as well. "Not at all. Feel for yourself." He takes my hand and drags it down, "Oh no. You're definitely not going soft. But you, sir, need to behave. We are in a hospital," I whisper.

When I pull my hand back, his gown lifts slightly, revealing a tattoo on his thigh. I'm intrigued because despite how much sex this man provides me with, he always keeps his pants on. He just lowers them enough to pull himself out. I've never seen the tattoos on his legs.

I pull his gown up more, revealing the entire tattoo, and I think my heart stops.

"Colette." His voice is a warning.

How did he . . .? What the hell is going on? I push out of his lap, and he reaches for me but winces when his injury halts his hand just shy of grabbing me.

"That's my painting. I painted that. Where did you get that?"

"Colette." The guilt in his eyes kickstarts my heart. Now it's pounding against my ribs, demanding to be released, like it wants to run to him as my body backs away. Silly little thing, doesn't it know it already belongs to him?

"I painted that for Arrow—" I back into the door, one hand on my chest, one on the handle. Oh my god. I—He. He can't be. He would have told me. Right? "No."

"Colette. Please. Listen to me—"

"You? You're—No. You lied to me." He stays silent, pleading me with his hazel eyes.

"How long have you known I was Raven? How long have you let me sit in guilt for loving you? For loving Arrow? For feeling like I had to choose! How long, Gage?!"

"You love me?" he whispers.

"Answer me!" The anger inside my body boils over because I do love him. I love him so fucking much it hurts, and he didn't care enough to tell me the truth.

"Your typewriter."

"My—" The memory hits me. He had such an odd reaction to seeing my dad's typewriter. Then at the door, he called me Raven. Oh my god. That was months ago. He knew when I told him about how I loved Arrow and how guilty I felt about having feelings for two men.

He's Arrow. How did I not see it before? It's all making so much fucking sense.

"I'm so stupid."

"No, Colette. Please—" He's up out of bed now, using the footboard for balance. I didn't even realize he was coming near me. I was too lost in the truth. But then I feel him grab my wrist.

"Don't touch me." I rip my wrist from his grip.

"Please, Colette."

I walk out. I need to process, but everything is so incredibly mixed up in my head. What was Arrow, and what was Gage? Why did he keep this from me? Did he use what I told Arrow to get close to me? To get me into his bed? We didn't like each other when we first met. Was this all a ruse to embarrass me?

"FUCK!" I hear his yell, so full of pain. Then a loud bang. I cover my ears and shake my head, rushing down the hall.

"Hey, is he okay?" LJ jumps up and wraps me in a hug.

"LJ, he's Arrow."

Her brows furrow. "What? Your Arrow?"

"Yes. He never—" I can't even get the words out. A cry breaks through, and she cradles my head in her neck, comforting me like only a best friend could.

"I'm going to go check on him." Everett pats my shoulder and walks away.

"Come on. I'll take you home. Everett will stay with him tonight."

"I don't care," I say with fire in my voice.

"Yes, you do, babe. Or you wouldn't be this hurt."

"I hate him, LJ," I cry.

"I know."

gage

It all blew up, literally.

I was happy for the first time in my goddamn life, but I ruined it. I was trying to protect her and ended up hurting her in the process. I should have told her. I should have been honest, but I was fucking terrified she would want something I couldn't give her.

I was going to tell her. I was. But I wanted to be a better man first. I wanted to heal on my own and then be everything she wanted.

And now, a week later, all I want is to give her everything. My good, my bad. Every fucking part of my soul. But she isn't responding to me. She's ignoring my calls; she isn't even staying at her apartment. I fucking broke into her apartment multiple times, and she wasn't there. I even pathetically slept in her bed just so I could be close to her scent again. Don't come for me. We're all aware I'm fucked up.

LJ told me she's staying with her mom and that she's pissed right the fuck off. Understandably. But more than that, I know she's hurt. I broke her trust. Now it's her who has left me, and I'm so fucking lost I don't even know what to do. How did our roles become so flipped, fucked, and reversed that I'm a sad sack of shit sitting in my apartment with a bum fucking leg and two broken ribs?

How did she consume so much of my life? When did I fall so desperately in love with her?

Everett comes over and sits next to me on the couch, handing me my Americano that he most likely fucking butchered. It's just espresso and hot water, but I bet he somehow fucked it up. "Give her time, man."

My best friend has been over taking care of me, and Hale takes his place when he has to work. I hate it. I hate people taking care of me like I'm a fucking child.

"I'm trying. But one minute without her feels like days. I'm going fucking mad, Ev."

"I know, probably more than anyone, how you feel." I look over at him as he sits down next to me on the couch.

"Right." Everett went eight years without the love of his life, Leo, and I'm barely surviving with my Chaos gone for a week.

"Hey, at least you know what you did, so you can fix it." The optimist in him tries to cheer me up, but we both know I don't know how to apologize all that well.

"I don't know how I can. Arrow was her safe space. She loved him, and I made her feel like she had to choose between us. If I had just told her, she would never have carried that guilt."

"Why didn't you tell her?" I glare at him, and he raises his hands like I have a gun to his head.

"Just a question."

I try to shake off my anger. It's not his fault I'm a fucking idiot.

"She always wanted more with Arrow, but I knew I could never give her the kind of relationship she wanted. I thought if I told her who I was, she would want it more now that we knew each other in person. And I was right. She did want it, but with Gage. Me. Fuck. Now I'm talking in third person."

I shake my head and run my hand down my face as if I could wipe all this shit away.

"What do you mean you couldn't give her the kind of relationship she deserves?" he asks as I take a sip of the Americano and thank fuck that it isn't grotesque.

"You know my past, man. Some of it. I'm fucked in the head. You know I don't like to be touched, and she . . . she craves a relationship that is filled with all that shit. I don't know how to love someone. She deserved more."

"You and fucking Leo, man. Both of you are such martyrs. Both of you decide for the other person what they deserve." He shakes his head, mimicking my same gesture.

"Yeah, that's why we get along so well. We understand each other."

"Yeah, and you're both fucking idiots." His eyes widen, realizing what he just said. "Don't tell her I said that."

I scoff at him. "Fucking pussy-whipped."

He punches me in the arm. "Welcome to the club, jackass."

I wince slightly at the shot of pain that radiates through my ribs at the abrupt impact. "What do I do?"

"Go back to your roots. She fell in love with you through your letters, right? So write her a letter. Be relentless."

It could work. Even though it all seems hopeless right now, like I'll never get her back, I know that I don't want to live without Colette in my life. So whatever it takes and however long it takes, I'll have her back in my life.

"Sometimes you're smarter than you look, you know that?"

"I'm a board-certified pediatric emergency medicine physician," he boasts with a prideful smile that I want to smack right off his face.

"Yeah, and you're still a dumbass 99 percent of the fucking time." I give him a smile.

"Yeah, well, I didn't run off to fucking God knows where and get my ass blown up." He smacks his hand down on my thigh, and my eyes roll back at the pain.

"Oops." He chuckles.

"Dick."

colette

A single letter. Left on the board of Henry Leo's. A single letter with three words.

Please come back.

Feeling him in my heart, my soul, it's crippling because I don't know who I'm feeling. Who is real? Are they the same? Or did I fall for two completely different people?

Why wouldn't he tell me? Why would he hide? Did he think I would run? Or did he think I would love him even more? Was he scared the latter would be true? I know Gage would rather be alone in this life, afraid to be loved. Is that why he didn't tell me?

As my heart begins to crack at the idea that he doesn't feel like he deserves my love, my anger spikes, filling that crack with stone. He doesn't get to decide for me. He doesn't get to take that away from me. I deserved to know.

"What's got you in a tizzy?" My mom runs her fingers through my twists.

"I—Nothing," I say as I dip my brush into the water cup resting on the stool beside me.

Perched up on my old wooden stool, I'm staring at this blank canvas with no idea or direction to go. I can't help but see the man I love, and currently hate, on my canvas. All I want is to paint his pain so I can then take a vibrant swash of color and erase it all away. As if it were that easy.

I thought coming up to my dad's old studio in the attic of our little house would help. But I was wrong. For the first time in my life, the raging storm inside my heart will not release onto my canvas.

"Honey. You're in your studio. Something is bothering you. I'm your mother. You can't hide from me."

How do I even put it into words? I'm not sure she would understand. I don't even fully understand everything myself. "I was lied to by someone I thought I was falling in love with."

She circles around to my side, pulling my chin so I'm looking at her. "Gage? Tell me more."

I do. I let it out all in the studio but not on my canvas, and as I think about it, this is the first time I have truly opened up to my mom and trusted her with my whole truth. My dad was always the one who got this side of me, but tonight, tonight it's my mother. And it's long overdue.

"Oh, sweetie." She embraces me in a hug, then pulls back, holding me by my shoulders and looking me in the eyes. Her brown ones radiate back at me with a love and understanding only a mother's eye could.

"You need to talk to him."

I let out a pout and drop my jaw. "Excuse me. You're supposed to support my decision to pout and ignore him."

She chuckles at that. "I'm always on your side, but that doesn't mean I'm going to tell you what you're doing is the best choice. I wouldn't be your mother . . . or friend if I did that."

"Dad would have been on my side." Crossing my arms over my chest, I turn back to my canvas.

"Yes, well, your father always did spoil you."

A pain in my chest ignites at the thought of him. What would he say in this situation? What would Arrow say? Oh right. Arrow is the cause of all this. Or Gage. Who-the-fuck-ever.

I grind my teeth together. This sucks donkey ass.

"I miss him." Her voice breaks, and I realize that I didn't notice her retreat to the attic window that overlooks our street. In my own grief of losing my father, I didn't realize a lot of what my mother was going through after losing her husband. The love of her life . . .

What would I do if I lost Gage? I can say with confidence that I would not have handled it as gracefully as my mother did losing Dad.

"He would know what to do. What to say. He would know how to help you. But I feel . . . helpless. Like everything I do will never measure up to what he could be for you."

"Mom. . ." I approach her and wrap my arms around her from behind.

Wiping tears from her eyes, she turns and wraps me in her arms.

"I miss him too. And you did help. You're right. I do need to talk to him. I just . . . don't know what to say. I don't want to fight with him, but I'm still so mad at him."

"Well, you know, when your father and I were mad at each other, we would strip down naked. Our philosophy was always, if you're fighting naked, you won't be fighting long."

"Mom!" I pull away from her as a smile and laugh lights up her beautiful face. Her smile lines that crease her eyes and the small little gap between her two front teeth show, and I realize this is the first time I have seen my mom genuinely laugh since my dad has been lost.

I'm shaking my head at her as our doorbell rings. "I did not need that image in my head."

Heading down the stairs, I hear her slow steps follow me. Her back isn't doing great recently, and she's moving slower and slower. I'm still smiling when I open the door. My smile falls. My heart races in my chest. Am I reliving a nightmare?

Two Marines, dressed in their Blues, stand at my door.

"Mrs. Corvina?"

"That's . . . that's my . . . my mother." I'm barely able to get out a full sentence. My stuttering evidence that my brain is short-circuiting. What are they doing here?

"Yes, I'm Mrs. Corvina. What can I do for you?" Her voice is shaken but stronger than my own.

"We found him, Mrs. Corvina. Sergeant Major Michael J. Corvina has been returned home."

I step back, away from the door. This must be a dream. Right? It can't be real.

"You've found him? Is he—" my mother's whisper breaks through. He has been found. This is real?

"Yes, ma'am. He's alive. He's in the hospital currently. If you would like to accompany us, we can take you."

She doesn't reach for her keys or purse. She walks out the door, and I follow. I'm finally going to see my dad. After all these years, he has been found. He's here. Home.

The drive to the hospital is short but feels like years. My mind is numb, not even registering that my body is moving. As we ride the elevator up, it dawns on me that I was here recently to see Gage.

The ding announces our arrival to the eleventh floor. The Marines lead us down a hall filled with quiet beeps and whispered conversations. All eyes are on us as we walk silently down the hall.

They stop in front of a closed door, and I'm almost afraid to open it. Will he really be there when I open it, or will I wake from this dream? Will I wake back in my room, my cold bed, sweat-soaked?

My mom grasps the silver handle and pauses. I see her inhale and exhale, probably gathering the courage she needs to also find out if this is real or not.

The door creaks as it opens and lying, with his eyes closed, is my father. He's skinnier, a shell of the broad, strong man I once knew, but when his eyes open and he turns his head, I know without a doubt. My father has been found. It's him.

My mother runs to him and collapses over him. He embraces her as she cries harder than I have ever seen.

I feel the tears running down my face, but no sounds leave me. My feet stay rooted in the doorway.

"It's okay, my little raven." The rough sound of his voice, a voice I haven't heard in nine years, breaks through every wall I erected. Every doubt. Every fear. He's home.

I run to him, and my mom tucks me under her arm. He's holding us both now, and suddenly, I'm a sixteen-year-old girl once again, clinging to her father, silently begging him not to leave, hoping he will come home.

And he did.

gage

"It's been a week, Leo. She isn't going to come back to me." At least not voluntarily, but I leave that part out. I'll drag her ass back here, tie her up and make her listen to my apology, then I'll make her come so hard that she can't even fathom how she forgot she belongs to me.

Leo sits at my kitchen island, stroking the rim of her mug. She has visited me almost every day since I told her about how I fucked up everything. How I fell in love with her best friend and then lost her. Sometimes she brings Rune, sometimes Everett. But today, it's just her, and I appreciate that more than I could ever admit.

There has always been something special about Leo's and my relationship, an understanding between the two of us. We both know how hard it is to love and be loved. We both suffer with monsters in our minds that were placed there by people who were supposed to love us. Her mother never loved her enough. My father loved me too much.

"She will. She's dealing with a lot right now. Her father is home and is going through intense therapy. It's a lot on all of them. She feels she needs to give all of herself to her family right now."

"He's home?" I question.

"Yeah, he's still in the hospital, but they found him, Gage."

Taking a deep breath, I close my eyes and imagine how happy she must be. I wish I could have seen her face when she saw him again. But I wasn't there like I should have been. "I'm happy for her and her mom. They really needed him."

"You have to give her time."

"Fuck. I get that, I do, but I miss her, and I'm terrified that I . . . " I halt my train of thought. I can't admit it out loud. I lean on the counter, my hands curling into fists on the marble. Closing my eyes, I do all I can to banish her from my mind. I shouldn't be so selfish. She needs to be with her family right now, not with me.

I feel Leo's hand lay atop mine and instinctively pull back at her touch and immediately regret it as I open my eyes to see Leo's blue ones staring back at me.

"I'm sorry." I lay my hand back on the counter, and she covers it again.

Leo is the first person who ever touched me gently, and I was able to allow it. I don't know if it's our shared past or just Leo, but with her, it wasn't hard to let her in. It took time, months of us seeing each other every day, her talking mostly while I pretended I didn't like her. Then she left, and that friendship was shattered; my progress was gone with her.

Now she's back, and we are slowly getting back to where we were.

"You're afraid she won't forgive you?"

She pulls her hand away, knowing I can only stand her touch for a short time. But progress is progress.

"I know she won't."

"Then you don't know Cole." She smiles a little. "Gage, she loves you, and when she loves someone, she doesn't let them go. She'll come back to you. But you need to be ready when she does. Maybe this distance will give you time to work on your past so that when she does come back, you'll be ready."

"I don't know that I'll ever be ready. I'll never amount to what she deserves."

"So you're deciding what she deserves? Isn't that her choice? Isn't it up to her to decide whether what you have to offer is enough?"

She decided for Everett all those years ago when she ran from him without being honest with him. "You're one to talk," I say with a little more fire than I mean to, but Leo is unaffected.

"I am. Because I made that mistake and lost eight years with the love of my life, so yes, I can talk."

I huff at her. Fuck her for being right. Looking down at the counter, I tap my fingers. Finally, I can't fight it anymore and pull out my coin, flipping it over and over between my fingers.

"You still have that old thing? Is it the same one?" She grabs it from my fingers, inspecting it with a smile.

Snatching it back, I narrow my eyes at her. "Yes. Don't touch it."

"Oh, hush. I gave it to you!"

"Exactly. It's mine now. Don't. Touch." At this point, it's not even a conscious response, just a natural instinct to intimidate, but it's completely lost on her.

She stands and digs into the pocket of her jeans, throwing the red Bic lighter I gave her years ago on the counter. My eyes shoot to hers, shock clearly written all over my face as she laughs at me. "Yeah, you ass. I also kept it."

"Why?"

She shrugs, taking the lighter back and flicking it on and off. "I used to be scared of these. Every time I held one, I could feel it pressed to my skin. The burn and the pain. I saw her face. When you gave it to me that day, it was the first time you let me touch you. This little thing became something I treasured. I looked at it and thought of you. Not her."

She looks up at me, and I see sorrow in her eyes. "Gage, you have to let go of him. You're giving him all the power. Look at what he's keeping you from."

"I can't, Leo. I wish I could. But every time she touches me, it's his words, his touch. You know, you understand."

"I do. But that's also how I know you can move past it." She lights the lighter and hovers her hand over the flame. "Did you know that after Ev found out about my mother and what she did, he threw away all his leather belts? I flinched one time when he removed his belt, and the next day, he had a fabric one. Told me he donated all his belts. And for his wedding gift, I bought him a custom, handmade leather belt. Because while we were apart, I worked on myself. I conquered my trauma. I keep this lighter to remind me that I'm in control. I have the power, not her."

"I wish it were as easy as you say." I walk away, collecting her cup and putting it in the sink. If I don't get out of here soon, I'll be late for my mandated therapy. My leg isn't healing like it should, and now I have been ordered to do physical therapy if I want to return to work anytime soon.

Fucking stupid. I can do this shit on my own. But no, I have to be the good little agent and follow the rules.

"Words spill easily from the mouth, Gage. You know this more than anyone. Actions are what prove you have or haven't changed. Don't just apologize. Make a change." She slides off the barstool and walks over to me. Her hand comes up and rests on my cheek. Gently first and I try to stay still, but I pull away only a second later as his eyes flash in my mind.

"Come on. Let's get you to therapy." Leo strides to my entry table and collects her keys.

"For the record, I think this is bullshit."

"It's not my fault you left against medical advice and didn't let your leg heal properly. Now you're stuck with me taking you everywhere since you can't drive your own car."

Fucking tell me about it. It's been torture. My car is a manual transmission, and my left leg is fucked. As much as I hate to admit it, I do actually need this therapy if I don't want to be dependent on others for transportation.

"I fucking hate doctors," I grumble as we descend the elevator.

"Hey, my husband, i.e. your best friend, is a doctor," she chastises as she bumps into my shoulder.

Yeah, and so was my father.

"Yeah, and look what he isn't doing, healing me. What a great friend."

She looks at me over her shoulder and rolls those pretty blue eyes. "Oh, stop being such a bitch. You're a big boy. It's not his job to take care of you."

"I miss when I didn't like you." I glare at her, but she's immune to me at this point.

"You always liked me."

Unfortunately, she's right. But I'll never tell her that.

***

After she drops me off at the physical therapy office, I check in and find a seat in the waiting area. I'm mindlessly killing time on my phone when I hear that name.

"Corvina. Yes, I have an appointment at ten fifteen."

Corvina. Her name. It's not her voice but a man's as he comes around to the waiting room. I recognize his eyes because they are hers. The deep brown eyes that haunt my dreams and talk to my monsters. He catches me staring and takes a seat across from me.

"Hello." He extends his skinny hand. The years of being a prisoner in Afghanistan have drained everything from him. "I'm Michael."

I shake his hand, gently squeezing the frail form. "Gage."

"Nice to meet you." I simply nod in response.

"What are you in for?" His eyes take in my body, assessing me for the injury that landed me here.

"Huh? My leg. I broke it a couple of weeks ago. It's not healing right."

He nods. I feel compelled to break our silence, so I return his question even though I'm pretty sure I already know. "What about you?"

He gives a small chuckle, as if he can't believe what he's about to say. "Well, I'm just here to gain back some muscle and strength I lost."

"I see."

Before our conversation can continue, a middle-aged woman comes from a door. "Mr. Eros and Mr. Corvina. We are ready for you both."

"Eros?" Michael gives me a puzzled look. "Gage Eros?"

"Huh? Yes, sir. That's me."

When I stand to follow the woman, he stands and pulls me into a hug, wrapping his small arms around my shoulders. I'm shocked by the sudden embrace and find myself returning it instead of pulling away.

"Thank you, son."

Pulling back, I see his eyes are glassy as if he's about to cry.

"I'm sorry, but I'm confused."

His hands are on my biceps, holding me in a firm grip as if he were to let go he might fall.

"I would know that name anywhere. You're the one who tracked me down. Found me. Brought me home."

I'm silent at his admission. He isn't wrong, but I didn't think they would tell him about the mission and how he was brought home so soon. I figured they would keep all that classified until he was mentally ready to hear it or if ever, even.

"If you're ready . . ." The woman motions through the door, and Michael follows, me reluctantly trailing him.

We are both silent while Bridget, the physical therapist working with us both, goes through our assessments and gives us exercises to work on. But during a break, Michael approaches me again.

"I'm sorry if I was a bit abrupt earlier. I was just a little overwhelmed. I never thought I would get to meet the man who saved my life."

"I didn't save your life. The team did," I reply as I take a sip of water. Who knew a few stretches and simple exercises would tire me so easily.

"But you did. I read the report, son. Your intel goes back *years*. How long were you looking for me?"

Fuck. I don't know how to answer him. This is why I didn't want him to find out. I'm not the type who wants or needs to be recognized for my efforts. I don't do my job for the recognition or glory but because I want to save as many as I can, and unbeknownst to him, his case was special.

"A while."

A small smile tugs at his lips. "And why me?"

Shit. Do I lie, avoid the truth, or just be honest? Avoiding the truth lost me the girl I love. I can't lie to her father.

"I knew your daughter. She told me about you and . . . well, I wanted to help her."

He nods in understanding, seeing more than I'm letting on. Colette was right; her dad is special. I can see it in his eyes, in his expression. He's reading me like an open fucking book, and I don't like it.

"And how long have you been in love with my daughter?"

I spit out the water that I just filled my mouth with. "I'm sorry?"

"I can see it all over your face, son."

"I'm that obvious, huh?" I say as we begin our walk back to our therapy area.

"No. I'm just that good," he replies as he places his hand on my shoulder. I flinch away, a reflex I wish I could control. His brows furrow for only a moment before he nods.

"I see you have more injuries than just your leg."

I can't help but pin him with my glare. I don't want nor need him digging into my life. It's not his business, and although he did nothing wrong, I can't help my defenses that rise to his inquisition.

"I'm not going to pry. It's not my business." He walks away from me, and I feel a little guilty.

"Mr. Corvina?" I call after him.

"Yes?"

"Could you keep this between us? I don't want Colette to know it was me."

He nods in understanding, then turns back to finish his therapy.

colette

I t's been one month since my dad has been home, and it's been the worst and best month of my life.

On the one hand, my dad is home. But on the other hand, he's not the same man as the one who was deployed all those years ago. He has changed, and although it isn't his fault, it's been an adjustment.

News reporters and radio and talk show hosts have been pestering us nonstop about wanting an interview, but my dad is nowhere near ready to talk about his years being a prisoner of the Taliban. I don't know if he will ever be ready. He hasn't even been able to talk with us about it.

He has therapy with a psychiatrist three times a week, physical therapy two times a week, and we try to keep his mind busy the rest of the time. We catch up over morning coffee and dinner. We try to take him out for lunch. Trying to get him used to this world again. We go up to the studio, and he watches me paint, but he has yet to pick up a brush himself.

I see the way his eyes go blank, and his gaze stares off, lost in his memories. I see the way he flinches at any fast movements or the way he ducks when Mom or I drop something and it makes a loud noise. Although he gives us hugs and kisses, something in his stiff posture tells me he isn't quite comfortable with it but simply does it to make us happy.

My dad was the type to always have a hand on my mom, on her leg or lower back. It seemed like he needed to be touching her in some way to be happy. But now? Now I see him flinch away or move back slightly when she approaches him. I see the hurt in her eyes and the regret in his own. I know he wants to, but his mind won't let him.

I know because I used to see the same look in Gage's eyes. I haven't talked to Gage in a month now. I wanted to. I had planned to, but then Dad came home, and I was so consumed with him and being present for him that I completely put Gage on the back burner. Now I feel like maybe it's been too long. Maybe he doesn't want to hear from me anymore. Perhaps I'm too late to apologize.

I never should have run out on him like that. I should have talked to him. Heard his side of things. Now that I have seen the trauma my dad is suffering from, how he longs to love my mother the way she wants to be loved but can't due to his mind being plagued with memories, I understand Gage. It's the same as Arrow—Gage described it.

A desire to be loved but an inability to be.

The hurt my mom is going through is unimaginable. She wants to be there for him but doesn't know how. How does one person save someone from their own mind? From their own trauma? From their own monsters?

It's this hurt that Gage was trying to spare me from, and despite every instinct in me telling me to run to him, all I want to do is embrace him. Kiss him. But that's exactly why he didn't want to be with me, couldn't be with me, because he would have to deny me. He would have to reject my need to comfort him, and even though I see why, it would still hurt.

I don't realize I'm crying till my father wipes my tears with his thumb. I look up at him, and I see the hurt in his eyes. "What's wrong, my little raven?"

"Nothing, Dad. I'm okay. It's just a lot. Everything."

He takes a seat at the kitchen table next to me. "I know it is. You have been so devoted to helping me and your mother. Have you forgotten to care for yourself?"

I smile, a sad one but still. "Maybe."

The bland coffee I sip from my cup is a stark reminder that this isn't the Americano Gage would make me each morning.

"You need to get out of the house. Do you have a friend or . . . a boyfriend you could go visit?" He says it like he may know something. I wonder if Mom told him about Arrow and Gage?

"No boyfriend, Dad."

"Are you sure?" He bumps my shoulder with his, and a coy smile graces his slight face. It's finally gaining some fullness back after eating proper meals and going to therapy. It makes my heart happy to see him come back into himself. Physically anyway. Mentally, he still has a ways to go.

"Yes, Dad. No boyfriend."

"Well, go on and get out of here anyway. I'm sure someone wants to talk to you." He stands, and as he walks away, I see him fiddling with something. Narrowing my eyes, I see him flipping a coin between his fingers.

"Dad?"

"Huh?" He turns, continuing to flip the coin.

"What is that?" I eye the coin, and his gaze follows mine.

"Oh this? Just a coin." He comes back toward me now, sensing that I want to continue to speak with him.

"Why do you have it?" Memories of Gage and his coin come to mind, and my heart hurts. I can still see Gage's eyes and his knuckles as they balanced the coin effortlessly. I still remember picking up his tails-up coin, challenging him to give me his worst. And when he did, I ran from him.

"A friend I met at therapy gave it to me. Told me it helps him when he feels lost. Reminds him that both sides of us, the side that no one wants to see and the side that we want to be, both have worth."

I smile to myself, knowing it was Gage who gave my dad the coin. It had to be.

"The craziest part is that friend. He's the man who found me." Sitting back down, across from me this time, he takes my hands in his. Holding them and the coin at the same time.

"What do you mean 'found you'? A team of men rescued you, Dad." Is he losing his mind fully now? Oh god, what am I going to tell Mom?

"Yes. A team rescued me, but a single man found me. He had been looking into my case for years, tracking intel and doing whatever other cyber things those tech guys do. Anyway, I don't know how, but he found my location and gave it to the right people. He brought me home."

My heart begins to pound recklessly inside my chest. The heart that belongs to Gage and has been looking for a reason to go home. Before I even ask my questions, a piece of me shatters and rebuilds simultaneously because I know the man I have been ignoring, my sweet yet flawed Gage, has not only been searching for my father . . . but he found him. "How long had he been looking? Do you know?"

"He didn't say exactly, just that he had been looking for a while. From the report I read on Operation Finding Raven, the first intel he gathered was from November of 2020."

My head rationalizes what my heart was hoping for . . . It can't be Gage. That was years ago. I had only met Gage recently.

"Anyway, Agent Eros is a nice man. I'm glad I met him." Dad stands and smiles, then winks at me.

Agent Eros. It hits me like someone threw a brick at my chest. I feel it cave in.

I may have only met Gage a few months ago, but Arrow, my sweet Arrow, I told him about my dad years ago.

Gage was looking for my dad all this time. Before he even knew me.

A second thought hits me—Gage's trip. Where he went for two weeks. It's the same time my dad was rescued. Oh my god, how could

I not put all the pieces together? That was the work trip Gage was on, the one where he was injured.

"You going to go see that boyfriend now?" My dad looks over his shoulder at me.

"Yeah, Dad. I am."

gage

"Okay, I see you, old man. Up to the five-pound weights now. You trying to show off?" I joke with Mr. Corvina as he grabs the weights from the rack. I'm stretching out my leg while he moves on to his own exercises.

"Someone has to keep you motivated. I figure I'm the best option, considering my good looks and chiseled physique."

I laugh at his sarcasm. Over the past month, Michael and I have grown close. Our physical therapy sessions together have done more for our mental health than anything. I gave him my coin last session when I saw him get down on himself.

One of the other patients dropped a large weight and the boom it made against the mats was loud. Michael fell to the floor on his belly and covered his head. When he looked up, I could see the realization in his eyes when he saw where he was and where he wasn't.

I knew that look. I'd seen it in the mirror many times. I didn't know if my coin would help, but I figured it couldn't hurt. I've seen him flipping it in his hands a few times now. Helping ground him, just as it does me.

Going through our exercises, we chitchat and tease each other like usual. Sometimes our conversations remain superficial, but on a few occasions, we've been able to get deeper. He knows a little bit about my own trauma, and I know about his. He opened up to me about how he's afraid he's going to hurt his wife or hurt Colette, and to say that didn't ruffle my feathers would be a lie. Any threat toward my girl puts me on edge.

I invited him to the boxing gym, and he promised he would check it out. I told him that I wouldn't be teaching him, but Sabrina would get him into shape.

As he lifts his little five-pound weights above his head, he surprises me with one of his off-the-wall questions. "So when are you going to tell my daughter that you're hopelessly in love with her? I'd like to make you my son for real."

"Michael." My tone has a warning in it. Colette and I are the one topic we avoid.

"Gage." He returns my warning, and I roll my eyes.

"Please take this in the most respectful way, but I'm not discussing your daughter with you. She and I will not work the way you want us to."

"And why is that?" He finishes three reps, then lowers the weights and takes a deep breath. I want to tease him about the low reps like I usually do, but the air in the room is thick, and I know it's not the time.

"I would think it's obvious?" I raise a brow at him, and he returns the same look.

"What, because you have some shit in your past? Because you have some trauma you're working through? Join the club."

"I need to be better for myself before I can be the man she deserves. I would think that you would appreciate that."

"The father in me does. The man in me, however, knows it's bullshit. We men are weak, feeble things. What makes us strong is the woman at our side. I would not be who I am today without my wife. And you can be so much greater with my daughter next to you."

I contemplate what he's saying as I retrieve my resistance bands. "I have too much fucked up inside my head right now. I'd only drag her down with me."

"My little raven is stronger than that, and you know it. You're just scared, and I get it. When I first came home, I wanted to do all this on my own. I wanted to be stronger mentally and physically before I went back to them. I was afraid I would hurt them. That I would ruin the life they had built without me. That after all I had been through, they wouldn't want the new me."

"What made you change your mind?" I ask as I go behind him to spot him as he starts his next set of reps.

"Laughter. I was lying in my hospital bed one night and one of the nurses laughed at something. It was the first time in nine years that I had heard a kind, genuine laugh, and the first thing I thought was man, I want to hear my little girl laugh again. I want to see my wife smile and hold her in my arms."

I smile at the memory of Colette's laughter. "She has a beautiful laugh." It's loud and obnoxious; it's shameless and alluring. When she laughs, she doesn't care who is around her. She does it without hesitation, throwing all of herself into her laughter. It's contagious and infectious, and it heals a broken part of all those around her.

"A laugh I have yet to hear." His voice is full of sorrow.

"You know I have found that trauma is like the sea. Sometimes it's calm and quiet and makes you feel at peace, forcing you to appreciate the beauty in all you have survived. But like the flip of a coin, it can turn violent, a raging storm that swallows you whole, drowning you in your memories. People focus too much on trying to tame their storms, but that's pointless. The storm can never be tamed. You must learn to sail."

"Even the strongest of ships capsize with the greatest of waves," I say like I'm fucking Edgar Allen Poe or some shit.

"You're right. Which is why we need someone to pull us from the waters."

"I'm afraid that I'll only pull her into the sea with me."

"Who said you were the one drowning?" I look at him, my brows creasing inward. What the hell does that mean?

"She hasn't laughed, and she barely smiles. She's lost in her mind, Gage, and I don't know how to find her. I feel like I don't know her anymore. Not who she became after she lost me. I feel as though you may be the only one who really knows her now. The only one who can find her in that self-destructive head of hers."

I can't find the words to speak. I'm lost in my mind now, focused on the single idea that my Colette is lost and I'm not there to find her. I promised I always would. Even though I made that promise as Arrow, I'm going to keep it as Gage.

My silence must stretch on longer than I realized when Michael speaks up again. "I'm not saying that you aren't struggling to stay above water, son. But I'm saying that you aren't the only one treading water, searching for a life raft. I know you're used to doing this thing called life alone, but you don't have to. Colette is strong. And so are you. Be strong for each other, with each other. When one is weak, the other bears the weight. When one is strong, the other rests. It's a give *and* a take. Not perfection."

He lays his hand on my shoulder and rubs his thumb gently over my collarbone. I nod and accept the words he has spoken.

After therapy, I head to the gym early, seeking a relief that only boxing can give me. When I get there, Natasha and B are in the ring, working on combinations. I notice that Nat's two lingering shadows are missing.

The two girls-turned-besties notice me and walk to the ropes, peering down at me. B reaches down and tries to ruffle my hair, but I slap her hand away.

"Hey big boy, want to get those hands wrapped and meet me in the ring?"

I ignore B and look straight at Nat. "Where are your boyfriends tonight?"

"Around." She flicks her blond braid over her shoulder like she doesn't have the two most deadly twins tailing her at all times.

"I'm surprised they give you such a long leash."

She sighs, clearly exhausted with my need to dig at her for as much information as I can get. Even on leave, my thirst for information is insatiable.

"Don't worry, they have their eyes on me. They always do."

"Weren't they supposed to be headed back to Seattle?" At least that's what my intel told me before my accident.

"I didn't want to go to Seattle. My life is in Boston now."

"And they listened?" I question, only half believing that the most notorious criminal hit men in the United States just listened to her when she batted those pretty lashes of hers.

Smirking, she turns and adds a sassy little sway to her hips as she reaches the opposite corner of the ring, she calls out, "For now."

"Your pussy that good, Nat?" I remark as I lift the shirt off my back, getting ready to dance with B.

"Gage!" The red-headed little devil hops down from the ring and punches me right in the ribs.

"Fuck. It was joke," I groan as I clutch the recently healed broken ribs.

"Don't talk about her like that."

"She has the Alessi twins doing her bidding. She has something over them. I'm just curious."

"I don't have anything over them. We have a history, and despite their reputation . . . I think they respect me. In some way. Either way, I told them I wanted to stay here, and they didn't argue. I'm not questioning it further, and neither should you."

The white bindings I'm currently wrapping around my knuckles give me a thrill of excitement. "Whatever."

"You ready to fight? It's been what . . . a month? We need to get you back in shape," B asks with a mischievous grin. She's clearly ready to beat the shit out of me for my comment earlier.

"Let's do it," I say as I roll under the ropes onto the canvas. Staying crouched down on the balls of my feet, my elbows resting on my knees, I watch as B bounces around me.

"Get up, big guy."

As she bounces around me, readying to pound her fists into my body, I recognize the amount of trust I have in B, and a thought strikes me. Like Leo with her lighter, maybe I need to desensitize myself. And what better way than with someone I trust?

"Actually, I need you to touch me."

"Touch you? Stand up, and I'll knock your ass to the ground." Her chin lifts in a challenge that makes me grin.

"Not like that, B. Come here, let me see your hand." I stand, and she extends her hand out, palm up.

"Okay, now what?"

I extend my own arms out to her, mimicking her pose. "I want you to place your hand on my forearm. Softly."

"Okay . . . " she says with uncertainty.

As she does, I try to keep my eyes open and on her—seeing her and not him—but as her touch sends goose bumps up my arms, my eyes close on instinct, and it's his face lurking in the darkness.

"Your skin is so soft." His fingertips trace over my forearms and then up my bicep, over my collarbone and down, down, down. My eyes stay tightly closed as I try to block everything out, but I can't stop the way shivers race across my skin. A natural reaction, a reflex of sorts. At least that's what I read in a book.

"See the shivers that race across your skin at my touch? Pretend all you want, boy, you enjoy my touch."

"Close your eyes. You know I never last long when I'm with you."

I grasp onto his wrists. "Stop!"

"Gage!"

"I won't let you touch me anymore!"

A sharp pain lashes through my nose, and I feel the hot blood dripping down my face before I taste it. My eyes fly open to find B covering her mouth with her hands.

"Sorry! Instinct. You wouldn't let me go."

I shake my head, clearing it of the pain. "Fuck. That hurt." Well, that plan went to shit. I didn't mean to grab her so harshly. At least I know she can defend herself from me if she needs to.

"What the fuck was that? It's like you weren't even here anymore."

"I was just trying something. It didn't work." I turn away from her, frustrated with myself. Why can't I be different?

"Clearly," she says as she throws a towel at me. I turn, catching it in one hand, the other clutching my nose.

"Wanna talk about it?"

"No." My anger is rolling through me like thunder. Angry that I tried. Angry that I failed.

"Will you talk to me, then?" The raspy, sweet voice echoes through the gym, or maybe it's all in my head again. I close my eyes because I'm not ready to face if this is real or not.

But I do. And my breath is taken from my chest, stolen by the one girl I could never resist. The one I couldn't deny. The one I can never let go.

Colette Corvina.

My Raven.

Chapter Thirty-Four

colette

"Colette." His voice is a defeated whisper as he says my name. I think more in disbelief than anything.

His muscles shake as he jumps down from the ring, shirtless and sweaty, and I momentarily forget why I'm even upset with him. Oh right, he watched and listened as I tore myself up over loving another man while also falling in love with him, and plot twist, he was my anonymous pen pal all along.

But he also searched for years for my father. And found him.

He makes it within arm's reach of me, and I smack him across the face. His head whips to the side, his dark, sweaty hair falling into his eyes. The muscles of his jaw tick, and I can't tell if I've pissed him off or turned him on. Maybe both . . .

"I deserved that," he says as he looks back at me.

"That's for lying to me and not telling me you were Arrow."

Then I grab his stupid, stunning face in my hands and rise on my tiptoes and place my lips against his. He's stock-still for a moment before reality catches up, and then I'm wrapped in his strong, warm embrace once again. Right where I belong.

Pulling away from this kiss, I take in his honey eyes and see nothing but regret inside them. All he ever sees is the bad in himself. But I know there's so much more. I see the man who searched for years for a man he never met. I see the man who is kind and expects no recognition for the simple acts he does. I see the man who just wants to feel love but doesn't recognize it when it's given to him.

"That's for finding my father," I whisper as I rest my forehead on his, but he pulls away slightly, breaking the contact.

"I know I fucked up, Colette. I'm so fucking sorry, baby girl."

His grip on me only tightens when I try to pull away. This man is a walking contradiction, pulling away from me but never letting me go. Placing my hands on his chest and pushing back slightly, I arch my back to look at him fully. "Did you not just hear me? You found my father, Gage. You're the reason he's home."

"I heard you; I just don't care. I fucked up. I hurt you. It doesn't matter what I've done, it matters how I made you feel, and I lost your trust. Colette, I—" His chest shudders as he releases a sharp exhale.

What I really want to do is wrap myself around him, cling to him like a fucking koala, and never let go. But I also know that would make him extremely uncomfortable because of his aversion to touch. That is exactly why we are in this situation; I want something from him that he isn't ready or able to give.

His grip loosens and then lets me go, and I hate the loss of him near me as he steps back. "I don't know what the fuck I'm doing here, Colette. You need to go. You need to—"

"Stop telling me what I need to do. Stop making decisions about my life for me. I'm a big fucking girl, and I can handle more than you think."

He reaches out for me but then stops. "I know you can, baby girl. I just . . . I don't want to be something for you to handle. You have already been through so much. I don't want to add on to all the shit you have been through."

I step up to him now, close enough to feel the heat radiating off his body again. Whether from his distress or from his workout, who knows, but either way, it's a comfort to me that I crave. I don't need to be touching him to feel him. "There you go again, making decisions for me. I get to decide what is worth my trouble and what isn't. And you, Gage Eros, I have decided are worth it. But you can't push me away."

"I know I've taken a few hits to the head, but if memory serves, you walked away from me," he teases, but he's right.

"I know. I might have a bit of a temper, and I was a little upset." I bit my lower lip in worry. But there really was no need to worry.

Before my eyes, Gage goes from unsure to cocky once again. "A little? If that was you 'a little' upset, I'd hate to see you pissed right the fuck off. Actually, it might turn me on a bit. Maybe I should ruffle those pretty feathers more often." He steps in closer to me, our chests almost brushing together. I feel as if I've been swept up in a tornado with all this push and pull we're going through. He trails his fingers up my arm, then my neck, and then brushes them across my cheek. Finally down to my lips, pulling at my bottom lip with his thumb.

"You ruffle them plenty just by being the asshole you naturally are. No need to go above and beyond," I snark back at him.

He hums in response, a devilish smirk gracing his pretty face. "So where do we go from here? We good?"

"Ha! Good. Oh buddy, we are so far from good. We are cosmically bad. But I want to be bad with you. I want to work on us so that we can be good. But we need to do it together. If you can promise me that, if you can promise me that you're trying, then I'm staying."

"God. You sound like a fucking romantic. It's disgusting." He wraps his hand around my throat and pulls me into him with such force that I have to catch myself on his chest. My nails dig into his slick, sweaty skin.

I let out a gasp at his quickness and strength, and he takes advantage of my mouth popping open. He slams his lips to mine, his tongue dances with my own, and a soft moan leaves him. "Fuck, I missed you, baby girl. Whatever I need to do, I will. How do I say sorry?" he whispers as he pulls away.

"Finding my father was a good start. Letting me come home would be good too?"

I reach up and place a soft kiss on his lips. He flinches away slightly and then shakes his head. "I'm sorry. I thought I was doing better but—"

"Hey. Healing isn't linear. You're going to have good days and bad days. And I'll be there for all of them. Okay?"

"Let me pack up, and I'll take us home." He lets me go and walks over to a bench that has his black duffel bag and water bottle on it.

"Hold up, lover boy, you have a class in twenty minutes, or did you forget? Gonna have to pause on taking your girl to pound town till after your class. Go wank one out if you need to, but you're not canceling on your other girls who need you," Sabrina calls out from her office. I'm not stupid enough to think she wasn't eavesdropping. Sabrina is many things, but subtle isn't one of them. And I know for certain she doesn't give a fuck if we knew she was listening in.

"Fuck. I totally forgot. Can we . . . do you want to join, and I can take us home after?" Gage takes a sip from his water bottle then squirts some over his head to cool off. Shaking out his dark locks like a freaking dog, he splashes a little on me.

"Ew, gross! Couldn't you be less . . . disgusting?" I say that out loud, but in my head, I think, *hot fucking damn that was hot*. And now he's smirking at me, giving me those I'm-going-to-pun-ish-you-as-soon-as-I-get-my-hands-on-you eyes, and I need to evac-uate before I let him.

"From what I know, you like when I'm disgusting. Turns you on." He steps toward me. I'm sure ready to make true on the promise his eyes hold.

"Oh no, you don't. No fucking in my gym . . . unless it's me." Sabrina steps between us, hands on her tiny little hips. "Cole, he's mine right now. Sorry, but I'm going to need you to leave because if you stay, I won't be able to keep this animal away from you, and I need him for the ladies' class. Shoo." She scurries me toward the door.

"Okay, B, you can have him. For now. I'll make myself scarce. But this isn't over, Gage! We are talking more about us, like real feelings and stuff!" I shout over Sabrina's shoulder.

"Yay. I'm thrilled." Gage holds up a finger gun and places it in his mouth, but before he metaphorically pulls the trigger, he sucks on his fingers, and his eyes roll back. Jesus Christ, I need to get out of here.

Feeling the cool night air on my skin calms my raging hormones, but only slightly. I dial Leo's number, and she picks up right away. Rune's laughter in the background fills the speakers before her own voice. "Hey, girl. What's up?"

"Nothing. Well, lots of things. Can I come over and talk?" LJ always knows the right things to say, and if she doesn't, her cuddles are the best. I don't know what it is about moms. Even if they aren't your own, they give the best snuggles. I have shamelessly tucked myself into LJ's bed on more than one occasion, wrapping myself around her. What can I say? I'm a stage-five clinger. Ironic since I'm in love with a man who can't stand to be touched.

"Of course. Rune and I were just watching a movie, and Ev is making dinner. Ev, make an extra! Cole is coming over," she shouts.

"Okay, be there . . . shit—"

"What?! Are you okay?"

"Yeah. I'm fine. My car, not so much. My tire is flat." I kick the deflated tube of rubber that is lacking the air it needs to deliver me to my best friend's house. Stupid piece-of-shit tire and stupid Boston street. Probably ran over a nail or something.

"Flat? Where are you?"

"I'm just leaving the gym."

"You don't go to the gym." I can hear the suspicion in her voice.

"Gage's gym. The boxing gym. I told you I was taking some lessons with him."

"Yeah, but I thought—" And then it clicks. "Oh, apparently, we do have a lot to talk about. Well, just go get Gage and have him drive you over."

I could, but he has a class to teach, and frankly, I'm a little afraid Sabrina might kick my ass if I pull him away. No, I'll just walk. Leo's apartment is like four blocks from here. I'll be fine. I could probably use the walk to clear my head a bit anyway.

"No. That's okay. I'll walk. Gage is busy, and Sabrina scares me. Don't tell her I said that . . ."

"You can't walk, Cole. It's night. In Boston. Ev can come get you."

"God, Mom. I'll be fine. It's like four blocks. Chill. I'm already walking. I'll see you in just a few."

"Cole—"

"Bye, Mom!" I interrupt before she can worry her little self into a tizzy.

I giggle at her absurdity as I tuck my phone into my purse. I've lived in this city all my life . . . well, most of my life, I guess. It probably should but it doesn't scare me to walk at night. In fact, I used to walk at night all the time to clear my head, especially after my dad disappeared. I couldn't stay in the house and feared sleep so much that I took nightly walks.

But as I'm thinking just how safe and welcomed I feel in my own city, chills run down my spine. That sixth sense we all have but never trust that tells us someone is watching. The feeling that something isn't right.

I quicken my steps. Pulling out my phone, I dial Gage's number. Praying with everything I have that he picks up.

"Come on. Come on. Pick up. Pick up." The feeling intensifies, and my heart is racing. I look behind me and see nothing. No one. I look to the sides. Nothing. Just darkness, illuminated only slightly by the streetlights. A few cars pass, and I jump.

Jesus, Colette. Get it together.

Gage's voicemail picks up. Shit. He has probably already started his class or is warming up. But I'm not thinking clearly, and I try again. He needs to pick up. I'm halfway between the gym and Leo's, and a part of me wants to turn back. Back to his safety but that would mean potentially walking into whoever is following me. If anyone even is. I quicken my steps again, practically running at this point.

I hang up as soon as his voicemail comes on again. I go to click on Leo's number when a hand reaches out, and pain lances through my scalp as someone grabs my ponytail and jerks me back. A large arm wraps around my throat, and I panic.

I scream out, but his hand lets my hair go and covers my mouth. I kick my feet and try to scratch at his arms, but nothing moves this solid form. I try to tuck my chin like Gage taught me, but I waited too long, and his hold is too tight now.

My heart racing, my throat burning from screaming, I realize I'm quickly running out of energy and getting nowhere. I'm pulled back into a dark alley between two brick houses and thrown forward onto my hands and knees. My joints slam against the concrete, and I feel like I have broken my kneecaps.

Before I can collect my thoughts, I'm pushed down and forced to my back, my attacker settling between my legs. He's wearing a dark hoodie, the hood pulled over his head, so I can't see his face. I feel like I can't breathe.

All in what seems like one moment, his hand is around my throat, the other pulling at my leggings. I continue to struggle, clawing at his wrist and forearm. A scream tries to escape, but his fingers tighten, and I feel the pressure not only cutting off my voice but my air as well. Then the hand that was pulling down my leggings, ripping them in the process, is reaching for his own waistband.

No. No. No. This is not happening. It can't be happening. Not to me. I was safe. In my city. I was safe. I've always been safe.

I can't let this happen. I feel my attacker's hands on my bare skin. His fingers brush against the most private parts of my body. He's taking things that aren't his. His touch is . . .

"I never want you to feel defenseless." His voice echoes inside my head. It's his voice I need. Keep talking to me, baby. Let me hear you.

"Panicking gives him more power. They are after your fear. Your struggle. Don't give it to them. Take a breath, then take control."

gage

"Oof, bitch. You know I recently just broke those, right?" I groan as B gets in a rib shot.

"That was a month ago, pussy. Plus, you should be focusing, G. You're distracted, and that's why I got that shot in." She floats around me, effortless on the canvas.

"Well, can you blame me? Colette just walked back into my life. I was ready to take her home and make her see stars when your bitch ass kicked her out." I hold my wrapped hands up, guarding my face. But B is small and fast, like a little fox. She works me out and keeps me on my toes.

"Good for you. But you have an obligation to your girls. They need you; no one can teach them like you do," she says as she kicks out, and I reach down to block.

And speaking of the girls, they start to filter in. "Alright, alright. I hear you. Let's go." I nod to the incoming women. Our warmup has my muscles loose and relaxed, ready to go. I greet some of the girls. I'm not usually a social person, but there is something about the women in this class. They have been through things no one should have to go through. I could never imagine being another man they are afraid of, so I do my best to smile when they come in.

"Hey, Gage."

"Layla, you ready for tonight?" Layla joined us three months ago after leaving her abusive boyfriend. She's a small thing, similar in build to B. I remember the first night she showed, she had a shiner to her left eye and a busted lip. It wasn't until her fifth class that she opened up about her past.

Now, she strides in here with confidence, holding her head high. She tried last month to take on Levi, one of the men from B's men's class, but as soon as he had her on her back, standing over her, her panic set in, and she tapped out.

"I think so. I've been doing a lot of mental prep, and I think I'm finally ready." Yet when she looks up, she can't hold eye contact longer than two seconds before they dip in submission and hit the floor.

"You'll do great. Just remember that you're not powerless, Layla. Take a breath, then take control."

"Thanks, Gage." She smiles as she continues into the gym. I'm hanging out by the old roll-up door, greeting all the women, when I hear hurried footsteps scuffing against the concrete.

"Help me!" The hairs rise on the back of my neck, and my hand fist at my sides. I begin to look around, but I don't see anyone. The streetlights are too dim in this part of town. I follow my ears in the direction I heard the steps, and then I see her.

She's running down the sidewalk, straight for me. She's hysterical. My Raven. "Colette!" I run to her, catching her in my arms as she collapses.

"Baby girl, what happened?" I try to console her, but she isn't calming.

"Colette, baby. You need to breathe. Come on, with me."

She's hyperventilating as she breaks in my arms. What the fuck happened? "I—He. Behind—me. Attack."

"Attack? Wait. Did someone hurt you? Colette. You need to breathe. Come on, baby. Look at me."

She's clawing at her throat, then her chest, then legs. She wiggles out of my hold in the process. Then her head is snapping in all directions, looking for someone.

"I—He. He came from behind. And I—couldn't see. His hood—black. My pants. I couldn't breathe."

"Fuck, baby girl. You're not making any sense. You need to breathe." I don't know what to do. I don't know how to get her to calm down. Before I can help her, I need to know what she's talking about. I do the first thing that comes to mind.

I grab her cheeks and force her to look at me. "Don't touch me!" she screams, and I immediately let go, as if her scream burned my own hands. Her hands are in her hair, and she's crouched down, whispering and mumbling to herself.

"Gage? What's—Oh my god! Cole?" B comes rushing up, crouching down next to her. She puts her hand on Cole's back, and she flinches away. "Don't touch me!" she screams again, then looks at B, and she immediately softens. "Please, B. I need Gage. Do you know where he is?"

"Honey, he's right in front of you," B reminds her. The concern and confusion on B's face have me worried. She isn't scared of anything; she's clear-headed and calm in even the most difficult situations. So to see her worried makes my chest tighten. Fuck, now I can't breathe.

Take a breath. Take control.

"Gage?" Cole looks up at me. "Gage." I kneel in front of her, and she knocks me on my ass as she crawls into my lap, wrapping herself around me. She's still breathing fast. But I can tell she's coming back to me now.

"Hey, what happened?" I say as she cries into my neck. B shakes her head at me like that was the wrong question to ask.

I get it now. This is not the time to ask her to retell what happened. This is a problem for me. The need to know is a weight that bears down on me. I need to know if she's hurt. Physically. I need to know if she knows who it was so I can fucking kill him. I need to know so much. But all she can give me are her tears right now.

She continues to cry into my shoulder, her hands wrapped around my waist. Her fingers claw into my back, and I can feel the skin tearing beneath her nails. But it doesn't bother me. No, I prefer this kind of touch, this kind of pain.

After what seems like hours, her cries have died down to occasional sniffles. And as her cries soften, so does her touch. But I can't bear to move her. I can't bring myself to ask her to get off me. I can't bear to remove myself from her, not in this state.

Her phone ringing pulls her out of her trance. She pulls it from her pocket, and I see Leo's face on the screen. Sliding the green button, she answers with more confidence in her voice than her physical appearance would lend me to believe she has.

"Hello."

I only hear a muffled voice.

"I'm okay. I just—umm. I needed to go back to the gym for something. I think I'll just stay with Gage. Rain check?"

Her eyes flash to mine, testing if I will call her out on the lie she just told Leo. But I don't. I know more than anyone that fear of the truth coming out and how weak it will make you not only look but also feel. Because that's the thing about vulnerability, isn't it? When you're the only one who knows you're weak, you bear it alone. But when everyone else knows, the ones you love now share a burden they were never meant to, and sometimes that hurts even more.

"Okay. See you tomorrow. Love you."

She hangs up and just stares at her phone.

"Baby girl?"

"Oh my god, I'm so sorry!" She hurries off my lap, standing in front of me. "I didn't mean to touch you like that. I'm so sorry."

I take in her full appearance now. Her leggings are ripped at the crotch, her shirt smeared with dirt. Her braids that were tied back in a pony when she left are undone and disheveled. She's missing one shoe, and I can see blood dripping at her knees where her leggings are torn.

A pounding in my chest makes me see red. I know exactly what the hell happened to her. The question is, how far did it go, and who do I need to kill? I may be a federal agent sworn to do good, but I will walk myself to hell with a smile on my face if it means I take that motherfucker who hurt my girl with me.

"Let's get you inside. I think I have some extra clothes you can wear, and we will get you showered."

"No." She hurries the phrase. I look at her, a bit confused.

"Colette, we need to get you cleaned up, baby."

"Yes. I know. I just—can you take me back to your place? I don't want to be here right now." She has her arms wrapped around her waist, phone clutched in one hand, searching the darkness for her monster.

"Yeah. Come on—" I reach my hand out to her, and she flinches away. "Let's go inside so I can grab my stuff. Then I'll take you wherever you want to go."

"I'm sorry, I didn't mean to—" She looks at me as if I'm the one who is hurt.

"Don't apologize. If anyone in this world understands not wanting to be touched right now, it's me."

She just nods as she walks in front of me to the gym. I walk to her side, making sure she can see me. She knows I would never hurt her, but still, I want her to be able to know who is with her.

B has taken over the women's class. A few of the girls take in Colette's appearance, and their faces hold nothing but understanding. Each one of them has been in her situation in one way or another.

After I grab my bag and keys, I walk her to my car and open my door, guiding her in without touch. The car ride is silent. But I have to break the silence. I need her to know she has options here.

"Colette, I need you to listen to me. You don't have to tell me what happened, but I need to know. Some things are . . . time sensitive. Do you want me to take you to the hospital?"

She looks down at her knees, brushing off some of the dirt. "What? No, they are just some scrapes. Nothing a first-aid kit can't handle."

"I'm not talking about your knees, baby. Do you need—want. Fuck." How do I ask this without asking this? I'm not good at these sorts of things. I'm not the caring, sensitive-to-your-feelings type. I'm the blunt, harsh, just-say-what-I-mean type. "Do you need a rape kit, Colette?"

Her eyes meet mine, but I can't hold them for long. I look back at the road, fingers curled, knuckles white as I grip the steering wheel. "Fuck. I'm sorry to ask, but I wanted to give you the option if you wanted one. They need the freshest sample—"

"Gage. Stop." Shit, I have hurt her now too. "I don't want one."

Before I can stop myself, the question leaves my stupid mouth. "Want or need?"

She straightens her spine, taking a big breath in and letting it out, and I feel as though my whole world is about to implode. She's going to tell me that she was just raped, and I'm going to hunt down and kill that motherfucker, then happily hold my wrists together and laugh as they slap the cuffs on me because I will not be quiet about it. I will make it known to the whole fucking world that I will kill anyone who touches what is mine.

"Need. I don't *need* one."

My head falls back on the headrest. Thank fuck. But it doesn't matter. I'm still hunting his ass down.

"I was able to stop him before he—did that."

I grin as it hits me. "You fought him off, didn't you, baby? You defended yourself."

She nods. "Thanks to you. You saved me."

I pull the car to the first empty spot I see on this crowded Boston street. My hand reaches out but then stops just before my hands pull her to me. "Can I?"

She nods again, and I wrap my hands around her beautiful face. "I'm so fucking proud of you." I kiss her hard because I don't do gentle. "And you saved yourself, Colette. You fought. You did that. Not me, you."

She leans her forehead to mine. "I love you."

I pull back, and my heart beats wildly inside my chest. The soft touch of her forehead to mine begins to take me into deep waters, but then those words pull me back to the surface. I've heard them from her before. But that was different.

"I—"

"Shh. You don't need to say it back. I don't want you to out of obligation or fear you might hurt my feelings if you don't. When you say it, I want you to mean it with every part of who you are. I don't want you to say it until you have given me every piece of you, Gage."

"But I have, baby girl. I—"

She gently lays her hand on my cheek, and I flinch away. A sad smile pulls at her full lips. "But you haven't. There is still a part of you that belongs to him. And that's okay. I—well, on a small scale, I understand a little now. I'm not saying what I just went through compares, but I can see it now."

"I don't know how to give that part of me to you," I admit, still holding her gaze.

"I know. That part of you is lost. But don't you remember what I told you? Share your monsters with me and let me find you. We will save each other."

colette

"You really need to knock it off with all this romantic shit. It's repulsive." He smirks as he says it. "Seriously, I want my little chaotic beauty back."

"News flash, I'm more than just a pretty face and a smart-ass mouth." But despite my joking, now that the conversation is coming to a close, the memories of tonight begin to filter back into the forefront of my mind. I was . . . I almost was . . . God, I can barely say it in my head. Just say it, Cole.

Raped.

I was almost raped tonight. I was assaulted. I was . . . scared. Terrified. I don't know if it's shock or my adrenaline wearing off, but all I want to do is curl into myself and cry for days. Just let everything out because right now, it feels too heavy to carry.

"Hey, you're safe." As if he could read my mind, Gage runs his knuckles down my cheek, forcing me to look at him. I don't say a word. If I open my mouth now, it will all come tumbling out. All the fear, the humiliation will spill into this dark car, and I'm afraid I'll never be the same after it does.

"Let's get you home." Gage shifts the car into gear, and we drive back to our apartment complex.

The drive home is silent, both our minds lost. But at least we are lost together, right? As much as I should focus on my own healing, I can't help but have Gage and his trauma at the forefront of my mind. Maybe it's my mind's way of protecting itself. Diving into and pulling someone else from the deep waters keeps me from looking in the mirror.

Gage goes to his bathroom, and I hear the shower turn on. Then, coming out and standing in the doorway, the soft light illuminated behind him, he stands like a broken god. Beautiful, fractured, powerful, calculated, guarded, compassionate, and above all else, mine.

"A shower will help wash him away. You ready?" He holds his hand out. And I take it.

I step into the bathroom and take a look in the mirror, and an audible gasp leaves me of its own accord. Shivers run down my body. I'm a mess. Physically, emotionally. I'm in ruins. I had been guarding myself, putting up a smoke screen in my mind, but I'm looking in the mirror now, seeing the physical evidence of the attack. All my walls come crashing down, and I can't stop them.

He steps up behind me, looking at my throat. I see his jaw clench, and his eyes go dark. "May I?"

I don't know what he's asking, but it doesn't matter because I would allow him anything right now. I need him to save me. Bring me back to who I was before . . .

He reaches up, brushing my hair off my back, and places a soft kiss on my neck. Then he slowly reaches to my waist and pulls my tattered leggings down, and I step out of them. My panties, he does next. As he bends to the floor, my torn lace in his hands, he places soft kisses on the backs of my thighs.

Once done, he tugs at the hem of my shirt and pulls it up. I lift my arms to allow him to remove the baggy cotton shirt. As he moves his hands up to unclasp my bra, his fingertips dance across my ribs. I close my eyes as he exposes me. I don't want to see the bruising to my throat, the split in my lip, the cuts on my knees. I don't want to see where my attacker touched me. Grabbed me. Stained my skin with his unwanted touch. But I do see it.

Even with my eyes closed, I see the damage that has been done.

"Open your eyes, Colette. See what I see." He isn't touching me, but I'm dying for him to. *Please, erase what has been done to me*, I cry out. But only in my head. I feel his presence at my back. So close but so far from me.

"I can't." I feel a single tear run down my cheek, then his lips catch the salty ruins of my fracturing composure.

"Yes, you can, baby girl. I'm right here. Together, remember?"

As I open my eyes, I see him behind me again. My dark angel.

"Where did he touch you?" the question asked in his deep voice makes my heart race. I don't want to relive this.

"What? No—I."

"Do you trust me?" His hazel gaze holds mine in the mirror. A challenge. A leap of faith he's asking me to take.

"Yes."

"Then where did he touch you? Show me."

I reach up to my hair at the back of my head. "He grabbed me here first, from behind."

Gage reaches up and runs his long fingers through my braids, gripping it at my scalp and for a second, the memory floods back. But when Gage pulls me back into him, his warmth entrapping me, he tilts my head back and kisses me viciously. I would know his lips in the dark. His taste. Him.

Breaking our kiss, he whispers against my lips, "You're mine. Not his. I will not let him have you. Where next?"

He loosens his hold on me, letting my hair go but keeping my back pressed to his chest. I reach up to my throat, tracing my fingers along the bruises already forming. "Here. First with his arm, then with his hand."

"Like this?" He wraps his hand around my throat, and I swallow at the feel of a hand around there again. The image of me trying to scream, clawing at this unknown hand, the tightening. The helplessness. I reach up instinctively and dig my nails into his forearms.

"Open your eyes," he commands.

I hadn't even realized I had shut them. But it's not a black-gloved hand. It's a tattooed ivory hand. The coin inking the back of his hand proves I'm with Gage. No one else. He traces his fingers gently down the column of my throat. Brushing soft touches across my skin, painting over the bruises left with forceful hands. He's replacing each memory with his own. Taking the rough, hard, uninvited touches with soft, gentle, welcomed ones. More tears fall from my eyes as I take in what this man is doing for me. He doesn't do soft, but he's giving me something he has never given anyone.

"Where next?" He keeps my throat in his grasp, but he isn't rough. It's a gentle embrace. Maybe more for himself than me.

"Here." I move my fingers to my center.

He tenses. All of him, hard as stone. "Did he—"

"No. He just touched—the outside. I was able to . . . I got away before—I got away."

It's him who closes his eyes now, releasing the breath that is filling his chest. "Fuck," he whispers to himself. Then his own hand comes around my body, and I know before he even touches me what is to come.

He traces his fingers up my center. Softly, not even pushing inside. My own body pulls up and tenses, but the memory doesn't come. My body knows who is touching me. She welcomes it. She craves it.

"Please," I whimper.

He brushes his fingers against my clit, circling softly and slowly. Teasing me. Gauging my reaction. The moan that releases from my mouth as it falls open gives him the reassurance he needs, and he speeds up. Moving his fingers down to my opening, he slips inside me. Collecting my arousal, he brings it back up and continues his welcomed assault against my body.

"Gage. Please—" He knows what I need without me needing to use my words. He reads my body better than even I can. Because before I know what I'm even begging for, his hand clamps down on my throat, cutting off my words. I'm not scared. I needed it. I needed to take back the pain I enjoy.

He continues playing with my body, and when he bites down on my shoulder, I shatter. The victim shatters—she's no more. I'm a woman who loves pain with pleasure, who loves to be dominated, who loves it rough and primal. One would think that after an attack like that, I wouldn't be able to be that woman, but on the same night, Gage showed me that I'm the one who has the control. The power. The choice.

I'm a shaking mess in his arms. He steps back and holds his hand out to me. I take it, gently laying my hand in his, and he helps me step into the shower.

"Your body is yours, Colette. No one else's. But it's not the body that carries the wounds in the end. Whenever your mind is lost, you come to me, and I will deliver your pain."

colette

"Tell me about your father?" I sit atop the kitchen counter, my hair wrapped atop my head and secured with a scarf, one of Gage's oversized T-shirts enveloping me in his clean, spicy scent. He's cleaning up the cuts along my knees. And a not-so-distant memory surfaces of a time when we were in a similar position.

"Colette," he warns.

But I'm not giving up on him. I don't care if I have to make him uncomfortable. I have a feeling no one challenges him like I do. Everyone is scared of him. No one has ever pushed him. But it's in the uncomfortable moments that we grow, and dammit, I'm going to make this man move. I don't care if we have to move backward first. We will move forward eventually.

The gauze dabs at my cuts. It's cold, and it stings a little. The smell of alcohol burns my nose. I reach up to place my hand on his cheek as he's distracted by my wounds. As I knew he would, he feels my hand and moves away.

"See. You asked me to trust you earlier. Can you trust me now?"

"What you went through was one night." He huffs with irritation as he steps back from me. I lift my head. Ready for this fight. He's going to say things he doesn't mean to push me away. Keep me out of his head and his heart. But I'm a fighter, and I'm not backing down. I'm not defenseless. He taught me that.

"What I went through was years, Colette. Years of abuse, years of being forced to feel something I didn't want to feel. Years of being used. By my father, no less. You can't expect me to trust you with that. You can't expect me to just open up and give you that piece of me. You cannot understand what I went through. You had a small taste of what I have carried for years. So drop it and let me do this my own way."

I slip down from the counter, my bare feet landing on the cold tile. "You have no right to compare our trauma. It's not a race. There is no winner here, Gage. You don't get a medal for diminishing what I went through because you have gone through worse. I'm not dropping anything because you don't have to do this alone despite what your stubborn head is telling you," I bite back at him.

He throws his head back and laughs. "You think I want a medal, baby girl? You think this is something I want to win at? I had settled my feelings about what I went through. I was content. I was living my life. And then you, like the fucking chaotic storm you are, rolled in and destroyed all that I had worked to build. You began demanding things from me that I wasn't ready to give. You made me want to give you things that I *couldn't* give. I told you, from the beginning, that I couldn't be what you wanted."

Stepping forward, I make a statement with my body that I will not let him run away from this. "That's the real issue here, isn't it, Gage? I pushed you out of your comfort zone. I made you *want* something more. Being content isn't enough. Don't you want to be loved? Happy?"

"No, I don't." He turns from me, running one hand through his messy dark hair. The other hand pulls his coin from his pocket, flipping it through his fingers.

He's on the edge. *Come on, break for me, baby, so that I can help you rebuild.*

"You're such a fucking liar!" I yell at him. "Look at me and tell me you don't want me to my face. If you can do that, I'll leave. Right now, Gage. I'll leave, and you can go back to being the miserable, grumpy ass you have always been."

He spins, steps chest to chest with me, his eyes burning bright. "I don't want you." He forces the words out. The clench of his jaw tells me he's lying, but the pain that hits my chest is like lightning. For a moment, it lights up something inside me. In any other relationship, I would have been long gone. But loving him *is* like breathing, intrinsic and necessary.

I know he doesn't mean the words he says, but I'm not going to sit here and take it lying down. I slap him across the face. My palm burns as his head whips to the side. "You're a liar."

He looks back at me, his nostrils flaring. I tilt my chin up. I'm not scared of him. He can't push me out like he does everyone else.

"You said you would leave," he grits out.

"I guess we're both liars, then."

"What can't you get through that pretty little head of yours? I. Don't. Want. This."

"Prove it." I push him further. He wants a fight, so I'll give him one. I'll push him so past his breaking point that the only option he has will be to rebuild with me. I shove at his chest, and he steps back, regaining his balance.

"Colette," he warns.

I push again. "Come on, Gage. Show me what you got."

"Colette. Stop. I'm fucking warning you."

I push again. "I'm not scared of you! You talk all this big talk of taking control and moving past your monsters. Facing your fears. You teach women how to move past their abuse. But you can't even move past your own. You're scared. You stand here as a man, big tough guy, but deep down, you're still that same scared little boy."

I go to push him again, but he catches my wrist, trapping my hands against his chest. I can feel his heart pounding under my palms. He steps into me, and I go to step back, but he doesn't let me. He's terrifying right now. I can practically feel the anger rolling off him. It's a palpable force that I have brought to the surface. But I'm not scared of him. I'm scared that if I don't fight for him, he will stop fighting for himself.

My heart is racing, my body trembling. But I'm ready for whatever defense mechanisms he's going to put up. I'm going to break them down. I need him to break.

"I know," he whispers.

My mouth drops open, and I look into his eyes and realize I didn't bring his monster to the surface. I brought the scared child that still lives within him.

"But I don't know any different," he confesses.

I meant to break him. But as I watch a tear fall from his broken eyes down his pretty face. I break.

"Oh god. Gage." I step fully into him, pulling my hands from his hold. I wrap them around his waist, and he wraps his own around my shoulders. "I didn't mean any of it. I'm so sorry."

"You did mean it. Own it. You were right. Don't apologize for that."

"But I shouldn't have—" I look up at him again.

"No. You shouldn't have. But maybe it's what I needed. No one has ever fought with me like you do. Fought *for* me like you do."

I reach up, placing my hand on his cheek. He pulls away, but I keep my hand right where he left it, suspended in the air. It's his choice now. Will he come back to me?

He leans back into my palm. Letting me touch him. His eyes are closed, eyebrows pinched as if he's in immeasurable pain. "Open your eyes," I whisper to him.

But he doesn't. Where is he? Where have his memories taken him? "Gage. Open your eyes," I say with more force.

He pulls back, stepping away from me entirely. No part of our bodies is touching now. But he did so well. He let me touch him or hold him. Even through his own pain, he held still in my love.

"I'm sor—"

"I'm proud of you." I smile at him, tears running down my cheeks.

"What?" His confusion is written all over his pretty face. His eyes hold bewilderment as he takes me in.

"I have an idea. Do you trust me?" I hold my hand out to him. He stares at it for what feels like forever before finally taking it.

gage

I gave her every vicious word I could think to force myself to say, meaning none of them but praying she believed them. And she didn't. She fought. She won.

Softly closing my door, she strips her body naked, and I watch as my shirt falls to the floor, then my briefs slide down her stunning legs. I take her in. Feeling completely in awe of this woman in front of me. Her resilience. Her compassion. Her. Just her.

She steps up to me, carrying with her the vanilla and cocoa scent that has become my aphrodisiac. Without a word. My mind is racing, my heart right along with it. What is she going to do? What is she going to ask of me? Can I give it?

Slowly, she wraps herself around me again in an embrace that feels cautionary. I'm on edge. I don't like not knowing. Her long, slim fingers caress down my bare back, sending shivers up my spine. The feather touch and sensation of pleasure coursing through my blood brings forth my nightmares.

"Your skin is so soft. There are no imperfections here. Do you like my touch? Does it do to you what it does to me? Ah, I see that it does."

His voice is in my head. I can't escape him when goose bumps coat my skin.

I release myself from her embrace, backing into the dresser. Books topple over, rattling the lamp that was softly illuminating the room.

"I can't. I'm sorry." My voice is shaky, giving away my fear despite the brave face I try to wear.

"It's okay, it's just me." She steps into me, and I flinch. It's just Colette, my Colette.

"Here." She reaches for my hand with a firm grip. Placing it around her delicate wrist, my thumb resting in the center of her palm. "Take a breath. You're in control. Guide my touch." I'm staring in wonder at her hand, not his. Hers.

Long, slender, decadent fingers glow a rich brown color in the soft lighting. Nothing like my father's pale, thick, calloused one. "Gage, look at me."

I couldn't resist her if I tried, my fragile mind seeking command at this moment. "My touch. Not his. Mine." She gives me a nod, and I bring her smooth, rich fingertips to my cheek, wanting her to wrap her fingers forcefully around my jaw. But she doesn't. She keeps her touch soft and willing. I close my eyes, but his face comes into my mind, and my hand instinctively tightens on her wrist.

"Open your eyes, Gage. Look at me, baby." And I do. My Colette. Just my Colette.

"Where did he touch you? Show me." She mimics my own words back at me. God, tasting your own medicine fucking sucks.

My breathing picks up as I drag her hand down from my cheek to my neck. The same neck his lips used to leave feather-like caresses. "He kissed me here."

Her eyes hold mine, sorrow and pain reflected back at me. Then those bright eyes flash to where her fingers rest. "Can I?"

I nod. Trusting her more than I have ever trusted another soul. She leans in, her long braids grazing my abs. She's so close now, I cannot see her face. Fear begins to seize me as her lips come closer to my neck, as I can feel his . . .

I stop breathing.

"Say my name, Gage."

Her voice.

Her breath.

"Colette." It's a plea. For her to stop. For her to never cease. I'm not sure exactly which I need more at this moment.

Her full lips graze my neck. The slightest of touch, the smallest of contact. The most I've ever allowed another person to do to me.

I'm still holding her hand, but my grip is tight, and I release slightly as she leans back and her stunning face comes back into my view. "It's just me. Say my name."

"Colette."

She nods and looks back at her hand. Silently commanding me to continue. I slowly drag her hand down to my collarbone and run it along the long, protruding bone. She feels the indent in the middle where it should be smooth, and a question crosses her face.

"Broken. I was seven."

I expect pity to shine in her eyes, but I'm wrong, as usual when it comes to her. Those whiskey eyes burn with rage like the sun shining through a bottle of the amber liquid. Then she leans in. "Say my name."

"Colette." As I do, she places a soft kiss on the once broken bone.

I continue to drag her hand down my chest, over my pecs, over my abs. The lower her hand travels, the more my breathing picks up again. When her touch glides along my happy trail, I'm lost to the memories.

"When you become a man, you'll have hair here." His fingers trail down from my belly button to the top of my jeans. "Hair will tarnish your beautiful skin, then you'll be a man. Useless to me."

I can't wait for that day, *I think to myself.*

"Gage. Open your eyes. Say my name, baby." Her grip is rough on my cheeks, holding my face in a tight grip. I'm pulled back to her by the pain she inflicts to my jaw.

"Colette. I ca—I can't," I stutter out. I'm losing it. He's here. He's in my head, and I need him out. I need—

"It's okay. You did good. Now, do what you need to."

Finally unleashing my monsters, I grab her wrists in a tight grip and walk her back to the bed, letting the bed collapse her knees as she hits it, her long braids fanning out behind her like dark wings.

"Safe word, Colette. Give me your safe word." It's a struggle to hold myself back at this point. I need to release the anger inside me, the darkness, the void. I need to feel something other than him all over my body. I have never been pushed to the edge like this.

"Raven," she begs on an exhale.

I reach to her delicate throat, grasping her dark skin with my tattooed hand and pull her up. Sealing my lips to hers, I command her oxygen to fill my lungs. Her taste to coat my tongue. Her smell to cleanse my mind. She's a delicacy that I want to savor, but I'm balancing at the edge of a cliff. And I need her to jump with me. I bite her bottom lip and here her suck in a breath as the tang of her blood coats my own lips and fills my mouth.

"This won't be kind. This won't be gentle," I whisper against her swollen lips.

"I don't want gentle. I want to play with your monsters. Unleash them."

Oh Fuck. "On your back." She lies back slowly, teasingly. The glint in her eye is always taunting. It excites me, and I need to ruin her. Put out that fire so all she has left is her submission. Her desire to please only me.

She's laid out like a feast before me, and I walk to the side of the bed, savoring every curve of her body. Hovering over her head, I look down upon this chaotic creature, and I can see the shivers run across her body. I trace the outline of her curves with my eyes, imprinting her on my mind.

"Hands." I snap my fingers and she reaches up, instinctively linking her wrists together.

"You tested me. So I'm going to test you, Colette. I'm not going to bind your hands, but you will keep them to yourself. Do you understand?"

She nods. I tilt my head. "Try again."

"Yes, sir," she mocks. Then dropping her hands, she keeps them locked at the wrist as if they were bound. Her eyes travel down her own body as if she's also imagining the invisible rope my command has wrapped around her wrists.

"Oh, and Colette?" Her eyes meet mine again. "Don't touch yourself."

"What?"

I click my tongue at her, and she glares at me. Those brown eyes are so completely discontent with following rules. It's comical she thinks she can challenge me when she's naked and at my mercy.

"Don't fucking test me, Colette. Not right now." I warn and I see her eyes heat at the vibration that rattles through my warning.

"I hate you," she says with narrowed eyes and devious uptick to those supple lips. Lips I have plenty of plans for.

"Turns me on."

"You're sick," she snarks.

"Hmm. Keep talking, baby girl." I stroke my cock, releasing some of the tension inside it. Looking down at her laid out body. All her curves and smooth skin on display for my viewing pleasure. I can see her fingers resting just above her pretty pussy, begging to tease herself. But she hasn't . . . yet.

"Are you just going to stare at me or are you going to put that cock to use and fuck me?"

"I think I'll shut that pretty mouth up first." I lean over and grab her wrists, then pull her to the edge of the bed so her head hangs off the side. She lets out a little screech, and I move my hand under the nape of her neck.

Pressing my pierced tip to her full lips, she immediately opens. "What a good girl. I didn't even have to ask."

She lifts her hand from her side and flips me off. I slap the defiant appendage back down.

My cock glides in and out of her throat, and I watch it move so gracefully as she takes me so fucking deep. "Fuck," I release on a moan, and she gives me one back. I glide my other hand over her throat, feeling her smooth skin. "Jesus, Colette, you take me so well baby. Look how good you're doing." I push a little deeper and she gags as I pull out, letting her breathe a moment before going right back in.

I started slow, testing how much of me she could take in this position, but now I know her limit and I push it. I thrust in and out of her sinful mouth and then pause, settled deep in the back of that cocky little mouth of hers. Choking her. Denying her the one thing all humans need and will fight for. Breath. When I see her body tense, I pull out and listen as she gasps. Music to my ears.

"Gage." She pants my name as I see her fingers go to her pussy.

"Don't you fucking dare touch yourself without my permission, Colette."

"Please." Her hips lift off the bed, seeking friction that only I will provide her.

"Is your pussy that desperate to be filled you would disobey me? Hmm?"

"I'll do anything. Please. Just touch me, Gage. I need you," she pants and I grin. Even if I want to prolong her torture, her pleas do something to my heart and body that I can't describe or deny.

"Fine." I growl out and round the other side of the bed. Grabbing her ankles, I pull her so her ass is right at the edge of the other side of the bed. Linking her ankles together, I put them against my shoulder, and I don't allow her the time to adjust. I run my tip up her center, collecting her arousal and thrust inside her.

She lets out a scream, gripping the sheets above her head. Her back arches off, pushing her perfect breasts up.

"Is that what you wanted? You wanted me to fuck you like no one ever has? You wanted me to push you, test you, *fucking own you*, isn't that right, Colette? You don't want to be treated with respect; you need someone to fuck that attitude right out of you."

"Yes, yes, yes," she lets out with each harsh thrust. I feel her clenching around me, suffocating my cock until finally, she soars. Releasing a moan so bewitching I almost release at the sound of it. Almost.

But I'm not done with her. So I pull out, smack her ass and roll her over. Pulling her hips up, her knees naturally go under her. Her body is like putty, melting into the mattress. Once she knocks off that fucking attitude, her body naturally wants to obey. And obey it will.

She stretches her arms out above her head and pushes her ass up, like a dangerous little minx, she teases me with a sway of her hips.

I run my hands down her flawless back, then back to her ass and let her flesh fill my palm as I slide back into her. "Fuuck," she moans out again into the mattress.

The feel of her around me is my home, my peace, my salvation. When I'm inside her, there are no monsters in my mind, no unwanted hands wrapping around my memories, there is only her.

Crowding over her lithe body, I grab her chin and push my fingers into her delectable mouth. She runs her tongue between my fingers, lapping them up, wetting them. When I slide them out and circle her clit with those same fingers, it takes only a few strokes before she's crumbling once again around me. Her body shattering under me.

"Gage. Please. I can't take anymore." She whines and I smile.

Her body trembles, her voice shaky, she can't even open her eyes as the top half of her melts into the sheets.

"Yes, you can, baby girl. Unless you're using your safe word?"

"Fuck a safe word. I'm no bitch. Give me . . . all you got." Her words are barely audible as she muffles them into the sheets, gathering her strength. I chuckle at her determination.

"That's my girl."

I pull out of her, rolling her to her back once again, and settle myself between her thighs. Her warmth envelopes me as she wraps her long legs around my waist. She keeps her hands above her head like a good fucking girl.

I feel the strong muscles of her thighs grip my hips and I savor the feel of them around me. I slide into her once again. Slowly this time and she hums out her pleasure. I do the same.

I rock my hips slowly, gently.

"What are you doing?" She whispers, her eyes more concerned than anything.

"Being gentle."

"But you said—"

Leaning in, I cut her sentence off with a kiss. Her arms come up automatically and wrap around my neck. My body tenses, a reaction I thought I could keep at bay. Regret fills me. I tried to be gentle to her and I couldn't. Once again. I could not offer her something she deserves.

Pulling back from her lips, I intend to completely pull away, body and mind. But she grabs my jaw between her slim fingers and grips it until a spark of pain scatters across my face. She must see the gratitude in my eyes at the sensation because her own eyes flare.

"Don't you dare leave me, Gage Eros. Fuck me like you hate me. Then treat me like the fucking queen I am when you're done with me."

"Fuck, baby girl." With that, I slam into her, over and over. As her grip tightens on my jaw and her pussy tightens around my cock, I feel her other hand softly trace up and down my back, caressing but also punishing me in more ways than my mind can comprehend.

With that, she obliterates me. I moan out my release as I collapse onto her, and like the fucking goddess she is, she continues to move her hips, fucking herself against me, finishing herself one more time and taking from me everything I have to offer.

Chapter Thirty-Nine

colette

Have you ever been in that state between sleep and wake where you feel weightless, like reality is a dream and your dream is a reality?

Same.

Gage is laid out next to me, bare except for the sheet lying across his hips. One arm is laid across his perfect abs and one slung over his dark head of hair. I watch as his chest rises and falls; he looks so peaceful. The ink on his skin ripples and waves as if it's an individual living breathing entity that's just attached itself to this man. I've never seen him sleep in a bed; it's always been on the couch. But sprawled out in this king-sized bed, he feels like a dream, this can't be reality could it?

His tattoos are on full display, except the ones that creep under the sheet, just poking out. Teasing me. The urge to pull back the sheets to see him fully is almost too strong to ignore. But I do. Because I want him to get this rest. He needs it.

Doesn't mean I can't admire him while he sleeps, though. His tattoos are all black and gray. No color on his pale skin. The contrast is mesmerizing. A black-and-gray moth covers his throat. I love the way the body ripples when he swallows. Down the center of his chest with an infinity symbol wrapped around it, is an arrow, pointing at the moth, the bow just under his pecs, stretching out across his ribs. Taking up almost his entire abdomen is a snake that circles around to eat its own tail. Right where his pants would hit, written from hip to hip are the words "Devil Doesn't Sleep." He has a coin tattooed over the back of each hand, one headsup, the other tails. Across his knuckles he has "Hate" and on the other hand "Love."

Scattered across his arms he has a patchwork of other images including butterflies, suns, moons, lighters, and one of my favorites, a little coffee mug. He also has a roaring lion on one of his shoulders. Any empty skin is filled in with dahlias and leaves. I recognize them easily as they are my favorite flower.

My second favorite tattoo covers his entire back, two large black wings that start at his spine, between his shoulder blades and cover the entire length of his back. And there is of course my favorite tattoo, the raven I drew that is on his left thigh. His legs are also covered in tattoos, but it's more of the same—daggers, butterflies, moths, arrows, and the occasional silly one like the smiley face and frowny face above both knees. I imagine he got those on a dare.

"Stop staring. It's creepy." His sleep ridden voice startles me out of my perusal of his perfect body.

"You're like an art museum. I can't help it. I want to paint on your skin, but I don't see any open canvas . . ."

"I have one spot left . . . your red lipstick would be the perfect medium, your lips the brush." He grins at me, and I've lost all thought at the image his words evoke in my head.

"Why don't you just ask what you want to know?" He continues when I don't say a thing.

He keeps his eyes closed, body in the same relaxed position. I keep my body from touching his. We made progress with the whole soft-touches thing during our fuck fest last night, but I don't want to push him. Two steps forward and one step back or whatever that phrase is.

"Okay. Tell me about them."

"Which one?"

"All of them."

He peeks one eye open at me. "That sounds exhausting." He turns so his body faces me now. Full frontal Gage, naked, in my bed, is intimidating to say the least. But I'm here for it. He'sn't nearly as intimidating as he thinks he is. Okay, maybe he is. But not to me anymore.

"You can pick one each night."

"You're covered! That will take forever!"

"Do we not have forever?" He keeps his face nonchalant, but my heart storms inside my chest.

"I—huh." *Collect yourself, Colette.* "Three."

"One."

"Two."

"Are we counting or negotiating?"

"You're not negotiating at all!" I stick my tongue out at him, and he leans forward, so fast I barely have time to pull my tongue back in as he slams his lips to mine. Collecting my hair at the nape of my neck he pulls on it, and a moan releases from my throat of its own accord. A pulsing sensation travels to my pussy.

Calm down, you hussy. We are trying to peel back his layers. Chill.

"One tattoo. And you can ask me one question about my past," he says as he pulls back from me, back onto his safe side of his bed where I can't easily touch him.

"That's very generous of you, Mr. Eros."

"What can I say? I'm a giver. Now ask away."

I rake my eyes across his body again, deciding which tattoo I will ask him about. I already know about the raven that I drew him. I think about the lion since it seems so out of the ordinary compared to his other tattoos, but that's most likely for LJ . . . or Leo as he calls her. The small suns and moons don't seem like they would hold much significance . . .

"This one." I point at the snake that takes up most of his abdomen. It has a beautiful design, bold lines. It wraps around itself, as if in a knot before circling back and eating its own tail. It has two roses, the stems forming an X that crosses behind the snake.

"Ouroboros."

"Huh?"

"Ouroboros. The eternal cycle of destruction and rebirth." He rolls onto his back again. I know opening up is hard for him and if he needs to look away to do so, I can accept that. As long as he doesn't leave.

"And that means a lot to you?"

He nods.

"Why?" I press on.

"With what you know about me, it should be easy to figure out."
His tone is a bit harsh, cold even. But I know it's his natural reaction
to someone getting close.

"Don't be an ass."

He looks at me, then rolls his eyes. "Yes, Colette. It means a lot
to me. There are many meanings you can take from the ouroboros,
for me it's about rebirth. How even if we are the ones to destroy
ourselves, we can always shed that part of ourselves and become
someone new."

"Thank you."

He looks back to me now. His cold demeanor melting away.
"You're welcome."

"And now my question!"

He runs his hands down his face, "Fuck, that wasn't intrusive
enough?"

"Nope," I say as I pop the P and sit up, cross-legged to face him.
His baggy shirt engulfs me, settling on my hips.

"Okay. Hmmm." I tap my fingers to my chin as if I need to think
about it but already know my question.

He just stares at me, one eyebrow cocked.

"Where is your dad now?"

"That's not a question about my past."

"Technicality. Answer the question."

His fingers lazily twirl one of my braids and the end tickles as it brushes against the skin of my thigh. "You're becoming quite brave."

I stay silent. Refusing to argue with him. And like I knew he would, he answers. After he lets out a pouty sigh.

"Fine. He's in prison."

"How do you know? Do you still talk to him? Did he go to jail for what he did to you? Or was it . . . someone else?" I lean in closer, the need to know everything consuming me to the point I completely forget that this is uncomfortable for Gage. Oops. Sorry, not sorry. He could use a little uncomfortability.

"I answered your one question. Don't get greedy. I'm going to make coffee. You, take a shower. You reek of curiosity and no boundaries."

"Ass."

And speaking of ass, I wipe the drool off my face as he gets up, butt ass naked and pulls his briefs on. Holy mother of a good one. That ass is fine as hell...

Practically falling and stumbling out of bed, I follow him to the kitchen like a lovesick little pup. As he starts up the espresso machine and grinds the fresh beans, I plop my butt down on his kitchen island countertop. The smell of the espresso brewing forces an audible moan from my throat.

"Since I'm feeling nice this morning, I'll let you ask about my past. It's only fair."

He peeks over his shoulder at me, the wings on his back moving as his muscles flex . . . what were we talking about again?

"I don't need to ask about your past, Colette. I just want to know about your future."

"Come on, there has to be something you want to know," I say as I swing my feet and they hit the cabinet causing a little bumping noise.

"I already know everything about you," he says as he glances to my feet then back up to my eyes.

"Bullshit. Come on, there must—"

"You were born on February 14th, 1999, at Camp Pendleton Naval Hospital, San Diego, California. Your full name is Colette Brianna Corvina. Aquarius with all the attributes of one. Including the pesky sensitivity and independence. Although you call Boston home, you spent the first nine years of your life in San Diego, which is why your Boston accent is not as annoyingly strong as others. You're intellectual and good with numbers, which is why you took over the financial side of your mom's business when you were only fourteen. Also why you didn't feel the need to attend college. Your first car was a 1992 Toyota Camry, which you were T-boned in four months after you got your license. Also why you have the scar above your left eyebrow. That's where I assume you hit the driver's side window on impact. Your credit score is 707. You twist your hair between your fingers when you're nervous, you talk in your sleep, you have exactly thirteen scars on your left thigh and five on your right because you're right-handed and favor the left side. Which is also the only side you can sleep on. You don't have any tattoos, you love Mexican food, and your favorite movie is *Clueless*. You tried volleyball, basketball, and softball but never stuck with any of them.

You enjoy painting, reading, and annoying the shit out of me. You have sectoral heterochromia in your left eye. You—"

"Jesus. Okay. You have proved your point, you freaking stalker."

He sets my Americano down next to me and opens my knees with his warm hands, then pushes my thighs open as he steps between my legs. His hands run down my legs, and he forces my ankles to cross behind his back, tightening the grip I have on him. "Speaking of stalkers, based on your browser history and Kindle library, you have a stalker kink, so I say that works in my favor." Then he fucking winks at me and reaches down, taking a sip of my drink.

His nose scrunches a second later as he pulls the mug from his lips. "Fucking disgusting. Entirely too sweet."

That fucking bastard. I can count on one hand how many times someone has made me speechless in my life. And this would be one of them. But not for long. "Okay, so you know practically everything about my past. What do you want to know about my future?"

His hands rub up and down my thighs, then settle over my scars as he brushes them with his thumbs. "For starters, am I in it?"

"I—Of course. Well, if you want to be. I do annoy the shit out of you, apparently . . ."

"You do." His hazel eyes are soft as he says it with no hint of malice in them and trust me when I say those amber eyes can be quite malicious when Gage Eros wants them to be.

"Do you want to run Henry Leo's till you retire, or do you have other dreams?"

"I enjoy my work with Leo." I sip from my mug and let the sweet but bold liquid travel down my throat, and I can't help but compare the Americano to the man currently between my thighs. "But I would . . . Wait. You already know the answer to this question."

He smirks, and I know I've caught him. "Guilty. I just wanted to see if anything had changed."

"Well, it hasn't. But it also isn't feasible right now. I would love to pursue a career in art, but I can't leave LJ behind, not right now. But maybe now that she's happily married and has her family together again, it's something I can look into."

"What about kids? Do you want them?" He takes another sip of his coffee. Why do I feel like I'm interviewing for a job here?

"Why the twenty questions? Am I interviewing to be your girl-friend or something?" I snarl my response at him. I don't like being put on the spot. I don't like being put under a microscope to see if I'm good enough.

His eyes hold mine, never wavering. "Actually, it's the opposite. I want to make sure I can give you everything you want, Colette. Because if I can't, I need to remove myself."

The burning desire to place my hands on his cheeks and give him comfort is a physical, palpable pain, but I know if I do, he'll back away. Instead, I keep my hands wrapped around the mug of coffee. "First, whether we disagree on some things, it doesn't matter to me. I want you, Gage. I don't really know when it all happened, but one day, I wanted to beat you with a portafilter, and the next, I couldn't imagine my life without you in it. Although, I do still want to beat you upside the head sometimes . . ."

When he doesn't pull away from my confession, I decide to try something harder for him. I reach up, placing my hand to his cheek, and he pulls away, but then lets me place my palm there once again. Baby steps. "I love you. For who you are, not what you can or cannot give me."

His jaw tenses, and so does the grip he has on my thighs, but he doesn't respond with words.

"Do you want kids?" I ask him this time.

"I didn't before. But after I met Rune . . . well, I think it could be a possibility. But if you don't want them, then I can be perfectly happy being the cool uncle."

"Right now, I'm happy being the crazy auntie, but I'm also open to kids. But first, I want to travel the world. Be young. I saw how LJ limited herself so much after Rune. I'm not saying that's a bad thing since that's what *she* wanted. She's a homebody and wanted to have a simple, quiet life, but I'm not like that. I want to see the world and try crazy things like skydiving or swimming with sharks. I want to go on a safari, pet koala bears in Australia, and eat real sushi from Japan."

"I can make that happen."

"Which part?" I giggle at him. The way he's looking at me right now is lighting me on fire. Like I'm the only thing he sees. The only thing he wants.

"All of it."

I shove at his shoulder, "You can't possibly."

"Hmm. I guess we'll see. Now, go take a shower like I already told you to do and get your ass off the counter I cook on, for fuck's sake. Also, I don't approve of your disobedience in my home."

"Get used to it. It's my new favorite hobby." I slide off the counter when he scoots back, leaning back on the counter opposite me, and I make sure I put a little extra sway in my hips as I make my way to his shower.

"Kill me now." I hear him grumble, but I know he loves it.

gage

I should have known that when I offered to let Colette choose a tattoo each night, she would make me live up to my word. The demanding little thing knows how to pull at my once nonexistent heartstrings. It's been a few days since she was assaulted, and we have been holed up in my apartment. She seems to be handling everything okay, but I'm still watchful over her body language. Reading her to make sure she isn't hiding behind her mask.

We're back to our little truth game, her straddling my lap, stunning in just my shirt that hangs off one shoulder and her lace panties.

Any man who says lingerie is the sexiest thing a woman can wear is lying. It's this right here. The apartment is solely lit by the soft glow of lamps and candles, and she's radiant as the golden light reflects off her warm skin. Her vanilla and cocoa scent invades my space, and I breathe it in like fucking cocaine, letting it light my brain on fire.

"This one. I want to know about this one." She points without touching the infinity symbol around the arrow tattooed over my sternum.

Fuck. Why did it have to be this one?

"If you chose any other one, I'll watch *Clueless* with you . . ."

My attempt at a bribe only encourages her more. "Oh, now I really want to know about it. You can't hide from me, Gage Eros. I'm going to unearth all your secrets."

"That's exactly what I'm afraid of." Running my hand down my face, I try one more time. "If you choose any other, I'll wear matching Christmas pajamas with you this year."

She leans in and kisses my nose . . . and I don't flinch away. The hell?

"Please, you'll be doing that anyway. As much as you want to act like you aren't, you're wrapped around my finger," she says as she holds up her pinky finger. I roughly grab her wrist and bring that finger into my mouth, biting on it and eliciting a gasp from her pretty little mouth.

As she pulls it away quickly, I can't help but take in the flush of her skin. The way her pupils dilate. The tensing of her thighs as they straddle my hips.

"Don't you dare try to distract me. The tattoo. Now. I want to know, and you agreed to this."

"Fine," I grumble.

Taking a deep breath in and out, I know full well that the memory I'm about to give her is my most prized one. The one I keep in my back pocket for my worst days. The one no one, not even Everett, knows I have. My only good one from my childhood.

"My mom died when I was five, so I don't have any memories of her. Except one. It's a glimpse in time, a moment that passes like the flash of a camera, but it's clear as day. I'm lying in bed, and my mother is lying beside me. Her hair is long and dark, tucked behind her ear to keep from falling in my face. She's singing a song and smiling. Her eyes, same as mine, are shining. Like she had just been crying despite the smile on her face. And with her finger, she traces a shape over and over on my chest."

Cole reaches forward with her finger and begins to trace the infinity symbol on my chest. And I allow her to do so. I close my eyes, feeling the run of her finger go up and around, then down and around again to reconnect where she started.

"I'll love you for infinity, my baby boy."

I feel her with me. Her touch. In this single spot over my heart. I feel her.

When I open my eyes, a tear falls, and Colette leans forward and kisses it away. She's still tracing the infinity symbol with the soft pad of her finger.

"Where did you go just now?"

"Somewhere good," I say with a smile.

I fist Colette's wrists in mine and bring those gentle fingers to my lips, placing a kiss on each one.

"Tell me about her. Please." Her voice is soft and soothing as if she were consoling a child. And for the first time, I want to talk about my past. My mother is the only good thing about my childhood, and I have a single memory of her. But that single memory has pushed me to survive all these years. Through all that he did to me, she's the reason I kept going. The deep longing I feel in my chest to know more about her is heavy.

It's a weight that could never be lifted because the fact is, I'll never get the chance to know my mother.

"I . . . honestly don't know a lot about her." I begin to talk as I trace the delicate lines of Colette's exposed collarbone. "Like I said, that's my only memory of her, and my father never talked about her. From what people around town have mentioned, she was kind. Compassionate. She was an elementary school teacher until she got sick. She died of leukemia. An aggressive form from what I'm told. When she died, my father went mad. He burned everything of hers in his grief. I know he loved her. I . . . I will never understand why he did what he did to me, but a part of me wonders if I didn't look so much like her, and if she never would have died, if he wouldn't have . . . but he did."

"So you don't have anything of hers?" She doesn't touch me, but as she fiddles with one of her braids, I know more than anything she wants to. And I hate that part of myself that won't let her.

"Nothing."

"There has to be something left. Maybe at the school? Or . . ."

"Colette. Stop. There is nothing. Nothing left of her except that single memory."

She flops down beside me, leaving her legs stretched out over my lap. I run my hand along her shin, down her feet, and back up again. For some reason, I have never had an issue with touching others, even if I'm doing it softly. It's just when they take the initiative, the control, that my mind goes dark. At least I can give her this. But I know Colette, and I can see how deeply she wants to return the comfort.

"Do you think you will ever talk to your dad again?" Her hesitation tells me she knows she shouldn't be asking. So why the hell is she? Why does she have to be so damn nosy?

"Don't push me. I've given you enough tonight," I warn.

"Don't be like that. You need someone to push you, Gage, and lucky for you, I'm just the girl for it. Yell at me, push me away, tell me you don't want me or don't love me. I know it's all bullshit. So just . . . let me in."

"I'm trying. But talking about my mom is a lot. And now my dad?" I defend my actions. She's mostly right, but she is wrong about one thing. I don't need *someone* to push me, I need *her*.

"What are you so scared of?"

Fuck.

Cole: 1 Gage: 0

"Hurting you," I answer honestly.

She reaches up and runs her fingers through my hair, and I move away. Then I roll my neck out and curse at myself.

"What's hurting me is seeing you still hurting and struggling. I think you need to bury your past and confront your monsters. I think you need to talk to your dad."

Whoops, there goes my control. I stand, pushing her legs off me. I can't fucking do this. "You don't know shit, Colette."

She stands, coming after me. Why does she need to fight me so much? Why can't she just back off? Why does she need to push and push and push?

"I know what you've been doing isn't working. You're still a ghost, Gage. You're surrounded by a family who loves you. Me,

Everett, LJ, Rune. We all love you and want to see you heal. But you refuse to take any steps to do that just because they will be painful."

"Leave me alone, Colette." I can feel her eyes boring a hole in the back of my head. She think's I'll give in because we fuck? She thinks she has a right to any part of me because I've given her a bit more attention than other women?

She's wrong.

Is she? Open up, let her in, a soft voice in my mind whispers, and I shake my head to clear it.

I feel Colette's presence at my back, knowing she's closing in on me, and I feel like a caged animal, getting ready to be let out to put on some performance just to make others happy. "I won't. I will not let you be lost. I will always find you, whether you want to be found or not."

"Leave me alone." Speaking more to the voices in my head than to the woman who is in a relentless pursuit of something I can't give.

"Let me come with you. I can talk to him with—"

"No." I swing around so fast that she actually backs up a single step.

I run my hands down the nape of my neck and pull at the hair there, giving me an ounce of pain, enough to clear my head, but it doesn't work. Inhale one, two, three. Exhale one, two, three. I dig my nails into my palms at the image of her near my father, his eyes on her. His eyes on me. I feel my back teeth grind, the click of my jaw resounding in my ears. I need to get out of here. I need to cool down before I say something I don't mean.

Going for my keys, she stops me in my tracks with her broken plea. "Don't leave me."

I turn to look at her and falter as I feel my armor crack.

Fuck. She's scared.

"You can be mad. That's fine but . . . How do I know you'll come back?"

Putting my keys back, I turn and crash into her as I grasp the nape of her neck in one hand, my other digging into her waist, and she holds me right back. Clinging onto me for dear life. The force of our collision makes her take a few steps back. After a moment of us just breathing as one, I move my hands to hold her face in my hands.

Looking straight into those broken, deep brown eyes, I make her a promise. "I'll always come back to you, my Raven. Always. But I . . . I can only take so much. I can only *give* so much. Am I not enough as I am?"

She's silent so long I don't think she'll answer, and I fear when she does. The desire to hear her voice but also to never hear her answer is a war inside my fucked-up head.

"You're enough," she whispers.

"Then show mercy, Colette. I'm doing everything I can to be what you deserve, but I don't know how. I need to do things on my own time. Please," I beg.

"I don't like to see you hurting," she whispers.

I kiss her forehead.

"Then don't hurt me in an attempt to heal me." I walk away from her but not out the door. Because despite how much I want to run, I won't from her.

colette

The November rain tip taps against my favorite glass window at Henry Leo's as I think about how I might have pushed Gage just a touch too far with his dad. I do think he needs to talk to him, but maybe he's right in that he needs to do it on his own time. I can't help but feel like something would mend inside him if he would just take those painful steps. It may not be pretty, but I've found that healing rarely is. A step in any direction is what he needs right now. He's stagnant. Even if he has to take a step back, he needs movement. Once he has the momentum, he can then change direction and move forward.

But the stubborn ass won't even take a step. Hell, he won't even take those pretty hazel eyes and look forward. He's too stuck living with his eyes closed.

But lucky for him, he has me. And I'm definitely one to push buttons until I get what I want.

Unfortunately, I can read him a little too well right now, and he's overworking himself, not even coming home. Okay, that's weird to say. Like we fucking live together or something.

Alright, maybe we kind of do since I haven't slept in my apartment since Gage and I reconnected.

Whatever, I'm rolling with it.

He hasn't been coming home until way later than he used to, and even though he's coming back to me, I can see he's stashing a piece of himself away. He still makes me my coffee, and we have simple conversations. But he hasn't allowed me to play our truth game. Every time I try, he excuses himself to bed. And then once I come to bed, he excuses himself back to the couch.

I swear I'm two seconds from selling that damn couch and forcing him to either sleep in the bed with me or on the fucking floor. Knowing him, he would sleep on the floor.

Calm yourself, Colette.

As I sit here, trying to focus on work, my mind keeps racing. I need to do something. I take to scrolling through Pinterest on my laptop, looking over the endless pins of artwork, book quotes and all things athleisure wear since that's my style when a hand wraps around my ponytail and I pull away fast, my heart races, and an image flashes in my mind.

"Whoa, babe." LJ throws her hands up in shock and I relax my posture, but my heart continues to race. "I'm sorry, you had a silly little braid sticking out all crazy. I was just trying to fix it."

I will my heart to calm down as I see the uneasiness in my best friend's eyes. I never told her about the attack. Something about sharing that burden with her felt wrong. She doesn't deserve to carry that with me. "It's okay. I'm just a little jumpy, I guess."

"Anything you want to talk about?" she says as she moves more to the table where I was working. I hate being trapped in my dark office all day. I enjoy the sunlight that comes through the windows and seeing all of our customers.

"No. Actually, I do have one question. What was the town called where you, Everett, and Gage grew up?"

Her brows pull in, and she tilts her head a bit. "Uh . . . Aurora."

"And it was in Oregon, right?"

"Yeah . . ."

"Okay. Thanks. Have a good day!" I jump up from the table, grab my laptop and coffee, and head to my office. I need privacy, and I don't need her nosy cute little ass digging into this little project of mine.

Googling Aurora Elementary, I dial the number in my phone. Someone there must have known his mom and might have something of hers. Anything. I'll take a fucking pen that belonged to her at this point so I can stab him with it . . . I mean, give it to him as a token of my love.

But it has been . . . probably twenty-two years, give or take, since she taught there.

"Aurora Elementary, this is Nancy, how can I help you?" Based on the gentleness of her tone, this Nancy woman seems to be older. Maybe she'll be able to help me.

"Hi, my name is Colette, and I have an odd request, but I'm hoping you can help me."

"I will surely do my best."

"Great. I'm looking for someone who might have known a teacher who worked there . . . maybe around 2000 to 2002? Her last name would have been Eros, I think."

A few moments of silence unfold between us. And I feel a heaviness in my gut.

"Oh . . ." There is a sadness to her voice now. "Evangeline Eros. She was a first-grade teacher. She passed away a year after she quit, I'm afraid. But I . . . Oh, I'm actually so glad you called! I have been trying to get into contact with her son or her husband, but I can't reach anyone."

I sit up in my chair. Oh. My. Fuck. Balls.

"Really. Well, I know her son, so I can help you."

"I actually just need his address. I have a letter here for him."

My heart is beating out of my chest, and I feel like I might vomit. "A letter?"

"Yes, her last year with us, 2002, we did a twenty-year time capsule. It's usually for the kids, but she wanted to put a letter in it. I think she knew she wouldn't be around long. She addressed it to Gage Eros. I looked him up in the phone book and even googled him, but I couldn't find an address. I even looked up Mr. Eros, but . . . well, I saw that he was incarcerated, and I didn't want to send it to him since it wasn't addressed to him. I don't know how all that works with him being in prison and all."

"Oh my god. This is amazing. I can give you his address."

"That would be perfect. Thank you so much for calling. I'm afraid this letter would have sat here forever had you not called."

"How long have you been holding on to it? And . . . why?" I ask with a little trepidation.

"Well, the time capsule was opened two years ago. And as to why . . . well, Evangaline was a friend of mine. I was sick to my stomach when I learned of her passing. She was always so happy, but it was . . ." She pauses as if trying to find the right words or maybe thinking about how much she should say. "Well, it just all seemed too good to be true. You know? Her husband seemed too nice and perfect . . . anyway. None of my business. Never was, but I'll say I wasn't surprised to see he was arrested."

I hear some shuffling, like she's going through drawers. Then she starts up again, "Ah. Yes. Here it is. Yes. Gage Eros. How is he? I think about him sometimes, how he managed living in a house with that man . . . He was always so sad as a child. I can see him now, walking through these halls; he didn't have any friends. At least not till that mayor's son came along, but even after that, there was always something . . . dark about that boy. I always thought it was the loss of his mother, but . . . Oh, it seems I have carried on a little too much. I'm sorry." She clears her throat as if it had begun to clog with tears. "That address, Miss Colette."

I give her the address, which is actually mine. I want to give Gage this letter and make sure he opens it. Hopefully, this is exactly what he needs to begin to heal.

When we hang up, I continue to scroll through the Aurora Elementary page and find a photo in their gallery of a flower garden and a bench dedicated to her. There is a picture of her on a plaque, and she's breathtaking. She looks just like Gage. Or I guess he looks like her. Same dark hair, hazel eyes, soft smile, and straight nose. I can't pick out a single difference between the two except his jaw is a bit more masculine, his eyebrows a bit fuller. Otherwise, they are almost identical.

The plaque reads her full name, and I feel a kick in my chest. "Evangeline Dahlia Eros. Beloved teacher and mother. Her love and kindness will live on for infinity." A small infinity symbol is under the words, and the garden bed is filled with dahlias.

gage

After our last little blowup, I let Colette have her space. Okay, I let myself have space. I've been working late so that by the time I got home, Colette was already asleep, and I knew she wouldn't come over. But not only that, I have been overworking myself because the Alessi and Natasha thing has my brain hurting.

And speaking of brain hurting. Colette is the migraine I always knew she would be, but don't I love the pain.

Like.

I like the pain.

Not love.

Fuck.

There is a clear shift between us. I felt like we were beginning to open up to each other. Both becoming a bit more vulnerable with each other. But then she had to go and push. I can only give so much, and she was demanding more. I felt like I was driving 100 mph, and she kept pushing on the accelerator till I was ready to crash and burn. I had to put the brakes on before I did just that and ruined her.

The fact is, I'm not a nice guy. I know my flaws. I will ruin someone before they can get close enough to ruin me. I will say things I don't mean. I'll gaslight and hurt until they decide I'm not worth the trouble. It's a dick move. I'm aware.

It's why I do it.

I never wanted to be the good guy, the knight in shining armor. I'll leave that shit for Everett and Hale.

Being the villian has kept me sane and steady all my life. No one has gotten close, not in an intimate way. Everett and Leo have wormed their way into my fortress, but they don't demand comfort and kindness from me. Colette would. She deserves those things from her partner. It's why I couldn't meet her as Arrow. Why I never should have entertained our relationship as us once I knew who she was. But like the storm she is, I can't help but be pulled into her vortex.

Now I'm running for my life, but it doesn't matter. We are both collateral damage at this point.

"Fuck!" The burn to my fingers from the damn oven singes, and not for the first time tonight, I question why in the hell I'm putting myself through this. I drop the pan of chicken that I just pulled out of the 450-degree oven and throw it onto the stovetop, the loud clatter making my brain hurt.

I fucking hate loud noises.

Flipping the water to cool, I run my hand under the water and let it temporarily ease the pain from the blister already forming on my hand.

Why I felt the need to cook for Colette is beyond me. I guess I'm trying to apologize without having to use the words. It's not like she's really going to appreciate this from me. She'd rather I eat her, but I'm trying to be Mr. Boyfriend over here, and I should not have under any circumstances listened to Everett when he told me the way to a woman's heart was with food.

I think the way to Colette's heart is my tongue in her pussy. That sounds a hell of a lot more delicious than my failed attempt at chicken parmesan.

Speaking of my favorite meal, she walks through the door as I'm drying off my hand. "What's that smell?" Her nose scrunches and I roll my eyes at my failure and her immediate notice of it.

"Nothing," I growl as I dump the chicken into the trash can.

"Hey! Wait! Was that dinner?"

"No." Throwing the kitchen towel down and pulling out the multitude of take-out menus from the drawer, I see from my peripheral vision Colette slinking over to me.

"Gage Eros, did you try to cook for me?" She bats her lashes and leans over the counter, pushing up her tits and giving me the best view.

All I give her is a scoff as I flip through the menus. She rounds the corner of the kitchen island, and my eyes finally lift to watch her. Her black sports bra that she says is "athleisurewear" and baggy nude-colored sweats have me practically drooling, but that's not what has left me speechless. No.

That would be her fucking curls.

Holy fuck.

I've only ever seen Colette with braids, but now she has her natural curls loose, and I'm fucking coming in my pants like a thirteen-year-old boy who just got his first *Playboy* magazine.

She was stunning with her braids; she's stunning with her curls, but there is something about seeing how wild they are that has my Chaos beaming with a radiance and confidence I haven't seen before.

"Your hair," I breathe out, and a shy grin breaks out across her perfect lips.

She runs her fingers through them, "I . . . needed a change. The braids . . . they . . ."

"You're stunning, Colette. I love your curls," I say as I finger one, twisting the strand around my finger and pulling it down slightly. When it's fully straight, it almost reaches her navel but when I let it go, it springs back to hit just under her breast. On one side of her head, she has three braids from her temple to just behind her ear, and I notice she kept three gold charms.

"You kept some charms?" I ask even though my fucking eyes can clearly see them. I don't know why I asked that dumbass question, but I'm a little starstruck right now.

"Yeah." She lifts her hand and runs her fingers over them. "The phoenix LJ gave me, the raven my dad gave me, and . . ." Her eyes meet mine, and I look at the last charm, and fuck me, but I actually smile.

"A bow and arrow," I finish for her.

"I couldn't let these ones go. Even though my curls will be a bit more to maintain . . . I just needed something different."

"I understand. And I'd love to help." I offer, but really, it's all for selfish reasons. All I want to do is get my hands in that mess of curls. I can imagine the feel of them wrapped around my fingers as I pull the most elicit moans from her mouth.

"You want to help me with my hair?" She lets out a small laugh like I'm joking, but I'm not.

"I'll do just about anything to get my hands on you, Colette."

Her blush turns her cheeks a deep rose color, and she looks at her feet. "Well, first, can we eat? I'm starving."

Stepping back from her, I nod to the menus, and she begins to flip through. "Do you want Chinese or Japanese?"

Jesus fuck, all I can think about is how fucking breathtaking she is right now. She expects me to think about food when she just sprang this entirely new and exotic side of herself on me? "All I want is you on your knees," I say before my mind can process.

Her brown beauties fly to my own eyes, and she snorts before bending over in laughter. "Oh my god! On your—Chinese, Japanese, on your knees." She continues to laugh, and I can't help it . . . one escapes me too.

Before I know it, we're both infected with the giggles that just continue to worsen when we look at each other. She's leaning forward, bracing herself on the kitchen island, and I'm mimicking her pose next to her. Moments pass and finally our laughter dies down. "Okay but seriously, what do you want?" she finally asks when she catches her breath.

"I meant what I said," I reply with a smirk and let my eyes show her that all I really want is to be buried inside her tight pussy, her bent over the counter with one hand wrapped in those curls and one around her throat.

She slaps my shoulder and pushes me away. "First, we eat, naughty, naughty boy."

"I agree. Come here and let me have a taste." I reach out for her, but she darts away and around the counter. "Colette," I warn, but it just makes her giggle more.

"Food! Gage!" She tries to get away again, but I'm faster as I wrap my arms around her waist and pull her back to my chest.

"Couldn't agree more, and now I've caught mine," I whisper in her ear as I walk us both to the couch. When we're close enough, I push on the space between her shoulder blades, commanding her to bend forward, and like the good girl I know she can be, she bends for me.

Her arms brace on the back of the couch and I slap her ass. "Knees up, baby girl."

She does as she's told, all while looking at me over her shoulder with eyes of fire. Once she has her knees planted on the couch, I pull at the waistband of her sweats and panties at the same time, exposing her supple skin and glistening pussy.

"So fucking perfect," I whisper and she moans at my praise, already anticipating what's to come. Getting on my knees behind her, I hold each of her round ass cheeks in my hands and give no warning before diving in. My tongue licks up her arousal, and her hips shoot forward as she lets out a cry.

My palm slaps her cheek, the sound filling the space. "Stay still, or I'll tie you down," I warn before going back for more.

My grip changes from her ass to her hips so I can keep her still because I know she won't be able to.

"Gage," she whines as I fuck her with my tongue, taking in her sweet taste. Her hips begin to rock up and down as she rides my face, trying to set the pace to get her to release as fast as she can, but I like to torture my chaotic little thing, just like she loves to do to me.

I tighten my grip on her hips and halt her movements. "I'll let you ride my face, baby girl. But I'm not ready for you to come. I like to savor my meal. So hold. Fucking. Still."

"I can't," she cries as I move my hand and begin to play with her clit. Her legs begin to shake, and her back arches as she tries to hold back her orgasm. She's so willing to follow my command, but her body is betraying her. I love to watch her writhe.

Once I feel satisfied by her taste and the fact that I have fully let her orgasm build so that when she falls, I know it will destroy her, I give her the okay to take what she wants. Flipping my body so my head is relaxed back on the couch, I pull her hips down forcefully and let her suffocate me with her thighs. "Ride my face like the greedy fucking girl you are."

And she does. All I have to do is continue my assault against her clit as she moves her hips back and forth over my tongue. One, two, three seconds later and her release coats my tongue as I swallow her down.

"Such a good girl, Colette," I praise, and she moans out as her muscles shake, and she collapses onto her back, laying across the couch. I wipe my lips with the back of my hand and then lay my head on her stomach, turning my head so I can take in her face. When her eyes meet mine, they are unfocused, still reeling from the orgasm that just wracked her body. Her hands thread through my hair, and I want to pull back, but I keep my eyes open and on her.

Moments pass as my head moves up and down with her breathing, and I listen to her heartbeat. Her fingers grip my hair in a tight hold, and she leaves them there, pulling enough to give me pain.

She's perfect. I can't even put into words how well she knows my body, probably as well as I know hers, I guess. She knows exactly what I need, and she isn't scared to push me.

"I'm sorry," I say, and her eyes open to meet mine again.

"I'm sorry too."

"Are you really?"

"No," she whispers. "But I don't want to hurt you. I just want to help."

Lifting my head, she sits up and swings her legs so they're on either side of me. Lucky for her, she already scooted her sweats back up, or I'd be having dessert right now.

I'm on my knees, kneeling in front of her, and she's looking down on me like the queen she is. "I love you, Gage, and maybe it's toxic, but it doesn't matter what you do or say, I'll still be here. I know that hurt people hurt people. I know you don't want to. I know it's all you've ever known."

I lay my head in her lap now, and she wraps her hands in my hair again, gripping it tight, and even this action is something I could not have handled before her.

"That doesn't make what I do okay."

"No, but even if I get hurt in the process of helping you heal, I'll be happy to end this war bloodied and bruised, as long as we come out together. That's what love is, Gage."

I can't tell her I love her even though in my fucked-up, twisted way, I do. Because she doesn't want me to say it till I can give her all of me. I'm not there yet, but she's right. I will come out of this with her, even if I have to break in the process because she's worthy of it all.

gage

"You're such a dick." Leo is behind the counter of Henry Leo's, making me an extra-hot Americano. She's also giving me her "mom" look, and it only slightly terrifies me. Poor Rune and Everett.

"You say that as if that's something new. I've always been this way."

"Exactly. Maybe it's time for a change." She shrugs.

"You don't like me the way I am?"

"I love you, Gage. But I also love Cole. And she's trying to help you."

"First of all. Ouch. I was your bestie first. And second, I never wanted help. I was fine with how my life was. Where it was at. She's the one who came into my life and flipped it on its fucking head. So excuse me if it takes me a minute to adjust."

"Yes. As she should have. You can't tell me that you were genuinely happy with your life. Maybe what you needed more than anything was a good kick in the ass. And trust me, if there is anyone who will eagerly give you one, it's Cole. She doesn't give up either."

"You're not wrong." I take the cup from her and back away from the counter.

"And don't even—wait. What did you just say?"

"I'm not repeating myself," I grumble as I turn for the door of Henry Leo's. "And thanks for the tips." I salute with my cup, and the ding of the bell signals my exit.

After I stop at the store, I head back to my apartment to find my favorite sight to behold—Colette in my T-shirt and her lace panties. Well, shit, I had planned a little pamper session for her, but I may have to take care of the now raging fucking boner that's pressing against my zipper first.

She must hear the door shut because her head spins to me, her curls bouncing with the movement, and I thank the good devil down below for that hair 'cause fuck, it has to be a sin to look as stunning as she does.

"You're home early?" she questions, and I answer her with a hum as I put my keys away and slip off my shoes.

I grab the bag of stuff I bought from the store and sit on the couch, then call her over to me. "Come here."

I watch her long legs unfold beneath her, and she saunters over, a little unsure of what I have planned. Good, I like to keep her on her toes. Or her back, or her knees, or her stomach with her face down and ass up.

"Yes?"

Oops, got a little lost daydreaming for a second.

"Sit." I glance down to the floor between my legs, and she kneels. Her big brown eyes look up at me from her knees. Goddamn.

Focus, Gage. This is about her.

"Turn."

Her brows furrow. "What?"

"Turn. Around." I speak clearly as I give her a smirk. I know she heard me; she's just being a brat.

She does, and I dig in the bag for the first thing I need. LJ said to use this oil first. I put a few drops in my hands, then rub them together before placing my hands on her traps. I gently squeeze, then slowly increase my depth.

"Oh, that feels nice." She hums as I feel her body relax more. She changes her position so that she's sitting on her butt instead of her knees now. I move my hands up from her shoulders to her neck and begin to work my way around her jaw and then down her neck.

When I finish with her skin, I grab the second oil that LJ recommended and put that in my hands. I begin at the base of her skull and thread my fingers into her curls, getting as close to her scalp as I can as I massage the oil into her hair and skin.

"Wait, you can't just use any oil on my curls! What are you using? Let me see." She tries to turn her head, but I force her to look back down as I continue to massage. "Simmer down, Chaos. I know what I'm doing."

"Bullshit." She huffs as she tries to look again and again. I keep her head forward and down.

"Would you just chill the fuck out? LJ helped me with what oils to use, so shut the fuck up and let me do this," I snap but keep my hands working.

"LJ helped you?" she asks a bit more timidly now.

"Yes. I can recognize that I had no idea what to use on your hair, so I pulled in some help. I did my research."

"Oh."

I continue to work the oil in as she hums her delight here and there. I watch in the reflection of the windows with the night sky beyond as her mouth drops open, and her eyes roll back when I get to the area around her temples.

"Mmm," she moans, and my dick twitches.

Finally, I place the last oil in my hands and begin working it through her curls with flat hands. LJ was specific in her instructions that I couldn't comb through her curls with my fingers, not right now anyway. She said I could do that when we were in the shower, and Colette was washing her hair. When it's dry, and I'm just using oil, I "must use flat hands, or I'll make them frizzy."

I don't fucking know, but I wouldn't dare mess with my chaotic beauty's curls, especially when I know exactly why she got rid of her braids in the first place. I know the memory of her attacker grabbing her from behind haunts her. It has to.

I covered my skin in tattoos. Colette unleashed her curls.

Last, I take a few of the curls that have begun to flatten and wrap them around my finger, giving them their bounce back.

Threading my fingers through the hair at nape of her neck, I tug on her hair and tilt her head back. "Done," I say just before I kiss the lips that haunt my dreams. The way our tongues meet, upside down makes me groan into her mouth.

"Fuck, baby girl. Your lips are a sin."

"Then let me sin just a bit more." She turns and reaches for my zipper. I let her pull me out as I relax back on the couch.

Find me in hell when I die 'cause that is where I will happily reside if it means I get to keep her.

gage

I'm making my way into headquarters the following morning when a text comes through from Colette.

My Raven

> I have something for you.

Fuck. Now we are gift giving? This is all moving so fast that it makes my head spin, but it also feels so fucking right.

> It better be a new toy to use on you. EC has been boring me lately.

She doesn't respond right away, so I slip my phone into my pocket as I walk into my office to find Hale already waiting for me. "Did you get your favorite boss a drink?"

"No." I set my stuff down on my desk, rounding to sit when Hale stops me.

"Dick. Don't get comfy. That special project you pulled me in on? I have something."

"Fuck, finally." I let out on an exhale and thank the devil below I'll have something more to work on than creeping on the fucking twins from hell.

Hale sits on the corner of my desk and hands me a manila folder. Opening it up, I set eyes on the man who attempted to hurt Colette.

"It's all there."

"Enough to put him away?"

"Oh, for sure. Now, all we have to do is find him."

A smirk pulls at my lips. "I'll find him. I always do." The hunt is what I live for.

With that, Hale leaves, but just before he does, he pauses and turns back to me. "Oh, Natasha returned to Seattle with the Alessis this morning. I want to keep tabs on her."

"You mean keep tabs on the Alessis?" I correct him.

Despite Natasha being an . . . acquaintance of mine. In a professional manner, she's simply another girl the Alessi twins have collected. From a legal standpoint, she has done nothing wrong, so therefore, we have no reason to keep tabs on her.

"Right." Hale's eyes drop to the floor—something they never do. The asshole has a bigger ego than even I do. He has to in his line of work, but I know that look better than anyone. Seems like maybe a certain high-maintenance blonde has gotten under his skin.

Pulling out my phone to reply to my little nuisance, I take in the photo she placed as my background. A photo of her flipping off the camera and sticking her tongue out. Such a little shit. I shake my head at her theatrics and type out my reply.

> I'll be home around 9. Does my gift include a new leather belt? My other one happens to have teeth marks in it . . .

The memory of when I tied her wrists together in the office of Henry Leo's flashes through my mind. She bit the belt so hard she left permanent marks on the leather. She blamed it on not wanting anyone to know I was fucking her into oblivion, but we both know she just wanted to leave me a reminder.

And she did, in fact, because every time I look at that belt, looping it through my belt loops, I think about her bent over the desk, her moans muffled by the belt, and her pretty pussy welcoming me home.

As much as I want to fight this, the truth is Colette will always be mine. I'm too selfish to give her up and too fucked up to give her what she deserves, but it doesn't matter anymore. I've already been caught up in her chaos, and I never want to leave it.

Booting up my systems, I get to work on the most important task. Hale reported they have enough to put this bastard away. All we need to do is find him. Multiple accounts of sexual assault, assault with a deadly weapon, and shoplifting. What a classy fella. He's been out on parole but has violated that parole and is now a wanted man.

I'll admit, finding out who he was proved to be a challenge, but it's nothing I couldn't handle. Hunting him gave me a challenge I hadn't had in some time. And with Colette not able to recall any of his worthless features, I had to rely on surrounding cameras. Once I had him, my team ran his face and easily enough, we got his name, date of birth, record, and supposed address, which I can tell you now he does not reside at.

Now, to find him.

And when I do, he will go to prison. And because his heart still beating is too good for him after he touched what's mine, his cell mates might happen upon some information about this waste of fucking breath that will put him in some precarious situations, which may or may not lead to an accidental slip on a razor blade.

Oops.

colette

It's here. Evangeline's letter. It's in an old, worn envelope, and her looping cursive adorns the front with Gage's name. I can't help but feel incredibly nervous with the looming fear that this letter will either give him everything he needs to move on or it will destroy him.

I'm either going to save him or lose him forever. But no matter the ending, this needs to happen. He needs to read this letter, so whatever the outcome, I do not regret reaching out to the school.

"Daddy, what if I'm about to lose him?"

"You won't." My dad's deep, soothing voice comes through the speakerphone. I'm pacing in my kitchen, knowing Gage should be home any minute.

I told my dad everything. From our letters as Arrow and Raven to meeting him, moving in next to him, falling in love with him, to pieces of his past and finding the letter. My father knows about some of these things already since he had therapy with Gage, and they became close, but he never heard my side of everything. And if there is one person I can count on to give me the truth, it's my dad.

"This letter could destroy him. And I would be the reason."

"My little Raven, that boy is already in pieces. If anything, this will give him the courage he needs to begin picking up those pieces."

"What if he leaves me?" The thought alone makes me want to fall apart. Jesus, when did I become so dependent on him?

"Then it will hurt. But you cannot continue to try to collect his pieces. You'll only continue to cut yourself."

Little does my dad know that cutting myself is something I had been doing way before Gage. It's a pain I relish and need. Needed. Before him.

"Honey, I've grown to love Gage as a son. He has an incredible heart underneath the armor he wears. But I don't want to see you hurt—"

"Dad," I defend.

"No, don't *dad* me. I know you love him. I didn't say you shouldn't be together. You just need to be careful and let him do things on his own time. From someone who knows, this is a journey he has to do according to his rules."

"So what? I'm just supposed to leave him to do this all by himself? I can't do that. I'm not that kind of person." I finally wear myself out and collapse onto the couch, his mother's letter staring at me from the coffee table.

"No. I think he needs you. But you two will be doing a balancing act with one another. Give him grace, Colette. That's all I'm saying."

"Do you think he'll ever be okay again, Daddy?" I hesitate to ask because I'm fearful of my father's honest answer, but if anyone is going to tell me the truth, it's him, and he has gotten to know a side of Gage not many people get to.

"Gage is treading water, reaching out for a life raft. As long as he's doing that, there is always hope."

I stay silent, contemplating his words. Gage seems to be going back and forth between wanting to heal and being content with drowning.

"I love you, Daddy, for eternity and beyond."

"For eternity and beyond."

Hanging up with my dad, I sit in all that he said to me. And I know, thanks to my stubbornness, that I will continue to search for Gage, I will continue to throw out the life raft, and I will continue to dive into those dark waters, even if I drown in them myself.

Is that toxic? Probably.

Do I give two flying fucks? Absolutely not.

Gage's storm has nothing on me. I'll make it my bitch because Gage is worth it.

He walks in, and just like every time I see him, I'm reminded how unbelievably beautiful he is. His black dress slacks, black belt, black button-up long-sleeved dress shirt all make him look like my dark angel. His dark hair is messed up a little, probably from running his hands through it like he does when he's stressed out.

He looks up from setting his wallet and keys in the entryway bowl, and his burning hazel eyes cut straight through me.

"Hi."

I pat the couch to encourage him to sit next to me, and he does. His thigh brushes against my curled-up ones. I don't think he realizes that even this touch is such an astounding step from where he used to be. He thinks he isn't making any progress, that all we have been doing is pointless, and that he will never change, but he doesn't see that he has made incredible progress. I'm so fucking proud of him.

"How was your day?" I ask a little shyly, knowing the bomb I'm about to drop on him.

"Fine."

I take a deep breath, dragging the heavy air surrounding us inside my lungs that are barely holding my racing heart in.

"I have something for you. And I want you to hear me out."

He narrows his eyes but doesn't say anything.

"I couldn't leave the fact you had nothing of your mom's alone—"

"Fuck, Colette." He runs that tattooed hand through his hair and goes to stand, but I catch his arm and pull him back down.

"Gage. Listen to me. Please."

I can see his jaw tense, but he lets me continue.

You can do this. Don't be a little bitch. Rip the Band-Aid off.

I hand him the letter.

"What is this?" He takes it, and I can tell that he doesn't even recognize his own mother's handwriting. Why would he, though? He only has one memory of her, and he doesn't own anything of hers.

"It's a letter. From your mother."

His head whips up, and his eyes meet mine. A collision of fear and confusion warring inside his all-consuming irises. "What—How?"

"I called your mom's school where she worked. The last year she worked there, before she quit, they buried a time capsule to be opened in twenty years. They opened it two years ago, but they didn't have any way to contact you, so it's just been sitting there."

"She—" He runs his fingers over her cursive letters that spell out his name. "She wrote me a letter?"

I remain silent. Letting him take this all in without any influence from me. I want him to decide the next step.

He sits there in silence, continuing to trace the letters of his name over and over. He's like a stone wall; I can't read him. I get no indication whatsoever of how he's feeling. Gage has always hidden behind his various masks he wears, but there was always something small I could pick up on. But not right now. No, right now, he's so lost in his mind.

The urge to reach into his mind and pull him back out is so incredibly strong that I have a hard time resisting, but I know, as sure as I know that we belong together, I know he needs to find himself this time. It's the only way.

"I'm here. For whatever you need," I say as I lay my hand on his cheek, and he flinches away.

"I—" He looks at me, and I can see right through his mask now. I see an emotion I have never seen in his eyes.

Fear.

He's terrified.

I imagine he doesn't even know what to do with this feeling.

"I need to go." He gets up, and this time, I let him leave.

The door slams, and I try my best to remind myself that he isn't leaving forever. He will come back.

I hope.

gage

The slam of my front door behind me jerks me from the daze I was in. When Colette handed me that letter, I felt like I couldn't breathe. Like I was suffocating, my lungs filling with water.

My mother wrote me a letter.

My mother.

I can't even think clearly, let alone get my fingers to function enough to open the letter. A part of me wants to burn it. Never open it. Never let her change a part of me. If I never see the contents of this letter, everything will remain the same. As it should. I'm happy where I'm at right now.

If everyone would just leave me the fuck alone.

I'm fine.

But you're not.

You need to open it.

That soft whisper creeps in again, and I shake it away.

But I know it's right. Because Colette and Leo are right. I need to do something, anything to get out of this limbo I've been living in.

If I want to be everything that chaotic little creature deserves, I need to take a step.

My chest burns right in the fucking center.

Like seeing a storm on the horizon, I know it's coming no matter how much I wish it away. I know damage is about to be done, but I also can't resist appreciating the beauty and power the storm holds.

For so long, I was content living with my monsters, letting them live inside me and occasionally letting them out to breathe, but in the end, it's keeping me from her. My Raven.

For the first time in my life, I have something to fight for. But it's not me. It's her.

My steps carry me through my living room and into my office, but my mind is in a drift. I fall into my desk chair. My old typewriter that I wrote all of my letters to Colette on, mocks me as I rip open the envelope containing my mother's letter.

The first thing I notice is the letter is typed out with the bold block, stamped letters of a typewriter. Looks like Mom loved them just as much as I do. I smile a little at knowing something about her that I didn't before. Something we have in common.

I take a deep breath, then take control.

August 2nd, 2002

My sweet boy,

I pray that we are reading this letter together, but I know that, more likely than not, you're reading this letter by yourself. And I'm sorry for that.

I never wanted to leave you, baby boy. But God had other plans for me. And I have spent a long time struggling with the thought of never getting to see you grow from the witty, silly, charismatic boy you are now into the intelligent, kind, and caring man I know you will become. But I'm okay with it now.

I know that despite the grief you will experience, you will endure. It's in your nature. Because more than anything, I'm with you. Always. I'm in your bones, your blood. I'm part of you, just as you are part of me.

I don't know what kind of life you will grow up in. I pray that your father was good to you. He has some struggles, but he's always been good to us. I'm not going to ask you to forgive him for whatever failures he may have had as a single parent because the truth is, I know something is lurking inside him. I see it when he drops his mask. Although he has never abused us, there is something dark under his surface, and I hate more than anything that I cannot do anything to shield you from it. All I can do now is hope and pray he keeps his monsters hidden. And if they do surface, I can only pray that you survive and remain that loving, sweet boy you are now.

But the stark reality is that I don't know who you are, at this moment, twenty years from when I'm writing this letter. I hope that you have found love, and more than that, I hope that you're allowing yourself to be loved. I hope that they drown you in their love, and I hope you allow yourself to be consumed by their love. It's terrifying to be so utterly consumed by another, but when you allow yourself to breathe their love in, let it fill you, it's incredibly liberating. You did that for me, Gage. I thought I knew what love was until you came into my life. You consumed me, and I drowned in your love, letting it show me that I was worthy of beautiful things. Of you.

Remember that no matter what happens to you, you cannot let your past own you, sweet boy. You have to win. You have to fight whatever fight you need to, and you need to win.

If your father was an amazing man and all this seems out of the blue and foreign to you, then my prayers were answered. But I'm a realist, and I have a feeling that you met his monsters. But your light is bigger baby boy, you endure, you survive. And one day, I'll see you again. I'll let you break in my arms for all that you had to endure alone. But until then, you live a life full of love. And when we meet again, you can tell me all about it.

I love you for infinity.

P.S. I wanted you to have something of mine. And if it wasn't given to you yet, find Ski at Mill's Coffee House. He will know what to do.

Find Ski? What the hell does she . . .

I look up at the typewriter.

The typewriter Ski gave me when I was sixteen.

Her typewriter.

I had no idea then. He didn't say anything. All he said was that it was meant for me. I assumed he had found it, seeing the custom arrow key and thought of me because of my last name. I never thought it was left for me by . . . my mom.

All this time, I had a piece of her with me.

All this time.

Her hopes and dreams for me make me feel like a failure. Because that's exactly what I have done. I have failed her. I became exactly what she feared I would be. Closed off. Afraid of love. Broken.

I let what happened to me confine me. Restrict me. I couldn't let anyone in, couldn't let anyone love me the way she desired for me. But the thing is, I don't even know if I'm capable of what she wants.

I failed her.

And worse than that . . .

I became like him.

A monster hiding behind a mask.

Chapter Forty-Seven

colette

It's been hours since Gage took his mom's letter back to his apartment, and I'm terrified. What if this is all too much?

The wear and tear I'm putting into these hardwood floors from my pacing will definitely come out of my deposit, but I can't stop moving. My curiosity is eating at me. What did that letter say? Will he be okay? Who am I kidding, of course he won't.

I should go over there. I should pound on his door until he opens up and lets me hold him while he processes all of this.

Yeah. That's what I'm going to do. He doesn't get to hide from me . . .

With determination, I stomp over to the door, set on pushing him so he lets me in. But then I stop.

I can't.

I have always been the type to go after what I wanted. I have had patience in my relationships—okay, maybe I wouldn't use the word patience . . . But I allow people to do things in their own time. Right?

Well, shit.

Okay, maybe I don't. But some people need that, like LJ, initially she was so closed off, but I remained persistent. I allowed her to open up in her own time, but I also made sure she was taking positive steps forward. Is it a character flaw of mine? Maybe. But I'd like to think that it's also good for people to be pushed outside their comfort zone.

But with Gage, I'm learning that I can't ignore people's boundaries, even when those boundaries are holding said person back.

I need to back off. I need to let Gage do this and let him come to me when he's ready instead of me chasing him down. I have to trust him.

Right there. That's the hang-up that doesn't let me allow people their space and boundaries because that would mean I'm trusting them to return to me.

Going against every instinct, I take a shower and make a cup of coffee to try to relax. Yes, I know it's contradictory to drink coffee to relax, but it's decaf. Don't come for me.

As I sip it, I put *Clueless* on and try to distract myself. But my mind is wandering, and I can't rein it in. My legs are shaking with nerves. God. This is killing me!

But then a knock on my door makes me shoot off the couch, spilling my coffee.

"Ow, motherfucking cunt balls!" I screech as I scramble to the front door. Not even bothering to clean up the coffee on me or the floor.

I fling the door open, and Gage stands there with the letter in his hand. His head is down, staring at it. I have to physically root myself in place because all I want to do is jump into his arms, hold him, comfort him, give him the love he deserves.

But I don't.

And then he looks up at me. His eyes are red, glassy. Tears track down his perfect face, and my heart breaks for him.

He steps into me and drops to his knees. His hands grip my hips as he buries his face into my stomach, and upon instinct, I run my hands through his hair. Clutching onto him as much as he is to me.

"I failed her, baby. I ca . . . can't do this anymore," he begs.

Has he finally broken?

Pulling my hands from his dark locks to his jaw, I hold the man I love in my hands. "I'm here."

I kneel and kiss him, telling him as much as showing him that I love him more than I ever thought possible, and I will always be here to find him. I lean my forehead to his after I release his lips. "Come with me."

I pull him up and lead him to the bedroom. Encouraging him to sit on the edge of my bed, I push my body between his thighs, and he gladly opens for me. His arms wrap around my hips as he buries his face into my stomach, and I hear him inhale me.

A confounding amount of emotions roll inside my body—hurt, anger, love, desperation. All for this man. I don't know what to say or do. But I know what I want to do. I want to comfort him and show him that he's mine. And always will be.

Running my fingers through his dark hair, I pull slightly, forcing him to look up at me and giving him the bite of pain I know his mind needs. "What did the letter say?"

He pulls his hand around and hands me the letter. One letter that changed everything.

I read it as I stand there. He drops his face back into my stomach, breathing deeply. I feel his breath against my skin, soaking through my shirt. He clings to me as if I were a life raft. His last hope at being rescued.

Tears stream down my face as I read the letter a mother left for her son, knowing she would not be there to protect him. It's heartbreaking, heart-shattering. And at the same time, healing in a way only Gage needed.

He needed this.

He needed her.

"Do you know what's at Mill's? What she left for you?"

Looking up at me now, his tears have stopped, but we both know that doesn't mean the pain has eased. If anything, it only means we have numbed ourselves. "Her typewriter."

My heart swells in my chest. I drop the letter to the bed and climb into his lap. He eagerly allows me to wrap him in my embrace, a far cry from where we began. "Gage."

His hands encircle my rib cage, holding my heart close, and I bury my lips into his neck, breathing in his scent. His deep voice vibrates against my cheek. "I never knew it was hers. Ski never told me."

"I think there is a reason she left it with Ski. Maybe that is what you need to do. Maybe you need to talk to him."

He shakes his head as I pull away slightly so I can look into his eyes. "No. I can't do that."

"Why not?"

"He—" He hesitates. His brows furrow, and I can see the clench of his jaw. "Ski is in Aurora. A place I swore I would never return to."

I place my hand on his cheek and smile when he doesn't flinch. He notices, and his eyes widen a bit in shock. "Sometimes to move forward, we need to go back."

"That makes absolutely no fucking sense, Chaos. And why do you have coffee all over you?"

"Shhh . . . Just let me have my moment." I lean in and place a gentle kiss to his lips, but it doesn't stay that way as he brings his hand to the nape of my neck and pulls me in tighter, demanding more.

His tongue collides with mine, as if he's punishing me for trying to be gentle. But I happily accept it. I was never one who wanted a gentleman anyway.

Releasing me, he rests his forehead to my own. "Will you come with me? I-I need you."

"Of course. But you have to do something for me." He groans out in protest, but we both know I will get whatever I want from this man. "We have to continue with our truth or touch game. And I'm going to start touching you. I'm going to push your boundaries, Gage. You need this to heal. Do you understand?"

"I don't like this game," he spits back at me, narrowing his eyes.

"Yeah, well, tough, because you chose me, and I'm your chaos, remember?"

"I regret all my choices," he deadpans, and I smack him on the cheek. Not hard enough to leave a mark but hard enough to feel the sting.

His eyes turn dark. "Oh, it's on, baby girl."

"Bring it, big gu—" Before I can even finish my sentence, he lifts me in the air, hands grasping my ass, and backs me up until I'm resting on the top of my dresser.

He grasps his shirt at the nape of his neck and lifts it over his head as I do the same to my own. He undoes his zipper and pulls out his perfect, pierced cock, and I swear I begin to drool.

The asshole takes notice as he lifts my chin. "My eyes are up here, baby girl."

My heel finds the dresser as I bring my leg up and spread my thighs wide, dipping my hand into my lace panties. I watch as his eyes travel down my body to where my fingers are playing with my pussy. Then I bring them to his mouth, and he opens for me. Sliding my fingers inside, I grip his chin with my thumb and pull him toward me. "My eyes are up here, baby." I snark back at him, using his own words against him.

He bites down on my fingers, not enough to hurt me but enough to leave a mark, and I pull them out and laugh.

"God, I can't wait to fuck the attitude out of you. Lift." He smacks my outer thigh, and I oblige as he slides my panties off me. "You want to be a tease, Colette? You want to play with me? Test me? Push my boundaries? Let me tell you something, I give as good as I get, so you better be prepared."

"That's what I'm hoping for. I don't want you to be gentle, Gage. I want you to ruin me. But know that I will do the same to you."

"Hmm." His eyes turn devilish as he accepts my challenge, and my pussy pulses in response. My breath catches inside my chest as he leans in close to my neck. Instinctively, I open more for him. As his teeth bite down, and he sucks on my neck, I bring my hands up and run them gently down his back.

I feel his muscles tense, his entire body turning as hard as stone. He lets go and places his forehead against my neck. "Colette," he whispers.

"That's it, baby, say my name. It's me. Just me."

I continue with running my fingers up and down his back. At first, he tenses even more, and when I pull back to look at his face, his eyes are closed tightly, his face in a grimace as if this touch is the most painful thing he has experienced. But I know that it's not a physical pain he's re-living inside his mind. It's his father's words, touch, and face that are ripping him apart inside.

"Open your eyes, Gage. Look at me."

He doesn't.

He's too lost.

His hands grip my thighs dangerously tight. Right on the verge of too much pain.

I need to find him.

I dig my fingernails into his back and leave my mark from shoulder to lower back. His muscles immediately relax as he lets out a long moan and opens his eyes.

"There you are," I say as he pants heavily.

"Colette."

"I'll always find you. When you're lost inside that dark head of yours, I'll find you."

Wrapping his hand around my throat, he pulls me into him, our chest colliding, our lips breaths apart. "Do it again," he demands against my lips.

I run my fingers gently down his back again. He tenses, but I don't let him retreat. I reach down between us with one hand and guide his tip to my entrance, then I scoot my hips forward and let him slide into me.

We both gasp at the feeling of him inside me. "I've got you, Gage. And I'm not letting go. I will not let him have you. No more."

He just nods his head against mine as he begins to thrust in and out of me. His grip remains firm on my throat, his fingers dig into the back of my neck, and I continue to gently touch down his back and his chest. Any place I can reach, I leave soft touches. Both of us give as much pain as we are receiving, but in two completely different ways.

"Colette. Colette. Colette," he chants my name like a prayer. A reminder. A plea. Imprinting into his mind who has him now.

He continues moving in and out of me, not in a punishing way like he usually does, but in a slow, torturous way. I feel the length of him glide in and out, his piercing eliciting more pleasure than I have ever felt before.

When I feel the ache building inside me, on the edge, ready to jump, he reads my body like only he can. He pulls his hand from my throat and presses his fingers to my clit as he circles. At the same time, he slams his lips to my own, and we both moan out our release.

"Fuck, baby girl," he pants as he pulls out of me.

My legs are a shaky mess, and my body feels spent. Despite that being the most gentle he has ever been with me, I feel like I just ran a marathon. He pulled from me an orgasm like no other, one that was earned with patience and coaxing, not brutality and demands.

He leaves me on the dresser as he walks to the bathroom and grabs a warm washcloth. The warmth of the washcloth sends tingles up my entire body, and I shiver. Grabbing me around my hips, he lifts me with ease. Carrying me to my bed, he pulls the blankets over me.

He slips in behind me and surrounds me with his body, his chest to my back, his knees curled behind mine. He has never snuggled me like this, and my heart beats wildly in my chest.

"Before you leave, can you wake me up and give me a kiss. I don't like falling asleep with you here and waking in the morning and you're gone."

He places a soft kiss on my neck. "I'm not going anywhere tonight, baby girl."

Chapter Forty-Eight

gage

"*You are my sunshine, my only sunshine. You make me happy when skies are gray.*" *Her voice filters into my sleepy mind as I watch her lips move, humming the song along with her. I feel her finger trace the figure eight she always traces over my heart.*

"*Close your eyes.*"

I slowly close them as they grow heavier, rubbing them to try to stay awake, to try to stay a little longer with her. Her smile blurs as I fail to fight sleep.

"*Mommy, five more minutes.*"

She giggles as she continues to trace the figure eight symbol over my heart.

"*Why an eight?*" *I ask, barely a mumble as I drift to sleep slowly.*

"*It's an infinity symbol, my love. It means my love for you has no boundaries, no limits, and it will live on, even after I'm gone, for infinity.*" *Her other hand brushes my hair back as she places a kiss to my nose.*

"*Hmm.*" *I try to make words, but I'm too tired.*

"*Like Buzz Lightyear? To infinity and beyond?*" *I murmur.*

"Something like that, sleepy boy. I love you for infinity."

"And beyond," I finish as I fall asleep to the small tracings of an infinity symbol over my heart.

"Gage."

"Five more minutes." I still feel her fingers. Round and round.

"Gage, wake up." Colette's voice infiltrates my mind now, but I don't open my eyes. I want to stay in this moment with my mother. The only moment I have with her. But I can feel Colette's eyes on me. I can always feel her.

"Stop staring, it's creepy," I murmur as I brace myself for the chaotic beauty lying next to me, tracing her finger over my infinity tattoo.

"You stayed." Her vanilla-and-cocoa scent finds my nose, and I inhale her as I feel her hand travel down from my sternum to my abs, to my—

I reach out, eyes still closed, and grab her by her wrist. I hear her gasp, and I finally open my eyes. "Small steps, baby girl. I stayed. You snuggled, I suffered. Don't push it."

Bringing her wrist to my lips, I kiss where her pulse pounds against her skin. "No wonder you don't snuggle. You're grumpy in the morning."

"I'm grumpy all the time," I say with a grin, and just like that, I see her melting once again.

As I get up and out of her bed, she reaches out and grabs my shoulder to pull me back down. I don't fight her like I should, so I let her lay me on my back, then straddle me with those beautifully scarred thighs. Gripping them in my hands, I look up at her, sitting atop me like the queen she is. I trace the ridge of her raised scars and see myself in her. Her need for pain. I feel a spark of joy in my chest, finding someone so similar yet completely contradictory to me.

"It's time to play our truth or touch game, big guy."

Joy gone.

"I just woke up. Can't you at least let me have coffee before you torture me?"

"I thought torture was one of your kinks?" The mischievous tone in her melodic voice pulls out a nefarious side of me. The side of me that envisions tying her up or bending her over, pushing her limits and making her scream.

"It is, when I'm the one doing the torture. Not the other way around, Chaos."

"Play with me and I'll make it worth your while?" She attempts to bargain, and I find it incredibly cute she thinks she has anything to bargain with that isn't already mine.

"Baby girl, that mouth and pussy already belong to me. What is it you think you have to offer that I don't already own?"

"I'll paint for you."

I tilt my head at her. Interesting. That isn't something I was expecting.

"Arrow said he could imagine me painting. I'll make that vision become reality."

As much as I hate answering her questions, the image of her painting has been a fantasy I relive almost constantly. The need to see her in her element, in her most happy moments, it's unbearable to know I have not experienced it yet.

"Fine. Ask away."

"Why is your dad in jail?"

I scoff at her question. "Going in hard this morning, huh?"

Her eyes roll, and her smile turns saucy. "You know I like it rough. Now answer."

"Isn't it obvious?"

"Not to me. I can guess, but I want to hear it from you."

Taking a deep breath, I run my hands up and down her thighs. As I do so, she begins tracing random lines and shapes along my abs. The touch is . . . uncomfortable but not as debilitating as it once would have been.

"He's in federal prison for human trafficking."

Watching her take in this information is comical. She's so innocent that an idea such as that is outlandish. She doesn't realize how common it is. Her naivety only ignites the need to protect her more.

"But—"

She doesn't even know what to ask, so I fill in the blanks so her naive, innocent little brain doesn't explode.

"When I grew up, my features became masculine, my voice deeper, my skin flawed with my tattoos, I was no longer what my father was interested in. Like most predators, he found enough satisfaction through videos on the dark web. But he had already had the real thing, so it wasn't long until he needed more again. When I was nineteen, three years after the abuse stopped, he reached out to a family who had connections to obtain what he wanted. He . . . purchased a nine-year-old boy. Someone had been watching, though. They alerted the FBI, and he was arrested."

"Why didn't you stop him before?" There is no judgment in her tone, but I can see her real question. Why didn't I stop his abuse? Why didn't I go to anyone? Why did it go on for as long as it did?

Running my tongue along the back of my teeth, I contemplate how to answer her question. It's one I have struggled with also. Why didn't I?

"I was scared that no one would believe me. My father was the town physician, well respected, well liked. In public, he was the type to give you the shirt off his back. A couple of times, he lost his cool with me in public, grabbing me a little too tightly, being a little too rough, but everyone looked at him with sadness. The poor man who lost his wife too soon and now had to be a single dad to a troubled kid while working a demanding job. It was nothing but sympathy for him."

She runs her hands along my forehead, moving my hair out of my eyes, and I continue. Letting it all out feels . . . different but light, and I eat it up.

"He had friends in high places too. From a young age, I knew his friends were just as bad as he was, and they were even in higher positions of power. One the mayor and another a wealthy man who funded most of the town. I didn't have anyone."

"Did you ever try to . . . fight him?"

I scoff at her question. "I fought every time. But I was little. Height-wise, I was growing taller and taller, but muscle-wise? I was a scrawny kid. Everett tried putting some muscle on me, but it just never came in, not till I was an adult and began boxing and eating healthy. Before that, any fight I gave didn't last long. As a boy, my body reacted even when I didn't want it to, and that reaction took over any fight I had. He knew how to play my body to his wants and needs, and I was helpless to it."

She remains silent for a while as I let her soak in the info dump I just gave her. It's a lot for someone who isn't exposed to or aware of the world I lived in every day. The world of sexual abuse. The world I'm incredibly happy she's not privy to. But then again, there has to be a certain level of knowledge she should have about this world, just enough to keep her aware, to keep her safe.

Finally, she runs her eyes over my entire body. "Is that why you covered your skin in tattoos? Because he didn't like them."

I contemplate how honest I should be with her. On the one hand, I don't want to hide anything, but on the other, I don't want her to know what happened to me . . . not details anyway. I don't want to expose her to my monsters. I don't want them to haunt her as they do me.

"I—"

"Gage, I want you to tell me the truth. I'm stronger than you think. I can handle it. I want to carry it with you." Silence carries on between us, weighing down the room before I decide to trust her fully.

"Okay, baby girl . . . yes, my father loved my skin. He commented all the time on how he loved how flawless it was. How pale and smooth. So as soon as I could, I started getting tattoos. I wanted to cover it, hide it, make it something that was disgusting to him. I got my first tattoo at fourteen from a guy in his garage. It was an awfully done dahlia." I chuckle at the memory of getting it. God,

I was fucking terrified. Not of the pain but of what would happen when he saw it.

"What happened when he saw it?"

I take her hand and bring it to my left pectoral muscle. I watch as she feels the scar on my skin that is hidden by my ink. Her face goes from confusion to horror.

"He cut it off."

"Oh my god. But—"

"He was a doctor. He had the skills and access to the tools he needed."

"Gage." She leans down and places a soft kiss on the scar. I flinch, but then allow her to continue leaving the kisses.

"I'm so sorry that happened to you."

"Please don't apologize for something out of your control."

"But you deserve to hear it."

"It changes nothing, Colette. It's just words."

She lets out a sigh and pouts out her lip. "Well, I'm still going to say it."

I roll my eyes as I pinch her ass. "Yeah 'cause you never fucking listen."

"Nope," she says with that attitude that I absolutely detest.

I continue with pinching and tickling her, loving the sound of her roaring laughter. As I begin to laugh with her, I flip her, so I'm settled between her thighs, and pin her down by her throat. "Take me down, Chaos."

Her eyes turn dangerous as she grins, I can see the confidence in her shining though. As she gets out of my hold with absolute perfect form, I feel so fucking proud of her.

"Good girl." I praise as she straddles me, topping me just like I wanted her to. The only man her body will ever be beneath is mine. She's an unstoppable force, made to sit atop the world, and I'll make sure she knows how to get there.

My phone ringing is the only reason I stop myself from taking her right here and now.

Reaching over, I see Hale's name, and I know before I answer it that I need to put a pause on our little wrestling match.

Fucking cockblock.

Chapter Forty-Nine

colette

"Do you think he's going to be mad at me?" LJ sits across from me on the couch, wineglasses in both our hands. I called her over for a Gage-vention as I'm calling it.

"Yes. He's going to be pissed, but that isn't necessarily a bad thing. I think he really needs this, Cole. I think you're really good for him."

It's been a few days since Gage read his mother's letter. He has had time to process, and now it's time to make some changes. So, naturally, I took the initiative and made arrangements to fly to Oregon so he can go talk to Ski. That part I'm pretty confident he won't be too upset with me over. In fact, I know he won't because he asked me to go with him. The part I'm terrified to present to him is that I looked up and contacted the federal prison his dad is held at and arranged for us to visit him.

"Yeah. You're right. Hey, great idea. Maybe you should tell him? He likes you more." I point my wineglass in her direction and put on my best pretty please face.

"Ha! Yeah. I want to remain alive and well, thank you very much."

"Oh, come on!"

"No. Plus, he can't fuck his hate out on me, you . . . he can." She smirks at me, and I feel myself blush.

Although I have never been shy about talking to LJ about my sex life, I don't think she would appreciate my going into detail about Gage's godlike dick and filthy mouth.

"I mean I guess you're right. If all else fails, I'll just drop to my knees, and I'll have him begging for my forgiveness for his asshole-ish ways."

"That's the spirit!" She takes a sip of her wine, and we both turn our heads to the front door as Everett and Gage walk in.

The smile that Gage wears when he's with Everett is indescribable. It's natural and unburdened.

LJ removes herself from my couch and goes to wrap Everett in her arms. He dips her and kisses her so fiercely that I'm overwhelmed at how much he loves her. As he should, she's fucking amazing.

"Cole, thank you for babysitting my wife." Everett smiles at me, and I raise my glass in salute.

"I'm sure it was the other way around. What nefarious things did you get up to while I was gone? Hmm?" Gage leans over the back of the couch, wrapping his hand around my throat and pulling me into a kiss.

Holy hell. Did he just . . .?

"Did you just . . .?" Everett's face is pure shock as he takes in the fact that Gage practically just made me cream my panties right here in front of everyone.

Gage releases me and spins, pointing his finger at Everett. "Shut the fuck up, dipshit."

"But you just . . . you kissed a girl! In front of me! This is like record-breaking shit. You've never done that. Honestly, I thought you might have been gay. I mean, nothing wrong with that if you are, I just . . . I've never seen you with a girl."

Everett pulls out his phone, "Do it again so I can record it."

Gage narrows his eyes. "Get the fuck out. I'm not a fucking exhibitionist."

"I mean, I'd be into it . . ." I pipe up. Gage's head swings to me, and he points his finger at me now.

"You shut your mouth," he teases.

"Oh man, I didn't mean it like that! You guys need a cute kissing photo together." Everett attempts to save his ass, but it doesn't work.

Gage shakes his head and digs the palms of his hands into his eye sockets. "You two will be the death of me."

LJ slaps Everett on the shoulder and shushes him as he looks at her innocently. "What?"

I finally stand as tipsy giggles leave my mouth and walk to Gage, stepping in front of him. He wraps his arms around my shoulders, and I immediately grab his forearms with my hands, gently stroking him.

"Wait. You're—you're touching him."

"Stop fucking talking, dude," Gage growls.

"Okay, okay, we're leaving." LJ pushes at Everett until he begins to back out the apartment door, still shocked at this newest revelation, and I just giggle . . . again.

Turning in his arms, I wrap my own arms around his neck and pull him close for a kiss.

"Please ignore that embarrassing mess of a human I call my best friend." His breath tickles my lips, and I want to giggle again, but I try to hold it in to hide the fact that I'm a little—okay, a lot—bit tipsy.

"Oh please, you act as if I don't know who he is. I'm just happy that you kissed me in front of them."

"Did you think I wouldn't?"

"I had my doubts. I know being intimate is difficult for you, and I wasn't sure when you would be ready to show that in public."

"Understandable. But I'm done hiding, Colette. Even if I have difficulty showing affection, it doesn't mean that I don't want to. I'm working on it."

"Hmm. Thank you." I hum before I kiss him again.

"But if he's going to act like that every time, I'll fucking kill him."

"No, you won't." I begin pushing into him, backing him up to the couch I was just snuggled on.

"You're right, but I might mess with his bank accounts and social media just a touch."

"Naughty, naughty." He lifts me, and I circle my legs behind him. He takes the hint, walking me over to the couch, and sits so I'm straddling him.

"Speaking of being naughty . . ."

"What did you do?" He levels me with a mock glare, one that is currently not serious, but I know will be soon.

"I booked our flight to Oregon for you to go talk to Ski. We leave tomorrow."

My heart is pounding. Maybe I will wait to tell him the other part of my plan until we're there. Yeah . . . that sounds like a good idea.

"And . . . "

"And nothing." I twist a curl in my finger.

"Colette, you're a shit liar. What else did you do because I know damn well that you aren't nervous over a plan we already made."

I swallow hard and work up the courage to tell him everything. "I also made arrangements for us to visit your dad," I mutter quietly as if the quieter I say it, the more he won't hear it.

His body stiffens under me, and his grip tightens on my thighs. "Colette," he growls, and I want to hide, but I won't. "You're going alone."

"Don't be—" He picks me up and drops me on the couch.

"You're going alone," he repeats with much more malice as he walks out my front door and slams it.

Infuriating, childish man who would rather throw a tantrum than talk about his feelings. I could kick him right in his baby maker if I didn't love it so much.

"Ugh!" I groan out and fling myself off my couch.

Fine, he wants to act that way. I will go alone. I'll talk to his dad. He wants to threaten me, thinking I won't go without him? Well, he's testing the wrong girl because I'm not afraid.

Opening my door, I go up to his and begin pounding on it. "Our flight is at six in the morning, asshole. And I'm going with or without you!"

I stomp back to my apartment ready to finish my bottle of wine but then remember I do in fact have to be up early in the morning. But I just can't let go of that anger in my heart. It's just festering, and I hate going to sleep on a note like this.

Opening my apartment door again, I drag myself across the hall and knock on his door, much softer this time. "Gage?"

Silence greets me, but I know he's in there.

I knock again. "Please open up."

Silence still. I understand that Gage sometimes needs to process alone but I'm not like that, which makes it incredibly difficult for me to allow it. All I want is to talk it all through right in the moment, but that's not what the man I love needs.

"I'm going to sit on the other side of this door. If you'll just sit with me. You don't even have to open it. Just let me know you're there."

Placing my back to the door, I slide down it and throw my head back. The thump causes a little sting of pain to my intoxicated brain.

"I can't look at you right now, Colette. I'm so fucking mad. I don't even know what I would do if I saw you. Probably something I could never take back." His deep voice is slightly dulled by the wooden barrier between us but at least he's sitting with me.

"I'm not afraid of you hurting me, Gage. I know you never would."

"What if I'm just like him?"

My heart physically hurts and all I need is to hold this man, but he won't let me. "Please Gage, open the door, let me be there for you. Let me show you that you're better. You won't hurt me."

Silence again.

"Gage. I—I'm sorry about going behind your back. Please go with me. I know it might hurt but I'm doing this because I love you."

"That's what he used to say too."

My eyes close as tears track down my face as I take in the incredibly different intentions behind the same words.

"The difference is my love isn't selfish, Gage. I'd take your pain if I could, but you need to feel this. You need to know that even if the pain breaks you, love will rebuild you, rebuild us."

When moment's turn to minutes, and minutes turn into an hour with no response from him, I finally get up and drag myself back to my bed where I cry myself to sleep, not knowing if my love is worth the pain.

gage

S he's the most infuriating woman, no . . . human I have ever met. She continues to push my boundaries beyond what I'm capable of. Doesn't she not see how fucking hard I'm trying to be different, better. All for her?

But at the same time, I'm fucking addicted to her.

And that is how I end up in her bed by midnight. I couldn't sleep without her.

I'm a fucking pussy, just like Everett. Great.

I haven't slept. My mind has an uncanny ability not to shut off when I'm stressed the fuck out. Which I am 99 percent of the time. Especially since Colette Corvina entered my life.

The blare of her alarm startles her awake, she jolts and turns, wrapping herself in the blankets like a fucking caterpillar in a cocoon. She slams her hand onto the nightstand with a loud slap, but the alarm continues to blare.

"Motherfucker, I'm up! Shut your shit." She continues to slam her hand down, not even looking at where she's hitting. By some miracle, she manages to hit the stop button but then just rolls around and closes her eyes again.

She's a fucking mess, my Chaos. She was also crying most of the night...I can tell by the way her eyes are a bit more puffy than usual. And I feel like shit because I caused those tears.

She fills her lungs, then her eyes snap open, and her cute dark eyebrows pull in as she looks at me.

"What are you doing here?" she mumbles.

"The hell if I know." Running my hand down my face, I flip the little remaining blankets off me and head for the kitchen.

"Wait—"

I stop, but I don't turn around. I'm still too pissed right the fuck off.

"When did you come to bed?" I hear her climb out of bed, but I still don't turn.

"We are leaving in forty-five minutes. Get dressed." It takes a considerable amount of effort to control myself right now. But the thing is, I don't even know which part of me I'm controlling. The part that wants to tear into her about how absolutely inappropriate sneaking behind my back to set up a meeting between my father and me was . . . Or the part of me that wants to turn around and taste that sweet pussy, devour her skin, and fill that bratty mouth with my cock before we partake on our little adventure.

Either way, my self-control wins, and I exit the bedroom to prepare our coffees because I'm already dressed and packed.

As I sip my Americano, hers still resting next to me as she makes crude comments. I hear multiple dresser drawers slam closed until she finally emerges after forty-four minutes.

"Okay, I'm ready."

She's in leggings and a pink crewneck sweatshirt with the words "UNWELL" in bold font across the front, and I have to resist the urge to comment on the accuracy of that statement.

"Why are you being a dick this morning?" she asks, hand on hip and full of attitude.

Fuck my resistance.

"Your sweatshirt is completely appropriate to your personality, Colette." I stand, dump her Americano down the sink as she was reaching for it, and lift my duffel bag onto my shoulder while also wheeling her hot-pink cheetah-print suitcase behind me.

"Hey! I was going to drink that!"

"You called me a dick."

"Well, you are one."

"Just trying to live up to your expectations."

Her addicting form steps in front of me, halting me right before I make it to the door. She wraps her arms around my waist and steps into me, and it's as if my whole body calms. I release a breath, and I feel a weight I didn't even know I was carrying lift.

Letting go of her bag and letting mine fall to the floor, I bring my arms over her shoulders and wrap her in a hug. I kiss the top of her head, and she reaches up and places one on my neck.

"I know you're used to doing everything alone, but you're not doing *this* alone. I know you're scared."

As she releases me, I feel my strength leave with her and as much as I know she means well, she doesn't understand. Against my father, I will always be alone. I will always be that pretty boy.

"Come on, we can swing by Henry Leo's, and I'll get you an Americano." Picking up our bags again, I head out the door and she locks it behind us.

***

One horrendous flight, an incompetent rental car attendant and an hour and half drive with a banshee who is tone deaf, and we are finally checked into Aurora, Oregon's one and only grand hotel—The Baldwin Inn.

The founding glory of the Baldwin's chain of hotels, now known as The Baldwin Resorts.

If I had any other option, I would have gone with it. But the good ole Baldwins have bought out or I'm sure threatened any other hotel that even attempts to make roots here in this small town.

"This place is so cute! Like a little bed-and-breakfast vibe. I love it!" Colette circles the room, opening drawers and closet doors, giving the place a thorough inspection.

Then I notice her settle on the bed and open the nightstand, pulling out the all too expected Bible. "What are you doing?"

"I heard this rumor once that people will sometimes leave money in Bibles. So I always check."

"Have you ever found any?" I've heard the rumor as well, but I've never checked. I don't want people's dirty money. Cash is fucking disgusting. I don't even want to imagine how many G-strings and ass cracks those bills have been in. And do you know what, no one washes their money. It all just gets passed around. Like I said, fucking disgusting.

"No. But I always leave a message."

Grabbing the pen from the nightstand, I watch as she vandalizes the poor book. Scribbling something inside the cover. I walk over to her and peer over, but she slams the cover closed and puts the book back.

"What do you say?"

As she stands, her body inches from mine, I feel her heat radiating off her. I lean in closer. Like a moth drawn to a flame, all I can think about is kissing her as I stare at her full lips, the top one slightly larger than the bottom. Then my eyes find hers, the small anomaly in her left eye so fucking beautiful.

"Whatever I want," she whispers, then brushes past me. As I look over my shoulder at her, she raises her brow in a challenge.

She heads into the bathroom and closes the door. I snatch the Bible from the drawer and read what she wrote. "If you exist, please help him."

Snatching up the pen, I scribble my own note under hers. *If you existed, you would have already.* I put the book back and let out a sigh. Sorry to disappoint, baby girl.

Coming out of the bathroom a moment later, she grabs her scarf and walks to the front door.

"If you play nice today, I'll give you a reward later," she says as she puts an extra sway in her hips and leaves out the front door.

I'm never nice.

Chapter Fifty-One

colette

If I have learned one thing today, it's that Gage Eros is the best person to travel with. First, he only flies first class. Bougie much? Yes. Am I complaining? Abso-fucking-lutely not. As soon as we got to the ticket counter, he upgraded us.

I may or may not have drawn some attention by bouncing up and down, throwing myself at him, and kissing his cheek, which he responded to by shrugging me off and mumbling something under his breath. But what I also saw was a hint of a smile. Such a sucker.

He also gives off this don't-fuck-with-me attitude, so no one sat near us while we were waiting at our gate, and every man who looked at me with even the slightest glimmer of attraction earned a death glare from Gage.

It's nice not having guys eye-fuck you when you're just trying to eat your hot dog in peace. Guard dog Gage for the win.

He also bought me all the alcohol I wanted on the plane, although now I'm thinking he was hoping I would pass out on the drive to the small town. Well, he learned his lesson because alcohol only gives me more energy, more don't-give-a-fuck attitude, and a better singing voice.

God, he's lucky to have me.

The little B&B we are staying in is adorable. It's totally *Gilmore Girls* meets *Pretty Woman*, like that hotel Mr. Lewis stays in but with a small-town charm.

A small bell rang out as we stepped through the frosted glass door, and the smell hit me like a wave of home. It smells just like Henry Leo's. LJ told me all about Ski and her little slice of heaven back home. She told me all about how Ski was kind to her, protected her, and taught her everything she knows about coffee and being a parent. Just like him she says, she parents with love, kindness, compassion, and forgiveness, but also accountability and no-bull-shit rules.

When I booked the tickets to come, I think that was what I was most looking forward to. Not only seeing Ski again but seeing what little shop birthed my best friend.

When we entered, no one was at the bar, and no one was even in the shop. Gage walks up to the counter to order, then we hear a deep, gravelly voice from the back. "Be there in a minute."

Mill's Coffee House is small, quiet, and charming. The old wooden coffee bar with stools lined up has areas of the deep blue paint chipping off and the tables are all different. A few diner-style red booths that line the wall with big pane-glass windows.

Gage holds my hand, and I feel his grip tighten as the old man walks out from a door behind the bar. He has a full gray mustache and beard now, whereas it was a clean face for the wedding. His eyes are comforting with many laugh lines creasing around them. His black T-shirt, jeans, and apron appear to be just as worn down as he is, but above all else, his smile makes me feel at home.

"Gage Eros. How've ya been, son?" He walks up to the counter opposite us and leans forward on his hands. I'm immediately washed over with a blanket of warmth at this man's presence. It's the same warmth that LJ gives off. Even though I know Ski isn't her real father, she shares so much with him.

"Ski." Gage just nods his head, and I look back and forth between the two of them. A multitude of unspoken emotions seems to pass between them before Ski glances at Gage holding my hand and then looks at me. "Colette, it's nice to see you again."

I smile up at him. Last time he saw me, I was just LJ's best friend, but now I'm with Gage. What will he think? "Good to see you again, Ski."

"Leo has told me that you and Gage are together now?" He trails off with a glint of mischief in his eye.

I look up at Gage, catching him already staring down at me with a softness in his usually hard eyes. "We are."

"You just love to collect the difficult ones, don't you, Miss Colette?" he says as he walks behind the counter and shakes his head. "Well, what can I get you? Gage, here, I know will be getting an Americano extra hot, unless something has changed?"

"No. Nothing has changed. An Americano for her as well, brewed over brown sugar."

"Ah. Yes, it does seem he has found his match, then." Ski turns around and begins making our coffee, and Gage leads me to a booth in the back.

When I slide into the fake leather booth with a tear in the middle, I see Everett's name carved into the tabletop, looking slightly to my left, the name Leo, and when I look across in front of Gage, his name is also carved.

A strange feeling swells inside my chest as I sit here in the booth they all sat in all those years ago. I can't imagine all the memories and bonds that were made right where I'm sitting. What all happened to them, the trauma they were surviving at that time in their lives. It's beautiful and heartbreaking all at once to be sitting here in their space.

When Ski returns, he sets our coffees down and pulls up a chair, sitting in it backward at the end of our booth.

"Well, Gage. What would you like to know?"

"How do you know I want to know anything?" Gage's guard is up. Immediately on the defense when he doesn't need to be. Can't he feel how safe this space is? Has he forgotten?

I reach over and lay my hand on Ski's arm, the warmth seeping into my own skin. "Please don't take offense to his asshole attitude. He really doesn't mean it." I shoot a glare over to Gage as he sneers back at me.

Ski's chuckle warms my heart and I look back at him. "Oh, I have known Gage since before he was born. I know he doesn't mean it, and I take no offense. In fact, I appreciate his attitude. Reminds me a lot of myself when I was young."

"What do you mean you knew me before I was born?" I can't read Gage's tone. Although I'm getting better at seeing behind his mask, he's level 10 on the mastery of disguise right now. He seems not quite angry but also not sincere. I resist the urge to bombard Ski with questions and decide this might be a good time to take a step back and let Gage lead.

"I'm going to assume you're here because you want to know about your mother. Am I right?"

Gage doesn't say anything. He keeps his cold, unaffected mask in place as he levels Ski with a glare. But he just smiles and nods his head.

"Be right back." He gets up and makes his way into what I assume is his back office.

I snap my fingers in front of Gage's face, which has gone blank, lost in his mind.

"Hey, I told you to play nice," I whisper-yell at him.

"This is me playing nice, Chaos. Stay out of it."

"Dick," I mumble as Ski returns.

He lays a photo on the table, and although I'm looking at it upside down, I can tell it's Evangeline, and she has a hand wrapped around a very pregnant belly. Her long dark hair is curled and draping over her shoulders, her eyes bright and her smile is infectious. Her dark green dress is loose except for where she has it shaping her belly. But what makes my breath catch in my throat is a much younger Ski with his arm wrapped around her shoulders. They are standing in front of Mill's. The photo is worn down as if it has been held many times. The edges slightly creased.

Gage's eyes are locked onto the photo.

"This was your mother on her first day as a teacher. If you couldn't guess, that's you in her belly." Then he lays down another photo.

Evangeline looks the same but in a yellow sundress, little cap sleeves, and she's holding a baby wrapped in a blue blanket. You can't see the baby's face, but Ski is there again in the same position but in this photo, he's looking at Evangeline, and she's smiling at him. Both smiling.

"The day she brought you home from the hospital, the first place she stopped was here."

Then another photo. Gage looks to be about two in this one. He's sitting atop Ski's shoulders with his hands wrapped under his chin. Gage's dark hair is past his ears and curly, his smile is big, and his chubby cheeks are a little red. He has a red scarf around his neck and red mittens. Evangaline and Ski are also bundled up in scarves and sweaters.

Ski and she are both looking up at Gage. Smiling again. All three of them.

"The Christmas after your second birthday."

Then another photo.

And another.

And another.

And another.

Then the last one.

Evangeline is sitting in a booth. This booth in the back corner. She's wearing a purple beanie, no hair coming out from it. Her skin is pale, her body frail. She sits next to Gage as he reads a book. Her hand stroking through his hair.

"A month before she passed away. And the last time I talked to you until that day you came in here with Everett when you were sixteen."

There are many moments of silence that pass as Gage stares at the photo. I see his eyes begin to glass over. His jaw clenching, the muscles rippling under his skin. His knuckles are white as he grips his mug in his hands.

I wait for his mug to shatter, but it doesn't.

"Gage, I've known you a long time, son. Your mother was like a daughter to me, and I loved her dearly. So, tell me, what do you want to know about her?"

gage

The pictures in front of me have my mind in another dimension. I have never seen her photo before. The only image I have of her is the memory in my fucked-up head. It's not that I couldn't have found a photo of her. I know where she worked. I know there is most likely a photo of her online somewhere that I could easily find, but I . . . I never wanted to see a photo of her.

If I did, she would be real. She wouldn't just be a memory. She would be a mother who lived. And died. But here they lay in front of me. I have been forced to accept that she lived and died and left me. She was real.

"Everything," I answer Ski without looking at him. I can't take my eyes off her. She's beautiful. She's ethereal. She's an angel.

I hear him let out a breath, then the scrape of the wooden chair legs against the floor. I don't follow him with my eyes. I can't look away from her. Her smile. Her radiance.

I hear the flip of the sign on the door. I hear the wrapper of something crinkle, and then I hear him sit back down as he sets a muffin in front of all three of us.

"We will be here a while. Might as well eat."

The idea of eating anything has my stomach turning over. I can barely form a thought that isn't about her. My mother. She's real.

"Let's start at the beginning. Your mother started coming into Mills when she was around eighteen. She was new in town, just moving here with your father. He was almost nine years older than your mom, and it always rubbed me the wrong way, but she seemed happy, so I stayed out of their business."

He takes a bite of his muffin, then looks at me, and reluctantly, I do the same. The blueberries explode in my mouth, and my stomach growls. I didn't realize how hungry I was. I look at Colette who is already halfway through hers, staring at me. Her eyes are cautious. Probably waiting for me to go off.

"She came in almost every day, always with a kind smile and bright, bubbly personality. We grew closer over the years; she spoke mostly to Millie when she came in. The two of them really bonded. Then about a year after your mom started showing up, my Mills passed away." He pauses, taking a moment to collect himself.

When he looks up, his eyes have a sheen over them, like he's holding back tears. "I was ready to join her, Gage. I tried to live life without her, and I couldn't. She was all I had. We never had any children of our own, I was estranged from my siblings. My Mills was my whole life and life wasn't worth living without her. But then Evangeline started coming in more. Every morning and every night. I knew it was just to check on me. Each day she came in, there was a little less pain in my chest. She reminded me of my Millie. Her joy, her laughter, her optimistic look on life."

Colette lays her hand on Ski's, where it's resting on the table. "I'm so sorry, Ski. Millie sounds like an incredible woman."

"She was, sweetie. She was my everything. I miss her more and more everyday." He takes his other hand, patting hers and they remain with their hands folded together.

"Anyway, I found that I began looking forward to when your mother would come in. It made me want to wake up each morning. I needed to be there to greet her and serve her an Americano each morning and give her one of Millie's famous blueberry muffins." He nods down to the muffin I'm fiddling with more than actually eating.

I continue to stay silent. I'm not sure what to say, all I want to do is listen. I want to know everything about her, and this seems to be the only person who can do that right now.

"Where was I? Oh yes. Evangeline was my new reason for living. It was effortless, our relationship. We just understood each other. She was brilliant, quick as a whip, and kind. I never heard her say a bad thing about anyone. She was always looking at the bright side, finding the silver lining in any situation. She was infectious. She was the type of person who walked into a room, and it lit up."

She sounds incredible, so how did she end up with a piece of shit like my father . . .

As if reading my mind, his eyes go distant, and he continues, staring off at the tabletop. "I never understood why she was with a man like your dad. He was never abusive with Evangeline; in fact, I would call him more obsessed. Dangerously so. I could see a lingering darkness underneath the mask he wore. He rarely came in, but when he did, something was always off. He almost seemed too perfect. I think your mother saw that too, but she felt like she owed him her life."

He takes a sip of his coffee and lets go of Colette's hand. "Four years after she started coming here, she showed up and told me she was pregnant. I was concerned." He looks at me with guilt in his eyes.

"I didn't want her to bring children near your father. I just felt in my gut that it wouldn't end well. But she was so fuckin' happy, Gage. It was such a wonderful sight to see her shining like that. In all honesty, I was worried that your dad might do something to mess with the pregnancy, but it carried on. Her belly grew and grew, and then she graduated with her teacher's credentials and got a job at the elementary school. Life seemed to be going well for her."

"When you were born, she brought you here before she even took you home. You were perfect, Gage. The most beautiful baby I had ever seen. I know they say babies don't really resemble their parents when they are born, but you looked just like her. Dark hair, bright eyes, cute little nose."

Ski smiles as if he's remembering the moment in time. He shuffles through the photos and picks up the one of her holding me. "Your dad took all these photos. He always seemed happy to do so, but I think it was because he knew it would make her happy. I don't know that he appreciated Evangeline being as close to me as she was, but she kept coming, and he never said anything, at least not to me. I asked her about it many times, but she always told me they were happy, and he was good to her. I never pushed too hard. It wasn't my business, but sometimes I think I should have been a bit more invasive."

Shaking his head, he drops the picture. "Then she got sick when you were four. A year later . . . well. You know."

I watch as a tear falls from his eye, and he takes his handkerchief out of his back pocket and wipes his nose.

"What about the typewriter?" I finally find my voice. Taking in everything about her is overwhelming and I don't know what to do with myself. But if he loved my mother so much, why wouldn't he tell me about her before?

"Ah yes. Her typewriter. She brought it in to me about a month before she passed and told me to give it to you on your sixteenth birthday."

"Why didn't you tell me it was from her? I have nothing of hers, Ski. My father burned everything. I had nothing. If I would have known that was hers . . . maybe . . ." My voice is rising. I can't stop the anger leaking out.

Ski lays his large hand on my shoulder and squeezes, pulling my attention back to him. His eyes are thick with worry. "You were so angry with the world at that age. I didn't know if it was from her death or your father and I feared if you knew it was from her, you wouldn't have accepted it. I think about it all the time. If I would have told you about her, maybe you would have turned out differently. Less angry. More like her. But . . . well, son, we can't play the what-if game. What has happened is set in stone but what we carve from that stone is still up to us. We can do better. Be better."

It's all fucking bullshit. Every last word.

I stand from the booth abruptly. I can't just sit here and let him spout off about how much he fucking loved my mother but then forgot about me. "If you loved her, why weren't you there for me? I came in here countless times! You never said anything! Did I mean nothing to you? You were there for Leo, what about me?!"

I needed someone in my life, so why wasn't he there. "You fucking failed her! You didn't care for me! You left me to survive him! I was alone! I was a child!" I can feel myself breaking. I can feel myself shattering, and I don't know what to do. How do I collect myself? How do I breathe? I feel my chest rising and falling, but I don't feel the air in my lungs. I can't breathe. He failed her. He failed me! He let me go through life without my mother.

My hands find my hair and pull, I need pain. I need to be grounded. I need to be pulled from the storm inside my head. There's no control. Everything is crumbling around me. I can't—I—

Then I feel him. Strong arms wrap around my shoulders, and they pull me in. I push away, trying to release myself from his hold, but he won't let me go. He has me, and he won't let me breathe.

"Get the fuck off me!"

"Shhh."

"No! You . . . She left me. I . . . I'm broken. I'm a fragment of her. Nothing more. I'm nothing." I can hear the weakness in my voice as it wavers, but I can't control it.

"Gage. She loved you. I love you." His voice is deep next to my ear, and I feel myself fall. I feel myself give in. My body, my mind . . . it all releases.

Sobs wrack my body as I wrap my arms around Ski's large torso. He pulls me in tighter.

"I'm so sorry, son. I'm so sorry. I know I failed her. I failed you. I'm so sorry. I can't change the past, but I can be there for you now. I promise. I'm here. You aren't alone."

But I am.

I'm always with you.

Her voice.

Chapter Fifty-Three

colette

Finally.

He's breaking.

Right before my eyes, the man I love is breaking, but I'm not the one who can put him back together.

I watch as Ski holds Gage like a father would hold their son. Ski holds him together as Gage breaks in his arms.

The words Gage yelled at him aren't untrue. They are horribly accurate. What if Ski would have told him about Evangeline? Would Gage have grown up knowing he was loved and wasn't alone. But would it have also made it worse for him since she died. Since he would never experience that love?

What would have been worse? The fact that he never knew his mother so he could never know what her absence felt like, or would it have been worse to live with her absence knowing he would never experience her love again?

Both situations are completely fucked up and impossible. And the decision was put on Ski. He had the best intentions with the worst situation.

Tears track down my face as I allow them to break together. As the moments stretch and a calmness falls over Mill's Coffee House, Gage pulls away, a resolve in his eyes, as he takes a deep breath and lets it out. Ski lets go of him. The two men just look at each other before Gage turns and walks away.

He goes out the front door, and I'm frozen. Do I follow him? Do I stay? Does he need a moment to himself, or does he need me? I don't know.

Ski sits and shakes his head. "I'm sorry, Colette. It seems I have failed the boy. I . . ." His wrinkled fingers intertwine on the tabletop, and I reach out, folding his hands in mine.

"You're here now."

"It doesn't matter. The damage is done, sweetie. I don't know what he went through, but . . ."

"You couldn't have stopped it, Ski. Trust me."

He looks up at me now, his eyes glassy with tears. "I could have been there for him. Just like I was for Leo. I just . . . I didn't know he needed me like that. His father never let me see him. And the boy never came into the shop until he was a teenager. I . . . I tried. But his father threatened me with a restraining order, and I . . . I couldn't risk losing the little I did see of him . . ."

My eyes go up to Gage as he walks back into the shop. "Gage."

Ski follows my gaze, but he doesn't say anything.

The silence is heavy in the air. No one knows what to do or say, or maybe having too much to say but not knowing where to start.

"Thank you, Ski," Gage finally says as he looks at him.

The shock on Ski's face is evident. He takes in a sharp inhale, and his body stiffens. "What?"

"Thank you for telling me about her. For the photos. For the typewriter. Thank you for showing me who I'm meant to be."

"Gage, I . . . I failed you. I should have told you—"

"Stop." Gage lays his hand on Ski's shoulder, clasping it in his grip. "You're right. I was so angry back then, and no matter what you would have told me or done, it wouldn't have mattered. I was meant to go through what I did. It's made me who I am. It's made me stronger. And now I know my mother because of you. I feel her kindness in the way you speak of her, I see her beauty in the photos you have kept, I know who she would have wanted me to be in the man I see before me. She loved you, Ski, and she would have forgiven you. So I'm choosing to do the same."

The tears fall from Ski's gray eyes. "Thank you, son."

Gage lowers his hand and begins thumbing through the pictures on the table. "If you have time, could you tell me more about her? I want to know everything."

They both smile at each other. "Of course."

***

Hours later, hours filled with tears and laughter and smiles, I let out a yawn, and Gage notices. We spent all day talking about Evangeline and young Gage. The imagery Ski painted of her is otherworldly. The memories he described will live in my mind forever. I know they will for Gage too.

All he ever had was his father, the scars and memories his father left on his body and mind, but now he has her too. The light to eradicate the darkness his father left.

A peace washes over me, and I can't even imagine how Gage is feeling.

"Well, old man, we should get going. We've had a long day." We all stand, and Gage grabs my hand and pulls me to his side, nuzzling his nose behind my ear. "No more yawning. You still owe me my reward."

I feel myself blush and push him off me jokingly. "Greedy bastard," I whisper, and he gives me a mischievous grin.

"When do you guys leave?" Ski asks as he leads us to the front door.

"Tomorrow," I answer.

Ski pulls me into a hug. "It was so nice to see you, Colette. Take care of my boy."

"I will. If I don't kill him, that is."

Ski just chuckles, and Gage shakes his head and rolls his eyes.

As we turn to leave, Ski catches Gage at the elbow, turning him back. "Gage, your father. He . . . He's in prison. I'm sure you already know, but in case you didn't, I thought you should know."

Gage just nods his head at him.

As we drive back to the inn, I can't describe it, but I can feel it. Something has changed in Gage. There is a lightness to him now. Like he has shed a layer of skin that was constricting him. The car is filled with silence as we make the short drive, both of us soaking up the events that just transpired.

He reaches across the center console and lays his hand on my thigh, I lay mine over his, and he looks at me with a grin and a lightness in his hauntingly hazel eyes.

He didn't flinch away.

I'm not sure this man next to me understands the gravity of what he just did. He had the option to turn away from Ski, to never speak to him again, to leave with hate in his heart, but he didn't. He forgave. He healed a part of his soul that was shattered.

He broke in Ski's arms and rebuilt a part of himself in those same arms.

The memories of who Gage was not that long ago surface, and I see how much he has truly changed. How much he has grown and taken his life back into his own hands.

No matter what comes tomorrow, I know that Gage can handle it. And I will be right there with him. For everything.

As we make our way into our room, Gage turns to me, pushing me back into the door as I shut it. His lips find mine, seeking and searching for salvation with his tongue as he kisses me like he never has before. He's gentle in his caresses, and I return the sentiment.

Snaking my hands under his shirt, I gently glide my fingertips along the muscles of his back, over where I know the tips of his feathered wings lie, and goose bumps break out across his skin. He shivers and moans. "Fuck, baby girl. Don't stop."

I don't.

I keep touching.

I keep exploring.

I keep showing him how a gentle touch is supposed to feel.

I keep reminding him that I'm here.

"I'll never stop, Gage."

He lets out a growl and picks me up, his hands grasping the backs of my thighs and lifts me. My legs wrap around his waist, and he lays me on the bed.

He's a dark angel hovering over me. I see his eyes trace over my features, taking me in as if he's reassuring himself that it's me.

"Say my name."

"Colette," he whispers.

I pull his lips to mine by the back of his head, and we kiss for what feels like hours. The kisses he leaves on my skin are soft, gentle, and kind. They leave an aftertaste of love and devotion. As he does, I trace my fingers along his face, feeling the corner of his mouth, his cheekbone, the arch of his brow.

I trace over every part of him, imprinting his edges into my heart. As if my fingertips are my brush, I paint an image of him in my mind through the textures I feel.

Pulling the straps of my dress off my shoulders, he dips his head, kissing over my heart. Peppering my skin with his breath. As he does that, I feel his hands run up the length of my legs, lifting my dress.

Then he grasps my panties and leggings, pulling them off in one swift motion. He unzips his own jeans and frees himself. Settling between my thighs, he slowly slides inside me, filling me.

Everything is slow, torturous, tame. It's everything he has tried to give me but never been able to before.

A moan leaves my throat on an exhale, and he returns with a kiss on my neck. He sucks the skin in slightly and then bites. "God, you're perfect."

His slow thrusts are driving me crazy. I push back on him a little, and he follows my lead, allowing me to flip us so I'm straddling him.

I take what I want as I ride him, lifting and rolling my hips. I chase my release. Throwing my head back, I feel my curls descend farther down my back, softly brushing my skin and eliciting goose bumps to erupt.

When I look down, his arms are tucked behind his head as he lets me take control. My nails dig into his chest and I explode.

"Oh fuck," he exclaims. "Jesus, Colette. You're fucking strangling my cock, baby girl. Take it from me. Take everything."

His hands finally grip my hips in a punishing release as I feel him pulse inside me. I collapse onto his chest, knowing he means much more than what he just gave me.

"I love you." I whisper as my fingers trace the scar on his pec, inked over with a dahlia, and his fingers run up my spine. "What I feel for you, Colette, is far beyond the definition of love."

gage

The hotel phone ringing wakes me. Based on the dim light coming through the window, I would guess it's pretty early. Colette has drool pooling on the pillow under her head, and she's taking up over half of the bed. I answer before it wakes her even though I know this woman could sleep through a fucking air horn.

"Hello?"

"Gage? It's Ski." The old man's voice comes through the receiver, and I sit up urgently, wondering if something is wrong.

"Everything okay?"

"Yeah. I was going . . . do you have an hour this morning? I'd like to show you something."

I look over at Colette, and something in my chest pulls me to answer yes to his question. I've never ignored that feeling, and I'm not going to start today. It's that feeling that gave me my Raven. That drew me to Colette. "Yeah. I can meet you in fifteen minutes at the shop."

"Meet me at Aurora Cemetery."

The line goes dead, and I can't help but smirk at both of our distastes for goodbyes. I leave a note for my Sleeping Beauty and place a kiss on her cheek before heading out.

The cemetery isn't far. Nothing really is in this small town, so I'm there within ten minutes, and I find Ski waiting, leaning up against his old truck with a bouquet. I recognize them easily since I have them tattooed all over my body—dahlias.

Greeting him with a head nod, he does the same, and no words are exchanged as he leads me to a simple headstone with an engraved inscription that reads *Evangeline Dahlia Eros.*

"I thought you might want to visit her, son," Ski says as he hands me the bouquet of dahlias.

I'm paralyzed. I'm not really sure what I'm supposed to do. I've never been here before. My fuckface of a father sure as hell never brought me, and . . . I guess as an adult, I never gave much thought to what happened to my mom after she died. But now I feel a rush of guilt for never looking it up. Why didn't I do that?

I notice Ski saying something in another language and kissing his fingers, then placing them on the top of the headstone. He looks at me. "I'll give you two time. It was good to see you again, son. Visit as much as you want. You'll always have a home at Mill's."

I nod again at him as I watch the old man walk away.

Leaning down, I place the bouquet I was holding in the same spot Ski placed his. When I lean in, I see a small inscription below her date of birth and death.

To my son, I love you for infinity . . .

My knees hit the wet grass in front of her headstone as the memory of our saying filters in like a soft voice spoken behind my eyes.

"And beyond," I whisper as my cheeks heat and tears begin to fall from my eyes.

***

The prison gates buzz as they open, letting in visitor after visitor. Colette has a death grip on my hand. "You're going to break the fingers you love to ride, baby girl. Ease up."

"Shit. Sorry. I'm nervous."

I raise a brow at her and tilt my head. "You're nervous?"

"God. Yes. I'm sorry. Fuck. Are you okay?" Her grip lightens as she brings her other hand up to grasp my bicep, tucking herself closer to me.

"I'm nervous for you. For me, I'd like them to let him out from behind that glass so I can shove my foot so far up his ass that if I wiggled my toes, they would tickle his brain."

I scoff at the imagery her crude mouth paints, and then I'm directed by a guard to station six. I can't see him, but I know when I approach, he will be behind the glass. My feet draw me closer to him, step after step, but Colette's arm pulls, halting me.

"I'm here, Gage. You're mine. Not his. Do you understand?" Her eyes are burning. Branding my soul with her determination and spirit.

"I'm yours," I say as I lean in and kiss her.

Coming up to the glass, I finally take in my father in his gray jumpsuit. He almost looks the same as he did when I left at eighteen. Just a few more wrinkles around his eyes, and gray has started overtaking his hair. But what makes me still is his smile at the sight of me. Then his eyes move to Colette at my side. He sees her clinging to me, and I want to rip him apart.

We sit a foot from him, separated by a thin piece of plexiglass. He picks up the phone, but I don't right away. My reality is moving in stills as if this is an old-time picture show. My vision blurs, and my chest tightens, but I know I need to do this.

I feel my back teeth grinding. I can do this. Colette squeezes my arm, digging her nails into my skin, and the bite of pain calms me. I feel her.

Only her.

Finally, I reach forward and hold the phone to my ear.

"Son."

"Don't you fucking call me that," I grit out.

His eyes fall for only a moment. "I'm happy you came. I've been waiting."

When I don't say anything, he continues.

"I need to make amends. I . . . What I did to you, it was wrong. My mind was sick, Gage—"

"Your mind isn't sick, Dad. You are." I swear the plastic black phone is about to break in my hands with the grip I have on it. Sick? He wants to blame what he did to me and other children on some sick mental illness? Fuck him.

"I see now, God has cured me of my sins, Gage."

"Oh, fuck you. So you're saved now, and all is forgiven? Is that it? I'm supposed to forgive you and move on now that you've found God. That's such bullshit."

"Gage—"

"No. I'm speaking now. You will listen. I will never forgive you. But I will move on knowing you will rot in the prison I put you in."

I hang up the phone and watch as his world crumbles. I see his eyes turn from light to dangerous.

There he is.

"You what?" I watch his mouth move as he whispers the words through the plexiglass.

Three, two, one. The mask fully drops, and the sinister man lurking beneath surfaces as he realizes that it was his son who was watching him all along, his son who turned him into the FBI and put him behind bars. His son who collected evidence for years and finally stood up for himself.

I watch as he slams his hands against the glass. "Gage, answer me? You did this?"

I sit there, Colette at my side, as I look at him through my brows, grinning.

I watch him break, only a fraction compared to how he broke me. "There you go you, just like that. What a good boy," I taunt, mimicking the tone and phrase he gave me for years.

"Gage!" he yells again as the guards drag him away.

That's all I needed. To see his reaction when he realized it was me who did this.

Fuck forgiveness.

I don't need it to move on.

I relish in the anger I have toward him. It's that anger that keeps me pushing to find every fucking criminal like him. A reminder to keep hunting the sick fucks who like to prey on innocents.

Fuck forgiveness.

I'm after revenge, and he's my muse.

"Gage?" Colette's voice brings me back to the surface.

Looking at her, I stand and pull her with me. "Come on, we have a plane to catch."

***

Colette heads for the domestic flights counter, but I grab her arm and steer her toward international.

"What are you doing? We need to check in."

"We are."

"Checking in?" the attendant asks.

"Yes," I say as I hand her my phone, and she scans the barcode. I hand her Colette's and my passports and luggage, and she does what she needs to.

"You're all set, Mr. Eros. Enjoy your trip to Japan."

"What the fuck?" Colette screams and jumps into my arms. I catch her under her ass as she kisses my lips, my cheeks, my forehead. Anywhere she can reach really. Eyes are drawn to us, and I just laugh. I fucking love seeing her happy, but even more than that I love being the reason for it.

"Ready to go eat some real sushi, baby girl?"

I set her down, holding on to her waist as she holds the back of my neck. "But wait, the shop, and your job, the girls at the gym? We have—" Ah, there she is. Colette is always react first, then logic.

"Stop. It's all taken care of. I will have to do some work, but I can do it from overseas. And Leo was more than happy to let you have a few weeks off. B has the gym."

Her eyes go wide as saucers. "A few weeks!" she shrieks.

"Four to be exact."

"I didn't pack for Japan! For a whole month! Are you insane?"

"I'll buy you whatever you want. I told you; I'm going to give you everything you want, baby girl, starting with the world."

Her smile stretches across her face, lighting her up. "I hate you."

"I love it," I say as I kiss her, her hands gently trailing through my hair.

Chapter Fifty-Five

colette

One month later

"You're home!" my mother cries as she runs up to me, embracing me in a hug. It's been a whole month since I saw her last. Our trip in Japan was over, and we were forced to come back to reality. But Gage has already booked us another trip in four months to Paris.

She fluffs my curls as I unwrap my scarf from around my neck, and snowflakes fall on her dark hardwood floors. The November fall-like weather of Japan is greatly missed as I step out of a Boston snowstorm.

The audacity of Boston to fill my favorite month with snow is beyond me.

"Did you get what I asked?" I whisper to her as she takes my scarf and hangs it up for me.

"Yes." She smirks and gives a wink. "He's going to love the ones I got for him."

A grin breaks out across my face as I feel the man in question approach behind me. "What am I going to love?" he says as he shakes out his dark hair.

"Oh nothing . . . " The feigned innocence in my voice doesn't fool him though as he narrows his eyes but luckily my mom interjects. "It's nice to meet you, finally." Gage reaches a hand out and my mom bats it away, embracing him in a hug which he returns.

"You too, Mrs. Corvina," he says gently as he returns her embrace.

"Gage! My boy!" My father rounds the corner from the kitchen and my mom pulls back. Beaming up at my dad. He wraps Gage into his arms and they both laugh.

"Good to see you, Michael."

"Wow, he gets a hug first? I'm offended." I cross my arms and pout.

"Oh, come here, my little raven." And he wraps me in a hug as well.

"Well, let's eat before it gets cold." Mom ushers us into the kitchen and hands us plates.

My dad and Gage are conversing in small talk as they scoop food onto their plate, and I take in the scene of their happiness. For the first time in a long time, my dad looks like the man he used to be, and Gage is lighter. Unburdened.

That's not to say he's magically healed in one day. During the month we were away, we worked heavily on touch and honesty. He shared with me horrendous stories of what his father did to him, and I listened. I had to practice incredible self-control as I wanted to march right back into that prison and shank a bitch, but you know, I didn't. So I think my self-control and patience are winning.

"He's happy." My mom sneaks up to my side, her own plate full of honey-glazed ham, mashed potatoes, and green beans. Mine is still empty. I've been too lost watching them to fill it up.

"Dad looks great, Mom. The therapy seems to be helping."

"I wasn't talking about your dad, honey." She bumps shoulders with mine.

"Oh. Yeah," I say shyly, but I'm not sure why. I curl my lips, thinking about how even someone who has never met Gage can see how happy he is.

"So . . . when can I expect grandchildren?" She winks at me, and I walk away.

"No. Nope. We are not talking about that. You're batshit crazy, Mother."

"Oh, come on, honey . . . " Her voice trails off as I make my way into the dining room to sit next to Gage. Looking through the arched, open french doors that lead to our living room, I see the fireplace, decorated with Mom's little village, the Christmas tree up and decorated in all my childhood ornaments.

My heart warms. Really all we are missing are matching Christmas pj's . . .

My dad and Gage continue talking about some cyber thing that I don't understand. Apparently, he has been helping my dad get up to date on the latest technology since he missed many advancements while he was gone.

I clear my throat, drawing my dad's and Gage's attention. "Excuse me, but I'm your daughter. Can you show me some attention?"

"Feeling a little jealous there, Chaos?" Gage's eyes darken, and his smirk immediately wets my panties.

"Shut up," I snap at him.

"Behave," he warns, his voice lowering to a whisper.

"Speaking of misbehaving, I have something for all of us," my mom calls out, and all our eyes turn to her. I, of course, know what she has since I arranged the whole thing. I bite my lip to try to hide my smile, but it doesn't go unnoticed.

"What the hell have you done, Colette?" Gage teases, and I shrug.

Mom pulls out four Christmas bags, fully decorated with tissue paper and handmade name tags, and passes them to each of us.

Dad goes first, throwing the tissue paper on the floor and pulling out a pair of Christmas pajamas . . . or should I say a Christmas onesie. The onesie is a full gingerbread man, and when Mom pulls hers out, a gingerbread woman onesie.

I snicker as Gage rolls his head to me, eyes narrowed, and I can tell his tongue just ran over the front of his teeth. "If I pull out a fucking gingerbread onesie from this bag, there will be hell to pay."

"I promise you, it's not a gingerbread onesie . . ." He opens the bag, neatly folding the tissue paper like the psycho he is, and pulls out a Christmas tree onesie, complete with actual twinkling lights and ornaments.

His eyes close, and he shakes his head. "You're a nightmare," he grumbles as I pull a matching one out of my bag.

"But you love me," I remind him with a kiss to his cheek.

"I hate you." He rolls his eyes just before pulling me in by the nape of my neck for a heated kiss. I taste the sweet cranberry sauce on his tongue and am intoxicated by all things Gage Eros.

"I love it," I whisper when he finally releases me.

gage

One and a half years later

I wake to an empty bed, and I hate it. I hate when she wakes before me, which is rare but nonetheless irritating. She knows I need her in the mornings. Her body, her attitude, her love. And I don't like being denied my fucking everything.

But I know where she is.

It's where she goes anytime she wakes before me.

Walking up to the attic of our new home we bought three months ago, I find her looking out the window, sitting atop her stool, draped only in a blanket, her chestnut skin shining against the cream cashmere of the blanket.

She hums to herself as her brush makes brilliant strokes across the canvas.

She's heaven.

The light from the window casts her in a celestial glow. My goddess.

The black feathers she paints are iridescent, and I question every time how she does that with paint and canvas alone. They look lifelike, like each feather was dipped in black oil, glimmering with blues and purples.

"You're staring. It's creepy," she sing-songs without looking at me as I lean against the doorframe.

"And you aren't naked in our bed. You know I don't like waking up without you."

"You'll survive, big guy. Come here. I need some inspiration."

I move to her like a sailor captivated by the siren's song. Standing in front of her, just to the side of her canvas, she looks at my bare chest, tilting her head. Assessing.

She does this often, finding inspiration for her paintings in my tattoos, my face, my body. She has painted countless depictions of how my hands grab her thighs and how my teeth bite into her flesh. All her figures of me are faceless, though. She says my face is for her and her alone.

But I know her. I told her once about how my father loved how pretty my face was. She doesn't want him ever seeing it again.

It's her own silent fuck you to the man who abused me.

Her paintings are sold around the world and she's opening up her own gallery soon.

But I'm hers and hers alone.

Reaching up, she quickly swipes the brush across my cheek. "Oopsies."

I level her with a glare and smile. "Oh, it's on, baby girl."

Grabbing her around the waist as if I were tackling her, I throw her over my shoulder and slap her ass.

"Gage! Put me down! We have a birthday party to go to!"

"Don't start a war you can't win, Chaos. Plus, Callahan won't notice if we are a little late. I'll buy him a PS5."

"He's five!"

"Semantics." I dig my hands into her thighs, and she squeals.

Walking her down to our room, then into our bathroom, I walk into our shower and turn the water on. The cold water hits her back, and she yelps. But it begins to warm as I lower her and wipe my thumb across her cheek, wiping off the paint she had on her as well.

She reaches up and gently wipes the paint from my own cheek.

I back her into the tile as I drop my now soaking sweats onto the tile floor. She's already naked, losing the blanket on the walk down here.

I continue to look into those captivating eyes as I push my body into hers. I lift one of her legs at the knee and guide myself into her. I couldn't wait to warm her up properly. I'm not a nice man, remember? But it doesn't matter. As soon as I'm fully inside her, I feel her pulsing around me.

Her gasp fills the shower as her eyes close and her head falls back. I take this moment to lick up her neck, collecting the water rolling off her flawless skin.

"Gage," she releases on a breath.

"You're so brave, baby girl," I whisper in her ear and she turns to look at me. Her brows pulling in.

"For what?"

"Loving me. I'm so fucking proud to be yours, Colette. Marry me, baby girl." I don't ask it as a question because there is no other option for her. She's mine. And now I finally understand why the stupid piece of paper matters. Everything in me needs to see that ring on her hand, my last name next to hers, and hear the absolute perfect way Colette Eros would sound when she introduces herself to others.

Some say a marriage should be selfless. I say fuck that 'cause I'm marrying this woman for only selfish reasons. She's mine, and the world will fucking know it.

"Wh-what," she stutters out, unable to fully catch her breath as each thrust of my hips steals everything from her.

Her fingers tangle into the hair at the back of my neck, then she trails them down my shoulders and arms as I move ruthlessly inside her.

Her touch lights me on fire. I would be lying if I said his touch doesn't haunt me anymore. For the briefest of moments, it's his hands I feel, but as soon as I see her, hear her . . . I feel her and know that it's my Colette. My raven who holds me in her hands.

My Raven who saved me.

My Raven who changed me.

My Raven who found me.

"Yes," she whispers in my ear as her fingertips dance gently across my back. She moans out as her body, mind, heart, and soul all become intertwined with my own.

Acknowledgments

If you have made it to this page, first off...good girl. Or good boy. *Insert winky face.* I hope that you love Gage and Colette as much as I do! Gage holds a special place in my heart because his story is so incredibly important to highlight what most people don't acknowledge. Men. Can. Be. Victims.

I could not have made this story a reality without some very important people and in no order of importance, here I go. First, my readers. How incredibly lucky am I to have you as a reader. Without you, the story would simply be words on a page. You are what makes it special, brings it to life, and allows it to live on.

Secondly, my group of friends–let's be honest, sisters–who encouraged me to continue writing. Elyse, Hannah, Nich and Alexis, you read my words and ran with them, demanded the happily ever after that my characters deserved and pushed me to bury my fears and share my book with others. You all have seen every beautiful and ugly side of this journey and have stuck by me through it all.

To my beta readers and editor, thank you for your insights, critiques, and hopes and dreams for the characters. Thank you for catching all my lazy finger mistakes and area's where my brain apparently took a break and just forgot to make any sense at all.

To my husband, tech guru and occasional muse (thanks for the Chinese, Japanese, on your knees scene. . .yes that actually happened), thank you for wrangling our tiny pterodactyls, cooking dinner, washing dishes and being Mr. Mom when I needed to write. Also thank you for fixing all my computer issues and reminding me to breathe when I wanted to throw my laptop. You inspire me. Fill me with love and confidence. You keep me grounded while letting my dreams take flight. I lava you.

There is a little piece of each and every one of you in this novel and I hope you feel that as you read it.

Till our next escape,

–S

S. E. Emory is a contemporary romance author who enjoys writing heart-wrenching stories. She loves taking real life struggles and heartaches and creating the happily ever afters that we all deserve. S.E. enjoys playing with her two kiddos, watching anime with her husband, and sipping coffee in her rocking chair with a warm blanket and her latest all consuming read.

Connect with S. E. Emory online

www.seemorybooks.com

g

goodreads.com/seemorybooks

instagram.com/s.e.emory

tiktok.com/@s.e.emory

Website
www.seemorybooks.com

Instagram
www.instagram.com/s.e.emory

Goodreads
https://www.goodreads.com/seemorybooks

Pinterest
https://www.pinterest.com/seemorybooks/

TikTok
https://www.tiktok.com/@s.e.emory